HANDEL COLLECTIONS
AND THEIR HISTORY

GERALD COKE

Handel Collections
and their History

Edited by

TERENCE BEST

Foreword by
Brian Trowell

MANNES COLLEGE OF MUSIC
HARRY SCHERMAN LIBRARY
150 WEST 85 STREET
NEW YORK, NY 10024

CLARENDON PRESS · OXFORD
1993

Oxford University Press, Walton Street, Oxford OX2 6DP

*Oxford New York Toronto
Delhi Bombay Calcutta Madras Karachi
Kuala Lumpur Singapore Hong Kong Tokyo
Nairobi Dar es Salaam Cape Town
Melbourne Auckland Madrid
and associated companies in
Berlin Ibadan*

Oxford is a trade mark of Oxford University Press

*Published in the United States
by Oxford University Press Inc., New York*

© *The several contributors 1993*

*All rights reserved. No part of this publication may be reproduced,
stored in a retrieval system, or transmitted, in any form or by any means,
without the prior permission in writing of Oxford University Press.
Within the UK, exceptions are allowed in respect of any fair dealing for the
purpose of research or private study, or criticism or review, as permitted
under the Copyright, Designs and Patents Act, 1988, or in the case of
reprographic reproduction in accordance with the terms of the licences
issued by the Copyright Licensing Agency. Enquiries concerning
reproduction outside these terms and in other countries should be
sent to the Rights Department, Oxford University Press,
at the address above*

*British Library Cataloguing in Publication Data
Data available*

Library of Congress Cataloging-in-Publication Data

*Handel collections and their history / edited by Terence Best ;
foreword by Brian Trowell.*

*Papers of a conference organized by the Handel Institute and
held at King's College, London, Nov. 24–26, 1990
Includes indexes.*

*1. Handel, George Frideric, 1685–1759—Congresses.
2. Handel, George Frideric, 1685–1759—Archives.
3. Handel, George Frideric, 1685–1759—Manuscripts. I. Best, Terence.*

ML410.H13H259   1993   780'. 92—dc20   93–22581

ISBN 0-19-816299-5

1 3 5 7 9 10 8 6 4 2

*Typeset by Seton Music Graphics Ltd., Bantry, Co. Cork, Ireland
Printed in Great Britain
on acid-free paper by
Biddles Ltd., Guildford and King's Lynn*

Foreword

❧❀❧

WHEN the Handel Institute was founded in London in September
1987, it set itself a number of specific objectives. One of these was the
organizing of meetings and lectures designed to improve knowledge
of Handel's music; among others are the support of scholarly
editions, principally by nominating two members of the Editorial
Board of the Hallische Händel-Ausgabe (HHA), and the encourage-
ment of performances of the composer's works by providing scholarly
advice. All three of these desiderata came together in the conference
on 'Handel Collections and their History' held at King's College,
London, from 24 to 26 November 1990, the scholarly proceedings of
which are presented here under the editorship of Terence Best. The
conference was timed to coincide with a London meeting of the
Editorial Board of the HHA, so taking full advantage of an occasion
which would bring together several of the distinguished participants;
it is intended to repeat this every three years, so that we may look
forward to a triennial pattern of conferences in the future. To open
the proceedings, the Carnarvon Baroque Players gave a concert of
unknown or little-known works taken from the collections under
discussion, in a programme prepared by Anthony Hicks; this event
was made possible by a generous grant from the Cicely Boyce Trust.

The inaugural conference was organized by Colin Timms and
Curtis A. Price; its theme, conceived by Donald Burrows, is one of
fundamental importance to Handel studies, particularly at this time
of renewed and intense editorial activity. While Handel was not the
first great composer to keep all his autograph manuscripts and performing material by him in what must have been a carefully organized
library, he is the first whose library survives more or less complete.
In an age when publication was a rare event—and even then offered
only incomplete versions of works such as operas, shorn of their
ensembles and recitatives—the personal collection of a composer or
choirmaster, whether of his own or of other composers' works, was
a valuable resource: it made him more attractive to a potential
employer, and he might also wish to revive and revise earlier music
since forgotten, or to borrow from it in order to create new pieces.
Both Handel and J. S. Bach consistently reused and adapted music
from their stock. In Bach's case, since his son Wilhelm Friedemann
did not take care to preserve his share of the *Nachlass*, many works

are lost, including a great number of the originals whose music is known to us only in the form of adaptations.

With Handel, however, we are more fortunate. He inspired unusual admiration and friendship, even hero-worship, among those around him. He was the first musical 'classic', whose works, with the exception of the operas, have never ceased to be performed, and he inspired the first substantial biography of a composer. It is not surprising that his personal library of music, though divided up after his death, should have been so carefully preserved by those who acquired it. It is less well known that several admirers and friends started to collect manuscript copies of his music during his lifetime, one of them (Charles Jennens) desiring such comprehensive coverage that he even acquired sets of performing parts. Usually these copies were derived from sources close to the composer and were written by his own copyists; sometimes they contain variants and revisions in his own hand, or preserve first thoughts and early versions of works which he altered before performing them in public. When performances led to a wider demand, music-publishers began to produce editions of his works, initiating, for example, the collections of operatic arias with which England long led the field. The circle of collectors correspondingly broadened to those who subscribed to such publications; eventually we find a growing public appetite for the music leading to the first attempts at collected Handel editions in England and Germany.

The nine collections discussed at the conference, along with the better-known Royal Collection in the British Library, offer a remarkably comprehensive record of Handel's mature work as a composer. They allow us to trace a composition through from its first draft into performance (and later revision for revival with different performers) and into publication and other means of dissemination. The picture that we are able to form of a highly professional composer at work, and of his reception by ever-widening circles of admirers, even long after his death, gives us a paradigm which helps us in the study of composers whose music has not survived in such quantities. Although the insight that we gain into Handel's own working methods, the chronology of his works, and the development of his musical language is fascinating in itself, the single case allows us to generalize. The same is true of the more detailed forms of research exemplified in this volume. In the case of music whose occasion and date is unknown, an examination of the handwriting of the composer and his copyists, taken in conjunction with analysis of paper-types based on watermarks and the ruling of the staves, permits us to see patterns associating undated with datable works, and to arrive at a

FOREWORD   vii

hypothetical ordering of the former. Again, the comprehensiveness
of the material is all-important.

The papers here presented respond to the richness of our Handel
heritage with an equal richness of method and detail. They constitute
a major advance in Handel studies, and we are grateful to the British
Academy for its financial help in assembling such a panel of experts,
as well as to King's College and Professor Price for offering house-
room and hospitality for the conference.

Finally we are delighted to publish, as a prologue to our proceedings, a unique document written by the most recent, and no doubt
the last, great collector of Handeliana, the late Gerald Coke. It is an
account of his own aspirations and methods in assembling the collection that bears his name. He was our first Patron, and a valued
practical adviser, as well as a source of inspiration during the first
years of the Institute's work. His example helps us to understand
the zest and the powers of discrimination that underlay the work of
collectors of earlier generations, though not all of them would have
offered to Handel scholars the warm welcome and ready assistance
that modern researchers have always received from Gerald and
Patricia Coke and their family.

BRIAN TROWELL
Chairman of the Trustees and of the Council of the Handel Institute

Contents

Notes on Contributors	xi
List of Illustrations	xiv
Abbreviations	xv
Editorial Note	xviii

1. Collecting Handel
   GERALD COKE — 1

2. The Hamburg Collection
   HANS DIETER CLAUSEN — 10

3. The Malmesbury Collection
   WINTON DEAN — 29

4. The Aylesford Collection
   JOHN H. ROBERTS — 39

5. The Shaftesbury Collection
   ANTHONY HICKS — 87

6. The Barrett Lennard Collection
   DONALD BURROWS — 108

7. The Chandos Collection
   GRAYDON BEEKS — 137

8. The Shaw-Hellier Collection
   PERCY YOUNG — 158

9. The Hall Collection
   J. MERRILL KNAPP — 171

10. The Santini Collection
    HANS JOACHIM MARX — 184

11. The Music-Paper used by Handel and his
    Copyists in Italy, 1706–1710
    KEIICHIRO WATANABE — 198

12. Italian Source-Studies and Handel
    PAUL EVERETT — 227

13. Early German Handel Editions during the
Classical Period
BERND BASELT   238

Index of Handel's works   249

General Index   251

Notes on the Contributors

BERND BASELT is Professor of Musicology at the Martin-Luther University in Halle, President of the Georg-Friedrich-Händel Gesellschaft, and General Editor of the HHA. He has published a thematic catalogue of Handel's works (HWV), and other books and articles on German music, as well as editions of works by Handel, Telemann, Gluck, and other composers.

GRAYDON BEEKS, Director of Music Programming and Facilities and Associate Professor of Music at Pomona College, Claremont, California, has worked extensively on the music at Cannons under the 1st Duke of Chandos, and completed a thesis on Handel's Cannons Anthems in 1981. He has contributed articles and reviews to numerous journals and collections of essays. From 1991–3 he served as President of the American Handel Society.

TERENCE BEST is a member of the Editorial Board of the HHA, and author of a number of articles on Handel. He has edited five volumes of instrumental music for the HHA, with four more volumes (including *Tamerlano* and *Radamisto*) in preparation, and also volumes of keyboard music, chamber music, and organ concertos for Novello, OUP, and Faber. He is a founding Council Member of the Handel Institute.

DONALD BURROWS is head of the Music Department at the Open University, Milton Keynes; a member of the Vorstand of the Georg-Friedrich-Händel-Gesellschaft and of the Advisory Board of the Maryland Handel Festival (USA). He is the author of a book about *Messiah* (Cambridge, 1991) and coauthor of *A Catalogue of Handel's Musical Autographs* (Oxford, 1993). Publications of Handel's works under his editorship include *Messiah*, *Belshazzar*, the Foundling Hospital Anthem, and the complete Violin Sonatas. In 1975 he conducted the first modern revivals of some of Handel's church music. He is a founding Council Member of the Handel Institute.

HANS DIETER CLAUSEN is the author of the catalogue of Handel's conducting scores (*Händels Direktionspartituren* ('*Handexemplare*') (Hamburg, 1972)). He is deputy headmaster of a comprehensive school in Hamburg.

WINTON DEAN is the author of many books and articles on Handel. He has a particular interest in music for the theatre, and is coauthor of the comprehensive study *Handel's Operas 1704–1726* (Oxford

1987); his book on the oratorios has been a standard work for over 30 years. He contributed the Handel article to *New Grove*, and he has done important research into Handel's copyists. He is a Vice-President of the Georg-Friedrich-Händel-Gesellschaft in Halle, and a founding Council Member of the Handel Institute.

PAUL EVERETT is Lecturer in Music at University College, Cork. A specialist in the analysis of Italian manuscripts, he has published *The Manchester Concerto Partbooks* (New York, 1989) and several articles on Vivaldi sources. While continuing to research the chronology of Vivaldi's music, he is currently writing a book for CUP on the composer's Op. 8 collection. He has edited many works, and serves on the committee of the Istituto Italiano Antonio Vivaldi responsible for the New Critical Edition of Vivaldi's music (Ricordi).

ANTHONY HICKS read mathematics at King's College, London, and has since pursued a career in computing. His musicological studies, undertaken in his spare time, have concentrated on Handel and baroque opera. He contributed the Handel work-list to *New Grove* and he has provided articles on Handel and Handel's operas for *The New Grove Dictionary of Opera*. His other publications include essays on individual Handel works, and notes for recordings and concert programmes. He is a founding Council Member of the Handel Institute.

J. MERRILL KNAPP (1914–93) studied music at Yale and Columbia Universities. In 1946 he became Assistant Professor of Music at Princeton University, later serving as academic Dean and Professor of Music. He was the author of *Selected List of Music for Men's Voices* (Princeton, NJ, 1952), *The Magic of Opera* (New York, 1972; 3rd edn. 1984), and coauthor of *Handel's Operas 1704–1726* (Oxford, 1987). He conducted the first performances in the United States of Handel's *Imeneo* (1965) and *Amadigi* (1969). He was a member of the Vorstand and sometime Vice-President of the Georg-Friedrich-Händel-Gesellschaft in Halle, and member of the Editorial Board of the HHA, for which he edited *Amadigi* and *Flavio*. It is with regret that we report the death of John Merrill Knapp while this book was in the press.

HANS JOACHIM MARX is Professor of Musicology at the University of Hamburg. He has published editions, books, and articles on the music of the Renaissance and the Baroque, especially Corelli and Handel. He is chairman of the Symposia of the Händel-Akademie Karlsruhe, and Editor-in-Chief of the *Göttinger Händel-Beiträge*. He is a Vice-President of the Georg-Friedrich-Händel-Gesellschaft in Halle, and member of the Editorial Board of the HHA, for which he has edited Handel's Italian Cantatas with instruments.

NOTES ON THE CONTRIBUTORS

JOHN H. ROBERTS is Head of the Music Library and Professor of Music at the University of California, Berkeley. He has written extensively on Handel's borrowings, and edited the facsimile series *Handel Sources* (New York, 1986). He is a member of the Editorial Board of the HHA.

KEIICHIRO WATANABE is Professor of Music History at the Toho Gakuen College of Music in Tokyo. He is an authority on the music of Handel's Italian years, and has done comprehensive research into the paper and copyists of the period.

PERCY M. YOUNG is the author of *Handel* (Master Musicians: London, 1947; rev. edn. 1975) and editor of *Saul* for the HHA. He has written much on eighteenth- and nineteenth-century subjects, and has recently published *The English Glee* (Oxford, 1990) and the Critical Edition of Elgar's *The Spanish Lady*. He has for many years been a member of the Vorstand and sometime Vice-President of the Georg-Friedrich-Händel-Gesellschaft in Halle, and member of the Kuratorium of the Händel-Gesellschaft in Göttingen. He is Honorary Fellow of the Institute for Advanced Research in the Humanities in Birmingham University.

List of Illustrations

Frontispiece   Gerald Coke

Chapter 2
1.   Performing score of *Radamisto*, Dec. 1720, beginning of the aria 'Sì che ti renderai'.

Chapter 5
1.   Anthony Ashley Cooper, 4th Earl of Shaftesbury, portrait by Joseph Highmore.

Chapter 6
1.   The Barrett Lennard Collection, as listed in the *Catalogue of the Valuable Musical Library of the Late T. Greatorex* (1832).
2.   Overture *Agrippina*, arr. Henry Barrett Lennard, and in his hand.

Chapter 9
1.   First page of the Sinfonia, Act 3, *Alexander Balus*.
2.   First page of the score of *Belshazzar*.
3.   Back of a libretto of *Muzio Scevola*, showing Handel's laundry list.

List of Figures

Chapter 7
1.   The Brydges and Leigh family tree.

Abbreviations

General

Grove	George Grove (ed.), *A Dictionary of Music and Musicians* (London, 1879–89)
HG	Händel-Gesellschaft edn., ed. F. Chrysander
HHA	Hallische Händel-Ausgabe
HjB	*Händel-Jahrbuch*
HWV	Verzeichnis der Werke Georg Friedrich Händels
MGG	*Die Musik in Geschichte und Gegenwart*, xi (Kassel, 1963)
ML	*Music and Letters*
MT	*Musical Times*
New Grove	S. Sadie (ed.), *The New Grove Dictionary of Music and Musicians* (London, 1980)
WM	watermark

Library Sigla

A: Austria

Wgm	Vienna, Gesellschaft der Musikfreunde

Aus: Australia

NSWpm	New South Wales, Powerhouse Museum, Ultimo
Sfl	Sydney, University of Sydney Library, Edward Richardson Collection

CH: Switzerland

Gbb	Geneva, Biblioteca Bodmeriana
Bfl	Basel, Floersheim Collection, private collection

ABBREVIATIONS

D: Germany

B	Berlin, Staatsbibliothek Preussischer Kulturbesitz
Bds	Berlin, Deutsche Staatsbibliothek (formerly Königliche Bibliothek; Preussische Staatsbibliothek; Öffentliche Wissenschaftliche Bibliothek), Musikabteilung
HAu	Halle an der Saale, Universitäts- und Landesbibliothek Sachsen-Anhalt
Hs	Hamburg, Staats- und Universitätsbibliothek
HVsb	Hanover, Stadtsbücherei
Maw	Munich, Arwin Wiegand Library, private collection
MÜs	Münster, Santini-Bibliothek (in Bischöfliches Priesterseminar und Santini-Sammlung)

GB: Great Britain

BENcoke	Bentley (Hants.), Gerald Coke, private collection
Cfm	Cambridge, Fitzwilliam Museum
Ckc	Cambridge, Rowe Music Library, King's College
H	Hereford Cathedral
Lam	London, Royal Academy of Music
Lbl	London, British Library, Reference Division (formerly British Museum)
Lcm	London, Royal College of Music
Lgo	London, Guy Oldham, private collection
Lpro	London, Public Record Office
LVmt	Liverpool, Michael Talbot, private collection
Mp	Manchester, Central Public Library, Henry Watson Music Library
Ob	Oxford, Bodleian Library
Och	Oxford, Christ Church

I: Italy

Tn	Turin, Biblioteca Nazionale Universitaria

J: Japan

Tn	Tokyo, Nanki Music Library, Ohki, private collection

NL: The Netherlands

DHgm	The Hague, Gemeentemuseum

ABBREVIATIONS   xvii

US: United States of America

Cn	Chicago, Newberry Library
CP	Maryland, University Library, College Park
Cu	Chicago, University Music Library
MT	Morristown, NJ, National Historical Park Library
NH	New Haven, Conn., Yale University, School of Music Library
NYpm	New York, Pierpont Morgan Library
PRu	Princeton University, Harvey S. Firestone Memorial Library
R	Rochester University, Eastman School of Music, Sibley Music Library
SFsc	San Francisco State College Library, Frank V. de Bellis Collection
SM	San Marino (Calif.), Henry E. Huntington Library and Art Gallery
Wc	Washington, DC, Library of Congress, Music Division
Ws	Washington, DC, Folger Shakespeare Libraries

Editorial Note

The authors of the papers read at the conference in November 1990 have revised their contributions for the present volume. Those by Dr Clausen and Dr Watanabe were composed and read in English, but at their request I have considerably rewritten their texts, without, of course, altering the substance of their remarks. Professor Baselt's paper was read by him in my English translation of his German original; this also has been thoroughly reworked for publication. It follows that in these papers any infelicity in the English expression is entirely mine, and is not to be laid at the door of their distinguished authors. I am also responsible for the English translations in Appendix 1 of Professor Marx's paper, for the various items entered as 'Ed.'s Note' and for the compilation of the index. The paper by the late Gerald Coke is a special case, as explained by Dr Burrows in his notes.

After the introductory essay the contents are arranged in a logical sequence. Five papers deal with the major eighteenth-century collections: the most important (Hamburg) is placed first, followed by the others in an order determined largely by the dates at which they were begun (Chs. 2–6). The next three describe minor eighteenth-century collections and a major one from the twentieth century (Chs. 7–9). Chapters 10–12 form a group devoted to aspects of Handel's years in Italy: the important Santini collection of works composed there, the music-paper used by the composer and his copyists, and the wider significance of Italian source studies for Handel scholarship. Finally Professor Baselt explores the early dissemination of Handel's work in the country of his birth (Ch. 13).

I am grateful to all my colleagues for their co-operation, and for their willingness to deal with points referred to them for checking; in particular to Anthony Hicks and Donald Burrows for their patience in answering questions arising from the need to achieve the greatest possible accuracy; and to Bruce Phillips and David Blackwell at Oxford University Press.

T. B.

I

Collecting Handel

GERALD COKE[1]

I STARTED my Handel Collection in the mid-1930s. Its genesis was an interest both in fine books and music, and the idea that the two interests should be channelled into the formation of a collection of fine and first editions of music. After a false start collecting Mozart first editions, which turned out to be too expensive (and over-collected), the idea of a Handel collection was born. This dream could not have been translated into reality without the help of Percy Muir of Elkin Mathews[2] whom I met through a mutual friend. Not only did he take immense trouble to learn about the subject—his firm had not previously done any business in this particular field—but he secured for me several indispensable guides, including a detailed list of the printed music in Newman Flower's collection and a copy of Schoelcher's catalogue of librettos. He introduced me to Willie Smith,[3] then in charge of the Music Room at the British

---

[1] Gerald Coke was born 25 Oct. 1907 and died 9 Jan. 1990. This article has been edited and annotated by Donald Burrows from the brief history of the Collection that Mr Coke included in a Memorandum to the Handel Institute (typescript, n.d. but prepared Autumn 1988). It is published with the kind permission of Mrs Coke, and thanks are also extended to David Coke, Valérie Emery, Alec Hyatt King, Barbara Muir, Basil Ramsey, William Reeves, and Stephen Roe for assistance with the preparation of the article in its present form. Typescript catalogues of the Coke Collection prepared by Gerald Coke are kept with the Collection at Jenkyn Place. There is no published catalogue of the Collection, but a list of the manuscripts and printed items that were filmed for the Harvester Microfilm Collection was published as *Music Manuscripts in Major Private Collections: The Gerald Coke Handel Collection, A Listing and Guide* (Brighton, 1988). The microfilms are available from Research Publications, Woodbridge CT 06525, USA, and from PO Box 45, Reading, Berkshire, RG1 8HF, UK. Since the volumes of the Coke Collection do not yet have shelf-marks, items which have been microfilmed are listed in this book by their Harvester numbers.

[2] Percy H. Muir (1894–1979), partner and director of Elkin Mathews Ltd. Obituary in *Book Collector*, 29: 1 (1980), 85–8, where he is described as the 'doyen of English antiquarian booksellers'.

[3] William Charles Smith (1881–1972, *not* 1973) entered the Dept. of Printed Books in the British Museum in 1900, on transfer from the Scottish Education Dept., as a second division Clerk. He began by cataloguing both books and music received by copyright deposit. In Mar. 1903 he was seconded to work entirely in the Music Room for Barclay Squire. Smith remained in the clerical grade until Jan. 1921, when he was promoted to Assistant (subsequently, the

[cont. on p.2]

2   COLLECTING HANDEL

Museum, who became a close friend and often stayed with us, especially when he was working on his *Descriptive Catalogue*.[4] This friendship ripened over the remaining forty years of his life and was to lead to an important addition to the Collection.

In the years before the outbreak of World War II I was able, with Percy's help, to build up the core of the engraved music and books in the Collection. Not so much was known about the bibliography of printed music in general (and Handel in particular) in those days and it was fairly easy to pick up first and early editions for a pound or two. Moreover, there were many more sales of music than there are today and Sotheby's in particular held several important ones in the late 1930s, including the disposal of the Willmott and Arkwright Collections.[5] In those years Percy secured for me two important items which were at the time in the United States—the holograph manuscript of Handel's will and four codicils, and the first (Dublin) edition of the libretto of *Messiah*. He also found, in this country, the extra-illustrated copy of the *Anecdotes*[6] formerly owned by Julian Marshall, some other unique items and some of the more important manuscripts, including the three-volume score of *Messiah*,[7] the Jennens (or Aylesford) copy of *L'Allegro*, the *Additional Songs in Rinaldo* (also an Aylesford MS) and other association volumes including *Joshua* from the Shaftesbury Collection, missing from St Giles's since 1756 but now united with the rest of the set of manuscripts.[8]

I also met several other booksellers who specialized in music— Cecil Hopkinson (1898–1977), Harold Reeves and William Reeves junior,[9] and Albi Rosenthal (b. 1914), a friendship which fifty years

grade was renamed Assistant Keeper) in succession to Squire who had retired in Nov. 1920. Smith's career in his first 20 years in the Museum is described in A. H. King, *Printed Music in the British Museum: An Account of the Collections, the Catalogues, and their formation, up to 1920* (London, 1979), 130, 149–50.

  [4] W. C. Smith, *Handel: A Descriptive Catalogue of the Early Editions* (London, 1960; 2nd edn., Oxford, 1970). A ch. devoted to the Coke Collection was included in Smith's book *A Handelian's Notebook* (London, 1965), which was dedicated to Gerald Coke.

  [5] Sotheby's Catalogues for the sales give the dates as follows: Miss Ellen Ann Willmott, 1–3 Apr. 1935; Godfrey Edward Pellew Arkwright, 13–14 Feb. 1939 (main sale: sales of the residue on 5 Dec. 1944 (Sotheby) and 31 Aug. 1945 (Hodgson) include nothing relevant to the present article).

  [6] [W. Coxe], *Anecdotes of George Frederick Handel and John Christopher Smith* (London, 1799).

  [7] The 'Coke' copy: see W. Shaw, *A Textual and Historical Companion to Handel's Messiah* (London, 1965), 75–6.

  [8] Gerald Coke describes his purchase of the main Shaftesbury Collection in the last paragraph of this ch.

  [9] William Reeves sen. (1853–1938) commenced bookselling in 1875 at 185 Fleet Street, moving in 1900 to 83 Charing Cross Road. He published the *Musical Standard*; subsequently music and books about music became a speciality. His son Harold Reeves (1880–1960) left him about 1918 to establish his own music bookselling firm, which he sold *c*.1946 to Kenneth Mummery. On William Reeves's death in 1938, his business was carried on by his other son Frank A. Reeves, moving in 1953 to 1a Norbury Crescent. Since Frank Reeves's death in 1958, his son William A. Reeves (b. 1916) has continued the business.

GERALD COKE 3

later was to bear rich fruit. Besides meeting some other British collectors of music I am also happy to have known Paul Hirsch (1881–1951), whose collection is owned by the British Library, and Jim [James Marshall] Osborn (1906–76), an American collector whose library exists as a separate entity at Yale.[10]

Perhaps most important, I was brought together with Otto Erich Deutsch.[11] I thought then, and I still think, that the writing and production of his *Documentary Biography* of Handel[12] was a most remarkable feat, comparable in a different context with Chrysander's almost single-handed production of a major part of the Händel-Gesellschaft music edition. After the outbreak of war Deutsch was an enemy alien working in a foreign country and a foreign language, but he managed to discover most of the important documents and contemporary references to Handel and after the war, against great odds at a time when even British authors had difficulty in getting books published, succeeded in publishing his important work. He came to Jenkyn Place for some weeks when he was producing the *Documentary Biography* and, since we were living in the cottage at the gate, he had to be put up at the hotel in Alton. Because of his status he had to report regularly to the police. I am glad to say that in 1951 I was able to help him by buying the manuscript of the *Documentary Biography* for a sum which assisted him to return to Vienna and continue his research.[13]

After the war I carried on, with Percy's help, with the build-up and consolidation of the Collection. The policy of buying any scores which differed from those already in the library was seen to have paid off when Willie Smith produced his *Descriptive Catalogue* in 1960 and it was possible to place in their correct order the various editions. The process of filling in gaps went on and continues until the present time. There are virtually no important gaps in the printed-music section and I have aimed at securing all the editions listed in Smith's catalogue.

Of course there were a number of items which were offered to me by friends in the trade, or which came up for sale in the auction-rooms, but which I could not afford. This was especially true of manuscripts, but over the years I have bought every manuscript which was within my means, even of works already in the Collection. On the whole this policy has turned out to have been worthwhile as,

---

[10] Of the book-dealers and collectors mentioned in this paragraph, Hopkinson, Rosenthal, and Hirsch have biographical entries in *New Grove*.

[11] 1883–1967: see the biographical entry in *New Grove*.

[12] *Handel: A Documentary Biography* (London, 1955).

[13] The connection here is uncertain: Coke bought Deutsch's materials in 1951, and Deutsch declared his intention to return to Vienna in letters (now in the Letter Books of the Coke Collection) from Sept. of that year, but he does not seem to have returned there permanently until Dec. 1954.

4 COLLECTING HANDEL

not being either a musician or a musicologist, I was not in a position to assess the importance or otherwise of a particular manuscript. Winton Dean's scholarly appraisal of manuscript sources for the operas up to 1726[14] has shown that nearly all the manuscripts relating to this period have something to offer in furthering our knowledge. Because so many of the full scores of oratorios were not published at the time of the first production, requiring those interested to have a manuscript copy made, comparatively large numbers of manuscript full scores are in existence for many of the oratorios. The Collection contains four manuscript copies of *Athalia*, five of *Israel in Egypt*, three of *Samson*, three of *Deborah*, two of *Belshazzar*, and so on, some of which may in the end turn out to be merely repetitive. Most of the manuscript items which I had to forego were scraps of Handel's autograph, manuscripts of comparatively unknown works and a few important association copies.

Whenever possible I tried to add to the engraved-music or books section copies in 'as issued' condition. Of course the value of a score of an opera to a musician or musicologist, or of a book to a student, is not affected by its condition, nor is its significance enhanced to the researcher or editor: but to the bibliophile the satisfaction of obtaining an item in the publisher's blue paper wrapper with its deckle edges uncut or perhaps in a contemporary binding, failing original boards, is enormous. On one occasion when Albi Rosenthal was browsing through the Collection, he stood almost in awe before a copy of the Trio Sonatas[15] which still has all its parts bound together in their blue-grey paper as issued by the publisher, and said that he had never seen a collection where so many items were still in their pristine state. On one of his visits to us Willie Smith became aware of the number of items in this category and went home to insert notes to this effect against some of the copies recorded in his *Descriptive Catalogue*.

During the early post-war period I was able to build up the fine-art section of the Collection. The Hudson portrait of John Beard, the Zoffany of J. C. Smith, the Frye of Leveridge, the Soldi of Geminiani, and other oil-paintings and drawings came in the 1950s and 1960s. I had not really had space to house many pictures until we moved into Jenkyn Place immediately after the war, and indeed the bookcases which I had installed when we first bought the house were soon full. When we had finished removing some Edwardian excrescences and cutting the kitchen area down to a reasonable size,

---

[14] In W. Dean and J. M. Knapp, *Handel's Operas 1704–1726* (Oxford, 1987).

[15] The 'Roger' ed. of Handel's Op. 2 set. See W. C. Smith, *Descriptive Catalogue*, p. 244, no. 1 and, on the origins of this publication, D. Burrows, 'Walsh's Editions of Handel's Op. 1–5' in C. Hogwood and R. Luckett (eds.), *Music in Eighteenth-Century England* (Cambridge, 1983), 79–102.

we decided to extend the top half of the music-room in order to improve on some ugly additions and to replace a conservatory which had become a danger through neglect. This had the further advantage—not altogether unanticipated—of providing additional shelf space. The various parts of the house gave wall space to display the pictures and a sizeable number of prints, the remainder being housed in solander cases. In order to obtain a number of prints of Handelian interest, I acquired three separate collections and decided to form the nucleus of a collection of musical prints.

One or two successes—and failures—may be of interest. When Novello the music-publishers moved from Wardour Street to Soho Square some of their collection was sold, and from this I gained a significant manuscript of *Teseo* and the near-contemporary plaster bust of Handel after the Roubiliac at Windsor.[16] Mrs Emery,[17] whose husband Walter was a dedicated musicologist, secured the latter for me and amongst other items over the years offered me the set of parts which contain, besides first editions of the *Water Music* and *Fireworks Music*, the only known contemporary copy of the four parts of the incidental music for *The Alchemist*.[18]

A minor triumph was the purchase of one of the Roubiliac models for the Westminister Abbey monument. A friend in the office of the National Trust told me that a friend of his had bought it in an antique shop in Bristol. I contacted the owner and bought the model from him without having seen it. I was especially pleased at having prevented this terracotta from passing into the dead hands of a museum. The Victoria and Albert Museum had decided in principle to acquire it but had not yet got financial clearance for the purchase and there were some glum faces when I went to collect it from the Museum where it had been temporarily deposited.

Another purchase illustrates how dotty the obsessive collector can become. As I have recorded, I bought a first edition of the *Messiah* libretto from America before the war. Another copy turned up in an auction-room, the only difference between it and my copy being that the slip pasted over 'Let all the Angels of God' to insert an additional

---

[16] Gerald Coke's text at this point was as follows: 'The fire at Novello's premises presented the opportunity for me to purchase a significant early *Teseo* manuscript—partially burnt— and also the near-contemporary plaster bust of Handel after the Roubiliac marble at Windsor.' The 'burnt' Teseo MS (described in Dean and Knapp, *Handel's Operas* 252–3 n. 14) was lot 360 in the sale of property of Novello & Co. Ltd. at Sotheby's (Sotheby and Co., 20 July 1965); the bust did not appear in the sale and may have been sold separately. The connection between the present state of the MS and any fire at Novello's is uncertain: employees of Novello's in the period before 1965 have no recollection of a fire.

[17] Valérie Emery, owner of the booksellers Travis and Emery.

[18] See W. C. Smith, *Descriptive Catalogue*, 8, and C. A. Price, 'Handel and The Alchemist', *MT* 116 (1975), 787–8.

6   COLLECTING HANDEL

recitative was inserted loosely.[19] I bought this copy also: now, of only five known copies of this libretto, two are in the Collection.

Not long after the war Percy Muir offered me a large collection of Burney papers. Much to my disappointment I could not afford to buy them all, though I managed to add to the Collection those concerned with the Handel Commemoration of 1784. The rest, which included manuscripts and proofs of the *History of Music*, went to Jim Osborn and are now with the Burney papers which form part of the large collection of eighteenth-century manuscripts which he bequeathed to Yale. Another of my regrets was to miss the chance of buying the Thornhill design, now in the Fitzwilliam Museum, Cambridge, for the lid of Handel's harpsichord. I did in fact bid for it but I set my limit rather low, because I had then and still have some doubts about it. It was exhibited at the National Portrait Gallery's Handel Exhibition in 1985 and the note in the catalogue summarizes some of my doubts;[20] but, as it carried an inscription linking it with Handel and was in itself a pleasant drawing, I am sorry not to have it, though, of course, part of the excitement of bidding at auction (whether by oneself or by proxy) lies in not knowing how far other bidders are prepared to go.

Three major acquisitions raised the interest and quality of the Collection. The first was the purchase of Willie Smith's entire collection. On several occasions when Willie was staying with us he discussed the future of his collection. His only son, who was a successful chartered accountant, predeceased him and his daughter was not interested in Handel and his works. After his wife died, Willie had to employ a housekeeper and his pension as a civil servant was not princely. He earned money from articles, books, and some advisory work for auctioneers and others but, in spite of his frugal habits, I was aware that he had not much to spare after his living expenses had been covered. So I proposed to him a solution which I hoped, like all the most satisfactory deals, would be advantageous to both sides. I suggested that I should buy and pay for his collection forthwith, but that it should remain in his possession for the rest of his life. This solution appealed to him and I was happy that it relieved his last years of some financial anxiety. As it happened, the collection came to me before his death because he had to move out of his house into rooms when his housekeeper left and he had insufficient space to house the collection.[21] But he came to Jenkyn

[19] The page concerned is illustrated in D. Burrows, 'The Autographs and Early Copies of "Messiah": Some Further Thoughts' in *ML* 66 (1985), 213.

[20] See J. Simon (ed.), *Handel: A Celebration of his Life and Times* (London, 1985), 179.

[21] Coke purchased Smith's collection in 1962, and it was transferred to Jenkyn Place in 1968: see W. C. Smith, *Descriptive Catalogue* (2nd edn., 1970), 331.

GERALD COKE 7

Place on a number of occasions to see it in its new setting and helped
to incorporate it into my catalogue. Items from Willie's collection
filled many gaps in my collection and brought five volumes of major
importance—for *Messiah*, unique first editions of the *Songs* and the
full score; the copy of *Admeto* with names of singers for the 1754
revival;[22] the only known copy of the pamphlet *Do you know what
you are about?*;[23] and an important manuscript of the 1732 version of
Esther. But perhaps of equal significance, I acquired all his papers
and a number of books with his marginal comments and corrections.
His papers are now contained in thirty boxes.

In the 1960s Lord Howe decided to dispose of the Handel items
which had once belonged to his ancestor Charles Jennens, and so
another opportunity was presented to add some especially important
items to the Collection. He sold the great Hudson portrait which had
been on loan to the National Portrait Gallery and which happily the
Gallery was able to purchase. The then Director, Dr Strong, asked me
not to compete for it, a request which I had no difficulty in agreeing
to because the picture itself is about nine feet high and is surrounded
by a frame which adds another three feet or so all round; I would
have had to enlarge the house to accommodate it. But in the same
sale was the portrait of Jennens by Mason Chamberlin and this fortunately I was able to buy. I also acquired an allegorical oil-painting
by Cipriani which had probably been commissioned by Jennens as a
design for a memorial print and which had, for some reason, been
sold before the main picture sale. In 1973 Christie's put up for sale
the nine autograph letters from Handel to Jennens, the Jennens–
Holdsworth correspondence and an enclosure to one of the letters in
the hand of J. C. Smith with a note by Handel.[24] This sale faced me
with a difficult decision; I obviously could not afford to buy all three
lots (the nine letters were sold in one lot), much as I should have
liked to do so; and after much cogitation I decided not to bid for the
autograph letters but to try to buy the Jennens-Holdsworth correspondence and the note by J. C. Smith. The Handel letters had all been
published by Erich Müller in 1935,[25] whereas the correspondence
(except for one letter published by Deutsch) was unknown and the
enclosure had been thought to have been lost. I was fortunate in

[22] See Smith, 'The 1754 Revival of Handel's "Admeto"', ML 51 (1970), 141–9. Smith erroneously believed that the annotations on the copy (some samples of which are illustrated with
the article) are in Handel's hand.

[23] *Do you know what you are about? or, a Protestant Alarm to Great Britain* (London, 1739),
listed by Deutsch (Handel, 868) as 'No Copy Known'.

[24] Autograph Letters of George Frideric Handel and Charles Jennens, Sale (Christie,
Manson & Woods), 4 July 1973.

[25] *The Letters and Writings of George Frideric Handel* (London).

8   COLLECTING HANDEL

securing both the lots, for which Laurie Deval[26] bid on my behalf (it
is not often that a private individual can claim to have bought two-
thirds of one sale!) but my good fortune did not end there, because
the letters were bought by Albi Rosenthal in partnership with an
American dealer [Bernard Breslauer]. Albi has a great sense of the
importance of placing things appropriately and he knew that I was
anxious to acquire the letter to which J. C. Smith's note was an
enclosure, so about a year after the sale he wrote and offered me the
letter which he had retained with this object. He also had another,
less important, letter still unsold and I was able to buy them both,
thus uniting the letter with its enclosure—the sort of happy outcome
which every collector hopes to achieve.

This extremely friendly act on Albi's part was followed about
fourteen years later by another. In 1987 I had a letter from him asking whether I would be interested in purchasing Lord Shaftesbury's
Collection of Handel manuscripts. With the exception of Lord
Malmesbury's Collection (originally commissioned by Elizabeth
Legh and given by Handel to Thomas Harris, Lord Malmesbury's
ancestor),[27] which is most unlikely to come to market, Lord
Shaftesbury's was the last contemporary collection still in private
hands, and indeed it was at that time still in the same house that had
been owned by the collection's founder.[28] If Lord Shaftesbury was
determined to dispose of his Collection, I felt that it would be an
important and interesting addition to mine. It would, moreover, save
the Shaftesbury Collection from going abroad. The British Library
had already said that they were not interested, and other public insti-
tutions to whom it had been offered had more urgent calls on their
funds. There was a real danger, therefore, that an overseas buyer
might have made an offer which Lord Shaftesbury could not refuse.
The 4th Lord Shaftesbury, who was Handel's friend and patron, had
formed a collection of the composer's works consisting partly of MSS
and partly of engraved music. Unfortunately his descendant had been
told that the whole was worth £1m. but Albi and Christie's managed
to convince him that this was a gross overestimate. I discussed the
purchase with Albi and told him that I was only interested in the
manuscripts, as I already had copies of all the engraved music—in
many cases in better condition. In agreement with Albi I made an
offer which, after some delay, was accepted. Lord Shaftesbury had told
Christie's that he was retaining the manuscript of *Judas Maccabaeus*

[26] d. 1982. Partner with Percy Muir (see n. 2, above) of Elkin Mathews Ltd. in Muir's later
years. From 1970, when Muir retired from London, Deval set up as a partner of Deval and
Muir, Elkin Mathews continuing successively under Muir and his widow.
[27] See Ch. 3, below.
[28] See Ch. 5, below.

and one of the two copies of *L'Allegro*, the latter because the volume also contained the *Comus* music which had a special connection with his family. I should probably have insisted on the Collection being kept together, but Lord Shaftesbury forestalled me by offering to have photocopies made at his expense. This was done for him by the British Library and the copies joined the manuscripts. Moreover, the manuscript of *Joshua* which I had bought before the war was at last reunited with its companions.

POSTSCRIPT

Ed.'s Note: It was Gerald Coke's intention that the Handel Institute should eventually be responsible for the care of the Coke Handel Collection; the permanent future location of the Collection is under review, and arrangements for access may be made through the Secretary of the Institute.

2

The Hamburg Collection

HANS DIETER CLAUSEN

HANDEL'S works have come down to us more extensively and more comprehensively than those of any other composer of the time. This is the result not only of the great popularity of their creator, but also of the great pains that he bestowed on their preservation. This seems to have been one of the tasks which he entrusted to Johann Christoph Schmidt (anglicized hereafter as John Christopher Smith), the friend who had followed him from Germany to England. It is surely unique for a composer to have assembled in his own home two separate archives, one consisting of autographs and the other of conducting scores, quite apart from other archives which were commissioned by individual collectors who wanted complete sets of the composer's works. That Handel needed two archives casts light upon his working method, which is characterized by an especially intensive exploitation of musical material as well as by the utmost economy in using his time.

His archive of copies has usually been called in German *Handexemplare* (= composer's copies), a term going back to Chrysander and to their entry into the old catalogue of the Hamburg City Library; but the term *Exemplar* or *Handexemplar* in German should really be used only to describe an item chosen from a number of others of the same kind, for instance a print into which corrections, addenda, etc., were inserted, usually when a new edition was being planned. The term *Direktionspartitur*—conducting score, theatre copy, performing score— seems to be more suitable; but it cannot be employed for all the Hamburg scores, since neither the contents of this collection nor those of Handel's original second archive totally coincide with the surviving body of conducting scores. Apart from the fact that some of these are not in Hamburg, and that some probably got into it by chance, the Collection has always contained manuscripts which did not serve as conducting scores but as archive or harpsichord scores; so *Handexemplar*, used in the sense of a 'copy at the composer's hand', may be adequate as a generic term.

There are reasons for supposing that Handel's collection of copies was originally intended to hold archive scores, not performing scores.

Two manuscripts have survived from his Italian period which most probably were conducting scores, of *Il trionfo del tempo* (D-MÜs 1896/1914a) and of *La Resurrezione* (D-MÜs 1873/1873a), and one which served as his archive score of *Il trionfo* (GB-Lbl R.M.19.d.9). The copying of the conducting scores was begun before the composition was given its definitive form; only the archive score was kept by Handel himself.

The conducting score of *Il trionfo* was written before the final version of the music was arrived at.[1] Moreover, this manuscript has additional directions for performance ('forte', 'piano', 'si sona senza cembalo', etc.) which are not in the autograph; probably they were important for the copyists of the parts. The history of this manuscript makes clear that Handel did not keep it in his archive.

The archive score of this oratorio dates from about the same period, though written a little later.[2] Handel subsequently pencilled into it directions for the copying of a new score for the 1737 performance; from these directions and from the history of the manuscript it follows that he kept it as his archive score.

Comparing the two manuscripts one can already observe a number of differences which are valid also for later periods. Most of the conducting score was written by the excellent copyist Angelini (and the rest certainly under his supervision), whereas the archive score is the work of inferior scribes. Mistakes in the conducting score were generally corrected, while in the archive score even major errors such as the omission of bars were not amended. The conducting score remained in the place of performance (for the time being), whereas the archive score came to England in the composer's baggage.

D-MÜs 1873/1873a was probably the conducting score of *La Resurrezione*. This may be demonstrated by the fact that the manuscript was written while changes in the libretto and the music were still being made. Only gathering-numbers indicate the original order of movements found in the autograph, but the score was then laid out in such a way that the music could be read easily without interruption. In the first part, Angelini is the main copyist, and Handel wrote corrections and additions for performance (additional trumpet

---

[1] It contains 2 versions of the recit. 'Questa è la reggia mia'. The 1st was abandoned before the text was written, for unlike the later practice in London the 1st procedure in copying a recitative was to write the music only. The most plausible explanation for Handel's rewriting emerges from a comparison of the musical and prosodic aspects of the 2 versions: Handel had omitted some words while composing, and this was noticed when the text was written, so he composed a new beginning into the autograph.

[2] The recit. 'Questa è la reggia mia' had reached its final form when the score was written.

parts in the Introduzione to the second part). Finally, in this manuscript there is for the first time an important indication that it served as a conducting score: there are traces of changes made during rehearsals or between performances—the shortening of a recitative and the elimination of an aria. In the aria, only the bars before the first page-turn were crossed out, which indicates that at that time the folios were stitched together.

From Handel's early London period almost no conducting score seems to have survived; at most, a fire-damaged manuscript in the Coke Collection could have been used in performance. The reason for the absence of all the others may be found in considerations of storage and ownership; like the instrumental parts, the conducting scores belonged to the theatres and disappeared with them. An example of this rule of ownership is Heidegger's note of 5 May 1711, concerning payments to 'Lunecan' (the copyist Linike), which certainly refers to the theatre copy of *Rinaldo* (probably score and parts, judging by the sum involved). These payments prove that it was not Handel who owned the conducting score, and that there was a close relationship between ownership and the place where the manuscript was kept ('Lunecan' was allowed to take the score 'in his custody' after every performance, until it was entirely paid for).

The fact that the conducting scores were not Handel's property explains why he collected archive scores. These are identified by the composer's markings referring to later performances or, in the absence of such markings, by belonging to the Hamburg Collection. It can be observed that manuscripts which are evidently archive scores contain very different amounts of correction: in *Il trionfo* and *Rinaldo* many serious errors are not amended, while *Teseo* and *Amadigi* are more extensively corrected.

Archive scores of Handel's two earliest London operas are preserved; they are not in the Hamburg Collection, but are clearly identified by Handel's directions for their adaptation in the 1730s. Whereas one of them (*Rinaldo*, GB-Lbl R.M.19.d.5) was without any doubt nothing more than an archive score, it has been thought that the other (*Il pastor fido*, GB-Lbl R.M.19.e.4) had already served as a conducting score.[3] As this question is important in some respects, I have to consider briefly the arguments and counter-arguments: the most important argument is that this score was copied before the first performance, and contains changes which were made either before it or soon afterwards, written as insertions. There are indeed some pointers to such an early date, but none which can be taken as conclusive. The manuscript certainly contained a B flat major version

[3] W. Dean and J. M. Knapp, *Handel's Operas 1704–1726* (Oxford, 1987), 226–7.

of the aria 'Di goder' before it was replaced by the A major version; but it is doubtful whether this was the B flat major version of the autograph, which does not correspond to the printed libretto, because this version was itself an insertion into the autograph at a place where the original contents are not preserved. Thus R.M.19.e.4 was not necessarily written before the first performance.

The most important obstacle to the classification of this manuscript as a conducting score is the way in which the aria 'Ho un non so che nel cor' was inserted: it was placed at the end of the manuscript with nothing but a cue in the context. Handel generally treated the conducting scores differently from the autographs and archive scores by having insertions stitched (not merely placed) exactly where they needed to be, and by having bars rewritten which had been covered by them. Apart from the da capo arias, the tiresome business of turning the leaves forwards and backwards had to be avoided.

So I consider it possible that R.M.19.e.4 was copied later than 1712, from the autograph, at a time when the conducting score was not available. Linike, the copyist, was not able to find the inserted music in that source; but one can easily imagine that Handel asked him later to update the archive score by copying into it material from the conducting score.

Linike was Handel's most important copyist between 1711 and 1720, like Angelini previously and Smith later; it cannot be doubted that he wrote Handel's conducting scores. If they had survived, we would have reliable clues for dating the early stages of his handwriting, that is the stages with the C clef of the 'comfortable armchair' type.[4] If R.M.19.e.4 is no longer to be considered as a conducting score, we lose one of the most valuable clues for dating. Before using the changes in Linike's handwriting for this purpose, it has to be decided whether the form of the crotchet-rest or that of the semiquavers is to be taken as a guide, since they lead to different chronologies. I suggest that we rely on the semiquavers and ignore the rests, which would result in the order given in Table 1, or face the possibility that two copyists shared the same clefs.[5]

The opera *Teseo* may be the only work from the second decade of which both the conducting score and the archive score have been preserved. In the early copy in the Coke Collection we find respected,

[4] W. Dean, 'Handel's Early London Copyists', in P. Williams (ed.), *Bach, Handel, Scarlatti, Tercentenary Essays* (Cambridge, 1985), 75–97.

[5] The clefs, esp. the C clef, have generally proved to be such a reliable criterion for distinguishing different copyists that one is tempted to believe in deliberately chosen marks, perhaps originally intended to facilitate the copyists' accounts rather than to be expressions of personal individuality. Thus 2 copyists may have used the same clefs when the money was paid into the same purse.

Table 1. Changes in Linike's Handwriting

| Title | Shelf-mark | Semiquaver stems | | Crotchet-rests |
		Upwards	Downwards	
Rinaldo	GB-Lbl R.M.19.d.5			
Teseo	GB-BENcoke MS 100			
Amadigi	GB-BENcoke MS 14			
Il pastor fido	GB-Lbl R.M.19.e.4			
Amadigi	D-Hs MA/1003			
Duets	D-Hs MB/2767			

though not totally applied, the rules of the layout of conducting scores mentioned above. The alterations made in this score, mainly cuts in the recitatives, can surely be dated back to before the first performance, because the printed word-book puts them in *virgolette*.

Handel's archive score of this opera was probably GB-Lbl R.M. 19.e.6, which may have the same origin as the archive scores of *Rinaldo* and *Il pastor fido*. Its arias have been copied from the autograph, its recitatives from the conducting score, taking account of the cuts. In the 1730s Handel pencilled in directions for the transposition of two arias which had to be transferred to other operas.

Of the works which followed *Teseo*, *Amadigi* and *Acis and Galatea* are represented in the Hamburg Collection. The score of *Amadigi* has been corrected by Handel, but neither of the two shows directions for the preparation of a later conducting score. With *Acis and Galatea* that is surprising; the version performed in 1732 was not prepared from this score. The same is true for the 1739 version, of which the conducting score is lost; while the draft for the 1732 version cannot be found anywhere, several directions in the autograph are related to the 1739 performance.

Wolfram Windszus[6] supposes that the manuscript of the masque owned by the Duke of Chandos was the conducting score. In Noland's catalogue of the music at Cannons it is called ' "O the pleasure of the plain", a masque for 5 voices and instruments, in score'. Brian Trowell[7] convincingly demonstrates the relationship of six manuscripts

---

[6] *Georg Friedrich Händel: Aci, Galatea e Polifemo, Cantata von 1708; Acis and Galatea, Masque von 1718; Acis and Galatea, italienisch-englische Serenata von 1732: Kritischer Bericht im Rahmen der Hallischen Händel-Ausgabe* (Hamburg, 1979).

[7] *Acis, Galatea and Polyphemus: A 'serenata a tre voci'?* in N. Fortune (ed.), *Music and Theatre: Essays in Honour of Winton Dean* (Cambridge, 1987), 33–5.

2.1. Performing score of *Radamisto*, Dec. 1720, beginning of the aria 'Sì che ti renderai'; the violin and viola parts as well as the music of the preceding recitative written by Handel, the rest by J. C. Smith sen. (D-Hs M A/1043, vol. II, fo. 23ᵛ).

to this source; we look forward to the fascinating experiment of reconstructing a conducting score. If it verifies Windzsus's assumption, the thesis would be confirmed that the organizer of a performance was the owner of the conducting score.

In 1720 Handel must have agreed with the directors of the Royal Academy of Music that he should keep and own the conducting scores, because beginning in December 1720 the first copies of his stage works, which were used for further copying as well as for rehearsals and performances, also served him as archive scores. This arrangement must have been the main reason why he ordered another conducting score of the opera *Radamisto*. Normally, later revisions (even extensive ones, as in *Scipione*, 1730–1) were made in the old conducting scores whenever they were in his possession.

The change in Handel's habits of preservation more or less coincides with the début of Smith as his principal copyist. Though comparison with older conducting scores is hardly possible, there is good reason to suppose that Handel's way of preparing a performance changed when a friend undertook the task. The character of the conducting scores came nearer to that of the autographs: they have more passages in the composer's own hand, and are sometimes—whether wholly or partly autograph—the originals of revised versions, both of single arias and of extensively transformed and pasticcio-like works.

In recasting *Radamisto* for the ensemble of the second season Handel made extensive use of this close collaboration. Not only did

16 THE HAMBURG COLLECTION

he write into the score the music of the recitatives which had to be rewritten because of changes in the cast, and instrumental parts which needed alteration because of transpositions, but he also wrote the whole of two revised arias into the manuscript while Smith paused, and Smith continued where Handel had left off. The fact that these arias are not insertions, but are part of the original paper-disposition, allows us to conclude from the watermarks (which give a probability of 32: 1) that the Berlin autograph fragment 'Alzo al volo' was part of the manuscript in 1720–1.

The high proportion of autograph sections in this score may be an exception resulting from the beginning of a new collaboration. Only a few later scores (most notably *Esther* and *Messiah*) are similar; but there are reasons for supposing that the autograph sections must have been larger than they are today, because after their rediscovery, and perhaps earlier, these scores were noticed and appreciated not for their value as sources—arising from their original function—but on account of these autograph sections. It may well be that they have occasionally been plundered; this cannot easily be proved when insertions have been removed from the manuscripts, but it is certain that autograph folios disappeared from the scores of *Esther* and *Joseph* after the manuscripts were foliated by the Hamburg City Library.

Handel's last purely archive scores (*Acis and Galatea* and the first version of *Radamisto*) were either only partially written by Smith or not at all, whereas he wrote the original contents of nearly all the conducting scores; an exception is *Muzio Scevola* in 1720–1, written by H1. Other exceptions are to be found mainly among the pasticcios.

The earliest copies were commonly made while Handel was still composing. From the datings in the autographs we know that he organized his compositional process in two phases: a first stage when he wrote the text of the recitatives and often only a draft of the arias, and a second stage when all was completely *ausgefüllet*. If time was short between composition and the first performance Smith followed Handel immediately; that is he did not wait until Handel had completed a section of the work, but copied whatever was to hand. This can be demonstrated in the case of works which had to be recast during composition. Sometimes Handel's and Smith's method of working allows us to distinguish between different stages of the composer's revisions; occasionally large sections of the conducting score had to be replaced before the first performance, to the extent that the score has to be considered a new manuscript which possibly includes small parts of the older one. In some cases it must be assumed that the replaced and lost parts of the score contained autograph directions and alterations.

The use by Handel and Smith of paper from the same batch confirms the especially close relationship between composition and copying in the case of *Floridante*, where several stages of reworking before the first performance can be distinguished. The paper used for this opera shows four different pairs of watermarks: two of them (Cb and Bd) appear together over a longer period and were in use for both scores when Handel and Smith started work. After a while both of them came by a small quantity of paper with the rare watermark Be. The same thing happened with Bb paper towards the end of their work. From the points where these papers appear for the first time in both scores it can be judged how closely Smith followed Handel as he worked on the composition.

Whereas after *Muzio Scevola* there are not more than four cases where secondary copyists were employed in writing parts of opera and oratorio conducting scores (mostly towards the end of the manuscript), they usually wrote important parts of the pasticcio scores, working closely with Smith. The same picture is found in two versions of Handel's works for which there are no autographs: the 1732 *Esther* and the 1734 *Il pastor fido*.

In the pasticcio scores the nature of the collaboration between Handel and Smith, and between Smith and other copyists, frequently changes, depending on the origin of the arias and the treatment of the recitatives.[8] In the conducting scores the recitatives were written completely by the copyists, or completely by Handel, or he wrote or sketched part of them into the blank staves where the words had already been copied. When Smith prepared the staves for the recitatives he reserved pages for arias depending on their length. Irregularities in the order of gatherings arose when the copyist needed more pages than Smith had estimated. Only in the case of *Venceslao* do the arias seem to have been copied first, the recitatives being inserted subsequently—nearly all the arias begin on fresh gatherings.

The harpsichord scores which form part of the Hamburg Collection date only from the second Academy period. This raises two questions:

1. Have the lacunae in the series of harpsichord scores from the second Academy been caused by loss?

2. Did scores for a second harpsichord also exist during the first Academy period?

[8] The discovery of Handel's source-scores by R. Strohm ('Handel's Pasticci' *Analecta musicologica*, 14 (1974), 208–67, repr. in id., *Essays on Handel and Italian Opera* (Cambridge, 1985), 164–211), and J. H. Roberts ('Handel and Vinci's *Didone abbandonata*: Revisions and Borrowings', *ML* 68 (1987), 141–50, and 'Handel and Charles Jennens' Italian Opera Manuscripts', in Fortune (ed.) *Music and Theatre*, 159–202) allows us to observe that Handel frequently used the music of their recits., or at least their prosody and/or their melodic ductus.

The lacunae in the series of harpsichord scores seem to be accidental, determined neither by the type of work nor by the place of performance. In a third of the cases where works are represented by two scores, one of them is not part of the Hamburg Collection. The reason may be that previous owners of the Collection were more inclined to give away single scores when there were two of the same work. Even the old catalogue of the Hamburg City Library designates these scores as duplicates, although there are sometimes important differences in scoring between conducting score and harpsichord score.

Some of these separated manuscripts have reappeared in one way or another; further harpsichord scores may yet be found. In addition to those which I included in my catalogue I can state that the full-score GB-Lbl Add. MS 31565 is the manuscript which Chrysander considered to be the harpsichord score of the opera *Orlando*. The copyist is John Christopher Smith junior, the paper C*d, which made its first appearance in Handel manuscripts only four years later; so in the absence of alterations made in this opera we have to leave open the question of whether Chrysander was right or not.

The total lack of harpsichord scores from the first Academy period cannot be the result of accidental losses, as pointed out above; it must be attributed to different conditions of storage or to a different performing practice.

A re-examination of the sources of *Floridante* leads to the conclusion that the early copy of the first act (GB-Lbl R.M.19.c.10) was written to be a part of the harpsichord score, but was replaced before use. Changes in the cast forced Handel to revise the opera drastically when he had composed one act and a half. These revisions reached the point where he had to replace the first volume of the conducting score as well as that of the harpsichord score. He used one or two gatherings of the original volume of the conducting score for the new one; all the others are lost, but the rejected first volume of the harpsichord score has survived in the Royal Music Library; Handel used one of its gatherings a year later as an insertion in the conducting score. In my catalogue I considered this manuscript to be the original conducting score; but between the autograph and R.M.19.c.10 we must assume an intermediate stage, a manuscript with autograph alterations, which can only have been the first conducting score. On the other hand, it makes no sense to take the fragment as the second version of the conducting score, and the Hamburg manuscript as the third, because there was no need to write a second one when Smith began copying R.M.19.c.10. Thus

this manuscript can only have been intended to serve as a harpsichord score.[9] A further clue to its intended function is the bass of the March introducing the second scene, which was added later on blank staves. With this addition the appearance of the fragment is like that of the harpsichord scores of *Poro* and *Arianna*. They are full scores, but for the inserted pieces they give only the bass part.

We can assume now that there existed harpsichord scores for all Handel's operas of the first Academy period; they were kept together with the instrumental parts and have been lost with them. Because R.M.19.c.10 was never used in performance it was preserved from this fate. From the start of the second Academy the question of preservation and perhaps also of ownership must have been settled differently; but I am unable to explain why all Handel's harpsichord and organ scores and parts for the oratorios are lost (except *Alexander's Feast*, GB-Lcm MS 900). Perhaps, unlike the opera manuscripts, they were all really parts (type 3, as defined in the following paragraph) and not scores, complete or incomplete.

Chrysander was the first to realize the function of some of these so-called duplicates, and it was he who called them *Cembalopartituren*. Besides the bass of all the movements, harpsichord parts generally contain only the vocal parts of the arias and recitatives. But up to 1732–3 all the harpsichord scores of the Hamburg Collection (except the pasticcios) are full scores (type 1). In 1733–4 they resemble harpsichord parts for the first time (type 3), and a year later one of them is restricted to the bass line in the arias (type 4). The latest harpsichord scores we have, those from the season of 1737–8, are laid out like full scores, but contain only the music which can be found in normal harpsichord parts (type 2).

The practical requirements of performance do not explain the enormous labour of writing a complete second score, nor the waste of paper in harpsichord scores of type 2. It may be that it was useful to have another copy because the writing out of the vocal and instrumental parts was largely based on a division of labour, and scores of type 2 also offered the possibility of being filled in at a later date. Comparison of the two manuscripts of *Poro* suggests the likelihood that all fully scored harpsichord scores first belonged to type 2, and were completed only when there was enough time.[10]

---

[9] In this matter I agree with Dean and Knapp, though we have differing opinions about the relationship between the MSS (see Clausen, 'Die Enstehung der Oper *Floridante*', *Göttinger Händel-Beiträge*, 4 (1991), 108–33).

[10] In the harpsichord score of *Poro* some bars in a sinfonia (Act 1 Scene 11) were cancelled between the 1st and 2nd working process, and therefore omitted when the score was filled in. That is why in the cancelled bars a treble part can be found, as a sort of place-keeper, only where the bass is silent.

Whereas the conducting scores of Handel's operas, with the exceptions already mentioned, were written by Smith, and those of the pasticcios were written at least under his supervision, secondary copyists predominate in the harpsichord scores. They often took notice of the page-division of the music which Smith, the more experienced copyist, had set out for them; as a result sometimes even the points where a new gathering begins are identical in both manuscripts.

However, sometimes it was necessary to observe this exact correlation between the two manuscripts simply because some sheets or gatherings which had been eliminated from the conducting scores were destined for use in the harpsichord scores. This probably happened when parts of the conducting score spoiled the general appearance of the manuscript in one way or another. If we compare five harpsichord scores where this procedure is followed—though in the case of *Didone* we must content ourselves with Arnold's description—we can discover what was considered a defect in this sense. Adapting *Rinaldo* for the 1730–1 season, Handel had saved work by writing the recitatives on the staves of the conducting score prepared by the copyist. The same thing must have happened with the pasticcio *Didone*. In *Ariodante* two copyists, Smith and S1, had copied the first act, but only the gatherings written by Smith remained in the conducting score. In the eleventh and twelfth gatherings of the pasticcio *Alessandro Severo*, changes had been made in the text of two arias, and corrections in the recitative. In *Poro* the notes of the last gathering in the first act were no longer easy to read because cuts had been made. In all these cases the changes of copyists and of scoring in the harpsichord score can have only this origin; it seems that in the 1730s the conducting score had to be a clean copy, written by one copyist only, and with writing which gave a homogeneous and tidy impression, when an opera was produced for the first time. This is surprising in view of the numerous alterations which spoiled the appearance of many conducting scores at later performances.

Generally one can take for granted that the harpsichord score is the later. In most cases it is possible to prove the priority of the conducting score by changes made in it that are incorporated into the second score. Moreover it was Smith, the man most familiar with Handel's handwriting, who alone wrote the conducting score, whereas there were several copyists who wrote the harpsichord score; this, too, proves the priority of the former. When a pair of scores can be traced back to a common origin (as pointed out above), one can assume that it was the conducting score which was completed first.

In the case of the pasticcio *Lucio Papirio* only one of Handel's scores is known, and it is difficult to decide whether it is the

conducting or the harpsichord score. The fact that some arias are written in half-score may indicate that it is the latter, but this can be explained by lack of time; for instance, arias which in the first process of copying were written only in half-score did not need to be completed when they were later eliminated, or when instrumental parts had already been taken from the source score. In any case the manuscript is the primary copy, in some respects even the original score of the pasticcio, and among the harpsichord scores of the pasticcios there is no example which corresponds even partly to type 1. Therefore I am now inclined to consider it a conducting score, contrary to the view I took when I wrote my catalogue.

After Handel had lost his sight it was the younger Smith who had to prepare the scores for the oratorio performances; for this purpose he applied the same techniques as Handel had done previously. If one dates the insertions into *Jephtha*, 'Freedom now' and 'All that is in Hamor mine', back to 1756,[11] it follows that beginning no earlier than 1755 Smith introduced into the oratorios revised versions of old pieces in increasing numbers and of increasing length.

Whereas Handel's autographs remained unbound until they came into the Royal Music Library, the conducting scores must have been bound very early because they were used more frequently. Unlike the autographs, their bindings are not uniform; the boards of the opera manuscripts have differences in appearance which, if they are not unique, can be arranged in three groups, each confined to a limited period: 1720–1, 1724–6, 1728–38. They may be the work of three different bookbinders, distinguished from each other by their style and their ornaments. The third binder, of whom Handel was a customer for a decade, seems to have enlarged his stock of ornaments about 1732. The oratorio manuscripts are bound in a plainer and more uniform way. The spines of the volumes date from the nineteenth century and give the titles in German, while the labels on the front boards—as far as they can still be found—give the original titles.

The extent of the Collection must have been greater when it was inherited by Smith senior after Handel's death. The fact that parts of single manuscripts (the 1732 *Acis and Galatea*, *Scipione*) went a different way from the rest, may be considered a parallel to the fate of the autographs, and it probably happened before 1778; but we do

---

[11] The reasons for this dating can be found in the *Jephtha* entry, omitted in error from Clausen's catalogue, *Händels Direktionspartituren ('Handexemplare')*, (Hamburg, 1972), and given in App. 2 to this ch. It supports Anthony Hicks's assumption that Smith did not only write from Handel's dictation, but made creative contributions himself; see 'The Late Additions to Handel's Oratorios and the Role of the Younger Smith', in C. Hogwood and R. Luckett (eds.), *Music in Eighteenth-century England* (Cambridge, 1983), 147–69.

not know when the apparent lacunae (*Admeto* and the missing volumes of *Ottone* and *Joshua*) occurred, although the separation of the old conducting score of *Messiah* from the Collection can be dated to the year when Lady Rivers, stepdaughter of the younger Smith, died, for in 1838 it appears for the first time in a testament. Lady Rivers's last will does not specify any music, but directed that all her property which was not specified should be sold by auction. Probably at that time only Handel's most popular work could command an appropriate price, and the other scores became the property of her son Henry Rivers.

Besides the *Messiah* conducting score we can distinguish—according to their final location—three groups of manuscripts which originally formed part of the Collection:

1. the archive scores of the operas *Rinaldo*, *Il pastor fido*, and *Teseo*, as well as fragments of the conducting score of the 1732 *Acis and Galatea*, today in the Royal Music Library;

2. the conducting scores of the pasticcios *Alessandro Severo*, *Didone*, *Elpidia*, and *Ormisda*, as well as the *Orlando* score mentioned above, which might have been Handel's harpsichord score, all housed today in the Department of Manuscripts of the British Library.

3. the conducting score of the opera *Ezio*, and the harpsichord scores of *Faramondo*, *Sosarme*, and *Venceslao*, today in the Chrysander collection in the Hamburg State and University Library Carl von Ossietzky.

The first of these groups may have been among the manuscripts which John Christopher Smith junior presented to the Royal Music Library. There is some reason to suppose that the second group was part of the Collection when the Bristol bookseller Kerslake, who acquired it sometime after the death of Henry Rivers in 1851, offered it for sale by catalogue. This catalogue lists the pasticcio *Elpidia* as well as a second copy of *Ormisda*, volumes which came into the library of Julian Marshall. The third group may have been separated at the same time because, like most of the volumes of the second group, it consists of scores which were considered duplicates. One of the scores from the library of Julian Marshall, the conducting score of *Didone,* must have been separated much earlier from the Collection, for it belonged to the libraries of Samuel Arnold and of his student W. Russell.

Unfortunately Kerslake's catalogue is incomplete, as shown by the words '&c. &c.'; therefore it is hardly possible to draw conclusions from it about the extent of the Collection at the time. It quotes two figures: 'above 160 vols.' for Handel's works, and 'more than

200 vols.' for Handel's and John Christopher Smith's works. As the listing of titles shows that the author of the catalogue was not able to distinguish correctly between the compositions of the two composers, it is possible that we have to subtract more than eight works by Smith junior from the total of 160 volumes.

Victor Schoelcher bought the Collection in 1856. His *catalogue raisonné* is not very helpful for determining the extent of the Collection at that date, because he applies the term 'Smith's collection' to at least three different groups of manuscripts. At Chrysander's suggestion he sold it in 1868 to a consortium of businessmen in Hamburg, who later gave it to the Hamburg City Library.

Since then the Collection has consisted of eighty-five scores in 123 volumes, which constitute Handel's *Handexemplare,* and six additional scores. If one adds to these figures the eighteen *Handexemplare* of the Royal Music Library and the libraries of Marshall and Chrysander, there will still be a gap of about ten volumes; and if one starts from the more probable assumption that the four archive scores had already gone to the Royal Music Library at that time, then the gap would be even bigger, by about four volumes. It can only be partially closed by works composed by Smith which Kerslake included in the count without specifying them. Therefore I think it possible that more of Handel's *Handexemplare* will surface in the future.

The greatest handicap in making the Hamburg Collection accessible and getting a clear idea of its value is, strange as it may sound, the extensive use which Chrysander made of it without leaving any kind of critical commentary. In some respects its contents have been known for more than a hundred years, but this does not necessarily help the modern scholar; the opposite may be true: instead of being able to begin his work with an open mind, he has to test the plausibility of Chrysander's decisions without knowing the reasons for them. My catalogue was written with the aim of providing some help in this situation. Moreover this Collection is unique in giving a basis for dating other collections by means of watermarks and copyists. Twenty years after the publication of my catalogue the demands have become greater in this respect; the forthcoming catalogue of the autographs will give us new standards and raise new questions. I am sure that Handel's conducting scores still have some surprises for us.

Appendix 1: Handel's Conducting, Harpsichord, and Archive Scores

Year of Performance	Title	Shelf-mark Conducting score	Harpsichord score	Archive score	Cover ornaments
1707	Il trionfo del tempo	D-MÜs.1896/1914a		GB-Lbl R.M.19.d.9	
1708	La Resurrezione	D-MÜs.1873/1873a			
1711	Rinaldo			GB-Lbl R.M.19.d.5	
1712	Il pastor fido			GB-Lbl R.M.19.e.4	
1713	Teseo	GB-BENcoke MS 100		GB-Lbl R.M.19.e.6	
1715	Amadigi			D-Hs MA/1003	
1720 (Apr.)	Radamisto	D-Hs MA/1043		D-Hs MA/1044	1, 2, A
1720 (Dec.)	Radamisto	D-Hs MA/1032			1, 2, B
1721	Muzio Scevola	D-Hs MA/1018			1, 2, A
1721?	Floridante				3, 4, C
1723	Ottone (Act 3)	D-Hs MA/1037			
1724	Flavio	D-Hs MA/1017			5, D
	Giulio Cesare	D-Hs MA/1019		D-Hs MA/996	6
1725	Tamerlano	D-Hs MA/1056			7, C
	Rodelinda	D-Hs MA/1047			
1726	Elpidia	GB-Lbl Add.MS.31606			
	Scipione	D-Hs MA/1049			8, 9
1727	Alessandro	D-Hs MA/999			10, E
	Riccardo Primo	D-Hs MA/1045			11, F
1728	Siroe	D-Hs MA/1053			11, A
	Tolomeo	D-Hs MA/1059			11, F
1729	Lotario	D-Hs MA/1028	D-Hs MA/1040		11, G
	Partenope	D-Hs MA/1039			11/11
1730	Ormisda	GB-Lbl Add.MS.31551	D-Hs MA/1036		-/11, 12, G

Year of Performance	Title	Shelf-mark Conducting score	Harpsichord score	Archive score	Cover ornaments
1731	Venceslao	D-Hs MA/1061	D-Hs MA/189*		I1, G/I1, 13
	Poro	D-Hs MA/1042	D-Hs MA/1042a		I1, G/I1, 13, G
	Rinaldo	D-Hs MA/1046a	D-Hs MA/1046		I1, H/I1, G
1732	Ezio	D-Hs MA/167*	D-Hs MA/1015		II/I1, I
	Sosarme	D-Hs MA/1054	D-Hs MA/185*		II/12, I
	Esther	D-Hs MC/261			
	Lucio Papirio	D-Hs MA/1029			I1
	Acis and Galatea	GB-Lbl R.M.19.f.7/Eg.MS.2953			
	Catone	D-Hs MA/1012			I1, I
1733	Orlando	D-Hs MA/1035	?GB-Lbl Add.MS.31565		I1, 14, I/-
	Deborah	D-Hs MC/258			
	Athalia	D-Hs MC/264			I1, 13
	Semiramide	D-Hs MA/1051			
	Cajo Fabbricio	D-Hs MA/1011			13, I
	Arbace	D-Hs MA/1004			I4, I
1734	Arianna	D-Hs MA/1005	D-Hs MA/1005a		I1, I/I1, I
	Il Parnasso in festa	D-Hs MA/1038	D-Hs MA/1038a		I1, I/I1, 14, I
	Wedding Anthem	D-Hs MC/266			
	Il pastor fido	D-Hs MA/1041	D-Hs MA/1057		13, I/-
1735	Oreste	D-Hs MA/1034	D-Hs MA/1034a		I4/-
	Ariodante	D-Hs MA/1006	D-Hs MA/1006a		I4, I
	Alcina	D-Hs MA/998			
1736	Alexander's Feast	D-Hs MC/263		(GB-Lcm MS 900)	
	Atalanta	D-Hs MA/1008			I1, 13, I
1737	Arminio	D-Hs MA/1007			I1, 14, I
	Giustino	D-Hs MA/1020			13, I
	Il trionfo del tempo	D-Hs MA/1060			13, I

Year of Performance	Title	Shelf-mark			Cover ornaments
		Conducting score	Harpsichord score	Archive score	
1737	Didone	GB-Lbl Add.MS.31607			
1738	Berenice	D-Hs MA/1010			
	Faramondo	D-Hs MA/1016			
	Alessandro Severo	GB-Lbl Add.Ms.31569			
1739	Serse	D-Hs MA/1052a			13, I
	Saul	D-Hs MC/267	D-Hs MA/169*		13, I/13
	Israel in Egypt	D-Hs MC/262	D-Hs MA/1000		
1740	Ode for St Cecilia's Day	D-Hs MA/1031	D-Hs MA/1052		
1741	L'Allegro	D-Hs MA/1002			
1742	Imeneo	D-Hs MA/1023			
	Deidamia	D-Hs MA/1013			
	Messiah	GB-Ob MS Tenbury 346/347			14
1743	Samson	D-Hs MA/1048			
1744	Semele	D-Hs MA/1050			
	Joseph	D-Hs MA/1025			
1745	Hercules	D-Hs MA/1021			
	Belshazzar	D-Hs MA/1009			
1746	Occasional Oratorio	D-Hs MA/1033			
1747	Judas Maccabaeus	D-Hs MA/1026			
1748	Joshua	D-Hs MA/1027a (pt. 2)			
1749	Alexander Balus	D-Hs MA/1001			
	Susanna	D-Hs MA/1055			
	Solomon	D-Hs MC/268			
1750	Alceste	D-Hs MA/997			
	Theodora	D-Hs MA/1058			
1751	Choice of Hercules	D-Hs MA/1022			

HANS DIETER CLAUSEN

Year of Performance	Title	Shelf-mark			Cover ornaments
		Conducting score	Harpsichord score	Archive score	
1752	*Jephtha*	D-Hs MA/1024			
1757	*The triumph of time*				
1759	*Solomon*	D-Hs MA/1060a			
1760	*Ode for Queen Anne's Birthday*	D-Hs MC/268a			
1760?	*Messiah*	D-Hs MC/265			
1760?	*Esther*	D-Hs MA/1030			
	Ode for Queen Anne's Birthday	D-Hs MC/261a			
1765	*Israel in Egypt*	D-Hs MC/183*	D-Hs MC/262a		

Notes: The archive scores which were written before 1720 have been arranged according to the date of performance, regardless of the date of copying. In the Cover Ornaments column those which are arranged in rectangular form have been marked by arabic numerals; floral corner ornaments—as far as they are still visible—by capital letters. Volumes without ornament marks are bound in a plain manner, or their original binding does not survive. The ornaments of the conducting score are given first, followed by those of the harpsichord score, separated by an oblique. Ornaments which occur more than once are shown below.

* MSS marked * were not part of the Collection when the Hamburg City Library bought it in the 19th century, but came into it from Chrysander's private library after the second world war.

1   2   11   12   13   14

A   C   F   G   I

THE HAMBURG COLLECTION

Appendix 2:
JEPHTHA, *Direktionspartitur M A/1024 v.1752 b. nach Händels Tod*

1. Bestand:
    - I.   1–58, 59ᵇ, 60, 59ᵃ, 61–81
        U: *2 Bin., 1 Un., 17 Bin.* = 1–24, 29–58, 59ᵃ, 59ᵇ, 60, 61–81
        E: 1) 25–28
    - II. 1–77 u. 1 unfol. Bl.
        U: *18 Bin., 1 Un.* = 1–19, 24–77
        E: 2) 20–23
    - III. 1–38, 38ᵃ, 39–64
        U: *13 Bin.* = 1–34, L (3Bl.), 38, 38ᵃ, 39–41, 46–55
        E: 3) 35; 4) 36–37; 5) 42–45; 6) 56–64 (eigentl. nach f.45)
2. Schreiber: U — Sm; E — Sm (1, Teil v. 2, 3, 4, 5), Smj
        (Rez. u. Teil des Arientextes v. 2), S1 (6)
        H — Mittelstimme der Sinfonia im 3. Akt
        X — Trp., Säng., Korr.
3. Wasserzeichen: U — Cp; E — Cp (3, 5), Cr (6), F2a (1, 2, 4)
4. Veränderungen:
    - I.   1752 (Libr.)
        - ■ *Zebul* (B — Wass)
            - ■ E3 "Laud her" neue Fsg., L
        - ■ *Iphis* (S — Frasi)
            - ■ E5 "Freely I to heav'n resign" (= "Laud her", urspr. Fsg.)
    - II. 1753
    - III. 1756 (Libr.[1]; X: Curioni, [Is.] Young)
        - ■ E6[2] Arie "Freely I to heav'n resign" → Quintett "All that is in Hamor mine"
        - ■ *Storge* (MS — Galli → S — Curioni)
        - ■ E1 "In gentle murmurs" e° → h°
        - ■ E4 "Sweet as sight" D⁺ → G⁺
        - ■ *Zebul* (B — Wass → B — Champness?)
            - ■ E2[3] "Freedom now once more" (= "La mia sorte fortunata", "Agrippina")
    - IV. 1758 (Libr.)
        - ■ *Storge* (S — Curioni → CA — Frederick)
            - ■ "Sweet as sight" elim.
    - V.   nach 1759 (X: Girl, Scott, Tenducci, Polly Young)
        - ■ "O God behold" elim.
        - ■ Kürzg. "These labours past" (urspr. Fsg. GA Version A)[4]

---

[1] undatiert; W. Dean (a.a.O. S. 619ff.) datiert es auf 1753, weil zu dieser Zeit Watts u. Dod ihre Libr. ohne Datum druckten. Wir nehmen dagegen als Datum der beiden Veränderungen, die sich auf einer Überkl. u. einem ausgetauschten Bl. befinden, 1756 an. Dafür spricht auch das Wasserzeichen der E 1, 2 u. 4 u. die Vermutung, daß es 1756 mit größerer Wahrscheinlichkeit als 1753 Neubesetzungen in den betroffenen Partien gegeben hat.

[2] Vielleicht ist die E6 nicht die E von 1756, sondern ein späterer Ersatz; denn der Part der Storge entspricht hier nicht dem Stimmumfang der Darstellerin von 1756. Für eine spätere Datierung sprechen auch das Papier u. die Altersschrift des Kop. S1, die beide, soweit sicher datierbar, nur 1758 erscheinen.

[3] Das für Zebul neu gesetzte Rez. "Again heav'n smiles" anstelle des Anfangs von Jephthas Rez. "Heav'n smiles once more" (GA—) schrieb Smj. Chrysanders Auffassung (GA, Vorw. S. IV), Händel habe Jephthas Rez. eigenhändig gekürzt, kann ich mich nicht anschließen.

[4] Chrysander (GA, Vorw.) nimmt an, dies sei vor der Urauff. geschehen.

3

The Malmesbury Collection

WINTON DEAN

THE Earl of Malmesbury's Collection is by far the most important body of Handel manuscripts still in private hands, and the only one in the possession of the same family since the eighteenth century. Strictly speaking it should be called the Legh Collection, for the original owner, for whom the manuscripts were copied, was Elizabeth Legh of Adlington Hall in Cheshire, a friend and fanatical admirer of the composer, an accomplished harpsichordist and possibly an amateur singer as well. From about 1715 until her death in August 1734 at the age of 39 she evidently had a standing order with Handel's copyists for everything he composed. She had each volume uniformly bound in leather with her arms stamped on the cover, and they remain today in their original condition.

In an unsigned draft will dated 1731 (still in the possession of the Legh family) she described herself as spinster in the parish of St George's Hanover Square (where the Leghs had their London house in the same parish as Handel's), and expressed a desire to be buried in Westminster Abbey with a memorial tablet saying that she 'was a great lover of Musick & all ingenious things'. She left 'all sorts of musicall Instruments as Harpsicords Spinets Virginalls' to her executor, but made special dispositions for the manuscripts.

I desire all my Musick books that are composed by Mr Handel may be put in some Library or publick Room at Cambridge there to be seen or copied, but will have all fastned by a chain to ye Wainscoat or Wall that so none of them can be caried [sic] away or stole, therefore desire my Executor to buy every one a chain, & to see this done himself.

Elizabeth was indeed buried in Westminster Abbey, appropriately in the same building as Handel, but Cambridge never received her music books; in fact she seems to have died intestate. The next glimpse we catch of them is a note inside her score of *Giulio Cesare*, signed by the second Earl of Malmesbury and dated 20 January 1829, headed 'List

of the manuscript Musick left by Handel to my Great Uncle Thomas Harris.' It specifies thirty-six volumes, the same number as today. Thomas Harris, one of three brothers, all friends of the composer, witnessed the first three codicils of Handel's will and received a legacy of £300 in the fourth codicil, signed three days before his death. The will says nothing about the Legh manuscripts, which Handel must have given to Harris in his lifetime. That they were indeed returned to Handel after Elizabeth Legh's death has been confirmed very recently by Terence Best's discovery, from internal evidence, that at least two volumes[1] must have been available in the early 1740s when Handel's copyists were preparing scores for Charles Jennens.

William C. Smith referred to the Malmesbury Collection in the catalogue of works appended to Gerald Abraham's Handel Symposium,[2] but evidently did not see it; he mentions only three works, the Chandos Te Deum, Six Fugues for harpsichord, and a group of '23 airs' from the *Water Music*. Only within the last twenty years or so has the Collection been available to scholars, thanks to the courtesy of the present Earl of Malmesbury.

The thirty-six volumes comprise twenty-five operas, the two major Cannons works *Acis and Galatea* and *Esther*, four volumes of keyboard music, one of sonatas and concertos, the *Ode for Queen Anne's Birthday*, and three sacred works, the Utrecht Te Deum and Jubilate, the Cannons Te Deum in B flat, and the *Brockes Passion*. There is nothing, not surprisingly, from Handel's pre-London years on the Continent. Otherwise the only major absentees are the Italian cantatas (a fair number of which were composed or rewritten in London) and the Chandos, Coronation, and Chapel Royal Anthems. Elizabeth did possess two volumes of Italian cantatas, dated 1718 and 1720 and bound with her coat of arms, but they escaped from the Collection in the middle of the eighteenth century and are now in the Bodleian Library at Oxford. She may not have been able to obtain copies of the Coronation and Chapel Royal Anthems, but the absence of the Chandos group is more surprising. If they too escaped, they have not been identified. There is one complete set, copied about 1719 and mostly in the Tenbury Collection at the Bodleian, that would fill the gap; but though the binding is original it does not carry the Legh arms. Another volume once belonging to Elizabeth and annotated by her is now in the Coke Collection. Entitled in her hand *Overtures & Lessons for the Harpsicord*, it was copied by Smith, H1, and H2 about 1721–2. It passed to the organist and composer Joseph Kelway, who gave it to his pupil the younger Charles Wesley (1757–1834). Most of

---

[1] The 1718 keyboard MS and *Tamerlano* [*Ed.'s note*].
[2] G. Abraham (ed.), *Handel: A Symposium* (London, 1954), 275–310.

its contents are duplicated in the Malmesbury Collection, but a number of modifications in Handel's autograph give it a particular interest.

Much of the importance of the Malmesbury Collection derives from its early date, and from the accuracy with which individual items can be precisely dated, partly from annotations in the manuscripts, partly from their contents, and partly from identification of the copyists. All the other substantial Collections of copies (other than Handel's performing scores)—Aylesford, Lennard, Granville, Shaftesbury—are later in date and, as it were, open-ended. The Malmesbury Collection necessarily stops with Elizabeth Legh's death in 1734; the latest work represented is the opera *Arianna*, produced in January that year. The texts cannot reflect later performances or revivals, which is often the case with copies elsewhere. This is obviously a prime source for all editors of the Halle edition.

No fewer than sixteen volumes, including the two in the Bodleian, are dated by the copyist or Elizabeth or both. Elizabeth also supplied full indexes to most of the volumes and a number of other annotations, tempo marks, ornaments (mostly trills), bass figures, and some comments on the music. It is clear that most of the music was copied very soon after its composition and first performance. The score of *Floridante* is dated 14 December 1721, the day after the second performance, and only five days after the première; the copyist (H3—the last fifty-three pages by Smith) must have begun it even earlier, and since the opera was subjected to a good deal of last-minute alteration it is not surprising that the text is confused and inconsistent. The only major works copied an appreciable time after composition are *Rinaldo* and the *Brockes Passion*. Elizabeth may not have known Handel as early as 1711, when he had only just come to London; her *Rinaldo* copy probably dates from the mid-1720s (its first appendix represents one of the earliest appearances of the copyist S2), and that of the *Brockes Passion*, copied by Smith and S1, about 1728.

The works for which the Collection is most important are the two Cannons dramas, most of the operas, and the instrumental music. *Acis and Galatea* and *Esther* are both dated 1718 and entitled respectively 'an English opera' and simply 'Oratorium'. The *Acis* score, copied by RM1 and Smith (his earliest known appearance in this capacity), answers several questions about the work's original form. It confirms a conjecture of mine many years ago that it was written for only five singers, who took the choral as well as the solo parts. The obbligato in 'O ruddier than the cherry' is for 'Flauto piccolo 8vo'. As in the first London performance in 1731 and a number of early librettos 'Would you gain the tender creature?' is sung by the third tenor in

the role of Coridon. This aria, which is not in the autograph, may well have been added to give him a solo; otherwise he would have been the only singer without one.

Every one of the opera copies, at least up to *Admeto* in 1727, contributes information not available elsewhere; most of them contain unpublished music, some of it unique to this source. They are particularly valuable where the autograph or the performing score is missing or defective. For *Amadigi* and *Admeto* both are lost. The Malmesbury *Amadigi*, dated 1716, contains three arias not in Chrysander's score, including what was at first thought to be a unique copy of 'Affannami, tormentami', an aria which is in the libretto and was sung at the first performance but then dropped; these have now been printed. The *Admeto* copy, dated 1727, is the earliest surviving score; the off-stage voice of Apollo in Act 1 not only has different music from all other sources, but is for a different voice. Elizabeth was present at the first rehearsal of this opera, on 25 January 1727, when Mrs Pendarves described her as so 'transported with joy' as to be '*out of her senses*'.

The *Radamisto* copy is the only complete score of the opera as first performed in April 1720. It differs in many details of words and music from later versions, and from Chrysander's edition, and includes three ballet suites, one at the end of each act, the third incorporated in the finale in a huge rondo structure unique in Handel's work. Chrysander's score is badly confused, since he mistook a later copy for the April performing score, which is lost. He included none of the ballets, the first of which survives only in the Malmesbury copy. The *Ottone* and *Scipione* copies likewise give the only complete scores of the first-performance version—or indeed of any other version. Both these operas, like *Floridante*, were much altered shortly before performance, and only one act of the *Ottone* performing score survives; the Malmesbury copies are essential for disentangling the text.

There are a number of quite surprising finds. *Teseo* had only a single run in 1713, but the Malmesbury copy includes alternative settings of two pieces in which Agilea and Teseo, sopranos in the original, are both altos. These are not just transpositions. The duet 'Cara, ti dono' is completely reworked, with a B-section on new material. Agilea's beautiful aria 'Deh! v'aprite', one of the gems of the opera, is differently scored with six extra bars in the middle, and both sections have tasteful vocal ornaments. They are in the hand of the aria's copyist (RM1) but may well derive from Handel. It would be interesting to know the occasion for which these pieces were written; there is no mention of a cast change. The performing score is lost, and only a fragment of the autograph survives.

The copy of *Il pastor fido* gives the fullest text of the 1712 D minor Overture, which in Chrysander lacks the B-section and da capo of the Adagio and the independent second bassoon part in the Bourrée. That of *Rinaldo* adds an unpublished B-section to Almirena's birdsong aria with three recorders, 'Augelletti che cantate', and no fewer than nine additional arias in two appendices. Four of these belong to the 1717 revival; the others are not elsewhere ascribed to this opera, but Elizabeth wrote 'Almirene' against one of them, and evidence turned up only in 1989 that Anastasia Robinson sang it in the 1715 *Rinaldo* revival, though it seems to have been composed for *Teseo* two years earlier. *Rodelinda* was copied after the first revival in December 1725, and the new music composed for that occasion was incorporated in the main text. This supplies one recitative otherwise missing and a beautiful little instrumental coda to Grimoaldo's tremendous accompanied recitative 'Fatto inferno' in Act 3. There are signs in the Hamburg performing score that something was pasted in here but subsequently fell out. It survives only in the Malmesbury copy.

The Collection is also important for the light it throws on Handel's copyists. No fewer than twenty are represented, of whom all but one (who copied only seven pages in one manuscript) occur elsewhere. Five of them are not among those given numbers by Larsen or Clausen; I have distinguished them by the letters of the Greek alphabet. We know the names of four: the two Smiths, father and son, Linike and Newman—the last two thanks to Elizabeth Legh herself. On her score of *Il pastor fido* she wrote: 'transcribed by Mr Newman February 1715' (that could be OS for 1716); and on *Teseo*: 'transcribed by Mr Linike June 1717'. This information enables us to identify many other manuscripts written by the same copyists. It is particularly valuable in the case of Linike, who was a viola-player in the Haymarket orchestra and the theatre's principal copyist. Larsen and Clausen ascribed many Linike copies to early Smith; but some of them can be positively dated as far back as 1712, several years before the earliest possible date for Smith's arrival in London. The mistake is understandable, since Smith—initially employed by Handel as a kind of secretary—seems to have begun copying about 1718–19 under Linike's instruction, imitating his hand in certain respects, notably the formation of clefs. Since many Linike copies can be exactly dated, it is possible to trace the development of his hand and assign an approximate date to the others; and thanks in large part to this Collection the same is true of Smith in the early years before his music hand was finally formed. It is sometimes said that the younger Smith never acted as a regular Handel copyist. Some of the Malmesbury copies—*Scipione*, most of *Alessandro*, and certain items

34 THE MALMESBURY COLLECTION

in two instrumental volumes—prove that he did so for a time around 1726–7 when he was a boy of 14 or 15.

We can also discover a good deal about how the copyists worked. Sometimes an experienced scribe would write the first page as a model and then hand over to a subordinate to carry on. For example RM1, who was active from about 1713 to 1725, copied the first page of the B flat Te Deum (dated 25 March 1719 by Elizabeth Legh) and Smith wrote the rest. Smith copied the first page of the *Brockes Passion* and S1 wrote the rest. S1 copied the first five and a half folios of *Sosarme* and S3 continued on the verso. S2 copied the first eight folios of *Alessandro*, and Smith junior almost all the rest. This may give us a rough indication of when each copyist joined the scriptorium.

The earliest keyboard volume, dated 1718 on the title-page and 1717 (OS) by Elizabeth Legh, shows four copyists—Linike, RM1, RM4, and Beta—sharing the labour in rotation, one ending on a recto and another continuing on the verso of the same page. Linike was clearly in command (this is pre-Smith): the order is Linike, Beta, Linike, RM1, Linike, RM1, Linike, RM4, Beta. During the early 1720s the majority of copies, not only in this Collection, were shared between several hands; the pressure on the scriptorium was evidently very great. It seems that when a copyist left the room, however temporarily, someone else had to carry on even if he only wrote a page or two. Once or twice each act of an opera would be assigned to a different scribe. Act 1 of *Flavio* was copied by H1, Act 2 by H3, and Act 3 by Smith. Occasionally we find an insertion copied by a different hand from the rest of the manuscript. The Linike *Teseo* contains one aria copied by RM1, S2's *Siroe* one copied by S1. *Rinaldo*, *Ottone*, and *Giulio Cesare* have appendices in different hands. These are contained within the original binding and not subsequent additions.

The other instrumental volumes, which also exhibit a variety of copyists, have a more complex history, especially the first volume of overtures for harpsichord, signed and dated by Elizabeth 30 August 1722. That date cannot apply to the whole volume, as a study of the paper, rastra, and copyists, and the industry of Terence Best have conclusively proved. The core of it, about eighty pages, was evidently copied by Linike and RM1 in the pre-Smith era, around 1718. This was then rearranged, presumably in 1722, and bound up with 110 pages freshly copied by Smith, H1, H3, and Gamma, and some fifty blank pages. On at least two occasions the volume was returned to the scriptorium and these blanks were filled, first by H5 (about 1724) and later by the two Smiths in turn. Since the Overture to *Admeto* is included, the process cannot have been completed before 1727. We know that Elizabeth was in London for at least part of this period,

WINTON DEAN   35

so she had merely to take the book round to Handel's house and hand
it over to Smith.

A second volume, unpaginated and undated, was then begun, on
paper consistent with the date 1728, with a substantial chunk written
by Smith. It went through the same process of return to the scriptorium, receiving additions from S2 and Hb1, and later from S3,
Smith senior assisting on each occasion. One or two other points
are worth noting. There is much duplication of contents between the
two volumes;[3] perhaps Elizabeth wanted to keep one in London and
one at Adlington. Some of the overtures are straight transcriptions
from the scores, but seventeen are in Handel's own arrangements,
recently identified and published by Terence Best. And not quite all
the contents are overtures; there are a few keyboard works, arrangements of orchestral movements from the operas, the *Water Music*
and two of the Concertos, Op. 3, and modified and embellished keyboard versions of three arias from *Radamisto* and *Muzio Scevola*.
These are clearly by Handel himself, and perhaps made specially for
Elizabeth, since they are found only in volumes associated with her.

The remaining keyboard volume contains Handel's twelve fugues,
copied by Hb1 about 1727. The sonatas and concertos, dated 1727,
comprise four of the Concertos, Op. 3, copied by S2 and Smith
junior, and five of the Trio Sonatas, Op. 2, copied by S2, together
with an otherwise unknown Sonata in G minor. This has been
published in the Halle edition as HWV 404. The instrumental works
are so far the only section of the Malmesbury Collection that has
passed through the digestion of scholars into print.

In studying the Collection I have found myself more and more
fascinated by Elizabeth Legh's personality and wanting to know
more about her. One curious fact has turned up, in a document
unearthed by Howard Serwer among the Sloane manuscripts at the
British Library. This is an agreement between her father John Legh
and Rachel Ormston, the wife of a London merchant, who seems to
have been an early chiropractor or osteopath. In return for the substantial sum of 150 guineas she undertook to cure Elizabeth, 'who at
present is awry', and to take her in as a lodger for £25 a year. The
date is 20 October 1709, when Elizabeth was about 15 and still
growing. It is evident from the physiological details supplied that
she suffered from a major deformation of the spine which seriously
distorted her ribs and shoulders.

Some of her written comments on the music help to bring her to
life, supplying an added human and even a zoological interest. Against

---

[3] Where there is duplication, the 2nd vol. was undoubtedly copied direct from the 1st
[*Ed.'s note*].

36   THE MALMESBURY COLLECTION

the duet 'Ah mia cara' at the end of Act I of *Floridante* she wrote 'O imortall' with one 'm' and two 'l's—spelling was never her strong point. Her copy of *Muzio Scevola* contains only Handel's third act, but she leaves us in no doubt as to her relative opinion of the three composers concerned. At the beginning the first two acts are 'both very bad Musick: but this 3d. Act is so very fine that the Musick speaks its own Praise.' And at the end: 'both excessive bad musick: but this 3d. Act was composed by Mr Handel, & is incomparable, as all his works are.'

Long after Elizabeth's death John Lockman in an introductory essay to his libretto of *Rosalinda*, set by J. C. Smith junior and produced on 4 January 1740, recounts an incident said to have been witnessed by Smith.

It relates to a Pigeon in the Dove-house of Mr *Lee* [*sic*] in *Cheshire*. That Gentleman had a Daughter who was extremely fond of Music, and a very fine performer on the Harpsicord. The Dove-house was built not far from the Parlour, where the musical Instrument stood. The Pigeon, whenever the young Lady play'd any Air, except *Spera si* in *Otho*, never stirred; but as soon as that Air was touched, it would fly from the Dove-house to the Window; there discover the most pleasing Emotions; and the Instant the Air was over, fly back again. The young Lady was so delighted with the Fancy, that she ever after called *Spera si* the *Pigeon's Air*, and wrote it under that Title in her Music-book.

Hawkins and Schoelcher both repeat this unlikely sounding story, but identify the air as 'Spera sì, mio caro' in *Admeto*. Lockman was right: 'Spera sì, mi dice' in the Malmesbury copy of *Ottone* bears the inscription in Elizabeth's hand 'The Pidgeon Song'. Jennens even wrote it in his copy as well. This anecdote, with Handel vicariously exercising the functions of Orpheus, seems a suitable occasion to take our leave of the Legh–Malmesbury Collection.

POSTSCRIPT

As Winton Dean has remarked, for over twenty years the present Earl of Malmesbury has made Handel scholars welcome at Greywell if their work required them to consult the Legh manuscripts; but given the increasing quantity and intensity of research on Handel's music in recent years, pressure for such access has gradually outrun the facilities that Lord Malmesbury could reasonably be expected to provide. In 1990 he generously decided to allow the Collection to be filmed, and a copy of the film to be deposited at the Hampshire Record Office; the filming was undertaken during 1990–1 by the Hampshire Archives

WINTON DEAN

Trust. We have compiled a guide which describes those essential features of the manuscripts that cannot be seen on the film, namely the paper-conjunctions, watermarks, and the rastra. It also contains information about the copyists: this is based on Winton Dean's pioneering work, to which we have been able to add further details, and is summarized in the right-hand column of the table. A copy of the guide is deposited with the films. Scholars who need to consult this material should apply in writing to the County Archivist, Hampshire Record Office, 20 Southgate Street, Winchester, SO23 9EF [D. Burrows and T. Best].

Appendix: The Contents of the Malmesbury Collection

Many of the dates given in the table are those written in the manuscripts by Elizabeth Legh (shown by (Legh) after the date); for most of the vols. which have no such annotations the evidence of their contents, the paper, and the copyists confirms that they were copied not long after the composition of the works they contain. For the few to which this principle does not apply, dates are given in square parentheses, and three dates written by copyists are also recorded.

Title	Date	Copyists
Operas:		
Rinaldo	[Main pt. copied 1725–8; app. by RM1 copied c.1718]	Smith, S2; apps.: S2, RM1
Il pastor fido	Feb. 1715 (?OS), (Legh)	Newman
Teseo	June 1717 (Legh)	Linike, RM1
Amadigi	1716 (Legh)	Newman
Radamisto	1720 (Legh)	Smith, Gamma
Muzio Scevola, Act 3		H2, Smith
Floridante	14 Dec. 1721 (Legh)	H3, Smith
Ottone	1724 (Legh)	Smith, ?H3, Zeta
Flavio		H1, ?H3, Smith
Giulio Cesare		Eta; app.: H5
Tamerlano		H5
Rodelinda		S2
Scipione		Music: Smith jun.; text: Smith
Alessandro		Music: S2, Smith jun.; text: Smith
Admeto	1727 (Legh)	S2
Riccardo Primo		S2
Siroe		S2, S1
Tolomeo		S1

Title	Date	Copyists
Lotario		Music: S1; text: Hb1 and one unidentified
Partenope		Music: S1; text: Hb1
Poro		Hb1
Ezio	1732 (copyist)	H8
Sosarme		Music: S1, S3; text: S1, Smith
Orlando		Music: S3; text: Smith
Arianna		S3
Other Vocal Works:		
Ode for Queen Anne's Birthday	[copied 1717–18]	Linike
Utrecht Te Deum and Jubilate	1718 (Legh)	RM4
Brockes Passion	[copied c.1728]	Music: Smith, S1; text: Smith
Acis and Galatea	1718 (Legh)	RM1, Smith
Oratorium (*Esther*)	1718 (Legh)	H2
Chandos Te Deum in B flat	25 Mar. 1719 (Legh)	RM1, Smith
Instrumental Works:		
Pieces for harpsichord	1717 (Legh); 1718 (copyist)	Alpha, Linike, Beta, RM1, RM4
Overtures for harpsichord, i	30 Aug. 1722 (Legh) [copied 1718–27]	RM1, Linike, H1, Smith, Gamma, H3, H5, Smith jun.
Overtures for harpsichord, ii	[copied 1728–33]	Smith, S2, Hb1, S3
Sonatas and Concertos	Dated 1727 (title-page)	S2, Smith jun.
Twelve Fugues for harpsichord	[copied c.1727]	Hb1
MSS formerly in the Collection		
Cantatas (GB–Ob MS Mus.d.61)	1718 (copyist)	Linike, RM1, Beta, ?H2, [Philip Hayes]
Cantatas (GB–Ob MS Mus.d.62)	1720 (copyist)	Smith, H1, S2 [Philip Hayes]
Overtures and Lessons for harpsichord (GB-BENcoke MS 119)	[copied 1721–2]	Smith, H1, H2 [and later hands]

4

The Aylesford Collection

JOHN H. ROBERTS

SURVEYING the chief Handel collections known to him in his *Account* of the Westminster Abbey Commemoration of 1784, Charles Burney called particular attention to 'the collection of the earl of Aylesford, formed by the late Mr. Jennings', in which 'are preserved in MS. many valuable works of our author'.[1] Mr Jennings was of course Charles Jennens (the pronunciation was evidently the same in those days, whatever it was), and the music library he had bequeathed to his cousin the 3rd Earl of Aylesford in 1773 was indeed remarkable, including as it did the largest and most comprehensive collection of Handel copies assembled by any of the composer's contemporaries along with many other important music manuscripts. For a hundred years this Collection remained safe in the possession of the Earls of Aylesford, but from 1873 it was gradually sold off, the bulk of the manuscripts being auctioned at Sotheby's in 1918. More than four hundred volumes were ultimately acquired by Newman Flower, the Handel biographer and collector, and are now in the Newman Flower Collection of the Henry Watson Music Library in the Central Public Library in Manchester. But the remaining prints and manuscripts were widely dispersed, some passing from hand to hand until the owners had no idea of their illustrious origin. Fortunately it is possible to trace most of the manuscripts to their present locations and to identify, at least in summary fashion, the contents of a number of others.

Charles Jennens (1700–73) was a man of high purposes, cultivated tastes, and strong opinions.[2] Son of a wealthy Leicestershire land-owner, he attended Balliol College, Oxford, without taking a degree, and it was probably there, in the wake of the Jacobite rebellion of 1715, that be became a nonjuror, upholding the claims of the displaced

---

[1] *An Account of the Musical Performances in Westminster-Abbey and the Pantheon, May 26th, 27th, 29th; and June the 3d, 5th, 1784. In Commemoration of Handel* (London, 1785), 45.

[2] For a detailed account of Jennens's life and views see R. Smith, 'The Achievements of Charles Jennens 1700–1773', *ML* 70 (1989), 161–90.

Stuarts against the ruling Hanoverians. Closely allied with his conservative political creed was an evangelical zeal in defence of traditional Christian doctrine that found ample expression in the oratorio librettos he wrote for Handel. Next to religion, music was perhaps his greatest passion, but he was also intensely interested in the fine arts and in literature. He assembled an outstanding collection of paintings and sculpture, and after inheriting his father's estate at Gopsall in 1747 he transformed it into a palatial retreat, crowned by a miniature temple dedicated to the memory of his friend Edward Holdsworth. Near the end of his life he published the first five volumes of an edition of Shakespeare, based on his own formidable Shakespeare collection. They provoked much ridicule at the time but have since come to be regarded as a minor milestone in the development of modern editorial principles.

The appearance of Jennens's name on the list of subscribers to four Handel operas published in 1725–7—the earliest Handel editions for which such lists were issued—indicates that already in his mid-twenties he had taken a place in the front ranks of the composer's admirers. By the early 1730s the two men had clearly become friends: shortly after Jennens received five opera scores from Italy in 1732 Handel started borrowing musical ideas from three of them and prepared pasticcio arrangements of the other two.[3] They first collaborated on *Saul* (1738, perhaps begun already in 1735), followed by *L'Allegro, il Penseroso ed il Moderato* (1740) and *Messiah* (1741), and Jennens may also have had a hand in compiling the text of *Israel in Egypt* (1738).[4] Then the relationship abruptly deteriorated, primarily because of Jennens's annoyance over what he saw as shortcomings in Handel's setting of his *Messiah*.[5] After the composer agreed to make some of the desired changes, however, they were reconciled and joined once again in *Belshazzar* (1744), though Jennens complained he had been rudely rushed. They seem to have maintained friendly relations till the end. In 1756 Jennens had Hudson paint Handel's portrait, and in 1757, in the third codicil to his will, Handel left Jennens two of his prize paintings.

It was probably around 1728 that Jennens began collecting Handel manuscripts. Most were made for him by copyists of the Smith circle,

[3] J. H. Roberts, 'Handel and Charles Jennens's Italian Opera Manuscripts' in N. Fortune (ed.), *Music and Theatre: Essays in Honour of Winton Dean* (Cambridge, 1987), 159–202.

[4] This was first suggested in A. Hicks, 'An Auction of Handeliana', *MT* 114 (1973), 893. Handel would not have needed much literary assistance except in pt. 2; perhaps that is why it was composed after pt. 3.

[5] On Jennens's conflicts with Handel over *Messiah* see D. Burrows, 'The Autographs and Early Copies of "Messiah": Some Further Thoughts', *ML* 66 (1985), 201–19, and id., *Handel: Messiah* (Cambridge, 1991).

JOHN H. ROBERTS   41

particularly S2; sometimes with older works he instead purchased
existing copies of an earlier vintage, probably also through Smith.[6]
Two Aylesford manuscripts, a volume of miscellaneous arrangements
(GB-Lbl R.M.19.a.8) and an unfinished keyboard-vocal score of
Messiah (GB-Lbl R.M.19.d.1), are in the hand of Jennens himself.
At first his aims as a collector seem to have been relatively modest.[7]
He was always a faithful buyer of the published editions (on every
subscription list, often for more than one copy), and many of the early
manuscripts of opera excerpts copied for him were obviously designed
to fill gaps in the printed scores or compensate for their other defi-
ciencies, not to replace them. As late as 1741 he obtained a copy of
eleven movements from *Imeneo* (GB-Lbl R.M.18.c.11, fos. 167ᵛ–214)
that exactly complements the fifteen 'favourite songs' brought out by
Walsh in lieu of a score.[8] In the 1730s he ordered manuscript scores
of only four new operas—*Sosarme*, *Arianna*, *Ariodante*, and *Alcina*—
precisely those for which initially only 'favourite songs' were issued.
At the same time he purchased copies of some earlier works, mostly
those for which no printed editions were available or only the
defective versions produced by Walsh in the early 1720s.[9]

Then sometime in the early to mid-1740s Jennens decided to embark
on a far more ambitious project: a sort of complete edition of Handel's
music, for the most part necessarily in manuscript form. Scores were
copied for all the operas and oratorios previously represented only
by selected fragments, resulting in widespread duplication, and at a
somewhat later date sets of performing parts were made to accompany
them.[10] Anticipating the care he would later take to establish a reliable
text of Shakespeare's works and offer all variant readings, Jennens
displayed an extraordinary concern for completeness and authenticity
in the Handel scores copied under this direction. The copyist seems

---

[6] Among these older MSS were scores of *Agrippina* (in pt.), *Amadigi*, *Giulio Cesare*, and
Teseo.

[7] This account of the development of Jennens's collection is based in large part on info.
about the paper employed in the MSS, generously provided to me by Donald Burrows.

[8] I am grateful to Donald Burrows for checking on the contents of this edn.

[9] The list includes the *Brockes Passion*, *Flavio*, *Floridante*, *Muzio Scevola*, *Ottone*, *Il pastor
fido*, *Radamisto*, *La Resurrezione*, *Rodrigo*, *Silla* (*c*.1740) and *Tolomeo* (the older copy divided
between GB-Lbl R.M.18.c.1, R.M.18.c.3, and R.M.18.c.10). The score of *Admeto* was also copied
at this time, but here Jennens's reason may have been a particular admiration for the work,
which he had bound in red morocco.

[10] On the question of whether Jennens's parts were copied from his scores see the sections
on copies in W. Dean and J. M. Knapp, *Handel's Operas 1704–1726* (Oxford, 1987) and P. J.
Rogers, *Continuo Realization in Handel's Vocal Music* (Ann Arbor, Mich., 1989), 62. Anthony
Hicks has claimed that the Aylesford pts. for *Saul* were copied from the autograph before the
Aylesford score, because in some cases they preserve earlier readings: 'Handel, Jennens and
Saul: Aspects of a Collaboration' in Fortune (ed.), *Music and Theatre*, 209–10. It must be borne
in mind, however, that Jennens also owned another score of *Saul*, now lost, from which the
parts might instead have been taken.

42   THE AYLESFORD COLLECTION

generally to have worked primarily from the autograph,[11] supplementing it as necessary from other sources, and he transcribed many numbers or parts of numbers never completed or performed—though it was not until the 1740s that he normally included the secco recitatives in the opera scores.[12] Jennens would then compare his copy with the original, checking for mistakes and omissions and entering Handel's dates of composition, as well as sometimes collating it with the composer's performing score. He also supplied many additional bass figures.[13] With the oratorios for which he had written the libretto Jennens evidently felt entitled to special liberties. In his copies of *Messiah* and *L'Allegro*, he altered the text underlay, most egregiously in 'I know that my Redeemer liveth', and, as Anthony Hicks has shown, he made numerous alterations, musical as well as verbal, in the autograph of *Saul*, all of which the copyist incorporated in his score, though some were eventually overruled by Handel.[14]

Whereas the oratorio parts usually provide everything needed for performance, the opera sets are much less complete, lacking the overture and virtually all secco recitative and having no separate parts for the singers. This distinction probably reflects Jennens's assumption, reasonable enough in the late 1740s, that while he might someday have occasion to sponsor the performance of a whole oratorio, he would never be called upon to supply more than excerpts from the operas. He would not have needed manuscript parts for the opera overtures because of the comprehensive collections published by Walsh. In any case the Aylesford parts show no signs of having been used in performance, unless Jennens's figures are to be viewed in that light.

As with so many grand designs it appears that Jennens's plan was never fully realized. No parts are known to have existed for *Semele* (1743) or any of the oratorios after *Solomon* (1748)—there should probably have been three sets of partbooks containing *Semele* and *The Choice of Hercules* (two secular works), *Solomon* and *Susanna*, and *Theodora* and *Jephtha*. It also seems likely that many keyboard parts were never copied as intended. Some fourteen harpsichord parts for oratorios and two for operas are nowhere to be seen, and

[11] In his Mainwaring annotations Jennens mentions that his score of the *Ode for Queen Anne's Birthday* had been 'transcrib'd from a copy which belong'd to L^d. Radnor'; see W. Dean, 'Jennens's Marginalia to Mainwaring's Life of Handel' in id., *Essays on Opera* (Oxford, 1990), 76.

[12] Of the opera scores apparently copied in the 1730s, only *Admeto*, *Alcina*, and *Ariodante* contain the recits. Since all 3 were bound in full leather as opposed to the normal half-calf, it is possible that Jennens still considered this to be special treatment. I am indebted to Martin Thacker, Watson Music Librarian, for supplying me with info. about the recits. in the Flower opera MSS.

[13] On Jennens's figuring see Rogers, *Continuo Realization*, 79–83.

[14] See Burrows, 'Autographs and Early Copies of *Messiah*' and Hicks, 'Handel, Jennens and *Saul*'.

JOHN H. ROBERTS

Jennens's tallies of the volumes in the sets where one would expect to find them make it clear they were never present.[15] He specifically notes their absence for six works (in two sets) and points out that the part for *Joseph* is bound elsewhere, implying that that for *Belshazzar*, its companion work, is not.[16] What may have caused the apparent cessation of copying, which must have taken place sometime after 1751 since the extant parts include additions composed for that year's revival of *Belshazzar*, we can only imagine. Perhaps S2, who had been producing all the parts, died or was incapacitated, and Jennens was unwilling to entrust the task to anyone else. Or it may be that the irascible Jennens came to a final break with Smith, whom he had once referred to as Handel's 'toad-eater'.[17]

In addition to his vast store of Handel copies Jennens probably also owned four small autographs preserved in the Aylesford Collection:

1. The Allemande in B minor, HWV 479, an early version of that in the D minor Harpsichord Suite, HWV 436 (GB-Lbl R.M.18.c.2, fo. 30).[18] It appears also in a Malmesbury manuscript collection dated 30 August 1722 (see Chap. 3).

2. The keyboard arrangement of the aria 'Sventurato, godi, o core' from *Floridante*, HWV 482^2 (GB-Lbl R.M.18.c.2, fos. 28–9).

3. The final chorus of *Floridante*, 'Quando pena la costanza' from the main autograph, bearing Handel's date of completion, 28 November 1721 (GB-Lbl Zweig Collection MS 37).

4. A single leaf from a lost aria closely related to 'Se povero il ruscello' in *Ezio*. Sold at Sotheby's in 1936, it subsequently disappeared without a trace. Donald Burrows has cited evidence that Handel contemplated introducing 'Se povero' into the May 1734 revival of *Il pastor fido* in place of Mirtillo's aria 'Lontan dal mio tesoro' and has proposed that the Aylesford leaf was part of a revised version made for that purpose.[19] But the surviving text of the lost aria, which speaks of refusing love and taking pleasure only in hunting wild beasts, points to Silvio rather than Mirtillo as the singer; presumably it was intended for Act 1, Scene 8, where it was eventually superseded by 'Quel gelsomino', likewise in G major.

---

[15] Missing are pts. for *Alexander Balus, L'Allegro, Atalanta, Athalia, Belshazzar* and its 1751 additions (2 different sets), *Deborah, Deidamia,* Dettingen Te Deum, *Esther, Hercules, Israel in Egypt, Joshua, Messiah,* Occasional Oratorio, and *Ode for St Cecilia's Day.*

[16] See A. D. Walker, *George Frideric Handel, The Newman Flower Collection in the Henry Watson Music Library: A Catalogue* (Manchester, 1972), 3, 18, 25.

[17] *Händel-Handbuch,* iv. *Dokumente zur Leben und Schaffen* (Leipzig and Kassel, 1985), 361.

[18] On this MS and the next see T. Best, 'An Example of Handel Embellishment', *MT* 110 (1969), 933.

[19] 'In Pursuit of "Lost" Handel Autographs', *Göttinger Händel-Beiträge,* 3 (1987), 192.

44   THE AYLESFORD COLLECTION

The first three of these autographs must have originated in late 1721 or early 1722, suggesting that Handel may have given them all to the same person around that time, probably some noble patron on whose support he depended. How and when Jennens acquired any of these manuscripts remains a mystery.

Handel was not Jennens's only collecting interest, however. He had a particular fondness for Italian music and was fortunate in having a friend well situated to gratify it.[20] Edward Holdsworth (1684–1746), whose monument would later adorn the hill at Gopsall, was a classical scholar, best known in his day for his satirical Latin poem 'Muscipula', whose nonjuring views had led him to renounce an Oxford fellowship in 1715. Thereafter he spent much of his life travelling on the Continent, where he bought many music manuscripts and printed editions on behalf of his younger friend. Their extant correspondence from the years 1729–46, now in the Coke Collection, contains much detailed information about these purchases. Though disclaiming all knowledge of music, Holdsworth was obviously a careful shopper and, once at least, an inspired one when in 1742 he obtained for Jennens, at the bargain price of forty shillings, a substantial part of the library of the late Cardinal Ottoboni, prince of Roman patrons. These 150 pounds of music (Holdsworth paid by the pound) included autographs of Alessandro Scarlatti and Vivaldi and a wealth of manuscript music by Albinoni, Pietro Paolo Bencini, Cesarini, Mancini, Marcello, Pollarolo, Sarro, and others.

Three of Jennens's Italian opera manuscripts were used by Handel as the basis of his pasticcio operas *Caio Fabbricio* (1733), *Arsace* (1734), and *Didone* (1737), as may be seen from his pencilled changes in the Aylesford copies. He also borrowed musical ideas from scores of Alessandro Scarlatti's *Dafni* (1700) and *Marco Attilio Regolo* (1719), a volume containing excerpts from Scarlatti's *Griselda* (1721) and miscellaneous Italian arias, and Vinci's *Didone abbandonata* (1726), the model of *Didone*. Jennens must eventually have detected these incursions, for he remarked to Holdsworth in January 1743 that he had caught Handel 'stealing' from both Scarlatti and Vinci.[21] In the same passage the composer is reported to have just made off with 'a dozen of the Pieces' from the Ottoboni Collection, but one suspects

---

[20] Jennens's Italian collection has been extensively studied by Michael Talbot and Paul Everett. See esp. Talbot, 'Some Overlooked MSS in Manchester', *MT* 115 (1974), 942–4, and id., 'Charles Jennens and Antonio Vivaldi', in Francesco Degrada (ed.), *Vivaldi veneziano europeo* (Florence, 1980), 67–75; and Everett, 'Vivaldi Concerto Manuscripts in Manchester', *Informazioni e studi vivaldiani: Bollettino dell'Istituto Italiano Antonio Vivaldi*, 5 (1984), 23–52; 6 (1985), 3–56; and 7 (1986), 5–34; and id., *The Manchester Concerto Partbooks*, 2 vols. (New York, 1989).

[21] See Roberts, 'Italian Opera Manuscripts', and id., 'Handel and Vinci's "Didone abbandonata": Revisions and Borrowings', *ML,* 68 (1987), 141–50.

JOHN H. ROBERTS 45

that if he borrowed from any of them he did so less transparently than before.

For all his partiality for Italian composers Jennens did not by any means disdain the music of his compatriots. He subscribed at one time or another to works by Alcock, Avison, Boyce, Clarke, Greene, Hayes, Kelway, Pixell, and J. C. Smith,[22] and he owned manuscripts of music by Alcock, Greene, Lampe, and Purcell. John Alcock (1715–1806), who as organist at Lichfield Cathedral and the parish churches of Sutton Coldfield and Tamworth lived not far from Gopsall, seems to have been a personal friend. Three volumes in Alcock's hand are listed in the Aylesford sale catalogue of 1918, and a score of Greene's oratorio *The Song of Deborah and Barak* at the Royal College of Music (MS 884) bears the inscription by Alcock 'This is the only copy of this Piece of Musick, except one I wrote for Chas. Jennens Esq.' That copy is in the Fitzwilliam Museum.

As his Collection grew—or perhaps only after it had become too large to manage more casually—Jennens organized and arranged it with characteristic care. His shelf-marks, still visible on many Aylesford volumes, consist of two capital letters (the first always M, N, or O) over a number, separated by a horizontal line. With part-books, only the set was numbered: a typical inscription reads 'NT/3ᵈ. set/7 Volˢ.' or simply 'NT/7 Volˢ.' Like manuscripts were frequently placed together, most Italian sacred music going into MS, many Italian operas into NC. But the way a logical sequence begun in one group is sometimes continued in another shows that the letters denoted not discrete types of material but physical locations, presumably bookcases. Thus the chronological series of Handel opera scores that starts in NP (following some orchestral music) concludes in NX, and the Handel performing parts form a continuous chain running through NS, NT, NR, NV, and NQ to NW, which also packs in several scores. NN seems to have been reserved primarily for folio volumes. Shorter pieces and fragments were bound into composite volumes, within which the contents were arranged largely in chronological order. For many of these miscellanies Jennens wrote out detailed tables of contents and also supplied cross-references linking them to each other and to the related scores. It is noteworthy that in the table of contents of GB-Lbl R.M.19.a.1 he describes the D minor Organ Concerto, HWV 303, another version of the first movement of Op. 7, No. 4, as 'a new Introduction of ye 4th Organ Concerto'. Since Walsh did not invent Op. 7 until 1761, this implies that at least some of Jennens's organizational efforts came comparatively late in the day.

---

[22] R. Smith, 'Achievements of Charles Jennens', 190.

46   THE AYLESFORD COLLECTION

Heneage Finch, 3rd Earl of Aylesford (1715–77), Jennens's good
friend as well as his relative, was the son of his first cousin Mary
Fischer, whose marriage to the 2nd Earl had brought the Finches
their great estate of Packington. In younger days, as Lord Guernsey
till 1757, he had been on warm terms with Handel, who mentions
the 'particular Esteem I have for His Lordship' in one of his letters
to Jennens and in another conveys 'my humble Respects and thanks
to My Lord Guernsey for his many Civility's to me'.[23] Later, as lord
of Packington, he became something of a patron of music, judging
by the dedications in a song collection published by the Birmingham
composer John Pixell in 1759.[24] A sprightly song, 'The Landskip', is
dedicated to the Countess of Aylesford, while the concluding duet
and chorus with full orchestral accompaniment is inscribed to the
Earl. The suitably devout 'Though in the paths of death I tread' carries
a dedication to 'Char. Jennins Esq:' (who repaid the compliment by
taking six copies of the collection).

In a small way very different from that of his cousin, Finch too
was a collector of music. He subscribed to Walsh's editions of *Giustino*,
Arminio (both 1737), *Alexander's Feast* (1738) and the Concerti grossi,
Op. 6 (1740), though not to *Atalanta* (1736) and *Faramondo* (1738).
His name appears also as a subscriber to Festing's *Six Solo's for a
Violin and Thorough-Bass*, Op. 7, of 1747, implying wider buying.
Presumably it was he who acquired a number of early manuscripts in
the Aylesford Collection that apparently did not come from Jennens. A
set of string parts for excerpts from *Arianna* and other music of Handel,
now in the Flower Collection, has the name 'Guernsey' written inside
the front cover of the first volume, and a similar inscription is found
on one of the Aylesford manuscripts in the Coke Collection that formerly belonged to William C. Smith.[25] If, as seems probable, Guernsey
wrote the tables of contents and some other text in the Flower partbooks, then he was also responsible for textual additions in several of
the other manuscripts. These Old Aylesford manuscripts—so far as
we can tell from those that have survived—were primarily Handel performing parts, not the orderly system of transcripts designed by Jennens
but a much more motley assortment clearly intended for domestic
music-making. Along with various overtures and other excerpts there
were sets for *Alexander's Feast* (with the recitatives), *Ariodante*, *Alcina*,
Atalanta, and *Arminio*, suggesting that Packington Hall in the late
1730s and 1740s may have enjoyed quite a lively musical life.

[23] *Händel-Handbuch*, iv. 353, 377. Further on Handel's relationship with Guernsey see ibid.
365, 400, 419.
[24] *A Collection of Songs, with their Recitatives and Symphonies* (Birmingham, 1759).
[25] The ripieno vn2 pt. for the 1st 2 mvts. of an anonymous concerto in A m, this MS is not
included in the microfilm edn. of the Coke MSS (see 26, below).

JOHN H. ROBERTS

Of special interest is a manuscript in the Coke Collection, a keyboard part for excerpts from *Arianna*, evidently all that remains of a larger set of parts.[26] Together with the bass of the Overture and the voice and bass of eleven arias (one incomplete), in the hands of two unfamiliar copyists with the texts of several arias supplied by the presumed Lord Guernsey, it contains full scores of the accompanied recitatives that precede two of the arias, copied by S2 and elaborately figured by Jennens. These recitatives are evidently an integral part of the manuscript, since in one case the ensuing aria follows directly on the same page. Perhaps they were a gift from Jennens, designed to supplement the published score of 1737, which Guernsey later incorporated in his keyboard part so they could be performed with their arias. Jennens also added a few figures to a group of three additional airs for *L'Allegro* probably from the Old Aylesford Collection.[27] Clearly he was intimately involved in the early development of his younger cousin's music-library.

Certain of these Old Aylesford manuscripts testify to a close association between the future earl and the clergyman-composer Richard Mudge. Mudge (1718–63), whose *Six concertos in seven parts . . . to which is added, Non Nobis Domine, in 8 parts* were published by Walsh in 1749, served as vicar of Great Packington (whose church lies within the grounds of Packington Hall) from 1741 to 1756. He then became rector of the neighbouring parish of Bedworth, also under the Earl's patronage, remaining there until his death. The Flower Collection contains three autograph manuscripts of Mudge:[28]

1. A complete set of parts for the concertos as published by Walsh, with two notes for the printer (MS 130 Hd4 v.86–92).

2. A second, incomplete set of parts—two concertino violins, viola, and cello—for a very different version of the concertos, including two entirely unknown works (uncatalogued).[29]

3. The violin part for a 'Sonata Cômposta a la gusto del Seign.or Bombardini' (uncatalogued). This is yet another version of the Concerto in D minor, Walsh's No. 2.

[26] MS 16, see Ch. 1. n. 1.

[27] The MS is GB-BENcoke MS. 12. An uncatalogued Flower copy of a 4th additional air for *L'Allegro*, 'Orpheus self', may have been part of the same set.

[28] Mudge's hand can be identified from a letter in the possession of the Earl of Aylesford, addressed to the 2nd Earl and dated 16 Feb. 1746. I am grateful to Anthony Hicks for alerting me to its existence and to his Lordship for making a copy of it available for comparison.

[29] There are 8 concertos in the set, related to the published version as follows: (1) Variant of No. 1, (2) Variant of No. 4, (3) Variant of No. 3 including a variant of the 2nd movement in No. 5, (4) New concerto in D major (Largo Andante–Allegro–Andante Larghetto–Allegro), (5) Variant of No. 2, (6) Variant of No. 6, (7) New concerto in Bb major (2 'stanzas' with a partial reprise of the first), (8) New except for the final 'Non nobis Domine', a variant of the published version.

48 THE AYLESFORD COLLECTION

Assorted material of Mudge, from the Aylesford Collection, formerly belonged to William C. Smith and is now in the Coke Collection. Together with miscellaneous parts for various concertos there are drafts and sketches and a copy of Old Hundredth, which Mudge may at one time have contemplated working into a concerto movement as he did 'Non nobis Domine'. Additionally, several of the Old Aylesford Handel manuscripts are partly in Mudge's hand. His keyboard reduction of the Overture to *Hercules* is found with a set of parts for that overture, and he copied portions of sets for *Arminio*, *Ariodante*, *Messiah*, and excerpts from *Esther* and *Judas Maccabaeus* in the Manchester 'Guernsey' partbooks, as well as a separate score of 'I know that my Redeemer liveth'.[30] One imagines him playing a leading role in the performances at Packington Hall, where his concertos may well have been heard for the first time.[31]

Under the terms of Jennens's will the 3rd Earl was to have received all his music, but in the event it appears he got something less than his full legacy. The University of Chicago Library has a group of twenty-six Handel manuscripts (MS 437), consisting of scores and parts for various anthems and three odd parts for the *Ode for Queen Anne's Birthday* and other works, that undoubtedly belonged to Jennens but seem never to have been in the Aylesford Collection.[32] They were purchased from the London book-dealer F. C. Carter in 1926 or 1927, and came, according to Carter's 'Hornsey Book List No. 71',[33] from the library of Baroness Angela Burdett-Coutts, the Victorian philanthropist and friend of Dickens, which had been sold at Sotheby's on 15–17 May 1922. It is surely no coincidence that the baroness was the great granddaughter of Sir Robert Burdett (1716–97), Jennens's first cousin on his mother's side (so not related to the Finches of Packington) and his executor. Possibly Jennens gave some of his music to Burdett before his death; more likely these volumes and perhaps others were retained by Burdett, perhaps accidently, when the estate was finally divided.

[30] *Hercules* and *Arminio* are in GB-BENcoke (MSS 55 and 17), *Ariodante* is divided between GB-Lbl (R.M.18.b.6) and GB-Mp (MS 130 Hd4 vv.64–5), and *Messiah* is in GB-Mp (MS 130 Hd4 vv. 201–4). The copy of 'I know that my Redeemer liveth' is in AUS-Sfl.

[31] The Aylesford Collection also included a copy of Walsh's 5th collection of Handel overtures for hpd bearing Mudge's signature and a note about hiring a hpd in 1737. See First Edition Bookshop, *George Frederic Handel: A Catalogue of First Editions, Early Editions, Contemporary Manuscript Music, Arrangements, Books, Portraits, etc.*, Catalogue 25 (Mar. 1937), no. 31. The present location of this copy of the Walsh print is unknown.

[32] For descriptions of the MSS see H. Lenneberg and L. Libin, 'Unknown Handel Sources in Chicago', *Journal of the American Musicological Society*, 22 (1969), 85–100; G. Beeks, 'The Chandos Anthems and Te Deum of George Frideric Handel 1685–1759' diss. (University of California at Berkeley, 1981), i. 202–11; and D. Burrows, 'Handel and the English Chapel Royal during the Reigns of Queen Anne and King George I', diss. (Open University, 1981), 148–49, 313–14, 319, 344–6, 349, 385–6, 391.

[33] There is a copy of this catalogue in US-Cn.

As it happened the Earl had little enough time in which to enjoy his new treasures. Less than four years after Jennens, on 9 May 1777, he died at the age of 61 and was succeeded by his son, another Heneage Finch. The 4th Earl (1751–1832) was a figure of considerable interest. While at Oxford he had studied drawing with John Malchair, the German-born violinist and water-colourist, and he later developed a distinctive style of drawing that was taken up by his younger brothers and sisters and his children.[34] He probably played a major role in the design of the church at Packington, a landmark in English architecture. What his musical accomplishments may have been we do not know. But the wealth of printed chamber music in the Aylesford Collection, much of which can only have been added during his time, suggests he was a string player, most likely a violinist.

Certainly he was an active patron of music. Felice Giardini, the violin virtuoso and composer who became a favourite of the British aristocracy, dedicated his six String Quartets, Op. 22 (London, 1779 or 1780) to the Earl, and the autographs of three string trios composed in June 1792 are also inscribed to Lord Aylesford.[35] The trios may well have been composed at Packington, since Giardini often visited the country seats of his noble patrons during the summer. On the autograph of a viola sonata 'Per Lord Aylesford', Giardini, who was famous for his mischievous wit, added under his patron's name the word *billiardo* (billiards), suggesting that their relationship was social as well as musical. Other musicians who enjoyed the favour of the Earl were Franz Kotzwara, celebrated for his noisy *Battle of Prague* and scandalous death, and Benjamin Cooke. Kotzwara's *Six Trio's for Two Violins & a Bass with an Occasional Accompaniment for Horns* Op. 5 (1776) carries a dedication 'to the Earl of Aylesford', and Aylesford manuscripts of four of these works are preserved in the Flower Collection. Among Benjamin Cooke's manuscripts at the Royal College of Music are six metrical psalm-tunes 'for the Earl of Aylesford', two dated 31 July and 7 August 1787.[36]

During the time of the 4th Earl there occurred a curious episode, hitherto unremarked, in which copies were made of a number of Aylesford manuscripts for the King's music-library. The origins of

[34] On the artistic contribution of the 4th Earl and other members of his family see M. Binney, 'A Pioneer Work of Neo-Classicism: The Church at Great Packington, Warwickshire', *Country Life*, 150 (1971), 110–15, and I. Fleming-Williams, 'The Finches of Packington', *Country Life*, 150 (1971), 170–4, 229–32.

[35] One of the trios is GB-Lbl Add. MS 57538. The other 2 are known only through their descriptions in Catalogue 32 of the Leamington Book Shop, Fredericksburg, Virginia (Feb. 1968), which are largely reproduced in the App., Sect. 2. On Giardini generally and his relationship with the aristocracy see S. McVeigh, *The Violinist in London's Concert Life 1750–1784: Felice Giardini and his Contemporaries* (New York, 1989).

[36] GB-Lcm MS. 807, f. 14, and MS. 812, fos. 113–14. One tune appears in both MSS.

50   THE AYLESFORD COLLECTION

this undertaking are closely connected with Burney's *Account* of 1785, in which, as already indicated, he devotes considerable space to various Handel collections.[37] He begins with an inventory of the 'Original Manuscripts in the Possession of His Majesty', the collection Smith had presented to George III in 1774.[38] To this he attaches a list of works 'Not in His Majesty's Collection' and goes on to comment in some detail on the holdings of the Earl of Aylesford, Sir Watkin Williams Wynn, and the Granville family. George III was an ardent Handelian. 'He hears no other music if he can help it,' reported Burney, who despite his impatience with the King's 'exclusive liking' was impressed with how well he knew Handel's music.[39] From the first the King took a great interest in Burney's *Account*, reading over the manuscript and reviewing changes, using Frederick Nicolay, the Queen's principal page and his *de facto* music-librarian, as a go-between. And even before the book was published he seems to have decided to fill the reported lacunae in his collection by obtaining copies of the missing works.

As regards the Granville Collection this is documented by two letters from George III to Mrs Delany, Handel's great friend and the aunt of the then owner of the collection, the Reverend John Dewes or Granville. Writing on 7 November 1784, while Burney's book was being printed, he informs her that,

The King is much pleased with the very correct manner in which Mrs. Delany has obligingly executed the Commission of obtaining an exact Catalogue of Mr. Granville's Collection of Mr. Handel's Music, and desires She will forward it to Dr. Burney; at the same time, as Mrs. Delany has communicated Mr. Granville's willingness of letting the King see those Volumes that are not in the list of His original Collection, He is desired at any convenient opportunity to let the following ones be sent to Town, and great care shall be taken that they shall without damage be returned

No. 19.   Opera of Ameneto
    22.   Teseo
    25.   Amadige
    35. & 36. Vols. of Duets
    37.   Miscellanies and Water Musick

as also the Quarto Manuscript of songs composed by that great Master in eight parts beginning *Still I adore You though You deny Me*.[40]

---

[37] pp. 42–6.

[38] Burney's list differs significantly from that given in Mrs Julian Marshall, *George Frederick Handel 1685–1759* (London, 1883), 133–6, which shows how the Collection looked prior to its rebinding under Squire's direction. Most notably he makes no mention of scores of *The Choice of Hercules* and the *Ode for Queen Anne's Birthday* and reports 5 vols. less of vocal and instr. miscellanies. This probably reflects the arrangement of the MSS while they were still unbound or only partially bound.

[39] *The Letters of Dr Charles Burney*, ed. Alvaro Ribeiro, i (Oxford, 1991), 437.

[See opposite page for n. 40]

In the second letter, dated 11 February 1785, he reports that he 'has just received copies of the three operas Mrs. Delany so obligingly borrowed for him' and is therefore returning all the manuscripts.[41] These three operas had been identified by Burney as lacking in the King's Collection, although in fact he probably already owned a copy of *Teseo*, GB-Lbl R.M.19.e.6, which has revisions in the composer's hand. The copies made from the Granville manuscripts are undoubtedly GB-Lbl R.M.19.c.2 (*Admeto*), GB-Lbl R.M.19.c.5 (*Amadigi*), and GB-Lbl R.M.19.d.8 (*Teseo*), all in the hand of S13.

Scarcely less certainly, eight other Handel manuscripts in the Royal Music Library were copied from the Aylesford Collection by either S13 or RM5 (also known as RM6), as indicated in Table 1.

Table 1. Royal Music Manuscripts copied from the Aylesford Collection

Title	GB-Lbl Shelf-mark	Copyist
Additional Songs, i	R.M.19.d.10	S13
Additional Songs, ii	R.M.19.d.11	S13/RM5
Foundling Hospital Anthem	R.M.19.e.8	RM5
'Nisi Dominus'	R.M.19.d.2	S13
Ode for Queen Anne's Birthday	R.M.19.e.1	S13
La Resurrezione	R.M.19.d.4	RM5
Silla	R.M.19.d.7	RM5
Te Deum in D major, HWV 280	R.M.19.e.2	S13

The derivation is most obvious with the two volumes of *Additional Songs, &c.*, R.M.19.d.10 and R.M.19.d.11, which contain a very unusual assortment of pieces that can only have been culled from Jennens's composite volumes, but tell-tale details confirm the other connections, even in two cases where the Aylesford score is lost.[42] As

---

[40] The letter, found at the end of the Granville MS of the *Water Music*, GB-Lbl Eg. MS 2946, is quoted somewhat inaccurately in R. A. Streatfeild, 'The Granville Collection of Handel Manuscripts', *Musical Antiquary*, 2 (1910–11), 211. There seems in fact to have been only 1 'song in eight parts', an English version of 'Pena tiranna' in *Amadigi*: see W. Barclay Squire, 'Handel's "Song in Eight Parts"', *Musical Antiquary*, 4 (1912–13), 223–4.

[41] Streatfeild, 'Granville Collection', 212.

[42] The Aylesford sources of the *Additional Songs* are Lbl R.M.18.c.4, R.M.18.c.5, R.M.18.c.7, R.M.18.c.11, R.M.19.a.1, and R.M.19.a.5; Mp MSS 130 Hd4 v.187 and v.268; and BENcoke MS. 10 (*L'Allegro*). From his detailed study of the MSS Burrows has concluded that R.M.19.e.1 and R.M.19.e.2 were copied from the Aylesford scores of the *Ode for Queen Anne's Birthday* and the D major Te Deum: 'Handel and the English Chapel Royal', 148–9, 180–2. The RM5 copy of the Foundling Hospital Anthem has, bound in at the end, the 1751 setting of 'The leafy honours of the field' in *Belshazzar*. This sort of odd coupling was characteristic of Jennens's collection, and he must have owned a copy of this aria, missing from his other composite MSS.

52   THE AYLESFORD COLLECTION

with the Granville operas there is a strong correlation with Burney. He locates *La Resurrezione* and the Te Deum 'composed for the Arrival of Queen Caroline' in the Aylesford Collection, along with the 'Dances' in *Arianna* and *Pastor fido* and the 'Harpsichord Lessons . . . for Princess Louisa', all of which are in the first volume of *Additional Songs*, and he cites the Foundling Hospital Anthem and the *Ode for Queen Anne's Birthday* as being in the Wynn Collection, though the Wynn manuscripts cannot have been the sources used by the King's copyists. Handel's scores of the *Ode for Queen Anne's Birthday*, *La Resurrezione*, and the Te Deum were in fact in the King's library, but this would not have been obvious from Burney's list, where none of them is separately mentioned except *La Resurrezione*, identified simply as 'Oratorio Italiano'.

We may presume that in dealing with the Earl of Aylesford the King followed the same strategy as he had with Mrs Delany, requesting a catalogue and then borrowing the desired volumes for copying. He must have had access to such a listing—unless he paid a long and very laborious visit to Packington—for he obtained copies of two works that Burney does not cite at all, 'Nisi Dominus' and *Silla*, as well as of the *Ode for Queen Anne's Birthday* and the Foundling Hospital Anthem, listed under Watkin Wynn. This catalogue must have been quite detailed ('an exact catalogue' as the King phrased it to Mrs Delany), since he was able to draw out of it such morsels as the song 'Love's but the frailty of the mind' and the Hornpipe in D major, HWV 356, which are bound into the back of one of Jennens's scores of *L'Allegro*. Even so, many volumes must have been transported to London: copying the *Additional Songs* alone would have required nine, and it seems likely that as with the Granville Collection the King did not order copies of everything he borrowed.

Thus the King's music-library was augmented by some new music, some he already owned, and some copies of copies of his own manuscripts. And in a few instances duplication became threefold when in 1918 the library acquired most of the Aylesford manuscripts from which the two volumes of *Additional Songs* derived. For the study of the Aylesford Collection these Royal Music manuscripts are perhaps most significant for what they can tell us about Jennens's lost scores of the *Ode for Queen Anne's Birthday* and the Foundling Hospital Anthem.

After the death of the 4th Earl in 1832 little or nothing seems to have been added to the Aylesford Collection. It became a static object, a more or less disused family heirloom, and when money needed to be raised it was an obvious choice for selling off. First, two years after the death of the 6th Earl, came an auction at Puttick & Simpson on

25 August 1873, a mixed sale in which the Aylesford portion consisted largely if not exclusively of printed music. Then on 13 May 1918 most of the rest of the Collection went on the block at Sotheby's. With the Great War still raging, it was a bad time for such a sale, and most of the lots went for extremely low prices. From the point of view of musical scholarship the results might have been more disastrous had it not been for the efforts of two self-appointed rescuers, Newman Flower, at the beginning of his career as a collector of Handeliana, and William Barclay Squire, approaching retirement as chief music-librarian at the British Museum. First from Harold Reeves and later from various other dealers (possibly through Reeves) Flower purchased the lion's share of the Aylesford Handel manuscripts as well as many Handel editions and a generous selection of music by other composers. With less capital at his disposal Squire confined himself to tracking down certain manuscripts he believed to be of particular historical value, some of which he donated to the Royal Music Library and the British Museum; others were sold to the Fitzwilliam Museum and the Library of Congress.[43]

Of the non-Handelian manuscripts not taken up by these two bibliophiles, some, it is interesting to note, proved remarkably difficult to sell. A group of seven manuscript scores of Italian operas by Hasse, Jommelli, Latilla, Porpora, and Vinci, bought in the 1918 sale by a dealer named Hunt, were eventually acquired by Harold Reeves, who offered them in his Catalogue 102 in 1932. Although presented with considerable fanfare concerning their rarity and provenance, all must have remained unsold, for in 1940 he offered them again, without fanfare and at substantially reduced prices. This time he succeeded in selling five of the scores to American libraries, but the two operas of Latilla were still on hand when his successor Kenneth Mummery published his first catalogue in 1949, in which they were marked down still further to £5. 5s. each (having begun at £12. 10s), and it was not until Mummery relisted them at the same price in 1957 that he finally found a buyer in Frank de Bellis of San Francisco.

Soon after the second Aylesford sale in May 1922, the Jennens manuscripts now in Chicago were auctioned at Sotheby's as part of the Burdett-Coutts library. The sale catalogue shows only two lots that could contain music from Jennens's Collection.[44] Lot 336 is a set of five manuscript partbooks for viol music by William Lawes and

[43] Two vols. of Astorga cantatas and duets that he gave to GB-Lbl (Add. MSS 39765–6) seem to have been purchased at the sale by Squire himself. No buyer is recorded for the lot they comprise (lot 285), and he presented them to the library on 14 May 1918, the day after the sale.

[44] Sotheby, Wilkinson & Hodge, *Catalogue of the Valuable Library, the Property of the Late Baroness Burdett Coutts*, 15–17 May 1922.

54   THE AYLESFORD COLLECTION

others, partly in Lawes's hand; purchased by Quaritch, it became
GB-Lbl Add. MSS 40657–61. That Jennens may have had some
interest in Lawes is suggested by the presence in the 1918 sale of a
copy of *Choice Psalmes* (1648) by William and his brother Henry (lot
301). Lot 337 of the 1922 sale is described as 'an Extensive Collection
of Manuscript and Printed Music, including Italian Oratorios and
Operas in MS., Part Songs, Ballads, etc. *a quantity*.' This must have
included the Chicago manuscripts but obviously much else, since it
seems most unlikely that the parts for *La Resurrezione* embedded in
two of the Chicago volumes could fully account for the reference to
'Italian Oratorios and Operas in MS.' Confirmation that this lot
concealed a multitude of riches is found in a brief autobiography
that Harold Reeves contributed to Andrew Block's *A Short History
of the Principal London Antiquarian Booksellers and Book-Auctioneers*
in 1933. Noting proudly that 'many famous music libraries have passed
through my hands,' he first cites the Aylesford Handel manuscripts
and then remarks that 'the Burdett-Coutts Music Library was
extensive and interesting.'[45] Between 1922 and 1927 Reeves listed in
his catalogues a number of printed items as from the Burdett-Coutts
collection, none of them probably deriving from Jennens.[46] But as
they could hardly be called either extensive or interesting by Reeves's
standards, we must presume that he sold the best things directly to
collectors or libraries. Whether these unknown treasures had any
connection with Jennens is of course a matter of speculation.

It has usually been assumed that the 1918 sale entirely disposed of
the historical music-library of the Earls of Aylesford, but this was
apparently not the case, for it seems that the Earl or possibly some
other member of his family had retained, perhaps accidentally, a small
remnant that was not sold until some years later. This part of the
story can be pieced together only incompletely. A central figure was
Cecil Hopkinson, the distinguished music bibliographer and antiquarian dealer. In March 1937 his First Edition Bookshop issued a
special Handel catalogue, in which he designated twelve manuscripts
and nineteen editions as being of Aylesford provenance.[47] The manuscripts were small and with exception of a set of four arias for the
1717 revival of *Rinaldo* not likely to have belonged to Jennens. Then

---

[45] (London, 1933), 47.

[46] See Catalogues 38 (1922), 45 (1923), 58 (1925), 62 (1926), and 69 (1927), and relistings in
Catalogues 89 (1930) and 95 (1931). A MS of 6 sonatas for 2 cellos and bass by Emanuele
Barbella, no. 429a in Catalogue 58 and no. 11610 in Catalogue 95, cannot have come from the
Burdett-Coutts library as stated, since Reeves had listed it already in 1921, tracing it to 'the
recently dispersed Hamilton Library' (Catalogue 33, no. 635). Channan Willner graciously
retrieved relevant entries from the earlier Reeves catalogues.

[47] See n. 31, above.

in April William C. Smith published an article about three Handel manuscripts in Hopkinson's hands—the *Rinaldo* arias and two autographs, the final chorus of *Floridante* and the leaf from a lost *Pastor fido* aria described above—all of which were said to have come from the Aylesford Collection.[48] Both autographs had recently been sold at Sotheby's, the aria leaf on 18 December 1936 for £185 (£2 more than the total proceeds of the 1918 sale), the chorus on 16 March 1937 for £500. In his preface to a facsimile of the *Floridante* chorus published in a limited edition of ten copies in 1936, Hopkinson indicated that the manuscript had come to light in London and had been 'in the possession of the family of the Earl of Aylesford until recently'.[49] A number of other small manuscripts, ostensibly from the Aylesford Collection, were obtained by Smith, who relates only that he bought them from 'a dealer'.[50] These too presumably came from Hopkinson's cache, as did two manuscripts he sold to James Hall that were never listed in his catalogues. It is not possible to demonstrate conclusively the Aylesford provenance of all this material, yet the manifest links between many of the manuscripts and Jennens, Guernsey, or Mudge would seem to establish sufficiently the origin of the collection as a whole.

But this is not all. Thirty years later further material purportedly from the Aylesford Collection turned up in the catalogues of the Leamington Book Shop of Frederickburg, Virginia. Catalogue 31 (April 1937) offered the autograph of Giardini's Trio in C major 'Per A G Lord Aylesford', and Catalogue 32 (February 1968) followed with three more Giardini autographs similarly inscribed, a manuscript volume of English church music from around 1775, and forty-two printed titles, mostly music of the late eighteenth and early nineteenth centuries.[51] According to the description of the trio in Catalogue 31 (no. 103), the manuscript had 'remained in the Aylesford Family until about 40 years ago, when it was acquired at auction by a leading Midlands book dealer, from whom it was purchased by the writer [Sidney Hamer] recently.' If we accept this at face value, it means that this music was sold at an auction around 1927, and the reference to a Midlands book-dealer suggests that the sale, of which music surely

[48] 'Recently-Discovered Handel Manuscripts', *MT* 78 (1937), 312–15.

[49] *Manuscript of the Finale from Floridante* (London, 1936). This preface largely corresponds to the description of the MS given in a supplementary catalogue issued by the First Edition Bookshop in May 1937: *George Frederic Handel 1685–1759: An Original Handel Manuscript of Great Importance and a Few First Editions, Addenda to Catalogue 25, no. 1*. In the Sotheby's sale catalogue of 16 Mar. 1937 the manuscript is said to be 'the Property of a Collector'.

[50] *A Handelian's Notebook* (London, 1965), 122–3. These MSS were later added to GB-BENcoke.

[51] Catalogue 32 was kindly brought to my attention by James Coover.

56 THE AYLESFORD COLLECTION

formed only a small part, might have taken place not in London but closer to Packington. One suspects, though we may never prove, that this was the same occasion on which the family divested itself of the manuscripts later 'discovered' in London by Hopkinson. It must be added that not all the printed editions in catalogue 32 probably derive from the Aylesford Collection, since a number reportedly bear the names of former owners not obviously connected with the Earls.[52] After forty years it would not be surprising if the Midlands dealer's memory of exactly what part of his stock had come from that source was somewhat hazy.

If indeed a catalogue of the Aylesford Collection existed in the days of George III, it does not seem to have survived into modern times. Thus in attempting to determine the contents of this great library we must rely heavily on various listings produced in connection with its dispersal. Of central importance is the catalogue of the 1918 sale.[53] It describes 129 lots of printed and manuscript music in some detail, often giving information on binding and other physical characteristics but nonetheless falling considerably short of a full and reliable inventory. Several large miscellaneous lots obviously embraced far more than their descriptions disclose. In lot 313 only three of the sixteen volumes are identified, in lot 326A only nine out of twenty-four. The thirty-two volumes of lot 286 are reduced to 'Anthems. A parcel, all MS.' Some titles betray the transcriber's un-familiarity with foreign languages, as 'Salve Regina' is transmogrified into 'Alve Salve Regi' and 'Vola cupido' into 'O la nola Cupido' (overlooking the ornamental capitals). Elsewhere he did not go far enough in exploring a composite volume. Lot 276 is said to consist of three operas by Porpora, *Ariadne* (i.e. *Arianna in Nasso*), *Il Mitridate*, and *Polifemo*, whereas in fact the first manuscript (in the Newberry Library) contains the composer's *Enea nel Lazio* as well as *Arianna*, and the second and third manuscripts (at Yale University) are mis-cellanies that happen to begin with selections from *Mitridate* and *Polifemo*. Not surprisingly, the many mixed partbooks caused trouble, especially when sets were not kept together but distributed among two or more lots. In an exceptional mix-up, the entire contents of lot 244 reappear as part of lot 258, leaving one to wonder what the purchaser, Coupland, may have had for his nine shillings when five of the seven volumes listed had already gone to Reeves for three shillings.

---

[52] A piano sonata by William Dance is inscribed to 'Mr. Hatchett', possibly Charles Hatchett whose collection was sold at Puttick's in 1848. Other items are signed by Thomas Davis and Mary Jane Williams.

[53] Sotheby, Wilkinson & Hodge, *Catalogue of Valuable Books & Manuscripts*, 13–16 May 1918. This is reproduced in the microfilm edn., Sotheby's & Co., *Catalogues of Sales, 1734–1945* (Ann Arbor, Mich., 1973).

JOHN H. ROBERTS   57

Whatever the limitations of this catalogue, it is far more satisfactory than that of the 1873 sale. Entitled 'Catalogue of a Collection of Music Including the Valuable Music Library of the Late Earl of Aylesford', it specifies a few of its 386 lots of prints and manuscripts as coming from the collections of Crotch, Gauntlett, and others but leaves it unclear how much of the remainder derives from the Aylesford Collection.[54] Some items can confidently be linked to Jennens, such as the editions of Tartini's Op. 1 Concertos and Locatelli's *L'arte del violino* (both of which Holdsworth had purchased for him at Amsterdam in 1733) or the nearly comprehensive collection of Vivaldi's printed *opera*. On the other hand one may wonder, lacking any other evidence of such breadth of interest, whether Jennens or the Earls of Aylesford ever owned the sixteenth-century Italian organ manuscript in lot 115 or the treatises of Galilei, Glareanus, Zarlino, and others. At least two items had figured in earlier Puttick sales, Coferati's *Corona di sacre canzoni* (1689) in the sales of 23 February and 26 April 1872 (the catalogue descriptions are virtually identical) and two autograph volumes of Pachelbel in the sales of 30 June and 31 July 1873; both came from the library of Joseph Warren.[55] After disposing of a large part of his famous collection in three sales in 1872, it appears that Warren placed many additional rarities anonymously in subsequent sales, and he may well be the source of some of the more eye-catching lots in the 'Aylesford' sale.[56] Most likely he contributed the five sets of manuscript partbooks in lots 151 and 279–82: one of them, GB–Ob MS Tenbury 369–73, is known to have belonged to him, and all five sets probably came from the same collection since they all derive ultimately from the library of Edward Paston (1550–1630).[57]

The 1873 Catalogue spawned a holographic ghost that has for some years hovered at the margin of Haydn scholarship. Lot 126 is a 'March in E flat, for 2 Vns., Va. and Bass, 3 first Vn.; 2 second Vn.; 1, Va. and 3 bass parts, *believed to be one of two Marches composed*

---

[54] The GB-Lbl copy shows the buyers on interleaved pages. I am indebted to Anthony Hicks for relaying much information from this catalogue.

[55] Bought at the sale by Ouseley, these vols. became GB-Ob MSS Tenbury 1208–9. On their provenance see E. H. Fellowes, *The Catalogue of Manuscripts in the Library of St. Michael's College, Tenbury* (Paris, 1934), 264.

[56] A. Hyatt King, *Some British Collectors of Music, c.1600–1960* (Cambridge, 1963), 56, suggests that the 16th-cent. Frankfurt fair catalogues in the 1873 Aylesford sale were 'probably those from Warren's library'.

[57] Fellowes says that Warren owned the MS in 1845 (*Catalogue of St. Michael's College*, 64). On Paston see P. Brett, 'Edward Paston 1550–1630: A Norfolk Gentleman and his Musical Collection', *Transactions of the Cambridge Bibliographical Society*, 4 (1964–8), 51–69. The 5 sets are listed in the App., Sect. I, under Collections, 'Motets'. Because of the sketchy descriptions of lots 279–82, the identifications of these MSS are necessarily somewhat speculative.

58   THE AYLESFORD COLLECTION

for the Captain of some Vessel while Haydn was in London'. The
manuscript is said to be 'in the Autograph of the Composer and
signed "Dr. Haydn"'. Although no known work of Haydn
corresponds to this description, this supposed autograph is dutifully
reported by Hoboken, who identifies it, somewhat improbably, with
a first draft of part of the 'March for the Royal Society of
Musicians', H. VIII: 3, acquired by the Staatsbibliothek Preussischer
Kulturbesitz in 1964.[58] In fact, the manuscript sold in 1873 has been
in the Library of Congress since 1937, understandably failing to
attract attention because it is plainly not in the composer's hand
(though a note on the cover claims it is). Nor is this a new piece of
any sort, being merely an incomplete set of parts for the 'March for
the Royal Society of Musicians', the strings without the winds, the
need for which becomes painfully obvious in the trio where they
would carry most of the melody.[59]

A valuable source of information on the contents of Jennens's collection is his correspondence with Holdsworth. The latter in particular
often waxes quite specific about what he has ordered or dispatched,
going so far on one occasion as to give the number of unbound leaves
of Marcello he is sending.[60] These letters confirm the Jennens provenance of quite a few manuscripts and prints known to have been in
the Aylesford Collection at a later date, while two of Holdsworth's
purchases—a score of Astorga's Stabat Mater and an edition of the
first thirty-five Marcello Psalms—are not otherwise recorded.[61] Sadly
Holdsworth left no detailed account of his Ottobonian shipment.

Some useful titbits can be gleaned from the catalogues of
antiquarian dealers through whose hands the manuscripts sold in
1918 eventually passed. Particularly informative are those of Harold
Reeves, the leading British antiquarian music-dealer of the 1920s
and 1930s, who not only bought more than any of his competitors in
1918 but later obtained many of the manuscripts they had originally
purchased. In his last catalogue in 1942 he boasted (chilling the heart
of the latter-day bibliographer) that a manuscript of sonatas by
Giuseppe Sammartini had belonged to 'the celebrated Earl of Aylesford
library, from which so many interesting volumes of musical manuscripts have now been distributed to collectors and libraries in all
parts of the world by Harold Reeves.'[62] This Sammartini manuscript

[58] A. van Hoboken, *Joseph Haydn: Thematisch-bibliographisches Werkverzeichnis*, iii (Mainz,
1978), 314–15.
[59] The MS was given to the library by Goodspeed's Book Shop together with a
corresponding score of much more recent date.
[60] Everett, *Manchester Concerto Partbooks*, i. 24.
[61] Ibid. 19, 25.
[62] Catalogue 127, p. 33.

JOHN H. ROBERTS 59

is one of several items listed by Reeves that are not mentioned in the 1918 catalogue, and his descriptions often go well beyond those of Sotheby's.[63] Another useful document is the catalogue of Newman Flower's Collection published privately in 1921.[64] It allows us to distinguish between his earlier and later Aylesford acquisitions and serves as another indicator of Aylesford provenance, since at that time he seems to have owned no manuscripts not derived from the 1918 sale.[65]

When it comes to linking the items listed in these sources to particular manuscripts or copies we are greatly assisted by internal evidence of several types. As already noted, many volumes from Jennens's library display his distinctive shelfmarks. With non-Handelian materials these usually appear on a circular label attached to the upper spine. They may also be written inside the front cover, the only place they are generally found in the Handel scores and parts. No such markings seem to have been made on unbound manuscripts. Unfortunately the spine labels have often been lost in rebinding or simply fallen off, and many interior shelfmarks have been obliterated as well. A number of manuscripts can be identified as belonging to Jennens's library through additions in his hand—figures, dates of composition, and other annotations—though this sort of evidence can be misleading since, as previously noted in connection with the Old Aylesford manuscripts, he did not write only in his own books. His figures, when present in any significant quantity, are easily recognized because of his fondness for long sloping sixes, and fives with the horizontal stroke curling upwards and back.[66] These shelf-marks and manuscript additions also allow us to trace to Jennens some volumes not mentioned in any catalogues or lists.

Jennens favoured half-calf binding with marble boards, but it would be a mistake to suppose that all his music was bound in this style. Many of the Italian manuscripts came to him already bound, and certain of Handel's works, apparently singled out for special treatment, were done in full calf or red morocco—a fact that has been somewhat obscured by the disappearance of most of the red morocco scores sold in 1918. In any case, half-calf with marble boards was so common in mid-eighteenth-century England that without supporting evidence it can scarcely serve as proof of provenance.

Bound volumes auctioned in 1918 usually have a number scrawled inside the front cover in bright red or orange crayon. These Sotheby's

[63] See e.g. the entry quoted under 'Lampe' in the App., Sect. 2.
[64] *Catalogue of a Handel Collection formed by Newman Flower* (Sevenoaks, 1921).
[65] The Handel MSS are headed 'The Aylesford Collection of Handel Transcripts' (p. 9), the non-Handelian ones 'Other Transcripts from the Aylesford Collection' (p. 24). None of the MSS listed can be shown to have come from elsewhere.
[66] A typical ex. of Jennens's figuring is reproduced in Rogers, *Continuo Realization*, 82.

60 THE AYLESFORD COLLECTION

inventory numbers rarely bear any relation to either the position of the volume on Jennens's shelves or its place in the sale. Their absence, in a volume that has not been rebound, may be taken as a generally reliable indication that it did not figure in the 1918 sale, though some fastidious dealers or owners did their best to erase them. Their presence, however, proves only that the volume in question was handled by Sotheby's during a certain period; the same sort of numbers are found in the Chicago manuscripts auctioned in 1922.[67]

Today Jennens and Aylesford manuscripts can be found in at least twenty-two libraries and private collections in five countries. Without question the most important repository is the Central Public Library in Manchester, which purchased Flower's Collection after his death in 1964. A catalogue of the Handel sources by Arthur D. Walker was published in 1972,[68] and Michael Talbot provided a valuable handlist of the major non-Handelian manuscripts in 1974.[69] Some unbound manuscripts, none of them probably from Jennens's library, have never been described, though most are listed in Flower's 1921 catalogue. The far-flung distribution of the remaining manuscripts is summarized in Table 2.

After Manchester, the most important group of Handel manuscripts is in the Royal Music Library in the British Library. Squire's detailed catalogue of the Collection identifies twenty-six volumes as having come from the Aylesford Collection,[70] and seven more can be added to the list. Two of the Handel manuscripts, Jennens's partial vocal score of *Messiah* (Lbl R.M.19.d.1) and a volume containing the score of *Muzio Scevola* and assorted opera excerpts (Lbl R.M.19.c.9), did not derive from the 1918 sale but had left the Aylesford Collection at an earlier date. This is revealed by a summary catalogue of the royal Handel manuscripts published in Mrs Julian Marshall's biography of 1883, which indicates that at that time both manuscripts were already part of the Collection.[71] It is surely unlikely that Jennens would ever had given Handel his unfinished vocal score (it breaks off in the midst of 'Glory to God'), much less an operatic miscellany bound for his own collection with a table of contents in his hand. We may hypothesize that these two volumes were among those George III borrowed from the Earl of Aylesford in 1784–5 and that through an oversight they did not get returned to their owner, just as the 'Song in Eight Parts' went astray on its way back to the Granville

[67] Some of the Chicago MSS in fact have the same nos. as vols. sold in 1918, further evidence, if any were needed, that they were not part of that sale.
[68] See n. 16, above.
[69] See n. 20, above.
[70] W. Barclay Squire, *Catalogue of the King's Music Library*, i (London, 1927).
[71] pp. 133, 135.

Table 2. Distribution of Jennens and Aylesford MSS not in the Flower Collection

Location	Handel MSS	Other MSS
AUS-NSWpm		1
AUS-Sfl	4	
CH-Gbb		1
D-HVsb		1
D-Maw	1	
GB-BENcoke	20	8
GB-Cfm		22
GB-Ckc		1
GB-Lbl	34	8
GB-Lgo		1
GB-LVmt		1
US-Cn		6
US-Cu	26	
US-CP	2	
US-MT		1
US-NH		2
US-PRu	3	
US-R		4
US-SFsc		11
US-Wc	17	5
US-Ws	1	

Note: MSS containing works by other composers as well as Handel are included under 'Handel MSS'. These totals do not include items sold in 1873 or the Lawes MS from the Burdett-Coutts sale.

Collection.[72] The King's interest in the *Messiah* manuscript may be explained by the fact that it was formerly considered to be a sketch, as stated on the original binding.

A further complication emerges from a note in Squire's hand attached to R.M.19.d.1 stating that folio 37 'was discovered in 1897 in a volume of Orlando Gibbons' Church Music formerly in the Sacred Harmonic Library & was restored to this volume in 1898.' The only volume in the Sacred Harmonic Society's library that comes close to fitting this description is the printed anthology *A Collection of Sacred Compositions of Orlando Gibbons*, edited by Ouseley and published by Novello in 1873. By 1897 it was in the library of the Royal College of

[72] Streatfeild, 'Granville Collection', 212. H. McLean states that the King failed to return a vol. of duets as well: 'Granville, Handel and "Some Golden Rules"', *MT*, 126 (1985), 663. George III did request 2 vols. of duets on 7 Nov. 1784, but his letter of 11 Feb. 1785 indicates that he had received only 1; probably the Granville catalogue was in error. Burney, who apparently used the same list, says the Collection contains only 1 vol. of concertos, whereas in fact there are 2 (p. 46), suggesting that 1 vol. may have been incorrectly described.

62 THE AYLESFORD COLLECTION

Music, which purchased the Society's entire collection in 1883, and hence in Squire's care. But how did the stray leaf come to be in the Gibbons volume in the first place? Its appearance in an edition published in 1873 suggests that it may have passed through the Aylesford sale of that year, perhaps in one of the two miscellaneous lots described by the sale catalogue as 'Manuscript Music (*bound and unbound*) a parcel' (lots 267 and 372).[73] But it is also possible that it made its way to the Royal College library along with the collection of the Concert of Ancient Music, which was housed in Buckingham Palace for many years before being presented to the new conservatory by Queen Victoria.

The greatest concentration of non-Handelian Aylesford manuscripts outside Manchester is in the Fitzwilliam Museum in Cambridge. Here one finds large-scale works by Cosimo Bani, Gasparini, Greene, Domenico Francesco Negri, Pietro Giuseppe Sandoni, and Alessandro and Francesco Scarlatti, along with instrumental music by Martino Bitti, Giuseppe Sammartini, Gaetano Maria Schiassi, and Tartini. Most of the nineteen volumes were bought from Squire, three being contributed much later by Edward Dent, one of the few private buyers in the 1918 sale. In the absence of a catalogue covering music added by the library since 1893 this rich body of source-material has remained largely unexplored. It is to be hoped that the recent publication on microfilm of all the Fitzwilliam's music manuscripts will lead to its increased use by musical scholars.[74]

Particular mention must be made of the pair of Fitzwilliam volumes designated MU.MS. 659, what has been taken to be a two-part Latin oratorio by Pietro Paolo Bencini. The title-page of volume i reads 'Oratorio/Prime Partis/del Sig. Bencini'; volume ii has merely the caption title 'Pars Seconda'. In fact these two volumes do not belong to the same work, though there is a noteworthy historical relationship between them. Volume i is part 1 of Bencini's *Introduzione all'oratorio della Passione*, composed in 1707 or possibly earlier to precede Alessandro Scarlatti's oratorio *Per la Passione di Nostro Signore Gesù Cristo*. This Latin version, entitled in the printed libretto *Ad sacrum drama de Passione Domini nostri Jesu Christi Introductio*, dates from 1725, when it was performed at the Oratorio del Crocifisso in Rome in the same Lenten season as Scarlatti's Passion. Oratorio performances at the Crocifisso had been suspended since 1710, but in the Holy Year of 1725 Cardinal Ottoboni sponsored a season of five

[73] Both lots were bought by 'Rob^n', presumably William Robinson, a well-known antiquarian music dealer of the day.
[74] *The Music Collections of the Cambridge Libraries* (Woodbridge, Conn., 1987–91), pts. iii–vi.

JOHN H. ROBERTS 63

oratorios, all in Latin, as was customary at the Crocifisso.[75] Volume ii of Cfm MU.MS. 659 must be part 2 of one of the three oratorios newly composed for the occasion, Carlo Antonio Monza's *S. Philippus Neri* (*San Filippo Neri*), based on the Italian text set by Scarlatti in 1705.[76] Ottoboni's collection, from which these scores surely came, must have contained copies of the full set of five, including *Santissima Annunziata* by Gasparini and *S. Caecilia* by the youthful Giovanni Battista Costanzi. But we have no evidence Jennens ever owned more than the two volumes now in the Fitzwilliam.

Even among the manuscripts known to have been part of the Jennens or Aylesford Collections there remain some that have yet to be accounted for. Where, for example, is the copy of Handel's *Deborah* that according to the 1918 sale catalogue 'has a solo Hallelujah for Senesino and alterations for Carestino [*sic*]'? Where is the 'calf gilt' copy of Steffani's *Arminio* with 'red and gold endpapers'? It is noteworthy that most of the missing Handel scores, at least eighteen volumes in all, were bought in 1918 by the dealer G. H. Brown, and that all but one of those volumes were bound in red morocco leather. Flower acquired every other manuscript in Brown's lots, no less than seventeen scores and ninety-five parts, and it seems unlikely that he would have passed up such prizes as Jennens scores of *Belshazzar*, *Israel in Egypt*, *Messiah*, *Samson*, and *Saul* had they been for sale at the time he made his purchases. It may be that Brown had already sold them all to a single customer, one perhaps more interested in fine bindings than in music—in which case we may yet find them together in one place.

Undoubtedly Jennens owned some manuscripts that have never appeared in any lists of Aylesford holdings. Most conspicuous is the absence of scores for most of the anthems. It is evident from Jennens's numbering that he had a set of six volumes containing scores of the twelve anthems in the Chicago parts (the eleven Chandos Anthems and 'As pants the hart', HWV 251c), of which only the one volume in Chicago has come to light.[77] He would probably also have wanted copies of the Foundling Hospital Anthem, the two Wedding Anthems, and some other works composed for the Chapel Royal, if not the

[75] See L. Bianchi, *Carissimi, Stradella, Scarlatti e l'oratorio musicale* (Rome, 1969), 271–4. For bibliographic descriptions of the 5 1725 librettos see E. Esposito, *Annali di Antonio de Rossi, stampatore in Roma 1695–1755* (Florence, 1972), 255, 265–8.

[76] I have not been able to examine the printed libretto for Monza's setting, but the connection with MU.MS. 659 is sufficiently indicated by the distinctive cast list (St Philip, Faith, Hope, and Charity) and unusual language as well as the presumed presence of the MS in Ottoboni's library.

[77] The Chicago score of HWV 255 and HWV 247 (MS 437 v.26) has the Jennens shelf-mark NY/14, and the other 5 vols. must have been NY/15–19, filling a conspicuous gap in the sequence of known numbers.

64   THE AYLESFORD COLLECTION

Funeral Anthem, though he might have been content with its identical twin, part 1 of *Israel in Egypt*. In addition Jennens surely possessed a score of Handel's last opera *Deidamia* as he did of all the others from *Rodrigo* onwards. The anthems may well have gone to the Burdetts together with the Chicago manuscripts and may thus have figured in the Burdett-Coutts sale. Alternatively, they could have been part of the 'parcel' of anthems in lot 286 of the 1918 sale, though the position of that lot in the second half of the sale implies the contents were not Handel. *Deidamia* could have been sold in 1918 but passed over by the cataloguer, like the scores of *Alessandro* and *Giulio Cesare* (assuming that all three were not part of the Burdett-Coutts library).

Scattered as they are, the manuscripts collected by Charles Jennens remain a major resource for Handel scholarship. They furnish significant sources for most of the composer's works and preserve many pieces not found elsewhere; among the things that have come to light through these manuscripts are the only surviving fragments of the Hamburg operas *Florindo* and *Daphne*,[78] the *Comus* music,[79] the Trio Sonata in E minor, HWV 395, the clock music,[80] many harpsichord pieces, and numerous additions and alternatives for the operas and oratorios. The voluminous Handel performing parts, the largest body of such material known, are helping us understand how the frequently ambiguous instrumentation of the scores was interpreted in practice, particularly the role of the oboes and bassoons. It must be borne in mind in interpreting Jennens's manuscripts, however, that they were often copied many years after the works were composed. And his penchant for relying primarily on the autograph and for including whatever music he could find regardless of its place in the textual history of the score meant that often the version produced by the copyist did not correspond to any Handel had ever performed. The editorial urge that makes Jennens's Handel manuscripts so fascinating as historical documents can also make them peculiarly misleading as sources.

In Jennens's Italian manuscripts we can study a collection of other composers' music that Handel knew and used. Besides adapting some of the operas for the London stage and mining several scores for ideas for his own works he may also have been influenced in subtler ways by certain samples of the latest Italian idiom. The Ottobonian hoard, moreover, is full of pieces that Handel may well have encountered during his years in Italy, perhaps even heard performed on one of his

[78] B. Baselt, 'Wiederentdeckung von Fragmenten aus Händels verschollenen Hamburger Opern', *HjB* 29 (1983), 7–24.

[79] A. Hicks, 'Handel's Music for "Comus"', *MT* 117 (1976), 28–9.

[80] W. Barclay Squire, 'Handel's Clock Music', *Musical Quarterly*, 5 (1919), 538–52.

visits to the cardinal's Roman palace. One could hardly find a better basis for analysing the stylistic context of his Italian period than some of Jennens's Ottoboni manuscripts.

Despite all that has been written about the Aylesford Collection, much essential work remains to be done. We need a detailed analysis of paper types and copyists' hands in order to establish a reliable chronology of the Handel manuscripts.[81] We need to investigate further what sources were used by Jennens and his copyists and what editorial principles they followed. Little attention has been paid to Jennens's printed music, but it is clear that he made no hard and fast distinction between the two parts of his Collection, and some of his prints bear annotations in his hand. The editions he received from the Continent may have interested Handel as much as the manuscript music. Lastly the search continues for the missing Jennens and Aylesford manuscripts. If we cannot reasonably expect to find them all, we may yet hope for a few more happy surprises.

Appendix: Handlist of Manuscripts in the Jennens and Aylesford Collections

I have attempted to list all manuscripts that are known or inferred to have formed part of either the Jennens or Aylesford Collections, with the exception of a few unidentified fragments in the Flower Collection. Unless otherwise stated, the manuscripts are scores; in sets of partbooks it is to be understood that the contents given in a WITH note are likewise parts. If a partbook contains parts for more than one instrument in the same work, only the principal instrument is normally cited.

For each manuscript included in the 1873 and 1918 sales or the 1937 Hopkinson catalogue I have cited the appropriate date, then the lot or catalogue number.

Among the manuscripts located to date (Section 1) Jennens's holdings are distinguished from the rest by the following symbols:

† = from the Jennens Collection,
(†) = probably from the Jennens Collection,
‡ = from the Jennens Collection but never in the Aylesford Collection.

With manuscripts not yet located (Section 2) the catalogue description, if any, is quoted in full and for lots sold in 1873 and 1918 the buyer's name is also supplied.

---

[81] Donald Burrows is preparing such a study.

66   THE AYLESFORD COLLECTION

1. Manuscripts located to date

ALBINONI, T., †*Balletti e sonate a tre*, Op. 8, SELECTIONS, WITH selections from *Concerti a cinque*, Op. 9: 1918 (lot 275), GB-Mp MS F501 Aj23.

—— Instrumental music: SEE Handel, Miscellany (1).

—— †*Zenobia regina de' Palmerini* (opera): 1918 (lot 274), US-Wc M1500. A72Z4,[82] facs. edn., New York, 1979.

ANFOSSI, P., *Il geloso in cimento* (opera), 2 vols.: 1918 (Act 1: lot 326A?, Acts 2–3: lot 281), US-SFsc.

ANON., Aria 'Al nome del mio ben': GB-BENcoke.

ANON., Concertos (2) in A m and E♭. Vn1 'concertino' pt., WITH (inserted) incomplete pts. for vn1 and vn2 'del concerto grosso': GB-BENcoke.

ANON., Minuet in C m for 2 trebles and bc, WITH unidentified aria in A, arr. for hpd: GB-BENcoke.

ANON., Overture in G m for 2 vns and bc: GB-BENcoke.

ANON., Recit., 'A danni miei stanca mai fu la sorte' and aria 'La speme del mio core' (A m, 3/8): 1918 (lot 310?), GB-Mp Flower Collection.

ANON., Trio Sonata in G m. SEE Handel, sonatas, solo with bc.

ARIOSTI, A., †Tito Manlio (opera): 1918 (lot 282), GB-Lgo.[83]

ARNE, T. A., *Comus*: SEE Handel, Miscellany (15).

ASTORGA, E. D', †Cantatas (42): 1918 (lot 285) GB-Lbl Add. MS 39765.

—— †Cantatas and duets (20): 1918 (lot 285), GB-Lbl Add. MS 39766.

BANI, [COSIMO] ('ABB. BANI'), †*Il figlio delle selve* (opera): 1918 (lot 302), GB-Cfm MU.MS. 659 (*olim* 52.B.13).

BENCINI, G., †Sonatas (4) for hpd: 1918 (lot 313?), GB-Mp MS 710.5 Bk51.

BENCINI, P. P., Cantata 'Li due volubili' ('Chi m'insegna una beltà'). (†)SCORE: GB-LVmt; †PTS. (vn1, 'Liso' / 'Clori'): 1918 (lot 287?) GB-Mp MS 480 Bk51.

—— *La Jezabel* (oratorio): †PTS., 9 vols.: 1918 (lot 287),[84] GB-Mp MS 580 Bk51 vv.11–19. †PT. for 'Il fanciullo': 1918 (lot 315), GB-Cfm MU.MS. 225A (*olim* 24.E.6), formerly bound with A. Scarlatti, Salve Regina. SEE ALSO *Il sacrificio d'Abramo*.

—— †[*Ad sacrum drama de Passione Domini nostri Jesu Christi Introductio* (*Introduzione all'oratorio della Passione*)] ('Oratorio'), Pt. 1: 1918 (lot 302), GB-Cfm MU.MS. 661 v.1 (*olim* 52.B.15).

—— *Il sacrificio d'Abramo* (oratorio). †SCORE: 1918 (lot 287), GB-Mp MS 580 Bk51 v.1, facs. edn., New York, 1986;

---

[82] Michael Talbot assumes (*Tomaso Albinoni: The Venetian Composer and His World* (Oxford, 1990), 191–2), that the US-Wc *Zenobia* is not the MS sold in 1918, but the vol. carries an unmistakable Jennens label, and the first aria is figured in Jennens's hand.

[83] The MS is described in O. Haas, *Rare Music Exhibited at the Antiquarian Book Fair, 1972* (London). It is not currently available for study.

[84] The sale catalogue lists lot 287 as containing 5 parts for *Il sacrificio d'Abramo* and seven for *La Jezabel,* suggesting that the vocal parts may not have been present. In place of the usual volume count the catalogue says simply '2 parcels'.

†SHORT SCORE (vn1 'concertino', vn2 'concertino', bc), WITH id., *La Jezabel*: 1918 (lot 287), GB-Mp MS 580 Bk51 v.6; †PTS., WITH id., *La Jezabel*, 8 vols.: 1918 (lot 287),[85] GB-Mp MS 580 Bk51 vv. 2–5, 7–10.

BESOZZI, CARLO, Quartet ('A Quattro') for ob, vn, va, and vc. Vn1 pt.: 1918 (lot 310?), GB-Mp MS 642.3 Bn75.

BITTI, M., †Sonatas (12) for vn and bc: 1918 (lot 313?), GB-Cfm MU.MS. 662 (*olim* 52.B.17).

BONI, G., †'Cantata a due voci per il santissimo natale di Nostro Signore Giesù Christo' ('Vedi Linco' / 'Silvio, come bella'). SCORE and PTS. for 'Silvio' and 'Linco'; 3 vols.: 1918 (lot 287), GB-Mp MS Q532 Br53.

BONONCINI, G., *Astarto* (opera). SELECTIONS arr. for hpd: GB-BENcoke.

CESARINI, C., (†)Cantata 'La rosa e il gelsomino' ('Il verde armato stelo'): 1918 (lot 287), GB-Mp MS Q544 Cj71.

COLLECTIONS:

Arias (15) by G. M. Orlandini, N. Porpora, L. Vinci, *et al.*, WITH H. Purcell, anthems 'O give thanks' (Z.33) and 'My song shall be alway' (Z.31); anon., Ode 'I'll sing of hero's and of kings', sop. part: GB-Mp MS Q520 Vu51.

†Cantatas (11) by P. P. Bencini, G. Bononcini, C. Cesarini, Severo di Luca, F. Mancini, G. Della Porta, A. Scarlatti and F. Scarlatti, *et al.*, GB-Mp MS Q544 Bk51.

†Cantatas (15) by C. Cesarini, Severo di Luca, F. Mancini, F. A. M. Pistocchi, D. Sarro, A. Scarlatti ('Tutto accesso d'amore'), *et al.*: 1918 (lot 315), GB-Cfm MU.MS. 230 (*olim* 24.E.11).

(†)Cantatas, etc. (14), by 'Abb[at]e Filippo Colonnese', F. Lanciani, G. Pancieri, B. Pasquini, A. Scarlatti, A. Stradella, G. B. Viviani, *et al.*: 1918 (lot 323), GB-Lbl Add. MS 39907.

(†)Cantatas (12) by G. Corsi, F. Collinelli, A. Scarlatti ('Vola Cupido'), A. Stradella, *et al.*: 1918 (lot 321), GB-Cfm MU.MS. 655 (*olim* 52.B.9).

†Concertos (80) by A. Vivaldi *et al.*, PTS., 14 vols., WITH inst. pts. for works by various composers, Vivaldi partly autograph MS: 1918, GB-Lbl R.M.22.c.28 (lot 267?), GB-Mp MS 580 Ct51, vv.7–8, 12–13 (lot 291), and GB-Mp MS 580 Ct51 vv.1–6, 9–11 (lot 325).[86]

Madrigals, etc. by Aichinger, Anerio, Baccusi, Colombano, Croce, Eremita, Marenzio, Pallavicino, Preti, Verdonck, *et al.*, Ptbks. (5), Aylesford provenance doubtful: 1873 (lot 151), GB-Ob MSS Tenbury 364–8.

Motets, anthems, etc. [by Byrd, Fayrfax, A. Ferrabosco sen., R. Johnson sen., Lassus, Tallis, Taverner, R. White *et al.*]. Ptbks. (3), Aylesford provenance doubtful: 1873 (lot 280), GB-Ob MSS Tenbury 1469–71.

Motets, etc. by Byrd, [Chaynée, Clemens non Papa, Deiss, Guerrero, C. Hollander, Ivo de Vento,] Marenzio, [Palestrina, Regnart, Victoria *et al.*]. Ptbks. (3), Aylesford provenance doubtful: 1873 (lot 282), US-Ws V.a. 405–7 (*olim* 460328).

---

[85] See n. 84, above.
[86] On these MSS see Everett, 'Vivaldi Concerto Manuscripts in Manchester' and id., *Manchester Concerto Partbooks*.

68 THE AYLESFORD COLLECTION

Motets, etc. [by Byrd, A. Ferrabosco sen., Tallis, Tye, Victoria, R. White, Zallamella *et al.*]. Ptbks. (5), Aylesford provenance doubtful: 1873 (lot 279), GB-Ob MSS Tenbury 369–73.

Motets, etc. [by Byrd, A. Ferrabosco sen., Johnson, Marenzio, Morales, Palestrina, Regnart, Tallis, Taverner, Vaet, Victoria, R. White, *et al.*]. Ptbks. (3), Aylesford provenance doubtful: 1873 (lot 281), GB-Lbl Add. MSS 41156–8

Viol music, etc. by Bull, Chetwood, Coprario, A. Ferrabosco jun., Ford, Guy, T. Holmes, S. Ives sen., W. Lawes, T. Lupo, Marenzio, Monteverdi, Pallavicino, O. Vecchi, Ward, W. White, *et al.* Ptbks. (5), partly in Lawes's hand: GB-Lbl Add. MSS 40657–61.[87]

CORELLI, A., Instrumental music: SEE Handel, Miscellany (1).

—— †*Sonate da chiesa a tre*, Op. 3, SELECTIONS, WITH selections from *Sonate da camera a tre*, Op. 4, and Concerti grossi, Op. 6: 1918 (lot 291), GB-Mp MS Q501 Cu62.

GALUPPI, B., *Scipione in Cartagine*: SEE G. B. Pescetti, aria 'Semplici amanti'.

GASPARINI, F., †*La fede tradita e vendicata* (opera): 1918 (lot 302), GB-Cfm MU.MS. 660 (*olim* 52.B.14).

GEMINIANI, F., Concerti grossi (12): 1918 (lot 298), US-SFsc. SEE ALSO Handel, Miscellany (9).

GIARDINI, F., Duet for vn and vc in C: 1918 (lot 310?), GB-Mp MS 620 Gk16.

—— *Solo per il violoncello* in B♭: 1918 (lot 310?), GB-Mp MS 832 Gk16.

—— Trio in C for vn, va, and vc, autograph MS: GB-Lbl Add. MS 57538.

GREENE, M., †*The Song of Deborah and Barak* (oratorio): 1918 (lot 306), GB-Cfm MU.MS. 212 (*olim* 1.G.27).

HANDEL, G. F., *Acis and Galatea*. †SCORE: 1918 (lot 257?), US-Wc M2.1.H2 v.1; SEE ALSO Miscellanies (10, 13, 18), *Ode for Queen Anne's Birthday*.

—— *Admeto*. †SCORE: 1918 (lot 204), GB-Mp MS 130 Hd4 v.2; SELECTIONS (v. s./kbd reduction): GB-BENcoke MS. 2; SEE ALSO Miscellanies (2, 11, 14, 17), *Il pastor fido*, *Scipione*.

—— *Agrippina*. †SCORE, WITH selections from *Florindo* and *Daphne* (incomplete): 1918 (lot 210), GB-Mp MS 130 Hd4 v.11; †SELECTIONS, PTS. (vn1, vn2, va, vc, ob1, ob2, hpd), WITH *Rodrigo*, 7 vols.: 1918 (lot 210), GB-Mp MS 130 Hd4 vv.12–18.

—— †*The Alchemist*, WITH *Jupiter in Argos*, *Ode for St Cecilia's Day*: 1918 (lot 259), GB-Mp MS 130 Hd4 v.187.

—— *Alcina*. †SCORE, WITH selections from *Oreste*: 1918 (lot 209), GB-Mp MS 130 Hd4 v.26; †PTS. (vn1, vn2, va, vc, ob1, ob2), WITH *Atalanta*, *Imeneo*, *Deidamia*, 6 vols.: 1918 (lot 209), GB-Mp MS 130 Hd4 v.20–25; †hpd pt., WITH *Imeneo*: 1918 (lot 209), GB-Mp MS 130 Hd4 v.19; Overture, p.1: 1937 (no. 11), AUS-Sf1; SEE ALSO *Ariodante*, *Il pastor fido*.

—— *Alessandro*. †SCORE: GB-Lbl R.M.19.c.3; SEE ALSO Miscellany (11, 14, 17–18), *Il pastor fido*, *Scipione*.

---

[87] Part of the Burdett-Coutts library, these MSS may have belonged to Jennens but have no connection with the Aylesford Collection.

—— *Alessandro Severo*. Overture, PTS. (vn1, vn2, va, bc): GB-BENcoke MS. 6; SEE ALSO Miscellany (2).

—— *Alexander Balus*, †SCORE: 1918 (lot 240), GB-Mp MS 130 Hd4 v.27; SEE ALSO *Judas Maccabaeus, La Resurrezione, Il trionfo del Tempo* (1737).

—— *Alexander's Feast*. †SCORE: 1918 (lot 250), GB-Mp MS 130 Hd v.27A; †PTS. (S1, S2, A1, T1, B1, vn1, vn2, va, vc1, ob1, ob2, bn1, bn2), WITH *Il trionfo del tempo* (1737), *L'Allegro, il Penseroso ed il Moderato*, 13 vols.: 1918 (lot 250) GB-Mp MS 130 Hd4 vv.29–31, 33, 35, 37–40, 42–5; †PTS. (A2, vc2, hpd), WITH *Il trionfo del tempo* (1737), 3 vols.: 1918 (lot 250), GB-Mp MS 130 Hd4 vv.28, 32, 41; †PTS. (T2, B2), WITH *L'Allegro, il Penseroso ed il Moderato*, 2 vols.: 1918 (lot 250), GB-Mp MS 130 Hd4 vv.34, 36; PTS. (vn1, vn2, vn1 'grosso', vn2 'grosso', va, ob1, ob2, bn1, bn2, hpd): 1937 (no. 2), GB-BENcoke MS 7; org pt.: 1918 (lot 267?), GB-Lbl R.M.19.a.10;[88] SEE ALSO Miscellanies (2–3), *Ode for Queen Anne's Birthday, Il pastor fido, Il trionfo del tempo* (1737).

—— *L'Allegro, il Penseroso ed il Moderato*. †SCORE: 1918 (lot 258),[89] GB-Mp MS 130 Hd4 v.189; †SCORE, WITH Song 'Love's but the frailty of the mind', and Hornpipe in D, HWV 356: 1918 (lot 258), GB-BENcoke MS. 10; SELECTIONS (1741): GB-BENcoke MS. 12; Air 'Orpheus self may heave his head' (1741): GB-Mp Flower Collection;[90] SEE ALSO *Alexander's Feast*, Miscellanies (3, 18), *Ode for Queen Anne's Birthday, Il pastor fido, Il trionfo del tempo* (1737).

—— *Amadigi*. †SCORE: 1918 (lot 204), GB-Lbl R.M.19.g.2; SEE ALSO Miscellany (6), *Rinaldo, Silla*.

—— ‡Anthems (HWV 246–8, 249[b], 250[a], 251[b], 251[c], 252–6[a]). PTS. (S, A, T1, T2, B, vn1, vn2, vn3, vc, ob1, ob2, org), 21 vols.: US-Cu MS 437 vv.1–9, 11–22.

—— Anthem 'As pants the hart', HWV 251[c]: SEE Miscellany (2).

—— ‡Anthem, 'I will magnify thee', HWV 250[b]: US-Cu MS 437 v.25.

—— Anthem, 'In the Lord put I my trust', HWV 247: SEE Anthem 'The Lord is my light'.

—— Anthem, 'O come let us sing', HWV 253. Overture. PTS. (vn1, vn2, ob): GB-BENcoke MS. 27.

—— ‡Anthem, 'The Lord is my light', HWV 255, WITH Anthem 'In the Lord put I my trust', HWV 247. SCORE: US-Cu MS 437 v.26.

—— Arias, obs, hns and bc, HWV 410–11: SEE Miscellany (4).

—— Aria, str and bc, HWV 355: SEE Miscellany (9).

—— *Arianna*. †SCORE: 1918 (lot 208), GB-Mp MS 130 Hd4 v.51; †PTS. (vn1, vn2, va, vc, ob1, ob2, hpd), WITH *Ariodante*, 7 vols.: 1918 (lot 209), GB-Mp MS 130 Hd4 v.52–8; SELECTIONS, PTS. (vn1, vn2, va, bc), WITH selections from *Esther* and *Radamisto*, fragmentary pts. for *Imeneo, Deborah, Judas*

[88] Concerning this MS and GB-R.M.19.a.1 see B. Cooper, 'The Organ Parts to Handel's "Alexander's Feast"', *ML* 59 (1978), 159–79; D. Burrows, 'The Composition and First Performance of "Alexander's Feast"', *ML* 64 (1983), 206–11; and related letters in *ML* 65 (1984), 324; and 66 (1985), 87–8.

[89] The 1918 sale catalogue refers to 2 vols.; in fact there were 2 scores.

[90] This unbound aria is listed in *Catalogue of Collection formed by Flower* (1921), 26.

70 THE AYLESFORD COLLECTION

Maccabaeus, Coronation Anthems 'Zadok the Priest' and 'My heart is inditing', 4 vols.: 1918 (lot 208), GB-Mp MS 130 Hd4 vv.59–62; †SELECTIONS, partly arr.: 1937 (no. 4), GB-BENcoke MS. 16; SEE ALSO *Ode for Queen Anne's Birthday, Il pastor fido.*

—— *Ariodante.* †SCORE: 1918 (lot 209), GB-Mp MS 130 Hd4 v.63; PTS. (vn1, va), WITH *Alcina*, 2 vols.: 1918 (lot 267?), GB-Lbl R.M.18.b.6 vv.1–2; vn2 pt., WITH *Alcina*: GB-Mp MS 130 Hd4 v.65; bn pt., WITH *Alcina* (vc): 1918 (lot 267?), GB-Lbl R.M.18.b.6 v.3; hpd pt., WITH *Alcina* (hpd/vc): GB-Mp MS 130 Hd4 v.64; SEE ALSO *Arianna*, Miscellany (3), *Il pastor fido, Rinaldo.*

—— *Arminio.* †SCORE: 1918 (lot 209) GB-Mp MS 130 Hd4 v.66; †PTS. (vn1, vn2, va, vc, ob1, ob2, hpd), WITH *Giustino, Berenice*, 7 vols.: 1918 (lot 211), GB-Mp MS 130 Hd4 vv.67–73; PTS. (vn1, vn2, va; Overture only: ob1, ob2): 1937 (no. 5), GB-BENcoke MS. 17; SEE ALSO Miscellany (2), *Il pastor fido.*

—— *Atalanta.* †SCORE: 1918 (lot 208), GB-Mp MS 130 Hd4 v.75; PTS. (vn1, vn2, va, vc, hpd): 1937 (no. 3), GB-BENcoke MS. 18; SEE ALSO *Alcina*, Miscellanies (2, 10).

—— *Athalia*: SEE *Deborah, Esther*, Miscellany (8), *Ode for St Cecilia's Day, Il trionfo del tempo* (1737).

—— *Belshazzar.* Overture, PTS. (vn1, vn2, va, vc): GB-BENcoke MS. 21; SEE ALSO *Esther, Joseph*, Miscellany (3), *Ode for St Cecilia's Day, La Resurrezione, Il trionfo del tempo* (1737).

—— *Berenice*: SEE *Arminio.*

—— †*Brockes Passion*: 1918 (lot 242), GB-Mp MS 130 Hd4 v.233.

—— †Cantatas (50), 2 vols.: 1918 (lot 241), GB-Mp MS 130 Hd4 vv.77–8; SEE ALSO Miscellany (2).

—— †*The Choice of Hercules*: 1918 (lot 203), GB-Mp MS 130 Hd4 v.79.

—— Clock music: SEE Miscellanies (2, 4).

—— †*Comus* ('There in blissful shades and bow'rs'), WITH *Concerto a due cori* in F, HWV 334, *Judas Maccabaeus*, March: GB-Mp MS 130 Hd4 v.300.

—— Concerto in D, HWV 335ᵃ. PTS. (ob1, ob2, org): GB-BENcoke MS. 39; PTS. (tpt1, tpt2, timp): GB-Lbl R.M.18.b.9, fos. 1–6;[91] SEE ALSO Miscellany (3).

—— *Concerto a due cori* in F, HWV 334: SEE *Comus*; Concertos, org, Op. 7 No. 1; *La Resurrezione; Water Music.*

—— †Concerti grossi, Op. 3 Nos. 1–3: 1918 (lot 270?) GB-Mp MS 130 Hd4 v.81.

—— Concerti grossi, Op. 3 Nos. 4–5: SEE *Rodrigo.*

---

[91] The Aylesford origin of these pts. may be inferred from their being in the hand of S13, who also copied the matching ob pts. in GB-BENcoke MS. 39; the org pt. in that set carries a contemporary inscription stating they are 'from the Earl of Aylesford's Collection'. According to a pencilled note from Squire on R.M.18.b.9, 'these parts were inserted in printed parts of the Fireworks Music', presumably those in R.M.6.h.12. It is not clear whether the other MSS bound into R.M.18.b.9—instr. pts. for the trio in *Alcina* and an ob pt. for an unknown F-major version of 'In the battle fame pursuing' in *Deborah*—came from the same source.

—— †Concerti grossi, Op. 6: 1918 (lot 270?), GB-Mp MS 130 Hd4 v.85.

—— Concerto grosso in C, HWV 318. PTS. (vn1 'concertino', vn1 'ripieno', vn2 'ripieno', vc 'concertino', bc, ob1, ob2): GB-BENcoke MS. 38; SEE ALSO Concertos, org, Op. 4.

—— †Concertos, org, Op. 4, WITH Concerto grosso in C, HWV 318: 1918 (lot 270?) GB-Mp MS 130 Hd4 v.84.

—— Concerto, org, in A, Op. 7 No. 2: SEE Miscellany (3), *Water Music.*

—— Concerto, org, in Dm:, Op. 7 No. 4: SEE Miscellany (8).

—— Concerto, org, in B♭, Op. 7 No. 6: SEE Miscellany (3), *Water Music.*

—— Concertos, org, HWV 295, 296ᵃ, Op. 7 No. 1. †SCORE: 1918 (lot 270?), GB-Mp MS 130 Hd4 v.80; †bn2 pt., WITH *Concerto a due cori* in F, HWV 334: 1918 (lot 270?), GB-Mp MS 130 Hd4 v.83; †org pt., WITH March in D, HWV 345; Concerto, org, Op. 7 No. 2 (score): 1918 (lot 270?), GB-Mp MS 130 Hd4 v.82; SEE ALSO *Water Music.*

—— Concerto, org, in D m, HWV 303: SEE Miscellany (2).

—— †Coronation Anthems (4): 1918 (lot 244), GB-Mp MS 130 Hd4 v.49.

—— Coronation Anthem 'Zadok the Priest': SEE *Arianna.*

—— *Daphne:* SEE *Agrippina,* Miscellany (4).

—— *Deborah.* †PTS (S3, B2, bn), WITH *Athalia,* 3 vols.: 1918 (lot 247?), GB-Mp MS 130 Hd4 vv.96, 102, 109; Air 'In the battle fame pursuing': GB-BENcoke MS. 43; SEE ALSO *Arianna, Esther,* Miscellanies (8, 13).

—— *Deidamia:* SEE *Alcina,* Miscellany (18), *Water Music* (printed).

—— Dettingen Anthem, 'The King shall rejoice'. †SCORE: 1918 (lot 244), GB-Mp MS 130 Hd4 v.48; SEE ALSO Dettingen Te Deum.

—— Dettingen Te Deum. †SCORE, WITH Dettingen Anthem, 'The King shall rejoice': 1918 (lot 243), GB-Mp MS 130 Hd4 v.348; SEE ALSO *Esther, Hercules, Ode for St Cecilia's Day.*

—— †'Dixit Dominus', WITH 'Laudate pueri', HWV 237; 'Nisi Dominus': 1918 (lot 241), GB-Mp MS 130 Hd4 v.205.

—— *Esther.* †SCORE: 1918 (lot 247), GB-Mp MS 130 Hd4 v.93; †PTS. (1732) (S1, S2, A1, A2, T1, T2, B1, vn1, vn2, va, vc, ob1, ob2), WITH *Deborah, Athalia,* 13 vols.: 1918 (lot 247), GB-Mp MS 130 Hd4 vv.94–5, 97–101, 103–8; †PTS. (1732) (tpt1, tpt2, timp), WITH *Deborah, Athalia, Ode for St Cecilia's Day, Hercules,* selections from *Belshazzar* (1751), Dettingen Te Deum, *Occasional Oratorio,* 3 vols.: 1918 (lot 247), GB-Mp MS 130 Hd4 vv. 112–13, 115; †hn1 and hn2 pts. (1732), WITH *Deborah, Athalia, Hercules, Occasional Oratorio,* 2 vols.: 1918 (lot 247), GB-Mp MS 130 Hd4 vv.110–11; †tpt3 pt. (1732), WITH *Deborah,* Dettingen Te Deum, *Occasional Oratorio:* 1918 (lot 247), GB-Mp MS 130 Hd4 v.114; SEE ALSO *Arianna,* Miscellanies (8, 10, 13), *Ode for Queen Anne's Birthday.*

—— *Ezio.* †SCORE: 1918 (lot 208), GB-Mp MS 130 Hd4 v.3; †PTS. (vn1, vn2, va, vc, ob1, ob2, hpd), WITH *Sosarme, Orlando,* 7 vols.: 1918 (lot 208) GB-Mp MS 130 Hd4 vv.4–10; SEE ALSO Miscellany (12), *Il pastor fido, Rinaldo.*

—— *Faramondo.* †SCORE: 1918 (lot 205), GB-Mp MS 130 Hd4 v.116; †PTS. (vn1, vn2, va, vc, ob1, ob2, hpd), WITH *Serse,* 7 vols.: 1918 (lot 205), GB-Mp MS 130 Hd4 vv.117–23; Overture, PTS. (vn1, vn2, va, bc): GB-Mp

72   THE AYLESFORD COLLECTION

MS 130 Hd4 vv.124–7;[92] SEE ALSO Miscellany (2), *Il pastor fido*.

—— *Flavio*. †SCORE: 1918 (lot 207) GB-Mp MS 130 Hd4 v.129; SEE ALSO Miscellanies (14–15), *Ottone*, *Il pastor fido*.

—— *Floridante*. †SCORE: 1918 (lot 203) GB-Mp MS 130 Hd4 v.131; Overture, arr. for hpd: 1937 (no. 6), AUS-Sfl; Chorus, 'Quando pena la costanza', autograph MS: GB-Lbl Stefan Zweig Collection MS 37, facs. edn., London, 1936; SEE ALSO Miscellanies (6, 11, 14–15, 17), *Muzio Scevola*, *Il pastor fido*, *Rinaldo*.

—— *Florindo*: SEE *Agrippina*, Miscellany (4).

—— *Giulio Cesare*. †SCORE: GB-Lbl R.M.19.c.7; SEE ALSO Miscellanies (11, 14, 16–18), *Muzio Scevola*, *Ode for Queen Anne's Birthday*, *Ottone*, *Il pastor fido*, *Water Music*.

—— *Giustino*. †SCORE: 1918 (lot 203), GB-Mp MS 130 Hd4 v.188; SEE ALSO *Arminio*, *Il pastor fido*.

—— *Hercules*. †SCORE: 1918 (lot 261), GB-Mp MS 130 Hd4 v.132; †S2 pt., WITH Dettingen Te Deum: 1918 (lot 267?), GB-Lbl R.M.19.a.11; †B2 pt.: 1918 (lot 267?), GB-Lbl R.M.19.a.9; Overture, PTS. (vn1, vn2, va, ob1/2, bc), WITH *Hercules*, Overture arr. for hpd: GB-BENcoke MS. 55; SEE ALSO *Esther*, *Ode for St Cecilia's Day*.

—— Hornpipe, str and bc, HWV 356: SEE *L'Allegro, il Penseroso ed il Moderato*.

—— *Imeneo*. †SCORE: 1918 (lot 203), GB-Mp MS 130 Hd4 v.133; SEE ALSO *Alcina*, *Arianna*, Miscellany (18).

—— *Israel in Egypt*. †PTS. (S1, A1, T1, B1, vn1, vn2, va), WITH *Messiah*, 7 vols.: 1918 (lot 239), GB-Mp MS 130 Hd4 vv.142–4, 146–9; †PTS. (S2, A2, T2, B2, vc, ob1, ob2, bn), 8 vols.: 1918 (lot 239) GB-Mp MS 130 Hd4 vv.134–41; Recits. 'For the horse of Pharaoh', 'And Miriam the prophetess': 1937 (no. 9), GB-BENcoke MS. 59; SEE ALSO *La Resurrezione*, *Il trionfo del tempo* (1737).

—— †*Jephtha*: 1918 (lot 240), GB-Mp MS 130 Hd4 v.150.

—— *Joseph*. †SCORE: 1918 (lot 262, 2nd score), GB-Mp MS 130 Hd4 v.151; †SCORE: 1918 (lot 262, 1st score), GB-BENcoke MS. 68; †PTS. (S1, S2, A1, A2, T1, T2, B, vn1, vn2, va, vc, ob1, ob2, bn), WITH *Belshazzar*, 14 vols.: 1918 (lot 265), GB-Mp MS 130 Hd4 vv.152–65; SEE ALSO Miscellany (3), *Ode for Queen Anne's Birthday*, *La Resurrezione*, *Il trionfo del tempo* (1737).

—— *Joshua*. †SCORE: 1918 (lot 262), GB-Mp MS 130 Hd4 v.166; SCORE, 3 vols.: 1918 (lot 262), GB-Mp MS 130 Hd4 vv.167–9; vn1 pt.: 1918 (lot 262), GB-Mp MS 130 Hd4 v.170;[93] vn2 pt.: 1937 (no. 7), US-PRu Hall Collection, MS 9; ob1 pt.: 1918 (lot 265?), GB-Mp MS 130 Hd4 v.171;[94] SEE ALSO *Judas Maccabaeus*, *La Resurrezione*, *Il trionfo del tempo* (1737).

---

[92] These pts. are listed in *Catalogue of Collection formed by Flower* (1921), 14. Having been bound only recently, they could not be expected to have Sotheby's inventory nos.

[93] This part has no Sotheby's inventory number, but there was a vn1 pt. in lot 262 of the 1918 sale, and Flower seems to have acquired everything else in that lot except a red morocco score of *Joseph*, which had probably been sold previously. None of the items from lot 262 are listed in *Catalogue of Collection formed by Flower* (1921).

[See opposite page for n. 94]

—— *Judas Maccabaeus*. †SCORE: 1918 (lot 264), GB-Mp MS 130 Hd4 v.173; †PTS. (S1, S2, A, T, B1, B2, vn1, vn2, va, ob1, ob2, bn), WITH *Joshua*, *Alexander Balus*, 12 vols.: 1918 (lot 264), GB-Mp MS 130 Hd4 vv.174–9, 181–6; †hpd pt., WITH *Joshua* (vc), *Alexander Balus* (vc): 1918 (lot 264), GB-Mp MS 130 Hd4 v.180; SEE ALSO *Arianna*, *Comus*, *Ode for Queen Anne's Birthday*, *La Resurrezione*, *Rinaldo*, *Il trionfo del tempo* (1737), *Water Music*.

—— *Jupiter in Argos*: SEE *The Alchemist*.

—— Keyboard music. SEE Miscellanies (3–9, 17), *Rodrigo*.

—— 'Laudate pueri', HWV 237: SEE 'Dixit Dominus'.

—— *Lotario*. †SCORE: 1918 (lot 202), GB-Mp MS 130 Hd4 v.190; †PTS. (vn1, vn2, va, vc, ob2, hpd), WITH *Partenope*, *Poro*, 6 vols.: 1918 (lot 202), GB-Mp MS 130 Hd4 vv.191–6; SEE ALSO Miscellany (12), *Muzio Scevola*, *Il pastor fido*, *Rinaldo*.

—— March in D, HWV 345: SEE Concertos, org, Op. 7 No. 1; Miscellany (2); *Ode for Queen Anne's Birthday*, *Water Music*.

—— *Messiah*. †SCORE, 3 vols.: 1918 (lot 245, 4th score), GB-Mp MS 130 Hd4 vv.198–200; SCORE, 3 vols.: 1918 (lot 245, 3rd score), vols. i, iii—US-Wc M2000.H22M25 1740z, vol. ii—AUS-NSWpm;[95] PTS. (vn1, vn2, va, bc): 1918 (lot 245), GB-Mp MS 130 Hd4 vv.201–4; †vc pt.: 1918 (lot 245), GB-Mp MS 130 Hd4 v.145; †kbd-v.s. (unfin.), hand of Jennens: GB-Lbl R.M.19.d.1; Air 'I know that my redeemer liveth': 1937 (no. 10), AUS-Sfl; SEE ALSO *Israel in Egypt*, Miscellany (3), *La Resurrezione*, *Il trionfo del tempo* (1737).

—— †Miscellany (1). Arr. of opera arias, etc., fl 2 pt., WITH arr. of instr. movements by A. Corelli and T. Albinoni, hand of Jennens: 1918 (lot 267?), GB-Lbl R.M.19.a.8.

—— †Miscellany (2). Cantatas, overtures arr. for hpd; selections from *Scipione*, *Admeto*, *Alexander's Feast*, *Arminio*, *Atalanta*, *Alessandro Severo*, and *Faramondo*; Anthem 'As pants the hart', HWV 251ᶜ; org pt. for *Alexander's Feast*; Concerto, org, in D m, HWV 303; March in D, HWV 345; clock music: 1918 (lot 267), GB-Lbl R.M.19.a.1.

—— †Miscellany (3). Concerto in D, HWV 335ᵃ; Concertos, org, Op. 7 Nos. 2 and 6; *Semele*, overture arr. for hpd; selections from *Ariodante*, *Ode for St Cecilia's Day* (1742), *L'Allegro, il Penseroso ed il Moderato*, *Messiah* (1750), *Joseph*, and *Belshazzar* (1751): 1918 (lot 267), GB-Lbl R.M.19.a.2.

—— †Miscellany (4). Hpd music and arr.; Arias, obs, hns, and bc, HWV 410–11; clock music; selections from *Florindo* and *Daphne* arr. for various ensembles: 1918 (lot 267), GB-Lbl R.M.18.b.8.

[94] The MS, which remained unbound until recently, is listed in *Catalogue of Collection formed by Flower* (1921), 16. According to the 1918 sale catalogue lot 265 contained 15 pts. for *Joshua* and *Belshazzar*, but the set in question is clearly that for *Joseph* and *Belshazzar*, which has only 14 pts. Probably the extra pt. was this one for *Joshua*, hence the confusion of titles.

[95] This is W. Shaw's 'Flower (ii)': see id., *A Textual and Historical Companion to Handel's Messiah* (London, 1965), 78. On the history of pt. 2, which Flower gave to singer Phyllis Lett as a wedding present in 1924, see R. Illing, H. Williams, and P. Perry, *An Illustrated Catalogue of the Early Editions of Handel in Australia: A Second Supplement* (Melbourne, 1990), 62–3. Pts. 1 and 3 were given to his grandson Nicholas Flower and were auctioned by Sotheby's on 14 Apr. 1982.

74 THE AYLESFORD COLLECTION

—— †Miscellany (5). Kbd music: 1918 (lot 267?), GB-Lbl R.M.19.a.3.

—— †Miscellany (6). Opera overtures, etc., arr. for hpd; selections from *Amadigi, Floridante* (1727), *Siroe*, and *Tolomeo*: 1918 (lot 267?), GB-Lbl R.M.18.c.1.

—— †Miscellany (7). Opera overtures, etc., arr. for hpd; selections from *Siroe*; Allemande in B m for hpd, HWV 479; includes 2 autograph MSS: 1918 (lot 267?), GB-Lbl R.M.18.c.2.

—— †Miscellany (8). *Orlando*, Overture arr. for hpd; Concerto, org, Op. 7 No. 4, 2nd Allegro; selections from *Ottone* (1733), *Esther* (1732), *Athalia*, and *Deborah*: 1918 (lot 267?), GB-Lbl R.M.18.c.6.

—— †Miscellany (9). Overture in B♭, HWV 336; hpd music and arr.; Aria, str and bc, HWV 355; Trio sonata in E m, HWV 395, WITH F. Geminiani, concertos: 1918 (lot 267), GB-Lbl R.M.19.a.4.

—— †Miscellany (10). Selections from *Atalanta, Acis and Galatea* (1736?), and *Esther* (1735–7): 1918 (lot 267), GB-Lbl R.M.18.c.5.

—— †Miscellany (11). Selections from *Floridante* (1727), *Giulio Cesare* (1725), *Tamerlano, Alessandro, Admeto, Riccardo Primo*, and *Tolomeo*:[96] 1918 (lot 267?), GB-Lbl R.M.18.c.3.

—— †Miscellany (12). Selections from *Lotario, Partenope, Scipione, Poro*, and *Ezio*, WITH *Sosarme*: 1918 (lot 267?), GB-Lbl R.M.19.a.5.

—— †Miscellany (13). Selections from *Orlando, Esther* (1732), *Deborah*, and *Acis and Galatea* (1732): 1918 (lot 267?), GB-Lbl R.M.18.c.7.

—— †Miscellany (14). Selections from *Ottone, Flavio, Floridante, Giulio Cesare, Tamerlano, Rodelinda, Scipione* (1726–30), *Alessandro, Admeto* (1727–31), *Riccardo Primo, Siroe*, and *Tolomeo*: 1918 (lot 267?), GB-Lbl R.M.18.c.10.

—— Miscellany (15). Selections from *Radamisto, Muzio Scevola, Floridante, Flavio*, and *Ottone* ('30 Songs, etc.'). PTS. (vn2, vc/bc), WITH T. A. Arne, *Comus*, 'Sweet echo', 2 vols.: US-PRu Hall Collection, MS 11.

—— †Miscellany (16). Selections from *Rinaldo* (1711–31), *Giulio Cesare* (1730), and *Radamisto* (1720–8): 1918 (lot 267), GB-Lbl R.M.18.c.9.

—— †Miscellany (17). Selections from *Sosarme, Giulio Cesare* (1725–30), *Floridante* (1722–7), *Ottone, Scipione* (1730), *Alessandro, Admeto* (1728–31), and *Partenope* (Dec. 1730); hpd music: 1918 (lot 267?), GB-Lbl R.M.18.b.4.

—— †Miscellany (18). Selections from *Il trionfo del tempo* (1737), *Acis and Galatea* (1739), *Rodelinda, Alessandro, Riccardo Primo, Siroe, Saul* (1741?), *L'Allegro, il Penseroso ed il Moderato* (1741), *Imeneo*, and *Deidamia*: 1918 (lot 267?), GB-Lbl R.M.18.c.11.

—— *Music for the Royal Fireworks* (printed pts.): SEE *Ode for Queen Anne's Birthday, Rinaldo, Water Music*.

—— *Muzio Scevola*, Act 3. †SCORE, WITH selections from *Teseo, Giulio Cesare* (1724–30), and *Lotario*; opera arias arr. for hpd: GB-Lbl, R.M.19.c.9; †PTS. (vn1, vn2, va, vc, ob1, ob2, hpd), WITH *Floridante*, 7 vols.: 1918 (lot 203), GB-Mp MS 130 Hd4 vv.206–12; Aria 'Pupille sdegnose' arr. for

[96] The selection from *Tolomeo* in R.M.18.c.3 together with the excerpts in R.M.18.c.1 and R.M.18.c.10—Miscellanies (6) and (14)—constitute a virtually complete score of the opera without secco recitatives. Notes by Jennens link the 3 MSS and show the correct order of the nos.

JOHN H. ROBERTS

hpd, HWV 482[4], AUS-Sfl; SEE ALSO Miscellany (15), *Il pastor fido*, *Rinaldo*.

—— 'Nisi Dominus': SEE 'Dixit Dominus'.

—— *Occasional Oratorio*. [†]SCORE: 1918 (lot 240), GB-Mp MS 130 Hd4 v.213; SEE ALSO *Esther, Ode for St Cecilia's Day, La Resurrezione*.

—— *Ode for St Cecilia's Day*. [†]PTS. (S, A, T, B, vn1, vn2, va, vc), WITH *Hercules* (S1), selections from *Belshazzar* (1751), Dettingen Te Deum (S1), *Occasional Oratorio*, 8 vols.: 1918 (lot 259), GB-Mp MS 130 Hd4 vv.214–21; [†]ob1, ob2 pts., WITH *Hercules*, selections from *Belshazzar* (1751), Dettingen Te Deum, *Occasional Oratorio, Athalia* (vn3, vn4), 2 vols.: 1918 (lot 259), GB-Mp MS 130 Hd4 vv.222–3; [†]bn pt., WITH Dettingen Te Deum, *Occasional Oratorio*: 1918 (lot 259), GB-Mp MS 130 Hd4 v.224; March arr. for hpd, WITH Anon., Suite in A m for hpd;[97] and [G B.] Pescetti, 'Aire in Diana & Endymion'; GB-BENcoke MS. 120; SEE ALSO *The Alchemist, Esther*, Miscellany (3).

—— *Ode for Queen Anne's Birthday*. [†]PTS. (S1, S2, T1), WITH *Acis and Galatea, La Resurrezione*, 3 vols.: 1918 (lot 257), US-Wc M2.1.H2 vv.9–10, 13; [†]A1 pt., WITH *La Resurrezione*: 1918 (lot 257?), US-Wc M2.1.H2 v.11; [†]A2 pt., WITH *Acis and Galatea* (T3), *Judas Maccabaeus*: 1918 (lot 257), US-Wc M2.1.H2 v.12; [†]T2 pt., WITH *Acis and Galatea, Judas Maccabaeus*: 1918 (lot 257), US-Wc M2.1.H2 v.14; [‡]B1 pt., WITH *Acis and Galatea, La Resurrezione*: US-Cu MS 437 v.10; [†]B2 pt., WITH *Acis and Galatea, Joseph*: 1918 (lot 257), US-Wc M2.1.H2 v.15; [†]PTS. (vn1, vn2, vc1, ob1, ob2), WITH *Acis and Galatea*; selections from *Acis and Galatea* (1732–6), *Esther* (1737), and *Il pastor fido* (1734); *Arianna* (Nov. 1734), ballet music, 5 vols.: 1918 (lot 257), US-Wc M2.1.H2 vv.3–5, 7–8; [†]vc2 'repieno' pt., WITH *Acis and Galatea* (vc 'repieno'/bn); selections from *Acis and Galatea* (1732–6) (bn), *Esther* (1737) (bn), and *Il pastor fido* (1734) (bn); *Arianna* (Nov. 1734), ballet music; *La Resurrezione* (db): 1918 (lot 257), US-Wc M2.1.H2 v.6; [‡]bn2 pt., WITH *La Resurrezione, Joseph, Judas Maccabaeus*: US-Cu MS 437 v.23; [†]tpt1 pt., WITH *Rinaldo* (tpt4), *Giulio Cesare* (hn4), *Alexander's Feast, L'Allegro, il Penseroso ed il Moderato*, March in D, HWV 345: 1918 (lot 257), US-Ws W.b. 527; [‡]tpt2 pt., WITH *L'Allegro, il Penseroso ed il Moderato*, printed pt. for *Music for the Royal Fireworks*: US-Cu MS 437 v.24; [†]hpd pt., WITH *Acis and Galatea*; selections from *Acis and Galatea* (1732–6), *Esther* (1737), and *Il pastor fido* (1734); *Arianna* (Nov. 1734), ballet music: 1918 (lot 257), US-Wc M2.1.H2 v.2.

—— *Oreste*: SEE *Alcina*.

—— *Orlando*. [†]SCORE: 1918 (lot 208), GB-Mp MS 130 Hd4 v.225; SEE ALSO *Ezio*, Miscellany (13).

—— *Ottone*. [†]SCORE: 1918 (lot 207), GB-Mp MS 130 Hd4 v.226; [†]PTS. (vn2, va, vc, ob2, hpd), WITH *Flavio, Giulio Cesare*, 5 vols.: 1918 (lot 207), GB-Mp MS 130 Hd4 vv.227–31; SEE ALSO Miscellanies (8, 14–15, 17).

—— Overture in B♭, HWV 336: SEE Miscellany (9).

---

[97] On the authorship of this suite see *New Grove*, viii. 136.

76 THE AYLESFORD COLLECTION

—— *Il Parnasso in festa*, selections: SEE *Il trionfo del Tempo* (1737).

—— *Partenope*. †SCORE: 1918 (lot 201), GB-Mp MS 130 Hd4 v.232; SEE ALSO *Lotario*, Miscellanies (12, 17), *Il pastor fido*, *Rinaldo*.

—— *Il pastor fido*. †SCORE: 1918 (lot 203), GB-Mp MS 130 Hd4 v.234; †SELECTIONS (1734), WITH selections from *Arianna* (Nov. 1734), *Flavio*: 1918 (lot 267) GB-Lbl R.M.18.c.4; †hn1 pt. (1734), WITH *Radamisto, Muzio Scevola, Floridante, Giulio Cesare, Alessandro, Admeto, Lotario, Partenope, Poro, Ezio, Sosarme, Arianna, Ariodante, Alcina, Arminio, Giustino, Faramondo, Alexander's Feast, L'Allegro, il Penseroso ed il Moderato* (hn solo): 1918 (lot 203?), US-CP M2.1.M2 v.1; †hn2 pt. (1734), WITH *Radamisto, Muzio Scevola, Floridante, Giulio Cesare, Alessandro, Admeto, Lotario, Partenope, Poro, Ezio, Sosarme, Arianna, Ariodante, Alcina, Arminio, Giustino, Faramondo, Alexander's Feast*: 1918 (lot 203?), US-CP M2.1.M2 v.2; SEE ALSO *Ode for Queen Anne's Birthday, Rinaldo*.

—— *Poro*. †SCORE: 1918 (lot 201), GB-Mp MS 130 Hd4 v.236; SEE ALSO *Lotario*, Miscellany (12), *Il pastor fido*, *Rinaldo*.

—— *Radamisto*. †SCORE: 1918 (lot 201), GB-Mp MS 130 Hd4 v.238; SEE ALSO *Arianna*, Miscellanies (15), *Il pastor fido*, *Rinaldo*, *Silla*.

—— *La Resurrezione*. †SCORE: 1918 (lot 265), GB-Mp MS 130 Hd4 v.239; †PTS. (vn1, vn2, va), WITH selections from *Saul* and *Joseph*, 3 vols.: 1918 (lot 262?), GB-Mp MS 130 Hd4 vv.240–2; †vc1 pt., WITH selections from *Saul* and *Joseph*; *Judas Maccabaeus*: 1918 (lot 262?), GB-Mp MS 130 Hd4 v.243; †vc2 pt., WITH *Joseph, Judas Maccabaeus, Concerto a due cori* in F, HWV 334 (bn1), *Rinaldo* (timp): 1918 (lot 262?), GB-Mp MS 130 Hd4 v.244; †ob1, ob2, pts., WITH selections from *Saul*, 2 vols.: 1918 (lot 262?), GB-Mp MS 130 Hd4 vv.245–6; tpt1 pt., WITH *Il trionfo del tempo* (1737), *Saul, Samson, Israel in Egypt, Messiah, Joseph, Belshazzar, Judas Maccabaeus, Joshua, Alexander Balus*: 1918 (lot 262?), GB-Mp MS 130 Hd4 v.247; †tpt2 pt., WITH *Il trionfo del tempo* (1737), *Saul, Samson, Israel in Egypt, Messiah, Joseph, Belshazzar, Judas Maccabaeus, Joshua, Alexander Balus*, printed pt. for Overture *Occasional Oratorio*: 1918 (lot 262?), GB-Mp MS 130 Hd4 v.248; †hpd pt., WITH selections from *Saul*, carillon pt. for *Saul, Joseph*: 1918 (lot 262?), GB-Mp MS 130 Hd4 v.249; SEE ALSO *Ode for Queen Anne's Birthday, Acis and Galatea*.

—— *Riccardo Primo*. †SCORE: 1918 (lot 209), GB-Mp MS 130 Hd4 v.250; †PTS. (vn1, vn2, va, vc, ob1, ob2, hpd), WITH *Siroe, Tolomeo*, 7 vols.: 1918 (lot 211), GB-Mp MS 130 Hd4 vv.251–7; SEE ALSO Miscellanies (11, 14, 18).

—— *Rinaldo*. †PTS. (vn1, vn2, va, vc, ob1, ob2, hpd), WITH *Il pastor fido, Teseo*, 7 vols.: 1918 (lot 210), GB-Mp MS 130 Hd4 vv.258–64; †tpt1 pt., WITH *Silla, Amadigi, Radamisto, Muzio Scevola, Floridante, Lotario, Partenope, Poro, Ezio, Ariodante*, printed pts. for Overture *Occasional Oratorio* and *Music for the Royal Fireworks*: 1918 (lot 210?), GB-Mp MS 130 Hd4 v.265; †tpt2 pt., WITH *Radamisto, Muzio Scevola, Floridante, Ariodante*: 1918 (lot 210?), GB-Mp MS 130 Hd4 v.266; †tpt3 pt., WITH *Judas Maccabaeus*, printed pt. for *Music for the Royal Fireworks*: 1918

(lot 267?), GB-Lbl R.M.18.b.5; [†] SELECTIONS (1717): 1937 (no. 1), GB-BENcoke MS. 87; SEE ALSO Miscellany (16), *Ode for Queen Anne's Birthday*, *La Resurrezione*.

—— *Rodelinda*. †SCORE: 1918 (lot 201), GB-Mp MS 130 Hd4 v.267; SEE ALSO Miscellanies (14, 18), *Tamerlano*.

—— *Rodrigo*. †SCORE, WITH hpd music; Concertos, Op. 3 No. 4, last 2 movements, and Op. 3 No. 5, last 3 movements: 1918 (lot 210), GB-Mp MS 130 Hd4 v.268; SEE ALSO *Agrippina*.

—— *Samson*: SEE *La Resurrezione*, *Saul*, *Il trionfo del tempo* (1737), *Water Music* (printed pts.).

—— *Saul*. †SCORE, 3 vols.: 1918 (lot 265), GB-Mp MS 130 Hd4 vv.269–71; †PTS. (S1, S2, A, T1, T2, T3, B1, B2, vn1, vn2, va, vc, ob1, ob2, bn, hpd), WITH *Samson*, 16 vols.: 1918 (lot 263), GB-Mp MS 130 Hd4 vv.275–90; Airs (5), incomplete pts. (vn1, va): GB-BENcoke; SEE ALSO Miscellany (18), *La Resurrezione*, *Il trionfo del tempo* (1737).

—— *Scipione*. †SCORE: 1918 (lot 210), GB-Mp MS 130 Hd4 v.291; †PTS. (vn1, vn2, va, vc, ob1, ob2, hpd), WITH *Alessandro*, *Admeto*, 7 vols.: 1918 (lot 210), GB-Mp MS 130 Hd4 vv.292–8; SEE ALSO Miscellanies (2, 12, 14, 17).

—— †*Semele*: 1918 (lot 204), GB-Mp MS 130 Hd4 v.299.

—— *Serse*, †SCORE: 1918 (lot 205), GB-Mp MS 130 Hd4 v.301; Overture, PTS. (vn1, vn2, va, bc): GB-BENcoke MS. 91; SEE ALSO *Faramondo*.

—— *Silla*. †SCORE: 1918 (lot 204), GB-Mp MS 130 Hd4 v.302; †PTS. (vn1, vn2, va, vc, ob1, ob2, hpd), WITH *Amadigi*, *Radamisto*, 7 vols.: 1918 (lot 204), GB-Mp MS 130 Hd4 vv.303–9; SEE ALSO *Rinaldo*.

—— *Siroe*: SEE Miscellanies (6–7, 14, 18), *Riccardo Primo*.

—— †*Solomon*, 3 vols., Act 1: GB-Lbl R.M.18.b.15; Acts 2–3: 1918 (lot 244), GB-Mp MS 130 Hd4 vv.310–11.

—— †*Sonatas*, solo with bc (10), WITH Trio Sonatas, Op. 2; Anon., Trio Sonata in G m: 1918 (lot 267), GB-Mp MS 130 Hd4 v.312.

—— Sonatina in G m, HWV 574 (Allegro only): GB-BENcoke MS. 96.

—— Song 'Love's but the frailty of the mind': SEE *L'Allegro, il Penseroso ed il Moderato*.

—— *Sosarme*: SEE *Ezio*, Miscellanies (12, 17), *Il pastor fido*.

—— †*Susanna*, 2 vols.: 1918 (lot 240), GB-Mp MS 130 Hd4 vv.315–16.

—— *Tamerlano*. †SCORE: 1918 (lot 206), GB-Mp MS 130 Hd4 v.317; †PTS. (vn1, vn2, va, vc, ob1, ob2, hpd), WITH *Rodelinda*, 7 vols.: 1918 (lot 206, except va), GB-Mp MS 130 Hd4 vv.318–24; SEE ALSO Miscellany (11).

—— Te Deum in A, HWV 282. †SCORE: 1918 (lot 243), GB-Mp MS 130 Hd4 v.325; †B2 pt., WITH Te Deum in D, HWV 280: 1918 (lot 243), GB-Mp MS 130 Hd4 v.345; †B3 pt., 1918 (lot 243), GB-Mp MS 130 Hd4 v.346; SEE ALSO Utrecht Te Deum.

—— Te Deum in B♭, HWV 281: SEE Utrecht Te Deum.

—— Te Deum in D, HWV 280. †SCORE: 1918 (lot 243), GB-Mp MS 130 Hd4 v.326; SEE ALSO Te Deum in A, HWV 282; Utrecht Te Deum.

—— *Teseo*. †SCORE: 1918 (lot 204), D-Maw; SEE ALSO *Muzio Scevola*, *Rinaldo*.

—— †*Theodora*: 1918 (lot 240), GB-Mp MS 130 Hd4 v.349.

—— *Tolomeo*. †SCORE: 1918 (lot 203), GB-Mp MS 130 Hd4 v.238; SEE ALSO Miscellanies (6, 11, 14), *Riccardo Primo*.

—— Trio Sonata in E m, HWV 395: SEE Miscellany (9).

—— Trio Sonatas, Op. 2: SEE Sonatas, solo with bc.

—— *Il trionfo del tempo* (1737). †SCORE, WITH selections from *Parnasso in festa* and *Athalia* (1735): 1918 (lot 267), GB-Lbl R.M.18.c.8; †hn1, hn2 pts., WITH *Samson, Alexander Balus*, 2 vols.: GB-Mp MS 130 Hd4 vv.351–2; †timp pt., WITH *Saul, Israel, Messiah, Samson, Joseph, Belshazzar, Judas Maccabaeus, Joshua, Alexander Balus, Alexander's Feast, L'Allegro, il Penseroso ed il Moderato*: GB-Mp MS 130 Hd4 v.353; SEE ALSO *Alexander's Feast, La Resurrezione*.

—— Utrecht Jubilate. †SCORE: 1918 (lot 243), GB-Mp MS 130 Hd4 v.172.

—— Utrecht Te Deum: †PTS. (S1, A2, T1, T2, B1, vn1, vn2, vc, ob1, ob2), WITH Te Deum in B♭, HWV 281; Te Deum in A, HWV 282 (B1); Te Deum in D, HWV 280 (B1), 10 vols.: 1918 (lot 243), GB-Mp MS 130 Hd4 vv.327–8, 331–3, 338, 341–4; †PTS. (S2, A1, va), WITH Te Deum in A, HWV 282; Te Deum in D, HWV 280, 3 vols.: 1918 (lot 243), GB-Mp MS 130 Hd4 vv.339–40, 330; †PTS. (bn1, bn2, tpt2), WITH Te Deum in D, HWV 280, 3 vols.: 1918 (lot 243), GB-Mp MS 130 Hd4 vv.334–5, 337; †vn3 pt., WITH Te Deum in A, HWV 282 (vc2); Te Deum in D, HWV 280 (vc2): 1918 (lot 243), GB-Mp MS 130 Hd4 v.329; †tpt1 pt., WITH Te Deum in B♭, HWV 281; Te Deum in D, HWV 280: 1918 (lot 243), GB-Mp MS 130 Hd4 v.336; †hpd pt., WITH Te Deum in B♭, HWV 281; Te Deum in A, HWV 282; Te Deum in D, HWV 280: 1918 (lot 243), GB-Mp MS 130 Hd4 v.347.

—— *Water Music*. †SCORE: 1918 (lot 271), GB-Mp MS 130 Hd4 v.368;[98] †vn1 and vn2 'concertino' pts., WITH March in D, HWV 345; Concertos, org, HWV 295, 296ª, Op. 7 Nos. 1–2, 6; *Concerto a due cori* in F, HWV 334; *Judas Maccabaeus*, March (all vn1, vn2); 2 vols.: 1918 (lot 271), GB-Mp MS 130 Hd4 vv.354–5; †vn1 'repieno' pt., WITH Concertos, org, HWV 295, 296ª and Op. 7 No. 1 (vn3); *Concerto a due cori* in F, HWV 334 (ob1): 1918 (lot 271), GB-Mp MS 130 Hd4 v.356; †vn2 'repieno' pt., WITH *Concerto a due cori* in F, HWV 334 (ob2); *Giulio Cesare* (hn3); printed pt. (hn3) for *Music for the Royal Fireworks*: 1918 (lot 271), GB-Mp MS 130 Hd4 v.357; †va pt., WITH Concertos, org, HWV 295, 296ª, and Op. 7 Nos. 1–2, 6; *Concerto a due cori* in F, HWV 334: 1918 (lot 271), GB-Mp MS 130 Hd4 v.358; †vc pt., WITH Concertos, org, HWV 295, 296ª, and Op. 7 Nos. 1–2, 6; *Concerto a due cori* in F, HWV 334: *Judas Maccabaeus*, March: 1918 (lot 271), GB-Mp MS 130 Hd4 v.359; †db pt., WITH Concerto, org, Op. 7 No. 1; *Concerto a due cori* in F, HWV 334: 1918 (lot 271), GB-Mp MS 130 Hd4 v.360; †ob1, ob2 pts., WITH Concerto, org, Op. 7 No. 1; *Concerto a due cori* in F, HWV 334; *Judas*

---

[98] See C. Hill, 'Die Abschrift von Händels "Wassermusik" in der Sammlung Newman Flower', *HjB* 17 (1971), 75–88.

Maccabaeus, March; 2 vols.: 1918 (lot 271), GB-Mp MS 130 Hd4 vv.361–2; †bn, WITH Concerto, org, Op. 7 No. 1 (bn1); *Concerto a due cori* in F, HWV 334 (bn1); *Judas Maccabaeus*, March: 1918 (lot 271), GB-Mp MS 130 Hd4 v.363; †hn1, hn2 pts., WITH *Concerto a due cori* in F, HWV 334; *Judas Maccabaeus*, March, 2 vols.: 1918 (lot 271), GB-Mp MS 130 Hd4 vv.364–5; †tpt1 pt., WITH *Concerto a due cori* in F, HWV 334 (hn1); printed pts. (hn1) for Overture *Samson*, and *Music for the Royal Fireworks*: 1918 (lot 271) GB-Mp MS 130 Hd4 v.366; †tpt2 pt., WITH *Concerto a due cori* in F, HWV 334 (hn2); printed pts. for Overture *Samson* (hn2), *Deidamia*, March (tpt1, tpt2, hn1, hn2) and *Music for the Royal Fireworks* (hn2): 1918 (lot 271) GB-Mp MS 130 Hd4 v.367.

HASSE, J. A., †*Cajo Fabricio* (opera): 1918 (lot 311), US-Cn MS VM 1500 H35c.

HAYDN, J., March in E♭, H. VIII, 3b ('Marcia') for 2 fl, 2 cl, 2 bn, 2 hn, tpt, and str. PTS. (3 vn1, 2 vn2, 1 va, 3 b), Aylesford provenance uncertain: 1873 (lot 126), US-Wc M1046.H4 HVIII, 3b.

JOMMELLI, N., †*Astianatte* (opera), 3 vols.: 1918 (lot 326A), US-Cn MS VM 1500 J75a.

KOTZWARA, F., Trio in C for 2 vn, b, and 2 hn ad lib., [Op.5 No. 1]. PTS.: 1918 (lot 310?), GB-Mp MS 630.3 Kv76.

—— *Trio concertante* in D for 2 vn, b, and 2 hn ad lib., [Op. 5 No. 3]. PTS.: 1918 (lot 310?), GB-Mp MS 630.3 Kv75.

—— *Trio concertante* in F for 2 vn, vc, and 2 hn ad lib., [Op. 5 No. 5]. PTS.: 1918 (lot 310?), GB-Mp MS 630.2 Kv79.

—— *Trio concertante* in E♭ for 2 vn, b, and 2 hn ad lib., [Op. 5 No. 6]. PTS.: 1918 (lot 310?), GB-Mp MS 630.3 Kv77.

LAMPE, J. F., †*Britannia* (opera), SELECTIONS ('Songs in the Opera Brittannia'), WITH *Dione* (opera), SELECTIONS ('Songs in the Opera Dione'): 1918 (lot 313?), GB-Lbl Add. MS 39816.

LATILLA, G., †*Il Siroe* (opera), 3 vols.: 1918 (lot 326A?), US-SFsc.

—— †*Il Temistocle* (opera): 1918 (lot 326A), US-SFsc.

LOTTI, A., †'Confitebor tibi' in A for SATB and orch.: 1918 (lot 302), GB-Lbl Add. MS 39817.

MARCELLO, B. †Cantatas (32) for S or A and bc: 1918 (lot 305), GB-Mp MS 483 Mf61.

[MONZA, C. A.], †[*S. Philippus Neri*] (oratorio), Pt. 2: 1918 (lot 302), GB-Cfm MU.MS. 661 v.2 (*olim* 52.B.15).

[MUDGE, R.], Concertos (6) and 'Non nobis Domine'. PTS. (vn1 'concertino', vn2 'concertino', vn1 'ripieno', vn2 'ripieno', va, vc, hpd), autograph MSS: GB-Mp MS 130 Hd4 vv.86–92.

—— Concertos (8). PTS. (vn1 'concertino', vn2 'concertino', va, vc), autograph MSS: GB-Mp Flower Collection.

—— Concertos. PTS., drafts, etc., mostly autograph MSS: GB-BENcoke.

—— *Sonata Cômposta a la gusto del Seign.*ᵒʳ *Bombardini*. Vn pt., autograph MS: GB-Mp Flower Collection

NEGRI, [D. F.?], (†)Gloria in D for SSTB, chor. and orch.: 1918 (lot 313?), GB-Cfm MU.MS. 657 (*olim* 52.B.11).

80 THE AYLESFORD COLLECTION

NOFERI, G. B., Trio for vn, va, and bc. PTS.: 1918 (lot 310?), GB-Mp Flower Collection

PESCETTI, G. B., Aria 'Semplici amanti' from pasticcio *Alessandro in Persia* (London, 1741), WITH B. Galuppi, *Scipione in Cartagine* (opera), SELECTIONS, arr. for voice and hpd:[99] GB-BENcoke.

POLLAROLO, C. F., †*Giulio Cesare nell'Egitto* (opera), 3 vols.: 1918 (lot 283), US-Wc M1500.P74G4.

—— †*Alfonso Primo* (opera): 1918 (lot 283), US-SFsc.

—— †*Ottone* (opera): 1918 (lot 283) US-SFsc.

—— †*Pastorale a 3 voci.* SHORT SCORE (vn1, vn2, bc): 1918 (lot 287), GB-Mp MS 580 Ps41.

—— †*Proserpina rapita* (opera), 3 vols.: 1918 (lot 284), GB-Lbl Eg. MS 3022–4.

—— †*Sansone* (oratorio): 1918 (lot 287), GB-Mp MS F530 Ps41.

—— †*Saule indemoniato* (oratorio): 1918 (lot 287), GB-Mp MS F530 Ps44.

PORPORA, N., †*Arianna in Nasso* (opera), WITH *Enea nel Lazio* (opera): 1918 (lot 276), US-Cn MS VM 1505 P83a.

—— *Mitridate* (opera), †SELECTIONS, WITH A. Scarlatti, *Arminio* (opera), selections; Porpora, *Siface* (opera), selections; and arias by G. M. Costanzi and L. Vinci: 1918 (lot 276), US-NH Misc. Ms. 75;[100] SEE ALSO *Polifemo*.

—— †*Polifemo* (opera), SELECTIONS, WITH Porpora, *Mitridate* (opera), selections; F. M. Veracini, *Adriano in Siria* (opera), selections; etc.: 1918 (lot 276), US-NH Misc. Ms. 78.[101]

—— *Siface* (opera): SEE *Mitridate*.

PURCELL, H., Anthems: SEE Collections: Arias by G. M. Orlandini, etc.

RICCI, F. P., 'Divertimento 1' for vn, va, and b. PTS. (vn, va): 1918 (lot 310?), GB-Mp MS 630.4 R121.

SACRAMOSO VERONESE, MARCHESE, †*Il Giobbe* (oratorio): 1918 (lot 326A), US-SFsc.

SAMMARTINI, G., †Sonatas (27) for fl (4), ob (7), rec (14) or vn (2) and bc, WITH Anon., Rondeau in D for vn and bc: 1918 (lot 326A?), US-R M241.S189.

—— †Sonatas (2) for fl and bc in D and G: 1918 (lot 313?), GB-Cfm MU.MS. 656A (*olim* 52.B.10), formerly bound with G. Tartini, Concertos in A and F. SEE *Addendum to Sect. 1*.

SANDONI, P. G., (†)*La pulcella d'Orleans* (oratorio): 1918 (lot 302), GB-Cfm MU.MS 658 (*olim* 52.B.12).

SCARLATTI, A., *Arminio* (opera): SEE N. Porpora, *Mitridate*.

—— †*Dafni* (opera): 1918 (lot 321), GB-Cfm MU.MS. 227 (*olim* 24.E.8), facs. edn., New York, 1986.

—— †*La fede riconosciuta* (opera), autograph MS: 1918 (lot 313?), GB-Cfm MU.MS. 229 (*olim* 24.E.10).[102]

---

99 'Semplici amanti' is attributed to Pescetti in the 1st vol. of 'favourite songs' from *Alessandro in Persia*, pub. by Walsh in 1741. The arias 'Pupille vezzosette', and 'Quando mira il ciel sereno' were included in Walsh's 1st collection of songs from *Scipione in Cartagine* (c.1742).

100 See R. Strohm, 'Scarlattiana at Yale' in N. Pirrotta and A. Zino (eds.), *Händel e gli Scarlatti a Roma* (Florence, 1987), 140–1, 148–9.

101 See ibid. 140.

102 See E. J. Dent, 'A Pastoral Opera by Alessandro Scarlatti', *Music Review*, 12 (1951), 7–14.

—— †*La Giuditta* (oratorio), 1693: 1918 (lot 320), US-MT.

—— †*La Giuditta* (oratorio), 1697, autograph MS: 1918 (lot 320), GB-Ckc Ms. 205.

—— †*Griselda* (opera), SELECTIONS, WITH arias (11) by G. Bononcini, F. Gasparini, G. M. Orlandini, D. Sarro, G. Vignati, etc.: 1918 (lot 314), US-Wc M1500.S28G5, facs. edn., New York, 1986.

—— †*Marco Attilio Regolo* (opera), arias: 1918 (lot 321), GB-Cfm MU.MS. 228 (*olim* 24.E.9).

—— †*Il primo omicidio* (oratorio), autograph MS: 1918 (lot 318), US-SFsc.

—— †'Salve Regina' for SATB, WITH A. Scarlatti, Cantata 'Sciolta de freddi amplessi', autograph MSS: 1918 (lot 315), GB-Cfm MU. MS. 225B (*olim* 24.E.6), formerly bound with P. P. Bencini, *La Jezebel* (oratorio), pt. for 'Il fanciullo'.

—— †*S. Cecilia* (oratorio), autograph MS: 1918 (lot 319), CH-Gbb.[103]

SCARLATTI, F., †*Il Daniele nel lago de' leoni*, 'dialogo' for 5 v, 2 vn, va and tpt: 1918 (lot 314), GB-Cfm MU.MS. 226 (*olim* 24.E.7).

SCHIASSI, G. M., †Sonatas (10) for vn and bc: 1918 (lot 313?), GB-Cfm MU.MS. 654 (*olim* 52.B.8).

STEFFANI, A., †*Orlando* (opera): 1918 (lot 298), D-HVsb.

TARTINI, G., †Concertos (2) in A and F: 1918 (lot 313?), GB-Cfm MU.MS. 656B (*olim* 52.B.10), formerly bound with G. Sammartini, Sontas for fl and bc. SEE *Addendum to Sect. 1*.

TOESCHI, [C. J.,] Quintet for fl, vn, va, vc, and b. Fl pt.: 1918 (lot 310?), GB-Mp MS 651 Tp27.

VENTO, M., [(†)]*La conquista del Messico* (opera). SELECTIONS: 1918 (lot 302), GB-Mp MS F520 Vk57.

VERACINI, F. M., *Adriano in Siria* (opera). †SCORE: 1918 (lot 277), GB-Mp MS F520 Vl61; SEE ALSO N. Porpora, *Polifemo*.

VINCI, L., †*Artaserse* (opera), 3 vols.: 1918 (lot 326A), US-R M1500.V777A.

—— †*Didone abbandonata* (opera): 1918 (lot 326A?), US-Cn MS VM 1500.V77d, facs. edn., New York, 1977.

VIVALDI, A., †Sonatas for vn and hpd (RV 3, 6, 12, 17a, 22, 754–60), partly autograph MS: 1918 (lot 325), GB-Mp MS 624.1 Vw81.

2. Manuscripts not yet located

ALCOCK, J., 'Book of Music in Dr. Alcock's hand-writing': 1918 (lot 278) (Airy).

—— Hymns; 'At the end is written: "John Alcock, Reading, Jan. 22, 1741 2"': 1918 (lot 278).

—— See also Collections, 'Anthems, by Greene, Kent, etc.'

ANON., 'Il Giobbe, Oratorio':[104] 1918 (lot 302, Lewine).

ASTORGA, E. D', Cantatas, WITH cantatas by A. Scarlatti, A. Stradella; 'Half calf oblong 4to': 1918 (lot 280, Sharp).

—— Stabat Mater; Letter of Jennens to Holdsworth, 29 Mar. 1743.

[103] The MS is described in detail in T. Seebass, *Musikhandschriften der Bodmeriana* (Geneva, 1986), 20–4.

[104] This may be another copy of the work by Sacramoso Veronese listed in Sect. I.

82   THE AYLESFORD COLLECTION

BENCINI, P. P., *La Jezabel* (oratorio). SCORE: 1918 (lot 287, Reeves).

BONONCINI, G., *Il trionfo di Camilla* (opera), Overture. PTS. (vn1, bc): 1937 (no. 13).

CARISSIMI, G., 'Vocal Solos, Duets, etc., fine manuscript volume, folio, red morocco, gilt frame sides and central panels of black elaborately tooled and name in gilt: "Sig: Iacomo Carissimo Maestro di Cap: in St: Appolinare" (rubbed)': 1918 (lot 289, Pickering).

COLLECTIONS:

Anthems, 32 vols.: 1918 (lot 286, James).

'Anthems, by Greene, Kent, etc.'; 'On fly-leaf: "This Book was wrote by Dr. Alcock, Organist at Lichfield"': 1918 (lot 278, Airy).

'Italian fantasias for the organ [or Virginalls]' by Merulo ('Claudio da Corregio'), Palestrina, Willaert ('Adrian Vouillart'), Lasso, Clemens non Papa, 'Ruggiero', Rore ('Cipriano del Rore'), *et al.* (35 pieces); 'Whole calf stamped', fol., c.1580–1600, Aylesford provenance uncertain: 1873 (lot 115, 'W').

'Psalms, Hymns, & Anthems. Transcripts, 57 in all, written on hand drawn staves in a fine calligraphical hand (often with the appearance of engraved music), for solo, 2, 3, 4 Voices with Thorough Bass. Included in this collection are works of John Broderip, Joseph Key, James Kent, John Weldon, & Samuel Wise; however, most are anonymous. (Unfortunately 4 lines of MS. that could perhaps have provided a clue as to the writer and date have been indelibly inked out.) 1-103pp. Tall folio, original marbled boards, worn. Very fine example of music penmanship. c.1775.': Leamington Book Shop Catalogue, 32 (1968), no. 205.

'Sonate, etc. for 1st Violin, 2nd Violin, and Viola da Gamba' by B. Richard, N. Schnittelbach, J. Rosenmüller, etc. 'One [piece] is signed "Balthazar Richardt." . . . Another piece bears the signature of the violinist, N. Schnittelbach', 3 vols. ('The Gamba parts are in the 2nd Violin volume.'), 'Calf': 1918 (lot 324, Hill & Sons).

GAFFI, B., 'Cantata "Farfalletta semplicetta" for solo voice with figured bass and an aria with violino solo obbligato, finely written throughout, contemporary MS, 32 pp., ob. 4to': Harold Reeves Catalogue 33 (1921), no. 642; 1918 (lot 296, Reeves).

GIARDINI, F., 'Solo per Alto Viola' and kbd in F; 'Per Lord Aylesford Billiardo' (Andante–Grazioso–Allegro S[c]herzando); 'Title, 6pp. Large Oblong 4to.'; autograph MS: Leamington Book Shop Catalogue, 32 (1968), no. 108.

—— Trio in F for vn, va, and vc; 'Per Lord Aylesford Giugno 1792' (Andante–Grazioso–Allegro); 'Title, 10pp. Oblong 4to. Uncut'; autograph MS: Leamington Book Shop Catalogue, 32 (1968), no. 109.

—— Trio in G for vn, va, and vc; 'Per Lord Aylesford Giugno 1792' (Andante 'with 5-bar correction in the hand of the composer'– Siciliano–[Allegro]); 'Title, 10pp. Oblong 4to. Uncut'; autograph MS: Leamington Book Shop Catalogue 32 (1968), no. 110.

—— 'Twelve manuscript Duetts for a Violin and Tenor',[105] 2 vols., 'Oblong 4to, calf gilt': 1918 (lot 313, Lewine).

[See opposite page for n. 105]

JOHN H. ROBERTS

HANDEL, G. F., *Acis and Galatea*: SEE *Ode for Queen Anne's Birthday*.
—— *Alexander Balus*: SEE *Esther*.
—— Anthems, HWV 246, 248, 249ᵇ, 250ᵃ, 251ᵇ, 251ᶜ, 252–4, 256ᵃ, 5 vols.
—— Anthems, HWV 248, 250ᵃ, 251ᵇ, 251ᶜ, 254, 256ᵃ. T pt. (T1 in HWV 254).¹⁰⁶
—— Anthem 'As pants the hart', HWV 251ᵇ; SEE ALSO *Ode for Queen Anne's Birthday*.
—— *Arianna*: SEE *Ode for Queen Anne's Birthday*.
—— *Atalanta*.¹⁰⁷ Tpt1 pt., ?WITH *Giustino*, *Serse* (tpt), *Deidamia*; tpt2 pt., ?WITH *Giustino*, *Deidamia*; hn1, hn2 pts., ?WITH *Serse*, *Deidamia*, 2 vols.
—— *Athalia*: 'Folio, red morocco'; inscribed 'S.D.G.; G.F. Handel. Lon. Jun. 7. 1733': 1918 (lot 250, G. H. Brown).
—— *Belshazzar*. SCORE, 'Red morocco gilt, tooled borders', [fol.?]: 1918 (lot 247, G. H. Brown); SEE ALSO Foundling Hospital Anthem.
—— *Berenice*: 1918 (lot 204, Lewine).
—— Chamber duets (7), 'Half calf, ob. fol.'; Aylesford provenance uncertain: 1873 (lot 273, 'Whitt[ingha]m').
—— Chamber duets and trios, 'Red morocco, gilt ornamental frame sides, g.e. 4to': 1918 (lot 241, G. H. Brown).
—— Concerto, org (hp), Op. 4 No. 6: SEE *Esther*.
—— *Deborah*, 'Red morocco gilt, tooled borders', [fol.]; includes 'a solo Hallelujah for Senesino, and alterations for Carestino', 2 vols.: 1918 (lot 247, G. H. Brown).
—— *Deidamia*. SCORE; SEE ALSO *Atalanta*.
—— *Esther*. Hp pt., ?WITH *Saul*, *Alexander Balus*, Concerto, org (hp), Op. 4 No. 6: 1918 (lot 247);¹⁰⁸ SEE ALSO *Ode for Queen Anne's Birthday*.
—— *Flavio*: SEE *Ottone*.
—— Foundling Hospital Anthem, 'Blessed are they that considereth the poor', ?WITH *Belshazzar* (1751), 'The leafy honours'.¹⁰⁹
—— *Giulio Cesare*: SEE *Ottone*.
—— *Giustino*: SEE *Atalanta*.
—— *Israel in Egypt*, 2 vols. 'fol.', 3 vols. 'oblong 4to', 'red morocco, gilt tooled sides, g.e.': 1918 (lot 239, G. H. Brown).
—— *Judas Maccabaeus*. PTS., 16 vols., Aylesford provenance uncertain: 1873 (lot 310, H. Turner).
—— *Lotario*. Ob1 pt., WITH *Partenope*, *Poro*.¹¹⁰

---

¹⁰⁵ These pieces are probably the 'Duetti per Violino e Viola . . . Per il Duca Dorsset' found in GB-Lbl Add. MSS 31695–6. See McVeigh, *Violinist in London's Concert Life*, 320.

¹⁰⁶ Jennens's numbering confirms that 1 vol. is missing from this set.

¹⁰⁷ It is possible that these pts. were never copied. No timp pt. would have been needed for the March in *Deidamia*, one having been included in Walsh's 8th collection of overture pts. (London, 1743).

¹⁰⁸ The description of lot 247 mentions 23 pts. for *Esther*, one more than are in the Flower Collection, and the vol. count confirms that a vol. is missing.

¹⁰⁹ The *Belshazzar* aria is present in GB-Lbl R.M.19.e.8, which may have been copied from this MS. See n. 42, above.

¹¹⁰ Jennens's numbering shows this set contained 7 vols., one more than in lot 202 of the 1918 sale.

84 THE AYLESFORD COLLECTION

—— *Messiah*. SCORE, 'Folio, red morocco, gilt borders and ornaments':
1918 (lot 245, G. H. Brown); SCORE, 'Oblong 4to, red morocco gilt',
3 vols.: 1918 (lot 245).

—— *Muzio Scevola*, Overture. Hpd pt., 1937 (no. 8).

—— *Ode for Queen Anne's Birthday*. SCORE, WITH Overture *Il pastor fido*,
last 2 movements[111] ('Serenade. The Birthday of Queen Anne. Overture
in full score, together with the Words and Music. Suite of ye ouverture,
in Pastos Fido. Full score of the last two strains'), '4to. Half calf': Maggs
Bros. Catalogue 476 (1926), no. 54: 1918 (lot 257?); va pt., WITH selections from *Acis and Galatea* (1732–6), [*Esther* (1737)] and *Il pastor fido*
(1734); [*Arianna* (Nov. 1734), ballet music]; *La Resurrezione* (va da
gamba) ('Additional Songs, in Acis and Galatea, Serenada. Viola. Songs
in Pastor Fido Reviv'd. Viola. Oratorio, della Resurrezione. Viola di
Gambo'), '4to. Half calf.': Maggs Bros. Catalogue 476 (1976), no. 56:[112]
1918 (lot 257, Maggs); bnI pt., WITH *La Resurrezione*, Anthem 'As pants
the hart', [HWV 251ᵇ]: ('Serenade. Basson Primo, Oratorio della
Resurrezione. Basson. Anthem: As pants the Hart, Basson and Contra
Basso'), '4to. Half calf': Maggs Bros. Catalogue 476 (1926), no. 55: 1918
(lot 257, Maggs).[113]

—— *Ottone*. PTS. (vnI, obI), WITH *Flavio*, *Giulio Cesare*, 2 vols.: 1918
(lot 207, Lewine).

—— *Partenope*: SEE *Lotario*.

—— *Il pastor fido*. ?Aria for Silvio (May 1734), last p., autograph MS:
Sotheby's Catalogue 18 Dec. 1936, no. 148 (Blancheteau);[114] SEE ALSO
Ode for Queen Anne's Birthday.

—— *Poro*: SEE *Lotario*.

—— *La Resurrezione*: SEE *Ode for Queen Anne's Birthday*.

—— *Rinaldo*: 1918 (lot 210, Hunt).

—— *Rodelinda*. Overture, 'Oblong 4to, blue morocco, gilt frame sides, g.e.';
1918 (lot 313, Lewine).

—— *Samson*, 'Red morocco gilt, tooled borders, g.e.', [fol.?]: 1918 (lot 265,
G. H. Brown).

—— *Saul*. SCORE: 'Red morocco gilt, tooled borders, g.e.', [fol.?]: 1918 (lot
265); SEE ALSO *Esther*.

—— *Serse*: SEE *Atalanta*.

—— *Siroe*: 1918 (lot 204, Lewine).

—— *Tamerlano*: 1918 (lot 204).[115]

—— Te Deum in B♭, HWV 281; 'Red morocco, gilt borders, g.e.': 1918
(lot 243, G. H. Brown).

[111] These 2 movements are absent from Jennens's score of *Pastor fido*.

[112] This catalogue listing and the next were first noted in Beeks, 'Chandos Anthems', i. 213.
I have assumed that 'Serenada' refers to the *Ode for Queen Anne's Birthday* and that that work
comes first as it does in the other partbooks in the set. On the same principle this partbook
must have included the *Esther* and *Arianna* excerpts.

[113] Beeks, 'Chandos Anthems', i. 213.

[114] A facs. of this p. is found in W. C. Smith, 'Recently-Discovered Handel Manuscripts', 314.

[115] The shelf-marks on Jennens's chronological series of opera scores suggest he had only 1
score of *Tamerlano*, the copy now in the Flower Collection.

JOHN H. ROBERTS   85

—— Utrecht Te Deum: 1918 (lot 243).

—— Wedding Anthems (2).

HAYDN, [J.], 'Echo' [H. II, 39?]: 1918 (lot 310, Lewine).

—— 'Haffmann' [= composition attributed to L. Hofmann?]: 1918 (lot 310).

—— 'Notturni' [H. II, 25*–31*?]: 1918 (lot 310).

LAMPE, J. F., 'Overture Songs and Arias in the Opera Amelia, words by
Carey, produced 1732, in score, 103 pp.', WITH [J. A.] Hasse, 'Duetto
"Tu vuoi ch'io viva o Cara," 40 pp., and Arie dell opera Catone, 64
pp.' and [M.] Green[e], 'Bass Aria "Great is the Lord," followed by
Contralto Aria with trumpet obbligato, written throughout in full score
in bold early 18th century handwriting, ob. folio, hf. bd.' (Harold Reeves
Catalogue, 33 (1921), no. 646): 1918 (lot 296, Reeves).

LIDARTI, C. J., 'Lamentazione 3za. del Mercoldi. So. a 2 Voci con Vllo. obb.
nice old Italian MS. score' 'oblong folio'; Aylesford provenance uncertain:
1873 (lot 357, Whitt[ingha]m).

PEPUSCH, J. C., 'Rules for Thorough Bass, etc. Autograph MS.—Organ
part of 12 Sonatas (MS.)—Thirty-nine MS. Exercises on Harmony',
WITH 'Bass part of Benj. Healy's Sonatas for 3 Violes, Auto. MS.';
Aylesford provenance uncertain: 1873 (lot 283, 'W').

STEFFANI, A., *Arminio* (opera), 'Oblong 4to, calf gilt, red and gold end
papers, g.e.': 1918 (lot 298, Coupland).

TARTINI, G., 'Concerti per il Violino Solo e Strum. Fine Old Italian MS. set
in case': 1873 (lot 278, Whitt[ingham]).

Addendum to Appendix, Section 1.

The following additional items were formerly bound with G. Sammartini,
Sonatas for fl and bc and G. Tartini, Concertos in A and F:

ANON., †Motet 'Cantate Domino tympanis celestes anime' for B and bc:
GB-Cfm MU.MS. 656E (*olim* 52.B.10).

[ARAIA, F.], †[*Lucio Vero* (opera), SELECTIONS]:[116] GB-Cfm MU.MS. 656D
(*olim* 52.B.10).

[ORLANDINI, G. M.], †[*Il marito giocatore* (intermezzo)] for vs and bc: GB-
Cfm MU.MS. 656C (*olim* 52.B.10).

---

[116] The MS contains 2 arias, 'Questa d'un fido amore' and 'Ombra che pallida'. The 2nd
carries a pencil attribution to Araia's *Lucio Vero* (Venice, 1735), and both texts (neither of
which comes from Zeno's original) are found in the libretto of that opera.

5.1. Anthony Ashley Cooper, 4th Earl of Shaftesbury (1711–71). Portrait by Joseph Highmore (1692–1780), signed and dated 1744 (the Earl of Shaftesbury; reproduced by permission of the owner and the Paul Mellon Centre for Studies in British Art).

5

The Shaftesbury Collection

ANTHONY HICKS

THE group of Handel scores first assembled by Anthony Ashley Cooper, 4th Earl of Shaftesbury (1711–71), was, until recently, the least known of the great Handel collections formed by the composer's early patrons. It was said to have been preserved at St Giles's House, the Shaftesbury family seat in Dorset, but no description of it had been published, and even its owner and his immediate predecessors were not fully aware of its contents. When finally brought to light it proved to be a remarkable combination of printed and manuscript scores covering the bulk of Handel's output. The discovery of its full extent in 1983 was a happy precursor of the Handel tercentenary celebrations of 1985, but also led to changes. In 1987 most of the manuscript volumes were acquired by the late Gerald Coke and were moved to his Handel Collection at Bentley in Hampshire, while the printed material and two manuscripts were retained at St Giles's House. Though the division may be regretted, there were good reasons for it, and it is fortunate that the early state of the Collection and its subsequent history can be described with reasonable accuracy. It is the purpose of this chapter to put on record the events of that history, especially those in which I had the privilege of playing a part, and to offer an overview of the contents of the Collection. I was pleased to have the company of Winton Dean at St Giles's House on the day when the most important items in the Collection were first uncovered, and I am grateful to him for help over a number of matters, notably the identification of copyists. Both of us would wish to thank the present Earl of Shaftesbury for his kindness in allowing access to the Collection and other material at St Giles's House on a number of occasions, and for assistance in other ways. The help and hospitality given by his staff in the estate office has also been much appreciated.

Several references to the 4th Earl of Shaftesbury as a patron and interested observer of Handel are recorded by Otto Erich Deutsch. He

88   THE SHAFTESBURY COLLECTION

first comes into view in a letter of Mary Delany's, written to her sister on 12 April 1734, in which she tells of a musical evening at her house in Lower Brook Street.

Lord Shaftesbury begged of Mr. Percival [one of Mrs Delany's invited guests] to bring him, and being a *profess'd friend* of Mr Handel (who was here also) *was admitted*; I was never so *well* entertained at an *opera*![1]

Shaftesbury was then 23 years old, having succeeded to the title at the age of 2. He subscribed to three of Walsh's editions of Handel opera songs in 1737 and 1738 (*Arminio, Giustino*, and *Faramondo*), as well as to *Alexander's Feast* (1739) and the Opus 6 Grand Concertos (1740), the last two in company with his wife and mother. In 1760, prompted by the publication of excerpts from Mainwaring's *Memoirs* of the composer in the *Gentleman's Magazine*, he wrote some biographical notes of his own, which Deutsch published in full for the first time from the manuscript in the Public Record Office. Deutsch remarks: 'It seems a pity that Shaftesbury confined himself to Handel's performances, telling us nothing of the man, whom he must have known very well. (At St Giles, the residence of the Shaftesburys, there is still a large collection of Handel scores.)'[2] This seems to be the first reference in print to the Shaftesbury Collection. William C. Smith's catalogue of Handel's works, published in 1954,[3] makes no mention of the Collection, nor does his later bibliography of Handel editions[4]— though, as we shall see, the Collection contains material relevant to both of these publications. In 1961 Betty Matthews published an article in which she quoted letters of the 4th Earl of Shaftesbury mentioning the loan of scores from his Collection.[5] In this connection Miss Matthews commented: 'It seems that Lord Shaftesbury had an extensive library of Handel scores, though these have never been traced.'

My own interest in the Shaftesbury scores stems from 1969, when I identified a so-called 'Serenata' found in one of the Aylesford manuscripts now in Manchester Central Library[6] as the music written by Handel for a version of Milton's *Comus* privately performed in 1745 by members of the family of the 4th Earl of Gainsborough at his seat

---

[1] O. E. Deutsch, *Handel: A Documentary Biography* (London, 1955), 363; *Händel-Handbuch*, iv. *Dokumente zu Leben und Schaffen* (Leipzig and Kassel, 1985), 240.

[2] *Handel*, 844–8.

[3] in G. Abraham (ed.), *Handel: A Symposium* (London, 1954), 274–310.

[4] *Handel: A Descriptive Catalogue of the Early Editions* (London, 1960; 2nd edn., Oxford, 1970).

[5] 'Handel: More Unpublished Letters', *ML* 42. 127–131. Miss Matthews's extracts from the letters are reprinted under their dates in *Händel-Handbuch*, iv, except for that dated 23 Feb. 1755/6, which is correctly reassigned to 1746. The letters referring to the loan of scores are those of 20 May and 27 May 1756, 23 Sept. and 31 Dec. 1757 (*Händel-Handbuch*, iv. 498–9, 510, 511).

[6] GB-Mp MS 130 Hd4, v. 300 (1).

at Exton in Rutland.[7] The evidence for the identification had come from an earlier article of Miss Matthews in which she published and discussed a number of letters preserved among the Shaftesbury archives at St Giles's House.[8] One of these letters, dated at Exton on 23 June 1745, was from Lord Gainsborough's brother James Noel and was addressed to Noel's brother-in-law, the 4th Earl of Shaftesbury. Noel described the entertainment at Exton and Handel's contribution to it, and added that he would 'take care to have the Musick exactly transcribed, as I have my Brother Gainsborough's Orders to get it done by the Musick-Master here'. This remark suggested that Lord Shaftesbury was to be supplied with a score of the *Comus* music, and the question naturally arose as to whether it still could be found among the scores stated by Deutsch to exist at St Giles's House.

Unfortunately it was a bad time to make such an enquiry. The 9th Earl of Shaftesbury had died in 1961, at the age of 91, and had been succeeded by his grandson, the present Earl. There was a heavy bill for death duties and St Giles's House was found to be severely affected by dry rot. Just at the time of my interest, the decision was being taken to remove the nineteenth-century additions to the house in order to reduce it to something like its eighteenth-century proportions. Accordingly the kitchen wing on the north side of the courtyard was demolished in 1971 and the long south-west wing in 1972.[9] Good accommodation for the estate office has since been established on the ground floor of the house, and a general programme of restoration is now under way, but, at the time of my enquiry it was not possible to visit the house.

I was nevertheless able to get information about Handel scores at St Giles's House from another source, to which Watkins Shaw had kindly drawn my attention. It is a manuscript document bearing the title 'A Catalogue of Musick Composed by the late Mr Handel (In the Library at St. Giles's House 1761)', preserved in the British Library[10] among a batch of papers formerly belonging to the Victorian musical scholar William Henry Husk (1814–87), though not in Husk's hand. (At that time I was unaware that a similar document also existed in the library of the Royal College of Music.) It was clearly a copy of a

---

[7] A. Hicks: 'Handel's Music for Comus', *MT* 116 (1976), 28–9.

[8] 'Unpublished Letters concerning Handel', *ML* 40 (1959), 261–8. The letters published in this article are reprinted under their dates in *Händel-Handbuch*, iv, except for the letter dated by Miss Matthews 'January the 23rd, 1745', which is redated to 'June the 23rd, 1745' in accordance with Winton Dean's comments in *ML* 40 (1959), 406–7 (the original actually reads 'Jun. the 23d: 1745'). Otherwise, the *Händel-Handbuch* transcripts follow those of Miss Matthews, which contain several minor errors. The letters referring to *Comus* are those of 23 June 1745 and 1 Aug. 1748 (*Händel-Handbuch*, iv. 393, 416).

[9] Two photographs by A. F. Kersting in A. Mee's *The King's England: Dorset*, rev. edn. by E. T. Long (London, 1967), facing p. 212, provide a glimpse of past glories.

[10] Add. MS. 39864, fos. 98–102.

90 THE SHAFTESBURY COLLECTION

catalogue drawn up in 1761, subsequently annotated in 1772 (the year following the death of the 4th Earl) and again in 1855, when the 7th Earl of Shaftesbury noted that all the items listed 'Excepting the Messiah' were still present, presumably at St Giles's. A transcript of the catalogue is given in Appendix 1. It lists the music under various categories subdivided into groups identified by letters. Individual volumes (or sometimes sets of volumes) are identified by numbers within each group. (In the catalogue, and throughout this chapter, the term 'volume' is used to denote any individually bound document. Thus two or more printed editions of different works bound together count as a single volume, while each partbook of a publication issued in parts is counted separately.) The letter-and-number combinations are probably shelf-marks referring to the original positions of the volumes in the library, but they have no obvious connection with the state of the Collection as subsequently found and their exact meaning is not now known. The catalogue does not indicate which volumes are manuscripts and which are printed copies, but a mixture of manuscript and printed material is implied, since works unpublished in 1761 could only be represented in manuscript, while such entries as 'Six Concertos for the Harpsicord' and 'Seven Sonatas, or Trios for 2 Violins' apparently refer to early printed editions. No mention is made in the catalogue of the *Comus* music, or anything that could be identified with it, so my query concerning the score apparently sent to Lord Shaftesbury in 1745 remained unanswered; but clearly the Collection as a whole, if still preserved, was of great importance.

Eventually it became possible for me to visit St Giles's House, and, thanks to the kindness of the present Lord Shaftesbury, I did so in October 1975. At that time the bookshelves in the library were entirely covered with protective black polythene sheeting, but Lord Shaftesbury had drawn back the sheet over one high shelf where he believed the Handel scores were kept and allowed me to examine what was there. He also showed me a typescript list of the scores, covering fifty-seven volumes, which had been prepared by the British Museum in 1928. The contents of the shelf agreed almost precisely with the British Museum list and the volumes listed had numbered labels corresponding to the numbers on the list. Of the 57 volumes, 13 were manuscript and 44 were early printed editions. However, there were also 11 other volumes on the shelf, not labelled or numbered. One of these contained printed copies of the first two books of keyboard suites and the six keyboard fugues; the remainder consisted of manuscript copies of *Theodora*, *Jephtha*, and *Susanna*, each in three volumes, and a one-volume copy of *Samson*, all in the hand of John Christopher Smith, Handel's chief copyist. Thus on that occasion I

ANTHONY HICKS

was able to list a total of 68 volumes, 23 manuscript and 45 printed, all of which could be identified with entries in the 1761 catalogue. Lord Shaftesbury was not aware of the existence of any other Handel scores at the house, apart from a few volumes of the English Handel Society edition, and the polythene coverings prevented further inspection of the contents of the library. Thus it seemed that about fifty volumes of the original Collection had gone missing, and, regrettably, it appeared that most of these were manuscripts. Nevertheless the manuscripts already found were of considerable interest, and I was able to inform other scholars, including Winton Dean, Watkins Shaw, Gerald Hendrie, and the late Cecil Hill, of items relevant to their work.

My next visit to St Giles's House was prompted partly by my own desire to study some of the manuscript items more closely, and by Winton Dean's need to examine the manuscript scores relating to the operas in order to complete certain chapters of the book on Handel's operas which he was then writing in collaboration with Merrill Knapp.[11] The manuscripts relevant to the operas then known were those of *Agrippina*—reference D7 in the 1761 list—and the set of so-called 'Additions' to the operas—references E14 to E17. (These 'additions' are actually supplements to the printed extracts of the operas published by Walsh and Cluer; they contain accompanied recitatives, sinfonias, dances, and other items omitted from the prints, but not the plain recitatives.) I drove to St Giles's House with Mr Dean on 3 August 1983. The polythene sheeting had by then been removed from the library and it was possible to view all the shelves fully. The scores I had seen in 1975 were on their high shelf as before, but it was now apparent that there was a second batch of musical volumes at ground level in the same stack. A brief inspection of one or two of these left little doubt that they were the 'missing' items of the Collection, or some of them. Sand used for drying the ink fell from several of the manuscripts as they were opened, a clear indication that they had remained undisturbed for many years.

While Mr Dean worked through the manuscripts noted on my earlier visit, I inspected the newly found volumes, collating them with the 1761 catalogue as far as possible. After checking the content of the new group, I found that about ten of the volumes listed in 1761 had not been accounted for, including such oratorios as *Deborah*, *Athalia*, and *Israel in Egypt*—works with big double choruses. The thought arose that these works might have been copied in large folio volumes which could not be accommodated in the stack of the library containing the other volumes of the Collection. This proved to be a correct inference: an inspection of shelves containing volumes of the

[11] *Handel's Operas 1704–1726* (Oxford, 1987).

92 THE SHAFTESBURY COLLECTION

expected height soon brought to light the final group of scores, all manuscripts in large folio. The full extent of the Handel scores at St Giles's House was then revealed: a total of 118 volumes, 69 in manuscript and 49 in print. This is precisely the total stated in the 7th Earl's annotation on the 1761 list, but the correspondence is not quite exact. The total number of volumes in the 1761 list is actually 119 (excluding the lost *Messiah*), and 5 items listed as present in 1761—probably 2 printed volumes and 3 manuscripts—could no longer be found. On the other hand, the Collection included 1 printed item and 3 manuscripts not mentioned in the 1761 list. Such discrepancies were not surprising in view of the 4th Earl's willingness (as revealed in the letters found by Betty Matthews) to lend items from his Collection to performing musicians. It was especially pleasing for me to find among the newly revealed manuscripts the copy of the *Comus* music for which I had long been searching, bound in at the end of one of two copies of *L'Allegro, il Penseroso ed il Moderato*; it had been prepared by the copyist also responsible for the Manchester manuscript (presumably the 'Musick-Master' at Exton Hall in 1745), but differed from it in several details. (I hope to discuss the Shaftesbury score, and other new material relating to the Exton performance of *Comus*, in a separate study.)

The letters published by Miss Matthews had meanwhile led to the discovery of a fugitive volume of the Shaftesbury Collection, not at St Giles's House and not on the 1761 list. In 1756 Shaftesbury had received (via his cousin James Harris) a request from William Hayes for the loan of scores of *Messiah*, *Judas Maccabaeus*, and *Joshua* for performances in Oxford. He raised no objection to lending the first two, because 'they have already been frequently performed'; but he was more cautious with *Joshua*, and waited until he had obtained permission from John Christopher Smith before he allowed it out of his hands. The following year *Joshua* was on loan again, together with the Dettingen Te Deum, for more performances under Hayes but this time at Salisbury (where concerts were often organized by Harris himself). It seems that the score of *Joshua* was never returned to Shaftesbury. The oratorio does appear in the 1761 list (reference C7), but the entry almost certainly refers to the copy of the Walsh edition of the songs still found at St Giles's House; the score lent to Hayes must have been a manuscript full score with the choruses. Happily, just such a score of *Joshua* does exist, its flyleaf bearing the name 'Earl of Shaftesbury' as is also the case with many of the volumes at St Giles's House. Gerald Coke acquired it before 1939 and it remains in his Collection. Though its earlier provenance is not known, it can hardly be other than the score lent by the Earl in 1756 and 1757, and hence must be considered as part of the original state of the Collection.

ANTHONY HICKS 93

Thus the content of the Shaftesbury Collection as revealed in 1983 was more or less as recorded in 1761, though the volumes were no longer in their 1761 order.[12] A notional reconstruction of the Collection as it existed in 1761 is therefore possible, and its content is set out in Appendix 2; in effect this is an amplified version of the 1761 list, with the items more fully described. An indication is given of the size of each volume, and whether it is manuscript or printed; the copyists of the manuscripts and the editions of the printed scores are identified wherever possible; items now extant but not in the 1761 list are inserted in what seem to be appropriate places. The reconstruction enables us to visualize the Collection in its original state: first comes a set of oratorio manuscripts in the usual oblong folio format; the large folio manuscripts containing the double-chorus oratorios and most of the anthems follow, interrupted by a group of printed scores containing the songs from the oratorios. Next come the opera volumes, beginning with the Walsh and Cluer prints of the songs (many of them bound in pairs), with the manuscript of *Agrippina* arias included among them in the same format; then more manuscript full scores in oblong format and another group of printed opera volumes followed by the manuscript additions corresponding to them. Finally there is a miscellaneous group more mixed in content and size, with the printed part-books for the Opus 4 Organ Concertos and the two sets of Trio Sonatas at the end.

With the full extent of the Collection uncovered, we can look back over its earlier history. One of the notes added to the 1761 catalogue by the 7th Earl (the 4th Earl's grandson) in 1855 declares the Collection to be 'Handel's Operas & Oratorios in M.S.S. bequeathed to my grandfather in 1761'. There seems to be ample evidence, however, that the Collection was formed by the 4th Earl himself, and was not acquired as the result of a bequest. The subscription lists for the Walsh publications of 1737–40 already mentioned confirm that Shaftesbury was buying printed music at that period (the Collection contains first editions of the three operas concerned and *Alexander's Feast*, though there is no copy of the Opus 6 Concertos); the letters dealing with the loan of oratorio scores in 1756 and 1757[13] show that Shaftesbury owned several Handel manuscripts by that time; finally there is the evidence of a household account book preserved among the St Giles's House archives, which shows several payments for music copying in the period 1738–50, including some to 'Mr Smith' and in particular

---

[12] The order in which the vols. were found on the shelves in 1975 and 1983 (which seems to be of no significance) is recorded in the typescript notes which I prepared after my visits. (Copies are retained in the correspondence files at St Giles's House.)

[13] See 5, above.

94 THE SHAFTESBURY COLLECTION

one 'to Mr Smith for Judas Maccabaeus Oratorio'. This surely refers to the manuscript score of *Judas Maccabaeus*, listed as A3 in the 1761 catalogue and still in the Collection, which is indeed in Smith's hand. The payment, for £5, is dated 31 July 1747, four months after the first performance of the oratorio at Covent Garden, and the version of the oratorio represented in the manuscript reflects that early date. I therefore have no doubt that the Shaftesbury Collection was assembled by the 4th Earl in Handel's lifetime, probably between the mid-1730s and the mid-1750s, and that the 7th Earl's reference to a bequest is simply a mistake.

After the death of the 7th Earl in 1885 the family somehow seems to have lost its awareness of the full extent of the Collection. The 9th Earl, grandfather and immediate predecessor of the present Earl, succeeded to the title in 1886 at the age of 17. Though he was an accomplished musician who sang solo tenor in concerts and enjoyed playing the organ, he is not known to have taken an interest in his Handel Collection until 1926, when he received a letter from the musical scholar and librarian William Barclay Squire (1855–1927).[14] Squire had then retired from his post in charge of the printed music at the British Museum and was working on a catalogue of the Handel manuscripts in the King's Music Library, then recently deposited in the Museum.[15] In his letter, dated 2 July 1926, Squire explained to Lord Shaftesbury that he had come across the copy of the 1761 catalogue of the Shaftesbury Collection in the Royal College of Music. He asked if the scores listed in the catalogue were still at St Giles's House and, if so, whether he could inspect them. He would be staying at Breamore (a country house not far from Wimborne St Giles) the following week and wondered if he could come then. He obviously got a positive response, as ten days later he wrote to thank Lord Shaftesbury for allowing him to visit the house and to inspect what he calls the 'volumes of Handel on the top shelf in the Library'— presumably the shelf which I inspected in 1975. Squire noted that the volumes formed 'only a very small part' of the items listed in 1761. He adds, obviously responding to a remark of Lord Shaftesbury's: 'As you say, it is rather puzzling to know what became of the rest'. Lord Shaftesbury must have asked further questions about Squire's findings and in reply Squire sent his own transcript of the Royal College copy of the 1761 catalogue and another letter, dated 21 July 1926, in which he makes some interesting observations about Handel collections:

[14] The correspondence referred to here is held at St Giles's House and is quoted by kind permission of the Earl of Shaftesbury.

[15] W. B. Squire: *Catalogue of the King's Music Library*, i. *The Handel Manuscripts* (London, 1927).

Many great houses had such sets of Handel's works in the 18th cent. & though generally they consist of duplicates, sometimes they contain copies of music not found elsewhere. A notable instance was Lord Aylesford's collection which was sold for disastrous prices a few years ago at Sotheby's— hardly fetching the value of old paper. I secured 30 vols. (now in the Royal Music Library) from which I collected enough unpublished harpsichord pieces to form a big volume—some day to be published.[16] For this reason it would be important if your collection could be found. It might contain copies of things not to be found elsewhere. The great Chrysander edition is by no means complete: the autographs in the Royal Music Library alone contain a good deal which Chrysander omitted.

Sadly, Squire died the following January, but his enquiry had stimulated family interest in the Handel scores. In April 1928 Lord Shaftesbury wrote to Sir Frederic Kenyon, Director and Principal Librarian of the British Museum, saying that he had a 'whole shelf full' of Handel scores, and asking if anyone could come down from the Museum and report on them. Sir Frederic suggested it would be better if the volumes were brought to the Museum and Lord Shaftesbury duly obliged by delivering them to the Museum himself on 5 May 1928. Within a fortnight he had received the Museum's typescript report mentioned earlier, covering 57 volumes, together with some additional handwritten notes signed 'R.F.S.'—i.e. R. F. Sharp, Keeper of Printed Books at the Museum from 1924 to 1930 (as Hugh Cobbe has kindly informed me). Sharp had presumably been asked to give a guide to the value of the Collection and commented as follows: 'The prevailing prices for first editions of Walsh and Cluer printed copies are from £1 to £3 per work. The MSS. might fetch a little more—say £3 to £5 per work. The most valuable would be no. 47 (Agrippina) and nos. 1, 2 and 17.' (Nos. 1 and 2 in the Museum's list are the 2 volumes of organ concertos, reference F13; no. 17 is the volume of miscellaneous operatic music, reference F7.) Lord Shaftesbury declared himself satisfied with the Museum's report—'just what I wanted to know', he said—and the scores were returned to St Giles's House. It is curious that William C. Smith, who had succeeded to Barclay Squire's post at the Museum in 1920, and had already acquired some reputation as a Handel scholar, was apparently excluded from the evaluation of the Shaftesbury scores, and never showed an awareness of their existence in his writings. One can only guess that Smith, described by his distinguished successor as 'an impossible little man, cordially detested by his colleagues',[17] was

---

[16] The edn. of what came to be known as the 'Aylesford pieces' was completed by J. A. Fuller-Maitland and published after Squire's death in 2 vols. as *Pieces for Harpsichord*, ed. W. B. Squire and J. A. Fuller-Maitland (London, 1928).

[17] A. Hyatt King: 'Quodlibet: Some Memoirs of the British Museum and its Music Room, 1934–76', in P. R. Harris (ed.), *The Library of the British Museum* (London, 1991), 241–98.

not considered by his superiors as suitable to engage in discussions with a senior peer of the realm.

The next exchange of correspondence concerning the Collection occurred in 1951. On 21 November that year Otto Erich Deutsch, then based in Cambridge, wrote to Lord Shaftesbury in connection with his Handel documentary biography, mentioning references to the 4th Earl. He asked if any manuscript copies of Handel's works were still in existence at St Giles's House. Lord Shaftesbury (then aged 82) responded by sending Deutsch the list of 57 volumes prepared by the British Museum in 1928, with the comment that the Museum had informed him that 'there are many sets of this kind in English country houses, therefore they are not of much value'. Deutsch indicated a particular interest in the manuscript of the *Water Music*, and Lord Shaftesbury very graciously arranged for it to be sent by registered post to the University Library at Cambridge so that Deutsch could study it. Deutsch expressed his gratitude, saying that he was preparing a paper on the *Water Music* with a colleague. He returned the score, and the British Museum list, to Lord Shaftesbury in January 1952. Deutsch's study of the *Water Music* never appeared, as far as I know, and the only reference he ever made in print to the Shaftesbury Collection seems to be the remark quoted earlier: his knowledge of the 'large collection of Handel's scores' to which he refers was obviously confined to the fifty-seven volumes listed by the British Museum in 1928. No further interest seems to have been taken in the Shaftesbury Collection until my visit to St Giles's House in 1975. It is, of course, surprising that the earlier enquiries did not bring to light all the volumes in the Collection—particularly Squire's investigation in 1926, when he actually visited St Giles's House and was aware of the original extent of the Collection from his knowledge of the 1761 catalogue. I can think of only one explanation. The two shelves in which the previously unnoticed volumes were eventually found are both at ground level; perhaps in earlier days they had been hidden behind pieces of furniture, and only when the library came to be in its present unfurnished state did it become easy to see what they contained.

The history of the Collection can now be brought up to date. In 1987 Gerald Coke acquired the manuscripts of the Collection from the present Lord Shaftesbury, except for two volumes which Lord Shaftesbury wished to retain at St Giles's House because of the specific references to them in the family archives. (These are the Smith copy of *Judas Maccabaeus*, the score mentioned in the household accounts; and the score containing the copy of the *Comus* music mentioned as being copied for the 4th Earl in James Noel's letter of 23 June 1745. The Coke Collection has photographs of these volumes.) The printed

ANTHONY HICKS 97

scores are also retained at St Giles's House; Gerald Coke did not wish to acquire them because they would have duplicated what he considered to be superior copies of the same scores already in his Collection. It is thus the case that the Shaftesbury Collection of Handel scores, originally created as a mixture of manuscript and printed material, and preserved almost intact for over two hundred years, is now divided. However, the original state of the Collection is on record and we may hope that one day (perhaps for a special exhibition) it may be brought together again and displayed in its 1761 order. The transfer of the manuscripts to the Coke Collection has also allowed them to receive sensitive conservation and made them more easily accessible to scholars, particularly through their inclusion in the Harvester Microfilm publication of the Coke Collection.[18] As a bonus, the fugitive manuscript of *Joshua*, divided from the Collection in 1757, is now reunited with its fellows.

It remains to evaluate the importance of the Shaftesbury Collection. Barclay Squire's hope that 'it might contain copies of things not to be found elsewhere' is fulfilled in two of the manuscript volumes. One of these is a score of the opera *Rodrigo* (reference D15) copied from Handel's autograph when it was in a state more complete than it is today. Other contemporary copies include numbers from Act 3 that are now missing from the autograph, but the Shaftesbury copy is the only one to include the Act 3 recitatives. Unfortunately it does not supply the beginning of the opera—a section of the autograph that probably did not survive the journey from Italy—but the new material is enough to make performance of the opera viable, and it was used for the Handel Opera Society's production at Sadler's Wells Theatre in London in 1985. The other piece of music uniquely preserved in the Shaftesbury Collection is found in the manuscript called 'La Lucretia' (reference E2), that cantata ('Oh numi eterni') being the first item in the volume. The rest of the manuscript consists of twenty arias which were almost certainly written for operas in the period 1711–17—they include, for example, the well-known additional arias for *Rinaldo* and *Amadigi*. One aria not identifiable with a particular opera is 'Lusinga questo cor', which is not known in any other source. Regrettably, it cannot be numbered among Handel's very best arias, and the musical text is slightly corrupt; but it has its interest and, like the *Rodrigo* recitatives, received its first performance in 1985— in Dorset, appropriately enough.[19] No other music not previously

[18] MSS Nos. 154–210. See Ch. 1, n. 1.
[19] European Music Year concert at Sherborne Abbey, 25 May 1985, with the City of London Sinfonia conducted by Richard Hickox. Sarah Leonard (soprano) and Ameral Gunson (mezzo-soprano) were the soloists in four arias transcribed from the Shaftesbury manuscript ('Sento primo le procelle', 'Sorge nel petto', 'Sa perché pena il cor' and 'Lusinga questo cor').

THE SHAFTESBURY COLLECTION

known has so far been found in the Shaftesbury manuscripts, but it is likely that the Smith copies of the later oratorios—mostly, one suspects, copied shortly after first performance like that of *Judas Maccabaeus*—should prove of value to editors, especially those working on volumes of the Halle Handel Edition.

Another manuscript of special interest is that of the Italian cantatas (reference E18), which contains forty-nine numbered items. (No. 39, however, is merely a truncated version of 'Ne' tuoi lumi', which also appears complete as no. 7). What gives the volume importance is a pencil note in Handel's own hand on the first page of the cantata 'Vedendo amor'. As in several other volumes of Handel's cantatas, this cantata follows directly upon 'Venne voglia ad amore' as if it were a continuation of it, though there is no suggestion of a connection in the autographs of the cantatas. Handel's note on 'Vedendo amor' reads 'continuatione della cantata precedente', confirming that 'Vedendo amor' is indeed to be considered as continuing 'Venne voglia ad amore'.

Obviously much work has still to be done on the Shaftesbury Collection. A more detailed study of the manuscript volumes by Winton Dean and the present writer is in preparation. The process of editing Handel's works, both for the Halle Edition and for other projects, will help in the assessment of individual volumes. Meanwhile Anthony Ashley Cooper, 4th Earl of Shaftesbury, has been established among the pantheon of major Handel collectors. We are indebted to him for forming a Collection that is comprehensive and in some respects unique, and we are indebted to his descendants for leaving it largely undisturbed and allowing us to benefit from it today.

Appendix 1
Catalogue of Handel Scores at St Giles's House (1761)

Two virtually identical copies of this document exist, both taken from a lost original. One of the notes added at the head indicates that in 1772 the original was 'Inserted at the end of the Catalogue of Books'—presumably the books in the library of St Giles's House—but neither the original catalogue of music nor the 'Catalogue of Books' itself can now be found at the house. Both the copies, one in the British Library and one in the Royal College of Music, appear to date from the nineteenth century, and must have been made after 1855, when the 7th Earl of Shaftesbury added to the original the two notes signed 'S.'. A third copy of the inventory, made by William Barclay Squire in 1926 and held with correspondence from him at St Giles's House, is simply a transcript of the RCM copy.

The British Library copy is fos. 98–102 of Add. MS 39864, a volume of papers formerly belonging to William Henry Husk (1814–87), librarian of the Sacred Harmonic Society. The papers were transferred to the Library's Department of Manuscripts from the Department of Printed Books in 1919. The transcript given here is taken from this copy.

The RCM copy is one of several insertions bound into a copy of Burney's *An Account of the Musical Performances in Westminster-Abbey, and the Pantheon, May 26th, 27th, 29th; and June the 3d, 5th, 1784. In Commemoration of Handel* (London 1785), where it appears between pages 44 and 45 of Burney's 'Sketch of the Life of Handel'. The volume was formerly in the library of the Sacred Harmonic Society, but its earlier provenance is not known. Its press-mark, formerly, XXXVIII.A.9, is now 61785.a.2.

f. 98r]

> *Musick. A copy of this is Inserted*
> *at the end of the Catalogue of Books.*
> *Jan^{ry}. 1772*

> *Memorandum of the Earl of Shaftesbury.*
> *Handel's Operas & Oratorios in M.S.S.*
> *bequeathed to my Grandfather in 1761.*
> *S. 1855*

f. 98v – blank]

f. 99r]

A Catalogue of Musick Composed by the late Mr Handel.
(In the Library at St. Giles's 1761)*

> * *Examined and found to contain 118*
> *distinct Volumes the whole of this list,*
> *Excepting the Messiah.*
> *S. Jan^{ry}. 1855.*

Oratorios.
  A.
No
1 Messiah.
2 Joseph.
3 Judas Maccabaeus.
4 Samson.
5 Alexander Balus.
6 Belshazzar.
7 Occasional.
8 Della Resurrezione.
9 Dell' Tempo e della Verita.

THE SHAFTESBURY COLLECTION

f. 99v]

B.

No
1 Susanna
2 Jeptha   in 3 parts each
3 Theodora

C.

No
1 Israel in Egypt.
2 Deborah.
3 Esther.
4 Athalia.
5 Belshazzar.
6 Alexander Balus.
7 Joshua.
8 Judas Macchabeus.
9 Solomon.
10 Susanna.
11 Theodora.
12 Jeptha.

f. 100r]

Anthems.
  C. (continued)

No
13 Three in large Folio
14 For Queen Caroline's Funeral.
15 Te Deum & Anthem
16 Four Anthems
17 For Q. Caroline's Funeral, 2d Part.

f. 100v]

Operas
  D.

1 Radamista & Rinaldo.
2 Porus & Ætius.
3 Arminius and Alcina.
4 Justin & Berenice.
5. Atalanta.
6. Ptolomy & Ariadne.
7. Agrippina.
8. Hercules.
9. Deidamia
10 Parthenope & Otho.
11 Orlando & Sosarmes.
12 Flavius & Floridant.
13 Xerxes & Faramondo.
14 Imeneo.
15 Esileno & Fernando.
16 Alcina.
17 Silla Metella e Lepido.

ANTHONY HICKS

f. 101r]
Operas
  D (continued)
  18   Radamisto.
  19   L'Allegro, il Penseroso ed il Moderato (2 parts)
  20   Tolomeo.
  21   Teseo.
  22   Ariodante.

f. 101v]
Operas
  E.
  No
  1   Ariadne.
  2   La Lucretia.
  3.   Muzio.
  4   Amadigi di Gaula.
  5   Pastor Fido.
  6   Prologue & Additions to Dº.
  7   Lotharius & Siroe
  8   Richard 1st & Admetus.
  9   Alexander & Scipio.
  10   Rodelinda & Tamerlane.
  11   Julius Cæsar.
  12   Additional Songs in Dº.
  13   Dº. in Il Triento del Tempo.
  14   Dº. in Richard & Admetus.
  15   Dº. in Lotharius & Siroe.
  16   Dº. in Alexander & Scipio.
  17   Dº. in Rodelinda & Tamerlane.

f. 102r]
Miscellaneous
  E. (continued)
  18   Cantatas
  19   Choice of Hercules.
  20   Lessons.
  21   Serenata for Queen Anne's Birth Day.
  22   Duetti.
  23   Te Deum et Jubilate.
  24   Te Deum.
  25   Jubilate.
  26   Te Deum.
  27   Song out of Jupiter in Argus.

f. 102v]
Miscellaneous
  F. (continued)
  No
  1   Water Musick.
  2   Act Tunes.
  3   Concerto per L'Organo.

102   THE SHAFTESBURY COLLECTION

     4   Song for St. Cecilia's Day (2 Parts.)
     5   Concerto
     6   Six Concertos for the Harpsicord
     7   Miscellaneous Musick
     8   Alexander's Feast (with a Head of the Author)
     9   Acis & Galatea. (2 parts)
    10   Additions to Dº.
    11   Choice of Hercules.
    12   Acis & Galatea.
    13   Concerto's (2 parts)
    14   Six Concertos for the organ &ᶜᵃ. (9 Parts)
    15   Seven Sonates, or Trios for 2 Violins &ᶜᵃ. (4 Dº.)
    16   Six Sonates à Deux Violons &ᶜᵃ. (4 Dº.)

Appendix 2
The Shaftesbury Handel Collection

This list of the contents of the Shaftesbury Collection of Handel scores follows the order of the 1761 catalogue, but identifies the content of volumes
more explicitly in modern terms, and shows which are manuscripts (titles in
small capitals) and which are printed (titles in italics). The identification of
the six lost volumes as manuscript or printed is deduced from their position
and the form of their titles on the 1761 list.

Copyists of manuscripts are identified, as far as possible, with the symbols
devised by J. P. Larsen and defined in his book *Handel's Messiah: Origins,
Compositions, Sources* (London, 1957). The particular issues represented by
the printed scores are identified by the numbers allocated to them in W. C.
Smith's *Handel: A Descriptive Catalogue of the Early Editions* (London, 1960;
2nd edn. Oxford 1970). Larsen's indicators of volume sizes are also used to
indicate the dimensions of each volume. With the addition of IIb (not used
by Larsen) to signify the normal size of a folio print, the approximate dimensions in centimetres signified by each indicator are:

I	29 × 23	II	22 × 27½	III	26 × 37	IV	26 × 42
Ia	29 × 27	IIa	24 × 30	IIIa	28½ × 39½	IVa	29 × 47
Ib	32 × 25	IIb	24 × 33				
Ic	37 × 26						

In 1987 all but two of the manuscript volumes formerly at St Giles's House
were transferred to the Gerald Coke Handel Collection, where, though clearly
marked as Shaftesbury volumes, they are distributed among the other manuscripts in the Collection; they do not have shelf-marks. (The Shaftesbury
MS score of *Joshua*, here listed as an additional item in section A, was already
in the Coke Collection.) The two manuscripts retained at St Giles's House,
together with the printed scores, are *Judas Maccabaeus* (reference A3), and the

volume under reference D19 containing the 1741 version of *L'Allegro* with *Comus*; the Coke Collection has photocopies of these two volumes. An em-dash in the first column indicates an item not listed in the 1761 catalogue.

1761 reference	Title	Size	Copyist(s) of MS	Issue of printed edition
	ORATORIOS			
A 1 [lost]	MESSIAH	[I?]	[?]	
2	JOSEPH AND HIS BRETHREN	I	Sm	
3	JUDAS MACCABAEUS	I	Sm	
4	SAMSON	I	Sm	
5	ALEXANDER BALUS	I	S8	
6	BELSHAZZAR	I	S5	
7	OCCASIONAL ORATORIO	I	S5	
8	LA RESURREZIONE	I	S1	
9	IL TRIONFO DEL TEMPO E DELLA VERITÀ (1737 version)	I	S1	
—	JOSHUA	I	?	
B 1 [3 vols.]	SUSANNA	I	Sm	
2 [3 vols.]	JEPHTHA	I	Sm	
3 [3 vols.]	THEODORA	I	Sm	
C 1	ISRAEL IN EGYPT	IV	S2	
2	DEBORAH	IV	S1	
3	ESTHER (1718 version with 1732 additions)	IV	S2	
4	ATHALIA	IV	S2	
5	*Belshazzar*	IIb		1
6	*Alexander Balus*	IIb		2
7	*Joshua*	IIb		1
8	*Judas Maccabaeus*	IIb		1
9	*Solomon*	IIb		1[a]
10	*Susanna*	IIb		1
11	*Theodora*	IIb		1
12	*Jephtha*	IIb		1
—	*Occasional Oratorio*	IIb		2
	ANTHEMS			
13 [3 vols.]	CHANDOS ANTHEMS (nos. 2–11)	IVa	?	
14	*Funeral Anthem*	IIb		1
15	DETTINGEN TE DEUM and ANTHEM	III	Sm	
16	CORONATION ANTHEMS	III	?	
17	*Funeral Anthem*	IIb		2
—	FUNERAL ANTHEM	IV	S2	
	OPERAS			
D 1 [lost]	{ *Radamisto*	[IIb?]		[?]
	{ *Rinaldo*			[?]
2	{ *Poro*	IIb		1
	{ *Ezio*			1

THE SHAFTESBURY COLLECTION

1761 reference	Title	Size	Copyist(s) of MS	Issue of printed edition
	OPERAS (*cont.*)			
D 3	{ *Arminio*	IIb		I[b]
	{ *Alcina*			9
4	{ *Giustino*	IIb		I
	{ *Berenice*			I
5	*Atalanta*	IIb		I
6	{ *Tolomeo*	IIb		6
	{ *Arianna*			5
7	AGRIPPINA	II	S2	
8	*Hercules*	IIb		I
9	*Deidamia*	IIb		2
10	{ *Partenope*	IIb		2[c]
	{ *Ottone*			3
11	{ *Orlando*	IIb		2
	{ *Sosarme*			4
12	{ *Flavio*	IIb		3
	{ *Floridante*			4[d]
13	{ *Serse*	IIb		I
	{ *Faramondo*			I
14	IMENEO	I	S2	
15	RODRIGO	I	S1	
16	ALCINA	I	S2	
17	SILLA	I	S2	
18	RADAMISTO	I	S4	
19 [2 vols.]	L'ALLEGRO, IL PENSEROSO ED IL MODERATO (1740 version)	I	S4, ?	
	L'ALLEGRO, IL PENSEROSO ED IL MODERATO (1741 version) with COMUS (HWV 44)	I	S1, ?	
20	TOLOMEO	I	S4, S2	
21	TESEO	I	S4	
22	ARIODANTE	I	S1, S2	
E 1	ARIANNA	I	S1	
2	LA LUCRETIA (with 20 ARIAS, 1711–17)	I	S4	
3	MUZIO SCEVOLA (Act 3)	I	S2	
4	AMADIGI (with MARCH, HWV 345)	I	S4	
5	IL PASTOR FIDO (mixed version, 1712/1734)	I	S4, S1	
6	PROLOGUE and ADDITIONS to IL PASTOR FIDO	I	S2	
7	{ *Lotario*	IIb		I[e]
	{ *Siroe*			I
8	{ *Riccardo Primo*	IIb		I[f]
	{ *Admeto*			I

1761 reference		Title	Size	Copyist(s) of MS	Issue of printed edition
		OPERAS (*cont.*)			
E	9	{ *Alessandro*	IIb		I
		{ *Scipione*			I
	10	{ *Rodelinda*	IIb		I
		{ *Tamerlano*			I[g]
	11	*Giulio Cesare*	8vo.		I
	12	ADDITIONS to GIULIO CESARE	II	S2	
	13	ADDITIONS to IL TRIONFO DEL TEMPO (excerpts from 1707 version)	I	Sm	
	14	ADDITIONS to RICCARDO PRIMO and ADMETO	II	S2	
	15	ADDITIONS to LOTARIO and SIROE	II	S2	
	16	ADDITIONS to ALESSANDRO and SCIPIONE	II	S2	
	17	ADDITIONS to RODELINDA and TAMERLANO	II	S2	
		MISCELLANEOUS			
	18	CANTATAS (49)	I	S4	
	19 [lost]	THE CHOICE OF HERCULES	[I?]	[?]	
	20	*Lessons (Keyboard music)*:	I		
		{ *Suites de Pieces*, vol. 1			6
		{ *Suites de Pieces*, vol. 2			5
		{ *Six Fugues or Voluntarys*			I
	21	BIRTHDAY ODE FOR QUEEN ANNE (with Op 3/4)	II	S4	
	22	DUETTI (12 duets, 2 trios)	I	Sm, S4	
	23	*Utrecht Te Deum and Jubilate*	IIb		2
	24	CAROLINE TE DEUM (HWV 280)	II	S2	
	25	JUBILATE (= CHANDOS ANTHEM no. 1)	I	S2	
	26	CHANDOS TE DEUM (HWV 281)	I	S4	
	27	JUPITER IN ARGOS (excerpts)	I	S4	
	—	IL PARNASSO IN FESTA (excerpts)	I	S2	
	—	SEMELE	I	Sm	
F	1	WATER MUSIC	II	S2	
	2	ACT TUNES (for THE ALCHEMIST HWV 43)	I	S2	
	3 [lost]	CONCERTO PER L'ORGANO	[I?]	[?]	
	4 [2 vols.]	SONG FOR ST CECILIA'S DAY	I	S4	
		SONG FOR ST CECILIA'S DAY	I	S2	

1761 reference	Title	Size	Copyist(s) of MS	Issue of printed edition
	MISCELLANEOUS (*cont.*)			
F 5	CONCERTO (in D, HWV 335a)	IIIa	S8	
6	*Concertos and Sonatas*:	IIa		
	⎰ *Six Concertos for . . . Organ* [Op. 4] (keyboard part),			5
	A Second Set of Six Concertos . . .			1ᵍ
	for Organ (keyboard part), *Solos . . . with a Thorough Bass* [Op. 1]			3
7	MISCELLANEOUS MUSIC (excerpts from Partenope, Alcina, Arianna, Poro, Sosarme, Orlando, Atalanta)	II	S1	
8	*Alexander's Feast*	IIb		1
9 [2 vols.; 1 lost]	ACIS AND GALATEA (1718)	I	S2	
	ACIS AND GALATEA [another copy?]	[I]	[?]	
10	ADDITIONS to ACIS AND GALATEA (excerpts from 1732–6 versions)	I	S2	
11	*The Choice of Hercules*	IIb		1
12	*Acis and Galatea*	IIb		6
13 [2 vols.]	CONCERTOS (Opus 4 with HWV 303, 318, 425)	II	S1, ?	
14 [9 vols.; 1 lost]	*Six Concertos for the Organ* [Op. 4] (8 part-books: *Basso Ripieno* missing)	IIa		4
15 [4 vols.]	*Seven Sonatas or Trios* [Op. 5] (4 part-books including 2 copies of *Violoncello e Cimbalo* part)	IIa		1
16 [4 vols.]	*VI Sonates à Deux Violons* [Op. 2] (4 part-books including 2 copies of *Basso* part)	IIa		3

[a] without Privilege but with advertisement leaf
[b] without list of subscribers
[c] without additional song
[d] with 5 additional songs (as Smith no. 2) without separate title-page and flute part.
[e] with Walsh sticker (as Smith no. 6)
[f] with Walsh sticker (not recorded by Smith)
[g] without Privilege

Summary of Volume Counts

	MS	Printed	Total
Listed 1761; still extant	66	48	114
Not listed 1761, but extant	4	1	5
Listed 1761; now lost	4	2	6
TOTAL	74	51	125
At St Giles's House (1992)	2	49	51
In Gerald Coke Handel Collection (1992)	68	—	68
TOTAL	70	49	119

6

The Barrett Lennard Collection

DONALD BURROWS

THE great collections of manuscript copies of Handel's music formed in the eighteenth century by such people as Elizabeth Legh, Charles Jennens, and Bernard Granville are dual testimony to the originators' devotion to Handel's music and to their desire for a distinctive personal library: these enthusiasts wished to own a collected edition of Handel's works in an age when such an enterprise could not have been expected of London's music publishers. Sometimes the identity of the original collector is disguised by the fact that the collection is now known by the name of a later owner, who may have added new materials to the received collection: thus, for example, 'the Newman Flower Collection' and 'the Aylesford Collection' describe entities that are not the same as the foundation corpus of material collected by Jennens. The problem of a collection's identity occurs in a particularly acute form in the case of the Lennard Collection. On one hand, the sixty-seven manuscript volumes now in the Fitzwilliam Museum, Cambridge, (MU.MS. 789–855; see App. 2) that have been conveniently described as 'The Lennard Collection' or 'The Barrett-Lennard Collection' in modern Handelian literature bear the name of a fairly recent owner, while the identity of the original collector remains unknown: on the other hand, these volumes formed only a part of the (now dispersed) library of Henry Barrett Lennard.[1] Since the manuscripts now in Cambridge are certainly the most significant part of Lennard's Collection, they will be the prime concern of this article, but attention will also be given to other manuscripts from Lennard's Handelian library.

[1] This form of the name, without hyphen, is found in Lennard's bookplates and signature, though it is sometimes given in ref. books as Barrett-Lennard (which is probably the strictly correct form), and appears thus in his obituary, *MT* 40 (Oct. 1899), 690. I retain Henry's preferred form in this article to distinguish his line of the family from that of his namesake. On the history of the family and the family name, see T. Barrett-Lennard, 3rd Bart., *An Account of the Families of Lennard and Barrett* (London 1908); also E. Brydges, *Collins's Peerage of England*, vi (London, 1812) under 'Brand, Baroness Dacre', 558–90, and

[*See opposite page for n. 1 cont.*]

DONALD BURROWS 109

In dealing with the principal Lennard Collection I shall first trace backwards what is known of its provenance, and then deal with the Collection's contents and possible date of origination. The sixty-seven volumes, contained within a book-case that is reputed to have been owned by Handel, were presented to the Fitzwilliam Museum in 1902: the acquisition was arranged through Arthur Henry Mann, organist of King's College, Cambridge, from Francis Barrett Lennard, who wished it to be regarded as a donation by his late father Henry.[2] At this point it is necessary to dispose of one confusion concerning the provenance of the Collection. The date of Henry Barrett Lennard's death, at which the Collection would have passed to his son, is some- times given as 1870,[3] but this is the result of a confusion between two men of the same name. The Revd Henry Barrett-Lennard, born in 1798 and fourth son of Thomas, 1st Baronet, did indeed die at Fontainebleau in 1870:[4] he had connections with the University of Cambridge, but he was not the owner of the Handel manuscripts. The Henry Barrett Lennard with whom we are concerned was born in 1818, third son of John Barrett Lennard, Chief Clerk to the Privy Council Office, and this Henry died at the end of August 1899.[5] John Barrett Lennard was the second son of Thomas 1st Baronet, so his son Henry was the elder Henry's nephew.[6] There is no documentary evidence that the elder Henry ever owned the Handel Collection and we can discount him from further consideration. The younger Henry seems to have had a commercial career as a bill broker in the City of London. He is sometimes referred to as being 'of Hampstead', perhaps in order to avoid confusion with his namesake. One of the two forms of his bookplate gives his address as 12 York Gate, Regent's Park: this was his family home, from which Henry Barrett Lennard moved

---

S. Lee (ed.), *Dictionary of National Biography*, xxxiii (London, 1893), under 'Lennard, Francis, Fourteenth Lord Dacre'.

[2] Indicated in a letter from Francis Barrett-Lennard (from Hove, Sussex, 11 Mar. [1902]) to the director of the Fitzwilliam Museum: Cfm MU. MS. 2749. See also the brief report of the collection's acquisition in the article by F. G. E[dwards], *MT* 43 (Apr. 1903), 232.

[3] See, e.g. the entry describing the provenance of the Handel bookcase in J. Huskinson *et al.*, *Handel and the Fitzwilliam* [no ed. named] (Cambridge, 1974), 31.

[4] See the entries for 'Lennard, (Rev.) Henry Barrett' in J. Foster, *Alumni Oxonienses* 1715–1886 (London, 1888) and J. A. Venn, *Alumni Cantabrigienses*, pt. II (Cambridge, 1951).

[5] See the entry for 'Lennard, Henry Barrett' in G. F. Russell Barker and A. H. Stenning, *The Record of Old Westminsters*, ii (London, 1928). This gives the date of his death as 30 Aug. 1899: 'Obituary', *MT* 40, says that he died in Brighton on 31 Aug.

[6] I am indebted to Revd Sir Hugh Barrett-Lennard (6th Bt.) and Revd John Pollock for clarifying this relationship from the family's records: unfortunately T. Barrett-Lennard's *Families of Lennard and Barrett* does not give comprehensive treatment to the 19-cent. branches of the family, though in the preface he refers to the younger Henry as his 'cousin'. Henry jun. married back into the family, marrying his cousin Elizabeth, the daughter of George Barrett-Lennard, in 1845.

110   THE BARRETT LENNARD COLLECTION

after his father's death in 1856, living subsequently in Marylebone and then (from 1876) in Well Walk, Hampstead.[7]

The situation immediately before the reception of the Lennard Collection at the Fitzwilliam Museum is revealed in a letter from A. H. Mann to the Museum's director, written on 5 March 1902 from Mann's house at King's Field, Cambridge (Cfm MU.MS. 2748):

Some time ago, a well known Handelian Scholar by name M[r] Henry Barrett Lennard died at Hampstead.[8] He left a very valuable MS Collection of between 60 and 70 vols. of Handel's works, chiefly written by the well known amanuensis Smith. Also a beautiful mahogany book-case, which was the property of Handel himself and in which Mr Lennard kept the Handel books.

Since the death of Mr Lennard I have had these books and case at my house where they are now.

A condition of the donation was that Mann should have the privilege of taking volumes from the Collection out of the Museum. He prepared a catalogue of them with the same meticulous care that is to be seen in his descriptions of the Handel autographs in the general catalogue of music in the Fitzwilliam Museum published in 1893:[9] in view of the specialized nature of the Lennard Collection, it is perhaps not surprising that his catalogue was never published, but remains in manuscript at the Museum today.[10] The collection of Handel manuscripts, as received, occupied only the upper part of the so-called 'Handel book case',[11] whose lower drawer and cupboard were used from time to time by the Museum to store other music, but as far as can be discerned none of these miscellaneous materials had come from Lennard.[12] So

[7] John Barrett Lennard, Henry's father, lived at 9 Queen Anne's Gate from 1823 to 1836 and at 12 York Gate, Regent's Park from 1836 until his death in 1856. Henry, whose own wife had died the year before, moved successively to 59 Upper Berkeley Street, Marylebone (1856–60), 29 Cumberland Street (subsequently Great Cumberland Place), Marylebone (1860–76), and Well Walk, Hampstead (from 1876). At Well Walk Lennard lived successively at Nos. 3 and 7: these are 18-cent. houses in the old part of Hampstead. I am indebted to John Greenacombe for these details.

[8] 'Obituary', *MT* 40, reported that he died in Brighton.

[9] J. A. Fuller-Maitland and A. H. Mann, *Catalogue of the Music in the Fitzwilliam Museum, Cambridge* (London, 1893): Mann's descriptions of the Handel autographs comprise pp. 159–227.

[10] A. H. Mann, *Catalogue of the Barrett-Lennard Collection* (MS, Keeper's Room, Fitzwilliam Museum). The catalogue remained as loose MS sheets, kept in the drawer of the Handel bookcase, until they were bound in Oct. 1979. Mann's expertise was naturally limited by the state of knowledge on Handel sources a cent. ago: his identifications of copyists are unreliable and his descriptions of watermarks vague.

[11] The exact provenance of the bookcase prior to 1832 is unknown. For a description of the bookcase see Huskinson *et al.*, *Handel*, 31; a picture of the bookcase (then in Lennard's possession) appeared in *MT* Handel suppl. (14 Dec. 1893), 31.

[12] I am grateful to Mr Paul Woudhuysen, Keeper of the Manuscripts and Printed Books at the Museum, for this information, and for drawing to my attention the letters from Mann and Francis Barrett-Lennard.

DONALD BURROWS 111

the 'collection unit' with which we are dealing consists only of the bookcase and sixty-seven manuscript volumes.

That unit can be chased back, through a succession of owners in the nineteenth century, to Thomas Greatorex. Greatorex was Joah Bates's successor as conductor of the Concert of Ancient Music from 1793 and, in association with William Knyvett and Samuel Harrison, a director of the revived Vocal Concerts from 1801.[13] He was appointed organist of Westminster Abbey in 1819 and the first professor of organ and pianoforte at the Royal Academy of Music in 1822. Greatorex died in July 1831, and the bookcase with his manuscripts appears as lot 252 in the sale of his library in April 1832.[14] In a prefatory note to the catalogue the auctioneer stated that 'the collection is in the same entire state as when examined by him at the Residence in Norton Street' which was presumably where the book-case was to be found up to that date. Its subsequent travels were among people with Westminster Abbey connections. At the Greatorex sale the bookcase and manuscripts were bought by Dr John Ireland, Dean of Westminster, for 115 guineas.[15] Ireland died in 1842, and the Handel materials passed to John Leman Brownsmith, a Lay Vicar of Westminster Abbey: it is uncertain whether they were a bequest or whether Brownsmith had previously received them from Ireland as a gift or by purchase.

Brownsmith was an organist, and indeed it seems that he would have succeeded Greatorex at the Abbey but for the senior claim of James Turle.[16] In 1848 Brownsmith was appointed organist to the Sacred Harmonic Society, and he officiated as organist at all the Crystal Palace Handel Festivals between 1857 (the first) and 1865, the year before his death. The Lennard volume containing Handel's Organ Concertos Op. 4 includes annotations in Brownsmith's hand which record that he played Op. 4 No. 4 'with orchestral accompaniments' at Exeter Hall in July 1844 and again at Hanover Square

---

[13] See the bibliographical entry on Greatorex by W. H. Husk in *Grove*.

[14] *Bibliotheca Musica: A catalogue of the valuable musical library of the late T. Greatorex, Esq. F.R.S. F.L.S. . . . which, by order of the family, will be sold by auction, by Mr. Watson, at the King's Concert Rooms, Hanover Square, On Tuesday, April 3rd, 1832, and following days, at Twelve O'Clock.* Lot 252 is described on p. 21. (see Illus. 1).

[15] i.e. £121. 15s; 115 gs. is the sum named in 'Obituary', *MT* 40, and in the contemporary report on the sale in *Harmonicon*, (1832), 118. There is one other authoritative report of the collection's provenance, in Schoelcher's catalogue (see below, n. 27): this gives the figure as £150. Ireland's interest in the MSS is perhaps rather surprising, since only two years later he attempted, in the name of the Dean and Chapter, to block George Smart's plans for the Handel Commemoration to be held at Westminster Abbey (Letters of 14 and 21 Feb. 1834, Westminster Abbey Muniments 57792, 57794).

[16] See W. H. Husk's biographical entry for Brownsmith in *Grove*, and the short notice in *MT* 12 (Oct. 1866), 388.

THE BARRETT LENNARD COLLECTION

Rooms in May 1847.[17] He performed from the volume itself—a copy by S1[18]—and the manuscript bears his organ registrations in pencil. The bookcase and manuscripts were purchased from Brownsmith by Lennard, reputedly for the same sum as Ireland had paid at the Greatorex sale. The date of Lennard's purchase is not known, but it must have been within the period between 1847, the year of Brownsmith's latest annotation, and December 1855, when Lennard's Collection is mentioned in a letter from Elizabeth Mason to Lady Augusta Hall.[19] The volumes carry Lennard's second bookplate—i.e. the one that bears his name without the York Gate address—but no definite conclusions about the date of acquisition can be drawn from this.

While, from the scrupulous perspective of modern ideas about conservation of materials, we may be somewhat critical of Brownsmith for scribbling over a significant eighteenth-century manuscript, the present-day scholar may nevertheless be grateful to him for signing his name. One of the problems facing anyone who subjects volumes from the Lennard Collection to critical examination is that they contain a variety of annotations whose origins are difficult to determine, especially in view of the succession of owners, known and unknown, that preceded Lennard. My impression, and the result of a complete survey of the Collection that has involved examining every page, is that none of the annotations need be taken seriously as recording essential information committed to paper during or soon after Handel's lifetime:[20] this applies to the sporadic outbreaks of pencil ornamentation

[17] MS 836, annotations on pp. 54, 55. The phrasing of the first annotation is ambiguous, but it may be read as implying that Brownsmith reorchestrated the concerto or supplemented Handel's scoring with 'additional accompaniments' for other instruments.

[18] Sigla for copyists are from J. P. Larsen: *Handel's 'Messiah': Origins, Composition, Sources* (London, 1957; 2nd edn. with additions and minor revisions, New York, 1972).

[19] Letter dated 13 Dec. 1855, part of a collection of letters (now in GB-BENcoke) relating to the sale of the Granville Collection. The earliest published ref. to Lennard's collection is in V. Schoelcher, *The Life of Handel* (London, 1857), where the 'List of Works consulted by the Author' (p. ix) includes 'Collection of the Works of Handel, copied by J. C. Smith, Esq., his amanuensis, now in the possession of Henry Barrett Lennard, Esq.' Refs. to Lennard's Collection are also found in Handel biographies published later in the 19th cent.: Mrs J. Marshall, *George Frederick Handel, 1685–1759* (London, n. d. [*New Grove* and Lbl catalogue give 1883]), 136, and W. S. Rockstro, *The Life of George Frederick Handel* (London, 1883), 429. The latter also identifies the works by Handel that were represented in the Lennard Collection vols. (table, pp. 432–9, see n. 63 below), but erroneously describes the owner as 'W. Barrett Lennard, Esq.' (p. 432).

[20] e.g. in MSS 795 (*L'Allegro*), 811 (Anthems), 823 (*Alcina*), 827 (*Giulio Cesare*) and 844 (*Messiah*—ornamentation in choruses as well as arias). Other practical markings in pencil include tutti directions in MS 813 and slurs to string parts in MS 821. I renew my thanks to Mr Woudhuysen for arranging generous access to the Collection and to the staff of the Butler Reading Room (Helen Godfrey, Elizabeth Orton) for their labours in bringing the volumes from the bookcase for examination.

DONALD BURROWS

in the music as well as to the verbal comments in various hands.[21] Nevertheless, it is tantalizing to be faced with additions whose periods of origin, let alone the identities of their authors, are uncertain. It is not even possible, at present, to identify with certainty the hands of those who provided lists of contents on the flyleaves of many volumes. Forty-two[22] volumes have lists of contents on front flyleaves written in a hand that A. H. Mann identified as that of the singer James Bartleman (1769–1821), but they seem more likely to have been written by Robert Turle, the younger brother of James Turle the organist who succeeded Greatorex at Westminster Abbey.[23] And even if they are in Robert Turle's hand, it is impossible to know whether they were written in Turle's youth (while the manuscripts were owned by Greatorex) or in his old age (when they were in Lennard's possession).[24] Contents pages in some other volumes were added in another four different styles of handwriting, two of which may (or may not) have been perpetrated by Lennard at different periods.[25] None of the contents pages was written by any of the main music-copyists,[26] and it seems likely that most, if not all, of the contents lists were written in the nineteenth century.

Of the history of the bookcase and the Collection prior to Greatorex's sale we have only the sketchiest knowledge. According to Schoelcher's description of the Lennard Collection in his unpublished catalogue of Handel's works,[27] the bookcase and its contents had passed from Handel to the John Christopher Smiths, father and son, and at the death of the younger Smith 'it came to public auction.

[21] e.g. in MSS 797, 798, 803, 813, 814, 824, 830, 840, 841, 844, 851, 855: this list is probably not exhaustive and excludes the 'engravers' marks' in MSS 793, 804, 806, 807. The author of most of the pencil annotations in MS 798 is identified later in this article.
[22] MSS 789, 790, 793, 795, 796, 798, 800, 801, 803–9, 814, 816, 818, 819, 822, 823, 825, 827, 829–31, 833–7, 841, ?842, 843, 847–54.
[23] Mann's identification (in his MS *Catalogue of the Barrett-Lennard Collection*) was probably based on the similarity of the handwriting on these contents pages to that of Cfm MU.MS. 1452, *A Catalogue of the Musical Library of the late Lord Viscount Fitzwilliam . . . by James Bartleman*, but below the title this has 'Robert Turle Scrip[sit]'.
[24] Robert Turle (1804–77) was organist of Armagh Cathedral 1823–77. He may have lived in London prior to taking up this appointment, and after his retirement he certainly visited his brother at Westminster: see F. Bridge, *A Westminster Pilgrim* (London, 1918), 70–1.
[25] Style I: MSS 792, 794, 802 (?possibly Lennard); Style II: MS 799; Style III: MSS 810–13; Style IV: MSS 846, 855 (?possibly Lennard). I have compared these with the hands of Brownsmith or Ireland in docs. from the Westminster Abbey Muniments, with negative results. I thank the staff of the Abbey Library and Muniment Room for their assistance in this matter. The remaining Lennard vols. do not include lists of contents.
[26] The only possible exception is the contents page to MS 699, which might just be in the hand of the music-copyist. In general the music-copyists paginated their own assignments: the 'Robert Turle' hand added paginations to some volumes that originally lacked them.
[27] A copy of Schoelcher's catalogue, from the collection of Julian Marshall, partly translated into English and partly in the original French, is Lbl R.M.18.b.2, where the section on the Lennard Collection, quoted here, occurs at fos. 31–2.

THE BARRETT LENNARD COLLECTION

Mr Saml Harrison, music-publisher, and Mr Greatorex who conducted the festival at York 1829, leader of orchestra, encountered each other there, each determined to be the purchaser. In order to avoid a ruinous competition, they agreed to buy it and keep it between them on the condition that it should belong to the survivor.' The outline of the last part of the story seems plausible: Greatorex was associated with Samuel Harrison (who was a professional tenor singer, not a music-publisher)[28] at the Vocal Concerts and, furthermore, Greatorex has a known track record of visiting sales to purchase music. At the house sale that followed Joah Bates's death in 1801, Greatorex purchased Bates's set of Arnold's Handel edition, as well as a double bass, a steel fender, and fire-irons.[29] The same sale included a large bookcase, but it does not seem to have been the Handel bookcase.[30] As yet, I have failed to find a London sale catalogue before Greatorex's that includes the Handel bookcase and manuscripts. Harrison died in 1812 so, if Schoelcher's anecdote is correct, it seems very likely that Greatorex and Harrison acquired the Collection in the first decade of the nineteenth century.[31]

As Schoelcher himself recognized, the earlier part of the Collection's reputed provenance is very uncertain.[32] In the absence of firm evidence, the link in the chain between Handel/Smith and Greatorex/Harrison must be viewed with caution. An alternative provenance is suggested by a single sentence in Burney's 'List of Handel's Works' in his

[28] See the entries for 'Samuel Harrison' (by W. H. Husk) and 'Vocal Concerts' (by Charles Mackeson) in *Grove*. Schoelcher's identification of Harrison as a music-publisher was probably the result of confusion with James Harrison (Harrison & Co. were publishers of several early editions of Handel's music).

[29] *A Catalogue of a part of the household furniture . . . of Joah Bates, Esq., Dec., at his late dwelling house, on the west side of John Street, at the back of Gray's-Inn Gardens, Bedford Row, which will be sold by auction, by Mr. Christie, on the premises, on Saturday June the 27th, 1801, at twelve o'clock.* The auctioneer's annotated copy of the catalogue records Greatorex's purchases as follows: 'Front Drawing Room[:] [Lot] 65 Handel's Works, in score, by Dr. Arnold, 180 numbers, compleat on imperial Paper—a fine and perfect set £18.18 Greatorex [*ink annotation*: 'At 1- [? first] Mr. Mumford Greville St Hatton Garden';] [Lot] 66 A remarkable fine-toned well known double Bass, with bow in a case £26.5 d[itto]. Parlor[:] [Lot] 74 A cut steel fender, fire irons and brush ['and brush' *deleted*] £1.5 Greatorex.' These extracts are quoted by courtesy of Christie's and I thank Jeremy Rex-Parkes, (Christie's archives) for facilitating access to the annotated copy.

[30] The description from the catalogue is: 'Study[:], [lot] 101 An elegant mahogany library bookcase, with Chinese glazed doors in the upper part, the bottom doors panelled, 8 feet 9 high, 8 feet 9 wide. £28.7 Griffin £5.5 [?deposit].' The Handel bookcase measures approximately 8 ft. 3 in. high by 4 ft. wide.

[31] In a letter dated 22 Dec. 1857, Schoelcher referred to the auction sale of Robert Smith's collection and stated that 'It is from there that Mr Lennard's Collection proceeds' (Lbl Eg. MS 2953, fo. 108^r). This seems very doubtful. There is nothing in the catalogue of Smith's sale (18–19 May 1813, copy Lbl Hirsch IV. 1091) that fits the description of the MSS from the Lennard Collection: in any case, the sale took place after Harrison's death. Had Robert Smith ever owned the Lennard MSS, he would almost certainly have added his bookplates to them.

[*See opposite page for n. 32*]

Handel Commemoration volume:[33] 'The late Mr. Walsh, of Catharine-Street, in the Strand, purchased of Handel, for publication, transcripts of the Manuscript scores of almost all the works he had composed in England; and Mr. Wright, of the same place, successor to Mr. Walsh, is still in possession of these Manuscripts, many of which have never yet been published.' Walsh must, of course, have received some sort of musical copy from Handel for the works he published, and a document, now lost, supposedly recorded Walsh's payments for such copy.[34] It is very doubtful that the Lennard manuscripts constituted copy-texts for any of Walsh's editions, but they may have had some connection with his successors. The comprehensive nature of the contents of the Lennard *Messiah* score (Cfm MU.MS. 844), for example, is suspiciously close to that of the edition by Randall and Abell in 1767,[35] and the basso continuo figurings added to one of the anthem volumes (Cfm MU.MS. 811) by a later hand may be connected with the preparation of an edition of Handel's anthems by Wright and Wilkinson in 1784.[36]

Four of the Lennard scores—those for *Theodora, Susanna, Deborah,* and *Solomon* (Cfm MU.MSS. 793, 804, 806, 807)—bear marks and annotations that seem to derive from the use of the manuscripts by editors and music-engravers in the preparation of Wright's scores of these works, published in 1784 and 1787.[37] The Wright editions reused and adapted plates from Walsh's previous publications of airs from the oratorios, as far as possible, adding new plates for choruses, recitatives, and additional airs as required. The following examples will suffice to show the type of evidence that links the Lennard

---

[32] 'It passes, upon not very conclusive evidence, for having belonged to Handel himself, but the costliness of the case & binding makes this very doubtful' (R.M.18.b.2, fo.31). In another part of the description, Schoelcher seems to have misunderstood the statement that Handel's 'musick books' passed from Smith (sen.) to his son: he remarks that Smith jun. himself had no son, and refers to the statements by W. Coxe in *Anecdotes of George Frederick Handel and John Christopher Smith* (London, 1799), 6, about the transmission of the younger Smith's collection of music to Lady Rivers, his 'daughter-in-law' (*recte* stepdaughter).

[33] *An Account of the Musical Performances . . . in Commemoration of Handel* (London, 1785), 44.

[34] G. A. Macfarren, *Sketch of the Life of Handel* (London, 1859), 22, rep. in O. E. Deutsch: *Handel: A Documentary Biography* (London, 1955), 468, and *Händel-Handbuch*, iv. 301.

[35] *Messiah: An Oratorio in Score*: see W. C. Smith, *Handel: A Descriptive Catalogue of the Early Editions* (2nd ed., Oxford, 1970), 124. The contents of the MS and the printed ed. may be easily compared in Schedule A of W. Shaw: *A Textual and Historical Companion to Handel's 'Messiah'* (London, 1965).

[36] *The Complete Score of Ten Anthems*: see W. C. Smith, *Catalogue*, 149. My comparison of the music text of 'Let God arise', HWV 256b, had already led me to this conclusion in 1983: see D. Burrows, 'Walsh's Editions of Handel's Op. 1–5' in C. Hogwood and R. Luckett (eds.), *Music in Eighteenth-Century England* (Cambridge, 1983), 95 n. 27.

[37] See W. C. Smith, *Catalogue*, 145 (*Theodora*, 1787), 144 (*Susanna*, 1784), 103 (*Deborah*, 1784), and 143 (*Solomon*, 1787).

116 THE BARRETT LENNARD COLLECTION

manuscripts to the Wright editions,[38] and the conclusions about the publisher's working procedures that can be drawn from the evidence.

1. Preparation of new plates: In many choruses small numbers in the manuscripts appear above and below the stave systems: these were added by the engraver when calculating the layout for the printed pages, and coincide with breaks in the systems or pages of the Wright editions. Examples: *Theodora* 'He saw the lovely youth' (final section), MS 793 pp. 135–8 marked for Wright edition pp. 136–9; *Solomon* 'Praise the Lord with harp and tongue' and 'The name of the wicked', MS 807 pp. 318–48 and 363–80 marked for Wright pp. 265–98 and 309–26 (the last in red crayon, remainder in pencil).[39] Sometimes recitatives are also similarly marked—for example 'O Barak' from *Deborah*, MS 806 p. 45 marked for Wright p. 46: the numbers indicate the ends of the stave-systems. Other tell-tale signs of the printer's activity include additional barlines in choruses to clarify alignment (e.g. MS 806 pp. 153–62) and specific cues in MS 793 (*Theodora*) such as 'to be engrav'd' (p. 10), 'not to be engraved' (p. 19) 'before "When sunk" No. 1 Third Part' (p. 142) and many similar. Many of Theodora's recitatives in MS 793, which have the voice part in the soprano clef, also carry the direction 'Two Notes lower in the Treble Clef', accompanied by the over-writing of new clefs and note-heads in heavy ink on the music itself.

2. Adaptations and additions based on previous Walsh material: MSS 806 and 807 have many figurings to the bass line which are clearly not in the hands of the original copyists and were almost certainly added when Wright's edition was being prepared, for the heavy figuring was reproduced in the edition.[40] Taking the air 'Golden columns' from *Solomon* as an example, the engraver apparently took the plates from Walsh's edition[41] and checked them with reference to MS 807 pp. 313–18, adding extra basso continuo figures from his copy-text where necessary: the amended plates became pp. 261–4 of Wright's edition. (The situation appears to be further complicated by some pencil marks in this movement—extra dynamics, string bowings— which were not reproduced in Wright's edition, and may well

---

[38] The MSS have been checked against exemplars of the earliest Walsh and Wright eds., as identified from Smith, *Catalogue*, as follows: *Deborah* Walsh no. 1, Wright no. 7; *Solomon* Walsh no. 1, Wright no. 3; *Susanna* Walsh no. 1, Wright no. 2; *Theodora* Walsh no. 1, Wright no. 4.

[39] In MS 804 (*Susanna*) similar pencil-marks are found in the choruses 'Righteous heav'n' (final section) and 'Oh Joachim'.

[40] This additional figuring runs through recitatives and choruses as well, and was printed by Wright.

[41] *Solomon an Oratorio*, W. C. Smith, *Catalogue*, 142, no. 1, 68–71.

have been added by a later owner.) The collation of musical texts seems to have been done quite carefully: an error in the viola part at bar 134 of 'Ev'ry sight these eyes behold' was corrected in MS 807, presumably in order to prevent Wright's engraver from misguidedly amending the Walsh plates, which had the correct reading at that point. Wright seems to have adopted a slightly different procedure in his preparation of *Theodora*, for MS 793 does not carry the additional copious figuring of the bass part that characterizes MSS 806 and 807. The situation with *Theodora* can be best illustrated from Didymus's air 'Sweet rose and lily' and the preceding recitative ('Or lull'd with grief'). On p. 119 of MS 793 Wright's text editor deleted 'Scene 5' and the stage direction 'at a distance, the Vizor of his helmet closed' before the recitative, and neither of these features appears in Wright's edition.[42] A locating cue was added at the same time—'at the top of the Old Page 59'. 'Sweet rose and lily' indeed began on p. 59 of Walsh's edition of the songs from *Theodora* but, even after the removal of the original heading ('Sung by Sigr Guadagni'), there was not enough room at the head of the plate to accommodate the recitative, nor was there sufficient room at the end of the previous page of the printed score to insert the recitative there. So clearly the aria, preceded by the recitative, had to be re-engraved afresh: this plate became p. 119 of Wright's score. Although the engraver followed the continuity cue from MS 793, he used Walsh's edition as his musical copy-text, following the heavily-figured version that he found there in preference to the sparsely-figured version in MS 793.

It seems very likely that Harman Wright owned the Lennard manuscripts by 1784: but whether they came to him by succession from Walsh, and if so what need Walsh had had for them, are issues that cannot at present be investigated for lack of evidence.

What we can do, however, is to examine the volumes themselves to see what their musical contents and their physical characteristics— bindings, paper and rastra types—can reveal about the history of the Collection. Fortunately, most of the handsome original eighteenth-century bindings have survived intact,[43] though perhaps the use of the word 'original' could be questioned here, since the music may have been loosely bound in the first instance and only put into

---

[42] This circumstance may explain their omission from HG viii, for which Chrysander seems to have used Wright's edn. as a basis for his copy-text. Scene divisions and stage directions were, by contrast, included in Arnold's edn. of *Theodora*.

[43] There has inevitably been some cracking of spine back-strips and detachment of cover boards.

THE BARRETT LENNARD COLLECTION

proper boards at a later date. Volumes in the Collection have various different and distinctive styles of bindings, some of them apparently rather later than others. Appendix 1 lists the manuscripts by binding style,[44] and volumes in each style are grouped according to paper characteristics. Within each group, the volumes are listed in composition order of musical works: the groups themselves are arranged in an order suggested by the flow in the paper characteristics.

In summary, I have drawn the following conclusions. The forty-nine volumes with Binding Style A (to which may be added sections of MS 798, to be discussed below) seem to form a coherent foundation collection, probably copied, according to evidence from musical contents and paper characteristics, c.1736–41. Most of the rastra types and watermark types from these forty-nine volumes are found in other Handel sources from that period.[45] To this foundation collection further volumes were added at various times in the 1750s and 1760s in order to bring in other works composed by Handel after 1741, and the process was concluded after 1810 (probably by Greatorex) with the purchase of two further manuscripts (now MSS 789, 790) of works that were not previously represented:[46] all these additional volumes received Binding Style B. It seems that the original collection was discontinued for some reason in 1741, before the most recent operas (*Imeneo* and *Deidamia*) were copied. Perhaps the original owner-collector died at that period, or the departure of Handel for Dublin, presumably taking Smith with him,[47] interrupted

---

[44] After completing my own classification of binding styles, I discovered that Mann had made a similar classification (in *Catalogue of the Barrett-Lennard Collection*, entry for 'Binding'), though he did not identify the binding type for every vol. and he did not attempt to draw general conclusions from the evidence.

[45] Rastra from App. 1 occur over the following date-ranges in Handel's autographs: type a 1734–43, type b 1738–40, type d 1737 (types c and e are not found in the autographs). Date-ranges for WMs from Handel's autographs are: C*c 1735, C*e 1738, Bg 1736–7, 1741. Types C*c2, E*a, and E*a2 do not occur in the autographs. E*a appears in Handel's conducting scores over the period between 1738 and 1751, and E*b over a similarly wide-ranging period between 1744 and 1751, appearing also in an autograph from 1748. C*c clearly remained in use over a number of years, during the preparation of the Lennard Collection, but it only made a brief and limited appearance in the autographs and conducting scores. This seems to support a pattern that I have suggested elsewhere, that certain types of paper remained on the stocks for the 'collection' projects but were only drawn on briefly—perhaps in an emergency—for the central 'practical' copies: see D. Burrows, 'Sources, Resources and Handel Studies' in S. Sadie and A. Hicks (eds.), *Handel Tercentenary Collection* (London, 1987), 27. It seems very unlikely, however, on the basis of the available evidence, that C*c paper was available to the 'Smith scriptorium' much before 1735.

[46] Both vols. have small labels on the front paste-downs reading 'RYAN / BOOKSELLER / Oxford Street', and a similar label is found on the 'earlier' vol. MS 801 (Binding Style B, Group 2). The labels may relate to the binding or repair of the vols., or possibly to their purchase.

[47] Insertions in the conducting scores that relate to Handel's Dublin performances are in the hands of Smith and S4, suggesting that these two copyists accompanied him to Ireland: see D. Burrows, 'Handel's Performances of "Messiah": The Evidence of the Conducting Score', *ML* 56: 3–4 (July–Oct. 1975), 322.

the previous arrangements for having copies taken. It may be a coincidence that the notional commencement date for the collection falls at about the same period that the younger Walsh took over the reins of the family's music publishing firm, following his father's death in 1736, and apparently began to develop a more positive relationship with Handel over the publication of his music.[48]

The volumes of Style A have spines and boards elaborately decorated with gold tooling, and labels on the front boards (gilt lettering on a red ground) giving titles in the following styles: 'Handel's Opera of Sosarmes' (for example) for operas, and 'Handel's Oratorio call'd Saul' for oratorios. It is perhaps worth noting that on these labels the operas are given titles in the English forms, as in Walsh's publications.[49] The later Style B is simpler, with plain brown boards, but some attempt was made to match the previous set in the style of the labels and tooling on the spines, and in the size of the pages, even if this meant some ruthless trimming.[50] The spine decorations of Style B are not so internally consistent as those of Style A, which may doubtless be accounted for by the fact that the volumes in question were bound up over a more extended period, perhaps as long as sixty years.

Styles C and D do not appear to go with the main Collection at all. Not only are the two volumes of Style C of a different size from those in Styles A and B, but the tooling of the boards and spines is in a distinctive style very different from Style A. Style C bears no labels on the front boards but the volume titles are picked out in gold at the centre. The binding style of these two volumes relates directly to that of the 'Granville' Collection,[51] which has the same format, tooling, and central gold titles, though in addition the Granville volumes have a heraldic device in the centre of the back boards and a two-colour treatment of the panelling on both front and back boards.[52] Furthermore, the two manuscripts from the

[48] See Burrows, 'Walsh's Editions', 94.

[49] The same is true of the titles found on the front boards of the Granville Collection, though in the form: 'SOSARMES AN OPERA THE MUSIC BY MR. HANDEL'. It is also a remarkable coincidence that a vol. from the Granville Collection that was apparently intended to include a mixed collection of instr. music (Lbl Eg. 2946), has an original label to the front board with the title 'MISCELLANIES BY MR. HANDEL'—compare Cfm MU.MS. 798.

[50] The cropping of pages is seen most dramatically in the additional movements at the end of *Judas Maccabaeus* (MS 809, pp. 181–202).

[51] Lbl Eg. MSS 2910–46. See R. H. Streatfeild, 'The Granville Collection of Handel Manuscripts', *Musical Antiquary*, 2: 4 (July, 1911), 208–24; also D. Burrows, 'The "Granville" and "Smith" Collections of Handels Manuscripts', in C. Banks, A. Searle and M. Turner (eds.), *Sundry Sorts of Music Books* (London, 1993), 231–4.

[52] The heraldic device is not the Granville arms. The 2-colour effect on the covers was produced by the varied treatment of a single piece of skin. I thank Arthur Searle (Dept. of Manuscripts, British Library) for his assistance on this subject.

Lennard Collection with Style C have the same watermarks and rastra characteristics as volumes in the Granville Collection, which was copied c.1740–5, on the end of the putative Style A period.[53] It is possible that two of the Lennard manuscripts (MSS 794 and 813) were rejects from the Granville assignment, a suggestion that may be supported by the fact that the gold decoration on the Odes volume has been left rather rough.[54] On the other hand, it may be observed that the existing Granville Collection has a volume including the Funeral Anthem for Queen Caroline, which is duplicated in MS 813.[55] But MS 813 also carries clear evidence that it was not part of the original sequence of Lennard manuscripts, because both its musical contents and its spine title ('Anthems Vol. 1') are duplicated in volumes from the Style A category.

Style D is rather easier to place: it seems to date from the nineteenth century, though once again some attempt was made to imitate the general lines of Style A. *Parnasso in festa* (MS 846)[56] is clearly an eighteenth-century manuscript in a more recent binding, the result of an unsatisfactory attempt to mount the smaller Format III pages into a standard Format IV cover. In spite of its early origin, it is doubtful whether this volume was part of the original series with those in Styles A and B. The volume comprising *Rodrigo* and *Silla* (MS 855) seems to have been copied in the latter part of the eighteenth century and was presumably added to the Collection after 1832 in order to make it more complete. Its oblong quarto format separates it from the upright folio volumes of the rest of the Collection: in recent (and probably not-so-recent) times it was kept in the central drawer of the book-case and not on the shelves.

[53] For the basis of this dating see Larsen, *Handel's 'Messiah'*, 210–12. The suggested period seems to be confirmed by the paper characteristics: in Handel's autographs and conducting scores, WM C*f occurs over a range c.1740–8, and rastra type a c.1734–43. Some Granville MSS have a different style of tooling from the remainder: this group consists of Lbl Eg. MS 2918 (*Ottone*), Eg. MS 2937 (*Messiah*), Eg. MS 2938 (*Samson*), Eg. MS 2939 (*Joseph*), and Eg. MS 2942 (Italian Cantatas). From the presence in this group of the three latest oratorios to be included in the collection, it seems likely that these vols. were last to be copied, c.1743–5. Cfm MU. MSS. 794 and 813, and Mp MS 130 Hd4 v.130 match the style of tooling of the remaining (and probably earlier) part of the Granville Collection.

[54] Against this suggestion, it may be argued that the covers of vols. intended for the Granville Collection would have been given the 2-colour treatment before the gilt titles were added. Ref. must also be made to a score of *Flavio* now in the Newman Flower Collection at Manchester though not, like much of that Collection, of Aylesford provenance: Mp MS 130 Hd4 v.130. This is in the 'simple' 1-colour style, and is identical in format, watermarks, rastra and cover decoration to Cfm MU. MSS. 794 and 813. As evidence of former owners, it carries the bookplate of the Honourable Anne Rushout and a signature 'R Bowles, No. 66'.

[55] Though it is true that the Funeral Anthem in the Granville vol. (Eg. MS 2913) is somewhat hidden in the midst of a series of Cannons (Chandos) Anthems. It is also noteworthy that *Flavio* (Mp MS 130 Hd4 v. 130) is not represented in the Granville Collection as it now stands.

[56] The title is given on the vol.'s labels as 'Pernasso in Festa', no doubt simply in error.

One other apparently anomalous volume is that of the 'Miscellanys' (MS 798) which also has a nineteenth-century binding imitating Style A, identical in type to MSS 846 and 855. The materials contained in this volume originated from the earlier periods of the Collection and my guess is the contents of at least two former volumes were combined here, perhaps after some accidental damage to the originals.[57] Most of the music pages in the volume clearly date from the Style A period, and I have distributed the contents accordingly in Appendix 1;[58] the final section comprising the *Ode for Queen Anne's Birthday* fits with Style B, Group 2. It might be mentioned that MS 799, a copy of the Concerti grossi, Op. 6, has an original Style A spine label reading 'CONCERTOS / VOL II':[59] this may be a hint that the volume stood originally as a companion to 'CONCERTOS & WATER MUSICK' (MS. 836), or alternatively that the contents of a hypothetical volume 'CONCERTOS / VOL. I' are now to be found within the covers of MS 798.[60]

This leads to a more general consideration of the question as to whether the Collection, as it now stands, is complete, or whether some volumes have been lost. Completeness in this context is something of a shifting target according to the stage in the Collection's development that you choose as your standpoint. In Style A there is a pretty complete run of Handel's London operas: if some circumstance had

[57] The contents list, in the 'Robert Turle' hand on the front flyleaves, does not include the final section of MS 798 (the *Ode for Queen Anne's Birthday*), suggesting that that sect. was not part of the vol. when the contents were listed.

[58] The sects. of the vol. are as follows: (1) pp. 1–56, Concertos from Op. 3 (HWV 313, 315, 312), paginated by copyist (S1). (2) pp. 1–18, Trio Sonata movements from Op. 5 (HWV 400, 401, 396), paginated by copyist (S1). (3) pp. 1*bis*–236*bis*, movements from operas and serenata (HWV 22, 34, 33, A¹¹, 27, 8ᵇ, 8ᶜ, 73), paginated by copyist (S5) to p. 144, and paginated in 'Robert Turle' hand thereafter: pagination error at the end, where '236' from penultimate verso is repeated on the following recto (see also next entry). (4) pp. 238 [*recte* 239]–244, miscellaneous instr. movements as printed in HG xlviii. 140–3 from this source, copyist Smith sen.; paginations in the 'Robert Turle' hand, correcting the former pagination error by p. 242. On the front of this sect. of the MS ('p. 237', the previously empty verso from p. 236*bis*) another copyist—probably S7—added the 1st 2 movements printed HG xlviii. 140; the tempo directions to Smith's copy on p. 238 also seem to be in the same hand. The title 'Sinfonie Diverse' was added later in pencil at the top of p. 237, probably by Rophino Lacy in the 19th cent. The G major movement on pp. 238–9 (HG xlviii. 141–2) bears additional bc figs. (not in Smith's hand) in red ink. (5) pp. 245–51, Overture *Alessandro Severo*, HWV A¹³, copyist S5, paginations in the 'Robert Turle' hand. p. 251ᵛ is an unnumbered page of empty staves. (6) pp. 1–44, *Ode for Queen Anne's Birthday*, HWV 74, paginated by copyist (S9).

[59] MS 799 appears at first sight to be a rather anomalous vol. because of the unusual copyist, but there is no reason to doubt that it was part of the original Style A series of the collection. The music text of this volume requires further investigation: it may have been derived from the copy-text for the printed edn. of Op. 6, or even from the published part-books themselves.

[60] It is also possible that the labels on the front and spine of MS 798 (reading 'MISCELLANYS BY G. F. HANDEL' and 'MISCELLANYS'), which are almost certainly of 19th-cent. provenance, repeated texts from the labels of a previous constituent vol.: compare Lbl Eg. MS 2946.

21

LOT 252

An excellent Mahogany Bookcase, with glazed Doors, Drawers and Cupboard under, surmounted with a Bust of Handel, and known by the designation of

THE HANDEL BOOKCASE,

(Having with the whole of its contents, formerly belonged to that great Master;)

CONTAINING

Splendid Copies of his Compositions, in the handwriting of his Amanuensis, Smith.

ORATORIOS.

ALEXANDER BALUS	JOSHUA
ATHALIA	JUDAS MACCABEUS
BELSHAZZAR	MESSIAH
DEBORAH	SAMSON
ESTHER	SAUL
HERCULES	SOLOMON
JEPTHAH	SUSANNA
JOSEPH	THEODORA

ISRAEL IN EGYPT.

Anthems, Four volumes,

Te Deums and Jubilates, Two ditto,

Odes, &c. One ditto,

Acis and Galatea,

Choice of Hercules,

L'Allegro ed Il Pensieroso, col. Moderato,

Organ Concertos, Select Harmony, and Water Music,

Miscellaneous,

Grand Concertos,

Serenata, Queen Anne's Birth Day.

ADMETUS	FLORIDANTE	PTOLOMY
ÆTIUS	GIULIUS CŒSAR	RADAMISTUS
ALCINA	JUSTIN	RICHARD 1st
ALEXANDER	LOTHARIUS	RINALDO
AMADIS	MUZIO SCŒVOLA	RODELINDA
ARIADNE	ORLANDO	SCIPIO
ARIODANTE	OTHO	SIROE
ARMINIUS	PARTHENOPE	SOSARMES
ATALANTA	PHARAMOND	TAMERLANE
BERENICE	PASTOR FIDO	THESEUS
FLAVIUS	PORUS	XERXES

TRIONFO DEL TEMPO

CANTATAS ———— *DUETS.*

6.1. The Barrett Lennard Collection, as listed in the *Catalogue of the Valuable Musical Library of the Late T. Greatorex* (1832).

abruptly called a halt to the original Style A sequence in 1741, then it is quite likely that the most recent operas (*Imeneo* and *Deidamia*) were not copied, in which case we should not be looking for 'lost' manuscripts of these operas. When the Collection began to be extended again about ten years later, this may have been done on a rather haphazard basis and it is perhaps not surprising that the occasional work was missed. If, for whatever reason, the two volumes in Style C had been added to the Collection in the interim, then there would have been no need for a new copy of *Alexander's Feast* and the *Ode for St Cecilia's Day* in Style B. Taking the repertory of Styles A and B together, *Semele* is the most obvious omission from Handel's major English pieces: but it was hardly a popular work by the 1750s.[61] Other significant works not represented include the *Occasional Oratorio*, *Alceste*, and the later Organ Concertos: it also seems that Handel's operas and oratorios composed in Italy fell outside the canon at that stage, though duets and cantatas from the same period were included in the Style A sequence.

One check on the history of the Collection's development is provided by the list of volumes that appears in the catalogue of Greatorex's sale. (See Illus. 1 and App. 2, col. 3.) From this it appears that MSS 846 and 855 in my Style D were not part of the Collection in 1832: they were presumably bought in by a subsequent owner. On the other hand, it seems that the two volumes in Style C were part of the Collection by 1832, and a 'Miscellaneous' volume is also listed—presumably MS 798 but not in its present form, because the 'Serenata, Queen Anne's Birthday' which is now included in that volume is shown as a separate manuscript. The only puzzle in the 1832 list concerns the entry for two volumes of Te Deums and Jubilates, since only one volume covering this repertory is present in the Collection today:[62] there may have been a mistake in the catalogue, or perhaps a volume including the Dettingen Te Deum has been lost since 1832.[63] There is

[61] *Semele* was not revived in London between 1744 and 1762.

[62] MS 814. The labels describe the contents as Te Deums and Jubilates: the contents are HWV 281, 246 [= Cannons Anthem 1], 278, 279, 280.

[63] Rockstro credits the Collection with a copy of the Dettingen Te Deum in his table (*Handel*, 432–9), and also with a copy of the A major Te Deum, HWV 282 (erroneously described as a 'Chandos Te Deum'). But Rockstro's list is inaccurate in detail: although he includes entries for *Oreste*, *Terpsicore*, and *Alessandro Severo* (extracts from these works are found in MS 798), he misses the vols. for *The Choice of Hercules* and the Concerti grossi, Op. 6. Furthermore his description of the Collection suggests that the main series contained exactly the same number of vols. as today: 'The collection consists of eighty-five volumes, sixty-four of which are uniformly bound, in tooled calf, and contained in an oaken bookcase originally made for their reception' (p. 429). The constitution of the 64 vols. is suggested below: Mrs Marshall's near-contemporary description of the collection as 67 vols. (*George Frederick Handel*, 136) tallies exactly with the present total at Cambridge. Rockstro's description gives the misleading impression that Lennard purchased all 85 vols. from Brownsmith.

124   THE BARRETT LENNARD COLLECTION

just one piece of circumstantial evidence that something else might have strayed from the Collection before 1832. GB Lcm MS 899 is a copy by the elder Smith of the anthem 'I will magnifie thee' (HWV 250a), that may have come adrift from a lost volume of the Collection: it has the same format, copyist, and paper characteristics as the Lennard MSS 810–12, and bears Smith's paginations 149–84.[64] Otherwise, there seems little support for the proposition that there have been any major losses from the core of the Style A manuscripts.

However, one piece of evidence that may have some bearing on this issue demands investigation. Two small circles of black leather were at some stage stuck on to the spine of each volume of the Collection bearing, respectively, a number and the letters 'MS' in gold. (See App. 2, col. 3.) Many of these circular labels have now fallen off, although a few more were present when Mann made his catalogue, where he fortunately recorded the numbers. The highest number surviving on the folio volumes was 66 in Mann's record (and remains so today). The volumes without surviving numbers were subsequently arranged by alphabetical order of work titles (in their anglicized forms) and assigned notional volume numbers continuing from 67 to 85.[65] The sequence thus produced defined the order of the accession numbers that were finally given to the manuscripts at the Fitzwilliam Museum. The merest glance at Appendix 2 will reveal that the succession of works according to these numbers makes no sense, whether in terms of compositional chronology, genre grouping, or binding style. The presence of a manuscript serial number as high as 85 would seem to indicate the possibility of considerable losses from the Collection, until it is remembered that that figure was merely the consequence of beginning the assignment of unnumbered volumes from 67. In total content the Collection is clearly substantially as it was in 1832, and the circular labels were added after that date because they are to be found on MS 855, one of the volumes added subsequently. So it seems that the spine labels were added by one of the nineteenth-century owners and the numbers probably had reference to some personal library catalogue: the present MSS 836–54 were no doubt originally distributed earlier in the series, where there are now gaps in the number scheme of the spine labels.[66] The only

---

[64] Lcm MS 899 is Format IV, WM E*a, rastra type a.

[65] The present MSS 836–54.

[66] The modern introd. pp. to Mann, *Catalogue of the Barrett-Lennard Collection* record some previous alternative numberings as follows: MS 836 formerly '11'; MS 838 formerly '34'; MS 840 formerly '40'; MS 841 formerly '13'; MS 842 formerly '41'; MS 843 formerly '15'; MS 844 formerly '24'; MS 845 formerly '45' MS 846 formerly '46'; MS 847 formerly '48'; MS 848 formerly '52'; MS 849 formerly '54'; MS 850 formerly '57'; MS 851 formerly '22'; MS 852 formerly '58'; MS 853 formerly '59'; MS 854 formerly '60'. The origin and authority of this

minor puzzle is why MS 855, as the sixty-seventh volume, bears the number 68.[67]

Allowance must be made for the probability that, when the volumes as a whole were removed from the bookcase (for example when the bookcase itself was moved on a change of ownership), they were not replaced on the shelves in the same order. The modern arrangement dates back, at the earliest, to the state of the Collection as received by Mann c.1900:[68] the spine labels give a clue to a previous nineteenth-century arrangement. Some other evidence provides a hint about the arrangement of the volumes during the period of Lennard's owner-ship. On the inside of the front boards, below his bookplate, Lennard added two small paper labels to most of the volumes,[69] reading either 'K / 3' or 'K / 4' (see App. 2). These designations cut across the numer-ical sequence of the black circles, and my guess is that they were shelf-marks indicating whether a given volume went on the first or second shelf of the Handel bookcase: such an arrangement would put most oratorios on the top shelf (K3) and most operas on the second (K4). The sixty-six folio volumes fit pretty well exactly the space available in the top section of the bookcase,[70] and this in itself supports the hypothesis of the Collection's integrity in its present form, though not in its present order. We cannot even begin to guess how Greatorex or any of the previous owners ordered the volumes of the Collection.

Lennard's library was described at his death as consisting of 'eighty-five volumes, sixty-four of which are uniformly bound'.[71] The sixty-four

info. is obscure, and it may well be the remains of a 'best guess' attempt by Mann to reinsert these vols. at appropriate places into gaps in the numbering sequence of the spine labels. It will be noted that the overall sequence thus produced cuts across the arrangement suggested in the next para. on the basis of Lennard's 'shelf-mark labels'.

[67] The 3 most likely alternative explanations seem to be (1) that a vol. of Eng. church music was lost from the Collection before 1902 (the least likely), (2) that the *Ode for Queen Anne's Birthday* was a separate volume when the labels were first prepared and then lost its identity (and number) when MS 798 was re-bound to incorporate the *Ode*, and (3) that 'MS 67' was some other vol., now missing, that was kept in the drawer of the bookcase and was not part of the main series of fo. vols.

[68] Unfortunately we cannot even be certain of the shelf order of the vols. as received by Mann c.1900, as the loose leaves of his catalogue describing individual vols. could have been shuffled several times in the extended period before they were bound. Presumably Mann, who was a very methodical scholar, made an initial list of the MSS when he received them, but this is not to be found today. I thank Margaret Cranmer for searching Mann's papers at Ckc.

[69] I make this assumption from the relative placing of the labels, and from the fact that other vols. from his Collection bear comparable labels.

[70] This statement is based on a recent inspection of the vols. *in situ*. I cannot account for Schoelcher's description: 'This fine collection . . . consists of 67 vols, and occupies a book-case of mahogany, eight feet and a half in height, with glass doors, which seems to have been intended to contain it, but from the vacancies which occur on its shelves, it is evident that several vols. have unfortunately been removed' (R.M.18.b.2 fo.31). Such conservation of the vols. as has been undertaken to date has not involved any rebinding or paper lamination that could have expanded the Collection's demands on horizontal shelf-space.

[71] 'Obituary', *MT* 40, probably derived from Rockstro's description (*Handel*, 432–9).

126 THE BARRETT LENNARD COLLECTION

'uniformly bound volumes' referred to were probably the manuscript groups with Binding Style A and B, plus the 'Miscellanys' volume (MS 798) and the artificially-created format IV volume for *Parnasso in festa* (MS 846). If the total figure of eighty-five manuscripts in Lennard's library is to be believed, and sixty-seven of them went to the Fitzwilliam Museum with the bookcase, that leaves eighteen other manuscripts that went elsewhere. There is no reason to believe that these eighteen form a coherent group: Lennard no doubt bought up individual items as they came to his attention, or as they became available, and as a collector he would never have been able to repeat the *coup* of the big collection he bought from Brownsmith. Of the eighteen dispersed volumes, I have been able so far to locate about one third (see App. 3).[72] It will immediately be apparent that the numbers on the spines duplicate and do not complement those in the main Lennard Collection: furthermore, the labels bearing these numbers are not of the same circular black type.

Of the six dispersed Lennard volumes, that containing music from *Serse* is the most significant because it is an early source for the opera: ironically, in view of the lack of obvious connection between the main Lennard Collection and the texts of the early Walsh publications, this manuscript may possibly be the parent text for Walsh's first edition of *Serse* songs in 1738.[73] The three duet volumes in the Coopersmith Collection probably originated in the late 1740s, and they are still in their original bindings. Binding styles E and F from Appendix 3 seem to date from the nineteenth century and it is likely that Lennard was responsible for them: their appearance may provide a guide in the search for other as yet unidentified volumes from Lennard's Collection.

The two volumes containing keyboard arrangements of Handel's instrumental music lead us to another side of Lennard's activities, one that is touched upon in the obituary of him that appeared in the *Musical Times*.[74]

Mr Barrett-Lennard was educated at Westminster School. During his pupilage there he attended the services at the Abbey. One day he heard some music by

---

[72] There is no way of knowing whether the MSS now in the Coopersmith Collection were counted as 1 vol. or 3 vols. out of the reported total of 85. I have made the assumption that the 85 vols. referred to by Rockstro (*Handel*, 432–9) and by 'Obituary', *MT* 40, were MSS, though this is not entirely clear. Nor is it certain whether the *Overtures* volume, being mixed printed and MS, should be included in the total. It seems probable that the miscellaneous MSS were sold either soon after Henry's death or after that of his son, who died unmarried in 1924.

[73] For details of the published edn. see W. C. Smith, *Catalogue*, 68. Lennard's MS of *Serse*, which on the evidence of the bookplate he probably acquired before 1856, contains the Overture and arias, to which the names of the original singers were added by the copyist.

[74] 'Obituary', *MT* 40.

DONALD BURROWS

Handel which so enthralled him that, without any premeditation, he then and there determined to study music. He at once began to take lessons on the organ, which instrument he played until within a few days of his death. He had a small organ in the library of his house at Hampstead, and if a visitor offered to play this instrument the genial old gentleman would always insist upon 'something by Handel'.

Lennard has obviously played from his copy of the Walsh edition of Handel's keyboard overtures,[75] for he added extra music—inner contrapuntal parts or notes to fill out chords—in some of them.[76] Where the repertory of keyboard arrangements from Walsh ran out, Lennard took over, in the manuscript book now in the Coke Collection, mainly copied in 1841. There various instrumental works of Handel's—including the Trio Sonatas, Op. 2 and Op. 5, the spurious 'Water Piece', the *Concerto a due cori*, HWV 332 and the Organ Concertos, HWV 304–5[77]—were, as he proudly noted, 'arranged for the Organ or Piano Forte by H B Lennard now for the first time'. For an arrangement of the *Fireworks Music* Lennard called upon the services of 'R Marquis',[78] who also copied 'A Fourth Set of LESSONS for the HARPSICHORD', which is apparently a straight transcript of the sixth book of Walsh's collection *The Lady's Banquet*.[79] Rophino Lacy (1795–1867), the Irishman who supplied considerable musical expertise to Victor Schoelcher's investigations of Handel's career,[80] went through the 'Fourth Set of Lessons' in Lennard's book and identified opera movements from extracts that appeared in score in the 'Miscellanys' volume of the main Lennard Collection (MS 798). His cross-reference annotations appear in both Lennard's keyboard volume and in the 'Miscellanys', and they seem to have been made in the

[75] *Handel's Overtures from all his Operas and Oratorios*, late 18th-century edn: see W. C. Smith, *Catalogue*, 287, no. 28. I have not searched for other printed vols. of music owned by Lennard, but following the 1990 Handel Institute Conference I received news of one in a private collection. It contains kbd scores of *Israel in Egypt*, *Saul*, and *Alexander's Feast* (John Clarke edn.). Spine decorations and labels are similar to those for the *Overtures* volume, with spine labels (or label impressions): 'HANDEL G. F.', '3', and titles of works; inside front board: Lennard 'York Gate' bookplate and labels 'K/2'.

[76] e.g. in the Overtures to *Lotario* and *Atalanta* (Walsh overtures nos. II and XXXIII).

[77] HWV 305 was arranged from the garbled version published in Arnold's edn.

[78] On the title-page of 'A fourth set of LESSONS' Lennard described him as 'R. Marquis, professor of music', but I have not been able to discover any further details of him.

[79] Edn. listed in W. C. Smith, *Catalogue*, 270.

[80] See the biographical entry for Michael Rophino Lacy by W. H. Husk in *Grove* and (with additions) in subsequent edns. Schoelcher acknowledged Lacy's assistance in his biography of Handel (*Life of Handel*, p. xxii). GB–Lbl Add. MSS 31555, 31573 contain Lacy's MS transcriptions of music deriving from his visits to examine the Handel sources at Buckingham Palace, and various Handelian MSS carry his annotations—e.g. GB–Lbl Add. MSS 14182, 31557, 31564, 31566. (The last three of these came to Lbl from Julian Marshall's library in 1881, but it is not known who owned them when Lacy saw them.)

period before Lennard himself had bought the Handel bookcase collection containing MS 798.[81]

Although Lennard credited Marquis with arranging the *Fireworks Music* for keyboard, the first two movements of this arrangement are in Lennard's hand and were probably his own work. Lennard also made a second copy of the Overture and Bourrée, now found (along with his arrangement of the Overture in *Agrippina*) on some manuscript leaves bound at the end of his 'Walsh' copy of the Handel overtures. His keyboard arrangements, though superficially resembling those published by Walsh, reflect nineteenth-century taste in their well-filled chords and constant octave doubling of the bass part: the arrangement of the *Fireworks Music* stands in sharp contrast to the simple two-part keyboard version that Walsh published soon after the first performance in 1749.[82] Of interest also are Lennard's occasional synchronized double dots in the *Agrippina* Overture (See Illus. 2). Whether Lennard intended his arrangements to have any circulation beyond his immediate circle is doubtful: he seems to have made them primarily for his own use. Lennard was clearly an enthusiastic amateur musician as well as an important collector, and it is fitting to conclude with Schoelcher's tribute:[83] 'Like a true amateur, Mr. Lennard is free from that selfishness which glories in the possession of treasures only for the pleasure of possessing them.'

Appendix 1: Binding Styles in the Lennard Collection

Key:

Copyists (Sm; S1–S9; Hb1; Lenn 1, 2, x) are identified according to the sigla in J. P. Larsen, *Handel's 'Messiah': Origins, Composition, Sources* (London, 1957; 2nd edn. with additions and minor revisions, New York, 1972).

Watermarks are identified according to the sigla in J. P. Larsen, *Handel's 'Messiah'* and H. D. Clausen, *Händels Direktionspartituren ('Hand-exemplare')* (Hamburg, 1972), with the addition of Bm2, Ha2, C*c2, C*g2, E*a2 (the latter are sigla for 'new' watermark types; C*c2 may be a variant form of C*c).

---

[81] This is apparent from the wording of some of Lacy's annotations on MS 798 (e.g. sect. (3) pp. 59, 99), which refer to the vol. now in the GB–BENcoke as 'Mr L's MS book' or 'Mr Lennd's MS book': if Lennard had also owned MS 798 at the same period, the annotations would probably have referred simply to 'the other MS', or something similar. MS 798 also includes some pencil annotations in other hands.

[82] *The Musick for the Fireworks Set for the German Flute, Violin or Harpsicord*, see W. C. Smith, *Catalogue*, 233–4. Lennard seems to have begun making his arrangement by transcribing and adapting the string/woodwind parts from a full score, probably Arnold's edition: there is a hiatus in bars 15–16 where the music of the trumpet/horn parts has not been fully incorporated.

[83] Schoelcher; *Life of Handel*, p. xxiii.

6.2. Overture to *Agrippina*, arr. Henry Barrett Lennard, and in his hand (Burrows Collection).

Rastra types (no. of staves/rulings/total span in mm) are as follows:

a   20 @ 2 30.5 (MSS 794, 813: 16 @ 2 30.5)
b   20 @ 5 88
c   24 @ 2 23.5–24 (MSS 794, 813: 20 @ 2 23.5–24)
d   20 @ 2 26.5–27
e   21 @ 4 56.5–57 + @ 3 40.5 (×3)
f   20 @ 4 69.5–70
g   20 @ 5 92
h   20 @ 4 68–9
j   20 @ 5 90.5
k   24 @ 6 92–92.5
l   20 @ 5 87.5
m   24 @ 2 24–24.5
n   20 @ 10 193.5–194
p   16 @ 4 75.5
r   20 @ 4 56.5 (or possibly identical to rastra type c)
s   10 @ 10 199

Binding Style A: Format IV (Decorated boards, with labels on front boards)

Group no.	Cfm MU. MS. no.	Title	Copyist	WM	Rastra type	Flyleaf WM
I	832	*Il pastor fido*	S1	C*b, C*c	a	C*c
I	831	*Teseo*	Sm	C*c	a	C*c
I	792	*Acis and Galatea*	Sm	C*c	a	C*c
I	830	*Muzio Scevola*, Act 3	Sm	C*c	a	C*c
I	821	*Floridante*	S1	C*c	a	C*c
I	828	*Ottone*	Sm	C*c	a	C*c
I	826	*Flavio*	S1	C*c	a	C*c
I	827	*Giulio Cesare*	Hb1	C*c	a	C*c
I	852	*Tamerlano*	Sm	C*b, C*c	a	C*c
I	825	*Scipione*	S1	C*c	a	C*c
I	839	*Alessandro*	Sm	C*c	a	C*c
I	837	*Admeto*	S1	C*c	a	C*c
I	822	*Riccardo Primo*	Sm	C*c	a	C*c
I	834	*Siroe*	S1	C*c	a	C*c
I	849	*Tolomeo*	Sm	C*c	a	C*c
I	845	*Partenope*	S3; text: Sm	C*c	a	C*c
I	848	*Poro*	S1	C*c	a	C*c
I	838	*Ezio*	S1	C*c	a	C*c
I	816	*Orlando*	S1	C*c	a	C*c
I	820	*Arianna*	Sm	C*c	a	C*c
I	823	*Alcina*	S1	C*b, C*c	a	C*c
I	824	*Ariodante*	Sm	C*b, C*c	a	C*c
I	791	*Atalanta*	Sm	C*c	a	C*c
I	833	*Giustino* [1737]	Hb1	C*c	a	C*c

DONALD BURROWS

Group no.	Cfm MU. MS. no.	Title	Copyist	WM	Rastra type	Flyleaf WM
2	797	Italian Cantatas	S1	C*e	a	C*e
2	829	Rinaldo	S4; text: Sm, S1	C*c, C*e	a	C*c
2	853	Sosarme [1732]	S5	C*e	a	C*e
2	[798(4)]	Instr. movements [latest 1739?]	Sm	C*e	a	
3	810	Anthems, i	Sm	E*a	a	E*a2
3	811	Anthems, ii	Sm	E*a†	a	C*e
3	812	Anthems, iii	Sm	E*a	a,b	C*e
3	814	Te Deums, Jubilates	Sm	E*a	a,b,c	C*e
3	835	Il trionfo del tempo [1737 version]	Sm	E*a	a,d	C*c
3	817	Berenice	S5	E*a	a,d	C*c, Bm2
3	808	Saul [1738–9]	S5	E*a	a, c	C*e
4	796	Italian Duets	Sm	E*a	d	C*c
4	840	Amadigi	S1, S5	E*a	d	C*c
4	800	Esther [1717/18 and 1732 versions]	S5	E*a	d	C*e
4	819	Lotario	S5	E*a	d	C*c
4	806	Deborah	Sm	E*a	d	E*a2
4	803	Athalia	S5	E*a	d	C*c
4	836	Concertos HWV 289–294 [Op. 4], HWV 303, and HWV 318 and Water Music	S1, S5, Sm	E*a	d	C*e
4	854	Serse [1738]	S5	E*a	d	E*a2
4	[798(5)]	Alessandro Severo Overture	S5	E*a	d	
5	850	Radamisto	S5	E*a, E*a2	d	E*a2
5	847	Faramondo [1737/8]	S5	E*a, E*a2	d	C*c
5	[798(1)]	Concertos, Op. 3	S1	E*a, E*a2, C*e	a	
5	[798(2)]	Sonatas, Op. 5	S1	E*a, E*a2	a	
5	[798(3)]	Movements from Operas	S5	E*a, E*a2, C*e	a	
6	799	Concertos, Op. 6 [1739/40]	Lenn1	Bg	e	C*e
7	802	Israel in Egypt [1738/9]	S5	E*b	a,c	lines‡
8	818	Rodelinda	S1	C*c, C*c2	a	C*c
8	815	Arminio	Hb1	C*c, C*c2	a	C*c
8	795	L'Allegro [+1741 variants]	S2	C*b, C*c2	b	C*e

Total for Binding Style A = 49 vols.

† except inserted pp. 126–7: WM ?Ch, rasta @ 2 31.
‡ lines only, prob. 18th-cent. paper.

Binding Style B: Format IV (Plain brown boards)

Group no.	Cfm MU. MS. no.	Title	Copyist	WM	Rastra type	Flyleaf WM
1	804	Susanna (except pp. 83–84)	Sm	C*g2, E*b	f,g	lines only, thin 19th-cent. paper
1	807	Susanna, pp. 83–4	?	C*c	a	C/EAH, thin 19th-cent. paper
1	842	Solomon	S5	C*g2, E*b	g	lines only, thin 19th-cent. paper
1	844	The Choice of Hercules	Sm	E*b	h	lines only, thin 19th-cent. paper
2	[798 (6)]	Messiah [incl. 1750 Guadagni mvts.]	S5	Cp	h	lines only, thin 19th-cent. paper
2	851	Ode for Queen Anne's Birthday	S9	F2b	j,k	lines only, thin 19th-cent. paper
2	843	Samson	S9	F2b, F*2	j,k,l	lines only, thin 19th-cent. paper
2	841	Joseph	S9	Ha, Ha2	j,k	C/EAH, thin 19th-cent. paper
2	809	Belshazzar [uncompleted copy]	S9	Cu, Ha	j	lines only, thin 19th-cent. paper
2 (see also 3)	809	Judas Maccabaeus, pp. 1–180	S9	F2b	j,k,l	lines only, thin 19th-cent. paper
2	801	Joshua†	S9	F2c, Ha	j,k,l	lines only, thin 19th-cent. paper
3	793	Theodora	Sm‡	F2e	h	lines only, thin 19th-cent. paper
3	805	Jephtha	Sm‡	F2e	h,m	lines only, thin 19th-cent. paper
3	809	Judas Maccabaeus, additions pp. 181–202	Sm,‡ S5	F2e	h,m	lines only, thin 19th-cent. paper
4	789	Hercules†	LennX	RUSE & TURNERS 1811, 1812; RUSE & TURNERS 1813	n	none
4	790	Alexander Balus†	LennX	RUSE & TURNERS*; RUSE & TURNERS 1811; RUSE & TURNERS 1811	n	none; Lewis engraving (1828) of Kyte Handel portrait inserted

Total for Binding Style B = 13 vols.

Notes: Group 1, ?c.1751; Group 2, ?c.1760; Group 3, ?c.1761–3.
† with 'Ryan' bookseller's plate
‡ final style of hand

Binding Style C: Format III (Decorated boards, titles in gilt on front boards)

Cfm MU. MS. no.	Title	Copyist	WM	Rastra type	Flyleaf WM
813	Coronation Anthems and Funeral Anthem	S1, S5, S7	C*f (c.1740–5)	a,c	lines only, 18th-cent. paper
794	Alexander's Feast and Ode for St Cecilia's Day	Sm, S7, S5	C*f (c.1740–5)	a,c	lines only, 18th-cent. paper

Total for Binding Style C = 2 vols.

Binding Style D (Boards with simple decoration, and front labels of a later type)

Group no.	Cfm MU. MS. no.	Title	Copyist	WM	Rastra type	Flyleaf WM
1	798	'Miscellanys'†				
2	846	Parnasso in festa	S5	C1, B1 (c.1746–8)	p,r	rear flyleaf: unidentified B type (not B1)
3	855	Rodrigo and Silla	Lenn2	J1*	s	

Total for Binding Style D = 3 vols.

Notes: Group 1, Format IV; Group 2, Format III in Format IV boards; Group 3, Format I.
† The title on the front label of this vol. is apparently stamped over 'Handel's Opera'. For contents, see Binding Style A (under Groups 2, 4, 5) and Binding Style B (under Group 2).

DONALD BURROWS

133

Appendix 2: Serial Numbers and Evidence of Provenance

Cfm MU. MS. no.	Work	Spine Label No.	Lennard Labels
789	*Hercules*	1	K3
790	*Alexander Balus*	2	K3
791	*Atalanta*	[3]†	K3
792	*Acis and Galatea*	4	K3
793	*Theodora*	5	K3
794	*Ode for St Cecilia's Day* and *Alexander's Feast*	6	K3
795	L'Allegro	7	K3
796	Italian Duets	8	K3
797	Italian Cantatas	9	K3
798	'Miscellanys'	10	K3
799	Concerti grossi, Op. 6	12	K3
800	*Esther*	14	K3
801	*Joshua*	16	K3
802	*Israel in Egypt*	17	—
803	*Athalia*	18	K3
804	*Susanna*	19	K3
805	*Jephtha*	[20]	K3
806	*Deborah*	21	K3
807	*Solomon*	23	K3
808	*Saul*	25	K3
809	*Judas Maccabaeus*	26	K3
810	Anthems, i	27	K3
811	Anthems, ii	28	K3
812	Anthems, iii (Coronation Anthems)		K3
813	Anthems, i (Coronation Anthems and Funeral Anthem)	[30]	K3
814	Te Deums, Jubilates	32	K3
815	*Arminio*	33	K3
816	*Orlando*	35	K3
817	*Berenice*	[36]	K4
818	*Rodelinda*	37	K4
819	*Lotario*	38	K4
820	*Arianna*	39	K4
821	*Floridante*	42	K4
822	*Riccardo Primo*	43	K4
823	*Alcina*	44	K4
824	*Ariodante*	47	K4
825	*Scipione*	49	K4
826	*Flavio*	50	K4
827	*Giulio Cesare*	51	K4
828	*Ottone*	[53]	—
829	*Rinaldo*	55	K4

Cfm MU. MS. no.	Work	Spine Label No.	Lennard Labels
830	*Muzio Scevola*, Act 3	56	K4
831	*Teseo*	61	K4
832	*Il pastor fido*	63	K4
833	*Giustino*	64	K4
834	*Siroe*	65	K4
835	*Il trionfo del tempo*	66	K4
836	Concertos and *Water Music*		K3
837	*Admeto*		K4
838	*Ezio*		—
839	*Alessandro*		K4
840	*Amadigi*		K4
841	*Belshazzar*		K4
842	*The Choice of Hercules*		K3
843	*Joseph*		K3
844	*Messiah*		K3
845	*Partenope*		K4
846	*Il Parnasso in festa*		K4
847	*Faramondo*		K4
848	*Poro*		K4
849	*Tolomeo*		K4
850	*Radamisto*		K3
851	*Samson*		K3
852	*Tamerlano*		K3
853	*Sosarme*		K4
854	*Serse*		K4
855	*Rodrigo* and *Silla*	68	K4

Note: All volumes except MSS. 846 and 855 are identifiable from the list in the Greatorex sale catalogue: for MS. 814 the catalogue mentions 'Two volumes', but only one survives.

† [ ] indicates that the label bearing this no. is no longer present on the vol., but its existence was recorded in A. H. Mann, *Catalogue of the Barrett Lennard Collection*, (MS, Keeper's Room, Fitzwilliam Museum).

Appendix 3: Other manuscripts of Handel's works from Lennard's library

Location/Shelf-mark	Work	Format (size in mm)	Copyists	Paper	Binding style	Spine labels	Lennard bookplate
GB-Ob MS.Mus.d.221	*Serse* (Overture and songs)	II (270 × 215)	S1 and anon	WM E*a	E	HANDEL /47	Style B
GB-BENcoke	Arr. of Sonatas, Concertos, etc. for kbd, 1841	IIa (290 × 232)	H. B. Lennard and R. Marquis	19th-cent. printed MS paper	F	HANDEL/14/ SONATAS &&c	Style B (and K/2)
GB-Private Collection	Walsh printed edn., 65 Keyboard Overtures, with MS addition of 2 further pieces	IIa (330 × 240)	H. B. Lennard	19th-cent. printed MS paper	F	HANDEL P.F.-/9/-OVERTURES	
US-CP MS 3	Duets from Italian Operas	I		S5	G	ITALIAN†	Style A
US-CP MS 4	Original Italian Duets	I		S5	G		Style A
US-CP MS 5	Duets from English Oratorios, etc	I		S5 {2 'crowned' fleurs-de-lis WMs: 1 with marks H/IV, 1 with VDL}	G	HAN(DEL)† VOCA(L) (vol) 3 English	Style A

Key: Binding styles: E—Marbled boards with calf corners (19th cent.), F—Plain boards with calf corners (19th cent.), G—Tooled full calf (18th cent.)
Lennard Bookplates: Style A—Heraldic device and 'Henry Barrett Lennard' (as in Cfm vols.), Style B—2 heraldic devices and 'Henry Barrett Lennard, 12, York Gate, Regents Park'.
†Backstrips on these MSS have collapsed and most of the original labels may be lost.

7

The Chandos Collection

GRAYDON BEEKS

ANOTHER patron who, like Elizabeth Legh, began a collection of Handel's music before 1720, was James Brydges, from October 1714 Earl of Caernarvon and from April 1719 1st Duke of Chandos. The music of Handel formed only a small part of his music-library, which was an adjunct to his activity as patron of his own private band— the so-called 'Cannons Concert'—which provided music at his newly built Palladian seat of Cannons near Edgware. This activity lasted from late 1715 to around mid-1721 when, in response to financial losses from the collapse of the South Sea Bubble (and perhaps also to the inauguration of the Royal Academy of Music), Brydges released almost all his professional musicians.[1] Although there was some musical activity over the next few years involving servants and London musicians imported by Cannons's musical director, John Christopher Pepusch, there is no evidence that the Duke continued to commission music or to add to his music collection in any significant way after 1721.

The Duke had his music-library catalogued in 1720. That catalogue, written by the Duke's librarian Mr Noland and subscribed by Pepusch on 23 August 1720, was supplemented by another in Pepusch's own hand dated 23 October 1721.[2] The Handel items from these catalogues are shown in Appendix 1. All these items, except for the copy of *Pièces de clavecin*, the *Songs in the Opera of Rinaldo*, and perhaps *Radamisto*, must have been in manuscript. A few printed items, also shown in Appendix 1, seem to have been added to the Collection after 1721, but there is no indication that Chandos commissioned an

---

[1] At New Year's Day 1721 the Duke employed some 15 or 16 players and 10 singers. By New Year's Day 1722 the numbers had dropped to only 4 or 5 players and 3 or 4 singers. See G. Beeks, 'Handel and Music for the Earl of Carnarvon,' in P. Williams (ed.), *Bach, Handel, Scarlatti: Tercentenary Essays* (Cambridge, 1985), 1–20, esp. pls. A and B and table 2.

[2] This latter document does not survive, but some notes comparing the two catalogues were made at a later date by Dr Baxter, the Duke's Chaplain, and those notes and the Noland catalogue constitute US-SM MS Stowe 66.

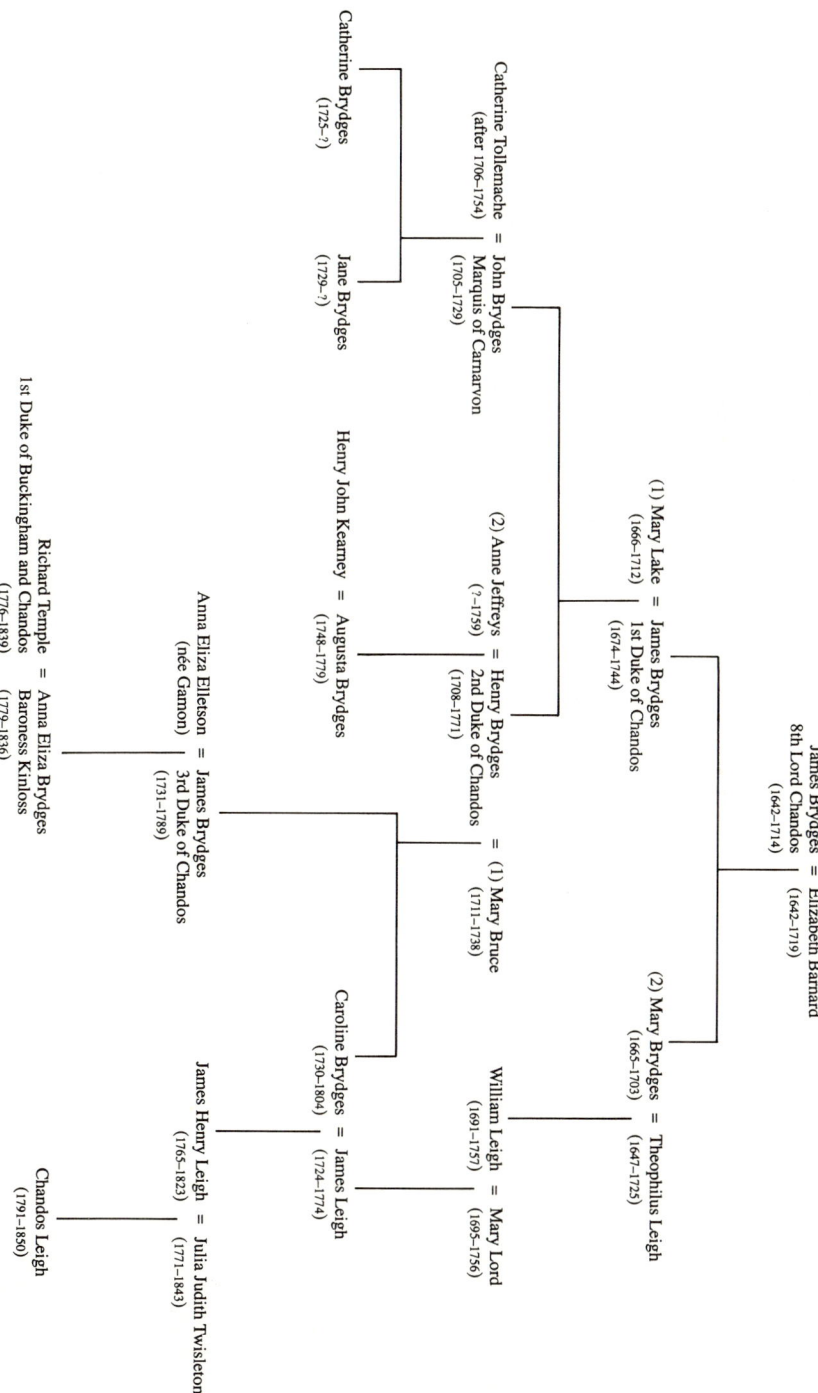

The Brydges and Leigh family tree.

ongoing series of manuscript copies from the Smith scriptorium in the manner of Elizabeth Legh.

The Duke died on 9 August 1744 and the music-library passed to his second son and heir, Henry Brydges, 2nd Duke of Chandos (see the family tree in Fig. 1) under the following terms of his will: 'To Lord Carnarvon plate, and pictures, books and manuscripts to go with Cannons as heirlooms.'[3] Unfortunately, the 2nd Duke was a spendthrift, and by the time of his father's death had already gone through most of his inheritance. In order to clear his debts, the trustees of the 1st Duke's will were forced to sell the property, beginning with the 'large and valuable library' in March 1747,[4] continuing with the paintings, and eventually including the contents and fabric of the house itself. In all these sales there was no mention of the contents of the music-library.

No items identified as being from the Cannons music-library surfaced, so far as I can tell, until 1915, when the collector Cummings described a volume in his own collection as follows:

The music-library of the Duke of Chandos was dispersed at the great sale by auction of the Palace and its contents in 1747. One large volume, handsomely bound in scarlet morocco and gold, still exists in my own library. It contains a collection of Handel's Church music probably written in the order of composition (from 1718 to 1720) by John Christopher Smith and his son. The manuscript presents several interesting differences from the admirable publications of the German Handel Society, edited by Dr Chrysander[5] . . .

Then followed a rather vague listing of variant readings. We know from surviving volumes not containing music that the 1st Duke had his manuscripts bound in several styles, including one similar to that described by Cummings.[6] At the sale of his library on 17 May 1917 it was purchased by Bernard Quaritch, Ltd., Booksellers, who in turn offered it for sale in their catalogues of October 1919 and 1921. The manuscript subsequently vanished and Quaritch have been unable to identify its eventual purchaser. I will return to this manuscript below.

[3] An abstract of the will is given in C. H. C. Baker and M. I. Baker, *The Life and Circumstances of James Brydges, First Duke of Chandos, Patron of the Liberal Arts* (Oxford, 1949), 465–8.

[4] GB-Ob MS Rawl.D.11, a MS copy of Clarendon's *History* i, includes a letter dated 'Whitchurch 25 Aug 1747' to Rawlinson from Daniel Perkins in which Perkins takes credit for preparing a MS catalogue of the Cannons library with the help of Cock the auctioneer and two booksellers. Perkins disowns the printed form of the catalogue as 'mangled'. From this letter we learn that the manuscript catalogue was complied in 22½ days under pressure of the sale, and that 8 days were spent on the manuscripts in the library.

[5] W. H. Cummings, *Handel, The Duke of Chandos and the Harmonious Blacksmith* (London, 1915), 11.

[6] c.f. GB-Lbl Stowe MS 772 with bookplate and GB-Ob MS Rawl. Poet. 229 without bookplate.

140   THE CHANDOS COLLECTION

The bulk of the manuscript documents from Cannons (letters, estate papers, etc.) descended through the 1st Duke's son, Henry the 2nd Duke, to his grandson, James the 3rd Duke, and passed to the Dukes of Buckingham by marriage to his great-granddaughter Anna Eliza. The documents were moved to Stowe, from where most were purchased by Henry Huntington in 1925 and transferred to what is now the Huntington Library in San Marino, California. In 1948 C. H. Collins Baker and Muriel I. Baker, after sifting through the bulk of the material, published the definitive biography of the 1st Duke: *The Life and Circumstances of James Brydges, First Duke of Chandos, Patron of the Liberal Arts*. In it the Noland catalogue of the Cannons music-library was made public for the first time and the extent of the music collection—all of it missing—became clear. The Stowe manuscripts at the Huntington contain not a scrap of music from Cannons.

Finally in November 1981 certain books and manuscripts from the library at Stoneleigh Abbey in Warwickshire were sold at Christie's.[7] Included were ten manuscripts and a number of prints which seem clearly to be identical with items in the Noland catalogue. Among these were six manuscripts containing works by Handel.

The whereabouts of this material for the past 260 years also became clearer. James Brydges's younger sister Mary had married Theophilus Leigh of Adlestrop, Glos. in 1689. James's granddaughter, Lady Caroline Brydges, married Mary's grandson, James Leigh, in 1755, and their only child, James Henry Leigh, inherited Stoneleigh Abbey from another branch of the Leigh family in 1806. Clearly these musical sources from Cannons passed to the Leighs at some stage, but just when I have not been able to determine. The 2nd Duke died intestate and generally insolvent in 1771 and his estate was administered by his widow. I have seen only a draft will for the 3rd Duke, dividing his estate between his nephew, James Henry Leigh, and his sister, Lady Caroline Brydges Leigh,[8] but this was made before his remarriage in 1777 and the birth of his surviving daughter Anna Eliza (1778/9–1836), and must surely have been superseded by a later will. He might still have left some or all of the music manuscripts to his sister, as she is known to have been fond of music.[9]

---

[7] *A Catalogue of printed books the property of The Trustees of The Stoneleigh Settlement, the Executors of the late 4th Lord Leigh, Stoneleigh Abbey Preservation Trust Ltd, and from various sources which will be sold at Christie's Great Rooms Wednesday 18 November 1981 at 11.00 a.m. and 2.30 p.m precisely* (London: Christie, Manson & Woods Ltd., 1981).

[8] GB-Lpro ACC 262 ST 49/100, Draft Will of James, Marquis of Caernarvon Sept 1768. It leaves his deceased wife's property to his nephew, James Henry Leigh; the goods at Minchenden House, including pictures but excepting plate, to his nephew, James Henry Leigh; and the rest and residue of his personal estate to his sister, Lady Caroline Brydges Leigh.

[See opposite page for n. 9]

In 1990, some seventy years after its disappearance, the 'lost' Cummings manuscript was identified by Dorothea Schröder as NL–DHgm MS A III 1.[10] Its contents are given in Appendix 2. The museum acquired it from the banker and collector Dr D. F. Scheurleer, who had apparently purchased it from Quaritch sometime before 1924. As Schröder points out, it appears likely that Cummings acquired the volume from Chandos Leigh (1791–1850), whose coat-of-arms appears on the inside front cover, or from his estate. A note on the flyleaf states that the volume is 'From James Henry Leigh's Library at Adlestrop', indicating that Chandos Leigh inherited the manuscript from his father,[11] presumably together with the items subsequently sold from Stoneleigh Abbey in 1981.

The fate of the remaining items from the Cannons music-library remains a mystery. There is no indication that they were ever in the possession of the Leigh Family, although it is just possible that material could have been lost in the transfer of their library from Adlestrop to Stoneleigh Abbey in the early nineteenth century. If they remained in the Brydges family and passed to the Dukes of Buckingham, it is curious that they do not appear in the surviving partial catalogues of the Stowe library or the catalogue of the great sale of manuscripts from Stowe of 1849,[12] and that they did not come to the Huntington with the Stowe papers—unless they were destroyed in the nineteenth century.[13] It is conceivable that they

[9] *Ed.'s Note*: The last will of the 3rd Duke of Chandos, dated 29 January 1780, with a codicil dated 12 Aug. 1782, and proved on 14 Oct. 1789 (Lpro. Prob 11/1183, fos. 381–3) contains the following: 'I confirm the settlement or articles made previous to my marriage with my present wife dated the twentieth day of June 1777. I also confirm the settlement which I have made on my sister Lady Caroline Leigh and my nephew James Henry Leigh her son bearing date the twenty fourth day of July 1777.' Apart from this he bequeaths all his 'real Estates' and his personal estate to his wife Anna Eliza, Duchess of Chandos; there is no mention of any musical manuscripts, nor any details of the settlements of June and July 1777, which may or may not have confirmed those in the draft will of 1768.

[10] 'Wiederentdeckt: die Kopie der Chandos-Anthems aus der ehemaligen Sammlung Cummings', *Göttinger Händel Beiträge*, 4 (1991), 94–107.

[11] It is just possible, though unlikely, that the MS somehow strayed from James Henry Leigh's possession and was subsequently purchased by Chandos Leigh in order to return it to the Leigh Family possession. He is known to have purchased the diary of Dr. Henry Brydges, younger brother of the 1st Duke, from a Mr Heber in 1836 for just such a purpose. See G. Beeks, ' "A Club of Composers": Handel, Pepusch and Arbuthnot at Cannons', in S. Sadie and A. Hicks (eds.), *Handel Tercentenary Collection* (London, 1987), 209.

[12] W. J. S., *Catalogue of the important collection of manuscripts from Stowe which will be sold by auction, by Messrs S. Leigh, Sotheby & Co. at their house, 3, Wellington Street, Strand, on Monday, 11th of June 1849, and seven following days.*

[13] In Messrs. Jackson Stops Sale Catalogue, *The Ducal Estate [of Stowe] and Contents of the Mansion*, 4–22 July 1921, items 2362–2499 are identified only as 'Manuscripts' while item 2202 is listed as 'Bound volumes of Music, 30 vols.; and a large quantity of loose music.' Both Brian Trowell and I remember having seen a ref. to quantities of material lying ruined in the rain at Stowe, but have not been able to trace it.

142 THE CHANDOS COLLECTION

descended to the 2nd Duke's last child, a daughter by his second wife. This child, Lady Augusta, died in 1779 having married one Henry John Kearney. At least one manuscript volume from the Cannons library, a history of the Willoughby family, survives bearing her bookplate and arms with the date 1766,[14] and it was apparently at Stowe in 1849. This suggests that she owned manuscripts from the Cannons library and at least some of her manuscripts may have returned to the Brydges family after her death. I have found no indication that she owned any music from the Collection.

The non-Handel items from the Stoneleigh sale seem clearly identical with the items listed in the Noland catalogue. For example, the volume of anthems by Nicola Francesco Haym, now GB-Lbl Add. MS 62561, contains a detailed dedication to James Brydges and an assertion that the anthems were written for performance by the Cannons Concert in the church of St Lawrence, Little Stanmore.[15] The volume of cantatas and arias for soprano by Thomas Roseingrave, now GB-Lbl Add. MS 62103, appears to be part of item 23 in the Noland catalogue: 'Two Books full of Cantatas for one voice and instruments by Mr. Rosengrave'. The three English cantatas included in that volume are to texts also set by Pepusch for Cannons—one of them, 'When Love's Soft Passion', is a text written by James Blackley who was employed at Cannons as a singer in 1718. The copyist of this volume is the same as the second scribe involved in the Cummings manuscript—Schröder's Hand B. Finally, the contents of the cantata miscellany now GB-Lbl Add. MS 62102 are identical with those of items 34–52 in the Noland catalogue and include Handel's cantata 'Sento là che ristretto' as item 36.

The other Handel items from the Stoneleigh sale consist of two volumes of Chandos Anthems (now GB-Lbl Add. MSS 62099 and 62100), a volume containing two Chandos Anthems and two anthems by Pepusch (now GB-Lbl Add. MS 62101), and two volumes of instrumental parts to Chandos Anthems (now in GB-BENcoke MSS 27 and 109). They are all presentation copies rather than performing materials, and they seem to correspond exactly to items 7–12, [12a], and [19a] in the Noland catalogue.

That these five volumes of music are from the library at Cannons is not in doubt, but questions have arisen as to whether they are identical with the items listed in the Noland catalogue of August

[14] GB-Lbl MS Stowe 656 [History of the various branches of the family of Willoughby . . .], 18th-century MS, 43 fos., bound in vellum. With bookplate and arms of Lady Augusta Anna Brydges, 1766. Since this is a Stowe MS it presumably returned to the Brydges family after her death, though whether by gift or purchase is not clear.

[15] The dedication is dated 'Cannons the 29th of September 1716' and signed by Haym.

1720. If so, for example, why do the descriptions not match? The catalogue describes item [19a] as 'A Score Book with a better cover than the rest of the Anthems'. Today the binding is virtually identical for all the volumes. The obvious answer would seem to be that they have been subsequently rebound, which would also explain why the anthems items 7–10 are grouped four-plus-two in the catalogue but are presently bound in two groups of three. The tooling on the binding of the mixed Handel/Pepusch volume (GB-Lbl Add. MS 62101) differs slightly from that of the other two Stoneleigh Abbey volumes (GB-Lbl Add. MSS 62099–62100), especially in the details within the central border on the covers and also in the details on the spine. This could indicate that the Handel/Pepusch mixed volume was bound at a different time. It might already have been bound at the time the Noland catalogue was made, with the remaining anthem volumes only being bound or rebound later.[16]

More difficult to answer are the questions which have been posed by Donald Burrows concerning paper-types found in the score volumes, and the discrepancies between the musical texts preserved in the parts and the scores.[17] Briefly stated, the two volumes of Chandos Anthem scores are written throughout on a paper with a watermark (Burrows's Bx) which makes no appearance at all in the conducting scores and appears in the autographs only in 1723/4 and 1729. In addition, Pepusch's anthem 'O be joyfull' in the mixed Handel/Pepusch volume from the Stoneleigh Abbey sale—a volume which must surely be identical with item [19a] in Noland's catalogue—is written on this same paper, although the remaining three anthems are on a different paper (Larsen's D1) whose lifespan in the autographs and other copies seems to be 1717–19.[18] As Burrows points

---

[16] GB-Lbl Add. MSS 62099–62100 both have the Stoneleigh Abbey crest stamped in gold on their front covers and have or at one time had labels pasted on their spines reading 'THREE / ANTHEMS / BY / HANDELL'. Add. MS 62099 also has a label on its spine reading 'VOL.I / M.S.S.' and presumably Add. MS 62100 formerly had a label reading 'VOL.II / M.S.S.' These two volumes also contain Stoneleigh Abbey bookplates, while Add. MS 62101 contains an older Leigh family bookplate. The volume of Haym anthems Add. MS 62561 also has the Stoneleigh Abbey crest on the front cover and bears evidence of having formerly had some sort of label on its spine. Presumably some or all of these alterations to Add. MSS 62099–62100 and 62561 are related to the presence on the inside front cover of each of a printed label from 'H.T. Cooke / PRINTER, BOOKSELLER / STATIONER & BINDER / High Street / WARWICK'. Add. MS 62101 lacks such a label.

[17] 'Sources, Resources and Handel Studies' in Sadie and Hicks (eds.), *Handel Tercentenary Collection*, 30–3.

[18] Burrows's Bx paper appears in the autographs primarily in *Giulio Cesare* of 1724 and *Lotario* of 1729. Larsen's D1 paper appears in the autographs in 1717–18 (Chandos Anthems) and in an early set of Chandos Anthems (GB-Ob MS Tenbury 881–3) which Winton Dean has dated c.1719 on the basis of the scribal hand. The instr. pts. in BENcoke are on a variety of Clausen and Burrows's Cb paper which falls in the autographs between the *Radamisto* autograph (begun autumn 1719 and performed Apr. 1720) and the *Floridante* autograph (completed 28 Nov. 1721). See D. Burrows, *A Handlist of the Paper Characteristics of Handel's English*

[*n. 18 continued on page 144*]

144   THE CHANDOS COLLECTION

out, it might be reasonable to suppose that watermark Bx appeared in the copies at an earlier date than it did in the autographs, especially since the scribes involved are not known to have had any direct connection with the Smith scriptorium and may well have had a different source of paper.

If the paper-types cast doubt on the identification of the two Chandos Anthem score volumes with items 7–12 in the Noland catalogue, the musical contents are even more puzzling, since the musical texts of the scores do not match those of the GB-BENcoke parts. These latter contain a version of Anthem 7, 'My song shall be allway', which preserves two movements not found in the autograph as it now stands or in any of the mainline manuscript copies.[19] They also include the longer version of Anthem 5a 'I will magnifie Thee', containing two 'extra' movements not found in the autograph but demonstrably early given their presence in GB-Ob MS Tenbury 881, dated c.1719 as mentioned above.[20] The fascicle structure of the Anthem 5a autograph (GB-Lbl R.M.20.d.6: fos.77^r–99^r) confirms that these two movements were later additions.

GB-Lbl Add. MS 62101 seems a curiosity in any case. Each pair of anthems is foliated separately (the Handel items as fos.1–84, the Pepusch fos.1–81) and copied complete. Yet in each case the space reserved in the upper left-hand corner of the opening folio of each anthem for a decorated initial, text *incipit*, and composer's name has been left blank. In addition, each anthem is duplicated elsewhere in the catalogue: Handel's Anthems 2 and 5a appear earlier as items 5 and 6, while Pepusch's 'O sing unto the Lord' and 'O be joyfull' appear later as items 97 and 100 (numbers 3 and 6 respectively of a set of eight anthems by Pepusch, perhaps bound in a single volume, now lost).

An expanded version of Pepusch's 'O be joyfull' survives in a collection of material which seems to derive directly from the composer (GB-Lam MS 86). Although there is no specific indication that this longer version dates from the Cannons period, it would be curious if

---

Autographs (Milton Keynes, 1982), 23–6, 34–5, 46; and W. Dean, 'Handel's Early London Copyists', in Williams (ed.), *Tercentenary Essays* 75–97, esp. 93–4 and plate G; a rev. version of Dean's article is published in W. Dean, *Essays on Opera* (Oxford 1990), 8–21.

[19] The shorter version of the sonata requires 54 bars instead of 75 and lacks the virtuosic solo passages so characteristic of the standard movement. It is also preserved in GB-Ob MS Tenbury 615, a mid-1730s copy in the hand of S3. The 'Celebrated Trio' is not found in any other MS source, but was printed by Arnold in *The Works of Handel in Score* (c.1790). Both movements are included in the Cummings MS.

[20] See G. Beeks, 'Handel's Chandos Anthems: The "Extra" Movements', *MT* 119 (July 1978), 621–3. My statement there that the 'Celebrated Trio' was included by Wright & Wilkinson in their 1784 print of *The Complete Score of Ten Anthems composed chiefly for the Chapel of his Grace the late James Duke of Chandos* is incorrect; it was first printed by Samuel Arnold.

it did not. This means that both Pepusch's 'O be joyfull' and Handel's 'I will magnifie Thee' exist in two versions, the later one being substantially expanded, which suggests that the shorter versions of both anthems found in item [19a] were superseded by the longer versions which one would expect to find in the missing items 6 and 100. If true, it would explain the presence of duplicates in the Cannons music-library, as well as the incomplete state of the copies in the mixed Handel/Pepusch volume and the fact that Noland did not assign the volume a number. They were earlier versions which had been superseded. The presence of the demonstrably early watermark D1 in the first three anthems in the volume may also support this hypothesis.

A further complication is provided by the Cummings manuscript, the contents of which agree substantially with those of the BENcoke parts. Both contain the shorter symphony and 'Celebrated Trio' in Anthem 7, and the 'extra' movements in Anthem 5a. The parts, however, also contain Anthem 9, 'O praise the Lord with one consent,' and Anthem 10, 'The Lord is my light', which are not included in the Cummings manuscript. Just how do these sources relate to the volumes of scores from Stoneleigh Abbey and to items 1–12 and [19a] in the Cannons library catalogue?

It seems to me that the volumes from Stoneleigh Abbey are almost certainly just what they seem; that they are identical with items 7–12 in the Noland catalogue of August 1720; and that watermark Bx just happens to appear in the manuscript copies three or four years before it appears in the autographs. Any other explanation which I have been able to propose to myself is unnecessarily complicated and creates at least as many unresolved questions as it answers. Furthermore, the case of library scores not matching library parts occurs again in the Aylesford Collection (e.g. *Esther/Oratorium*).

The Cummings manuscript, as suggested by Schröder, seems to be an earlier manuscript, presumably copied before the last two Chandos Anthems were written. Its oversized format and sumptuous binding probably indicate that it was to be displayed in the main library at Cannons rather than in the music-library, and thus was not mentioned in the Noland catalogue.[21] It may even have been copied from a lost conducting score, if such a thing ever existed, and reflect versions actually performed at Cannons.[22]

---

[21] Schröder advances the intriguing suggestion that the Chandos Te Deum may have been composed to celebrate the Peace of Passarowitz (21 June 1718), which ended the Second Turkish War, or in anticipation of James Brydges's elevation to the dukedom of Chandos (29 Apr. 1719), and that the Cummings MS may have been compiled in celebration of one of these events. See Schröder, 'Wiederentdeckt', 106.

[22] Conducting scores for a number of Handel's pre-1720 works are lost but must have existed. The existence of a now-lost conducting score for *Acis and Galatea* is the only way to

[*n. 22 continued on page 146*]

146 THE CHANDOS COLLECTION

The principal scribe, Schröder's Hand A, is also the copyist of the Stoneleigh Abbey volumes of Handel and Pepusch anthems. He was clearly an experienced copyist, otherwise unknown in Handel manuscripts but perhaps to be found in other circles. The secondary scribe, Schröder's Hand B, also appears to have been a professional and, as mentioned above, was the copyist of the volume of Roseingrave cantatas now GB-Lbl Add. MS 62103. The scribe labelled by Schröder as Hand C, who was also responsible for the BENcoke parts, was clearly a novice, and some of the curiosities in the derivation of the contrabasso part from the score noted by Burrows may be attributable to this fact.[23] Certainly some of the alternation of scribal hands in the Cummings manuscript is attributable to one of the experienced scribes establishing the layout of a piece with the work to be continued by Hand C.[24]

The discovery of the Cummings manuscript allows us to reconstruct with some certainty the development of Anthem 7, 'My song shall be alway'. In its original form it seems to have lacked both the duet 'The heav'ns are thine' and the trio 'Thou rulest the raging of the sea', and to have begun with the short version of the opening sonata. The duet was added before the Cummings manuscript version was copied, and this is the version of the anthem preserved in GB-Ob MS Tenbury 615 which apparently dates from the 1730s. The trio was added after copying was completed but before the volume was bound.[25] Subsequently, but before either the Stoneleigh Abbey score (GB-Lbl Add. MS 62099) or the Tenbury score (GB-Ob MS Tenbury 882) were copied, the short version of the sonata and the trio were removed from the autograph and the longer 75-bar sonata substituted for them. The question remains

account for the two separate traditions of early copies described by Windszus and Trowell. See W. Windszus, *Georg Friedrich Händel, Aci, Galatea e Polifemo, Cantata von 1708; Acis and Galatea, Masque von 1718; Acis and Galatea, italienisch-englische Serenata von 1732: Kritischer Bericht im Rahmen der Hallischen Händel-Ausgabe* (Hamburg, 1979), 81–183, esp. 1.3 'Stemma der Handschriften und Drucke'; and B. Trowell, '*Acis, Galatea and Polyphemus*: a "serenata a tre voci"', in N. Fortune (ed.), *Music and Theatre: Essays in honour of Winton Dean* (Cambridge, 1987), 31–93, esp. 32–8 and table 1. See also Clausen, Ch. 2 above.

[23] Others may be attributable to the fact, remarked upon by Schröder, that the scoring of the instrumental bass in the Cummings MS differs markedly from that indicated in the autograph or preserved in the mainline manuscript copies. Whether these differences reflect Handel's original intentions which were subsequently altered in the autograph, or changes which were made in a now-lost conducting score but never transferred to the autograph, or scribal unfamiliarity with Handel's method of working, remains to be determined.

[24] Good exx. are found in Anthem 5a, 'I will magnifie Thee', where Hand A sets the initial layout on fo. 61ʳ and Hand C continues the movement on fo. 61ᵛ, and in Anthem 8, 'O come let us sing unto the Lord', where Hand B sets the format on fo. 105ʳ and Hand C continues on fo. 105ᵛ. Similar behaviour by copyists is described in Dean's 'Handel's Early London Copyists'; see esp. p. 93 concerning copyists RM1 and Smith.

[25] This is indicated not only by the insertion of a separate bifolium containing the trio (fos. 26–7) in the hand of a different scribe (Hand B) as noted by Schröder, but by the notation at the bottom of the previous page in the hand of the original scribe 'Segue a Duetto' (fo. 25ᵛ).

open as to whether the trio could have been written by someone other than Handel.

If we can accept this as a tentative explanation of the Cummings manuscript and the Stoneleigh Abbey volumes, what can be said about the remaining Handel items from the Cannons music-library? Have they vanished—perhaps destroyed in the nineteenth century or lurking in private collections—or can they be identified among the single copies scattered in various libraries?

Before attempting to answer this question, I should note that at least one additional Cannons manuscript appears to have escaped from the Collection and to have survived. This is GB-Lcm MS 1097, a collection of cantatas by Pepusch and Galliard which seems clearly identical with items 24–5 in the Noland catalogue. There it is described as 'One Book full of Cantatas 3 of them for two Voices and Instruments 4 for one Voice and Instruments one for a Voice alone by J. C. Pepusch. One for one Voice and a Hautboi by Mr. Galliard.' This describes precisely the contents of Lcm 1097 (see App. 3), and these pieces occur in no other known source, let alone together in the same source. The chance that Lcm 1097 is a later copy of a lost Cannons volume is virtually eliminated by the fact that the principal scribe of Lcm 1097 is the one responsible for the Stoneleigh/Cannons volumes (GB-Lbl Add. MSS 62099–62101) and is also the principal scribe of the Cummings manuscript (NL-DHgm A III 1)—Schröder's Hand A. Furthermore, Schröder's Hand B from the Cummings manuscript makes a brief appearance in Cantata 6 (fos.53–4 and 77).

On the other hand, there are a number of items from the Noland catalogue which seem clearly not to have resurfaced and may very well be irretrievably lost. Among these are item 80 'A Book of Songs in the Opera of Titus Manlius in Score by Mr. Attilio', which cannot be identified with either of the surviving scores of the opera;[26] and item 105—'Six Concertos in 6 parts in Score consisting of 4 Violins one Tenor 1 Violoncello wth. the Organ compos'd by Mr Turner', for which no sources are known.

The one Handel item which seems clearly not to have surfaced is item 117—'Sonata for 2 Violins 1 Hautboi and a Bass composed by Mr Hendel', which I take to be the Sonata in G Minor, HWV 404, edited by Terence Best from its only known source, a manuscript in the Malmesbury Collection[27] which was almost certainly prepared

[26] GB-Lbl Add. MS 16156, a manuscript with no composer named which was owned by Philip Hayes in 1763, and a copy from the Aylesford Collection (lot 282 in the 1918 sale) which was identified by Anthony Hicks in 1972 but whose present whereabouts are unknown; see O. Haas, *[A Catalogue of] Rare Music Exhibited at the Antiquarian Book Fair 1972* (London, 1972).
[27] HHA/IV/15 (1979), 27–40.

148   THE CHANDOS COLLECTION

for Elizabeth Legh. The copy in the Cannons music-library must have been a different manuscript, now lost.

Since there is a possibility that some or all of the other Handel items might be sitting on library shelves somewhere awaiting identification, it may be useful to visualize what these fugitive Cannons manuscript volumes might look like. Based on what we know from the Stoneleigh Abbey anthem volumes and what we can infer from the Malmesbury volumes—surely a somewhat comparable collection—these missing volumes might display some or all of the following characteristics:

1. They will be demonstrably early copies, on paper types and in scribal hands consistent with a date before 1721; in a best-case scenario they would be in the hand of one of the scribes responsible for the Cummings, Stoneleigh, and Lcm volumes.
2. They will probably be in Larsen's upright II format, although oblong I and even upright III should not be completely ruled out.
3. They may be bound in red or black morocco leather with gold tooling, perhaps similar to the tooling of the Stoneleigh volumes.[28]
4. They are unlikely to show any evidence of use for performance.
5. They may, in some cases, be identified from clues present in the Noland catalogue description.

With these characteristics in mind, and with the understanding that I have by no means examined all the manuscripts which make up this proverbial haystack, it may be well first to consider briefly the eight Handelian items with no connection to Cannons which are listed in the Noland catalogue. Two of these—item 63 'The songs in the Opera of Rinaldo' and item 132 'Suite des Pieces pour le Clavecin'—were almost certainly prints. The other six are the *Ode for Queen Anne's Birthday*, the Utrecht Te Deum and Jubilate, and the operas *Amadigi*, *Radamisto*, and the third act of *Muzio Scevola*.

Item 104 in the Noland catalogue is described as 'A Piece of Musick compos'd for Queen Ann's Birth Day'. Only a few early copies of this work survive, and there was certainly a tradition in the late eighteenth century that few copies had ever been made. The most intriguing of those I have seen is GB-Lbl Add. MS 35347 (format IIa, paper B, copyist X), formerly owned by Dr John Randall of Cambridge University and headed 'Serenata on Queen Anne's Birth Day, 1714. / Compos'd by Mr Handell'. Unfortunately,

---

[28] Red morocco seems to have been a favourite at Cannons and numerous other volumes, both musical and non-musical, survive in such bindings, including two dedicatory volumes of Pepusch's published cantatas from Stoneleigh Abbey (items 127–8 in Christie's 1981 sale = item 107 in Noland's catalogue). Item 127 was purchased by Richard Macnutt for £286 and item 128 by Pickering for £264.

it has been rebound and there is nothing to indicate any connection with Cannons.

Items 121–2 in the Noland catalogue seem clearly to be the Utrecht Te Deum and Jubilate. Several early manuscript copies survive, the most interesting I have seen being GB-Lbl Add. MS 4323 (format II, paper B, copyist Linike), presented to the Museum by John Hawkins in 1789 and rebound in 1961.[29] Dean identifies it as probably the earliest surviving copy and suggests a date of 1713.[30] It is unlikely to have been made for Chandos, who seems not to have been collecting Handel's works before 1717, and there is nothing to connect it with Cannons. However, the Cannons copy must have had a similar appearance since the peculiar scoring for the works listed in the Cannons music-library catalogue can only have been derived from reading the first page of a layout which omits mention of all solo voices and a number of required instruments (e.g. oboes and bassoons in the Jubilate).

With the operas one tends to face the problem of too many early copies. The Noland catalogue describes item 87 as 'Amadis an Opera in Score by Mr. Handel'. The copies of the complete opera I have seen tend to be in oblong I format and designate the work 'Amadigi di Gaula' (e.g. GB-Mp MS 130 Hd4 vol. 46, GB-Lbl Add. MS 47848, and US-Wc M1500.H13 A44). At least two of the aria collections use the spelling 'Amadis'. GB-Ob MS Tenbury 884 (format II, paper C, copyist Sm), which contains arias without recitatives and one instrumental number, is called on the title-page 'Opera of Amadis & Other Songs by Mr Handel' and is dated by Dean and Knapp as c.1719.[31] It has, unfortunately, been rebound, so that potential characteristics cannot be checked. It was owned by Thomas Chilcot, from 1728 until his death in 1766 organist of Bath Abbey. Since Chilcot is thought to have been born c.1700, it is extremely unlikely that this and other early manuscript copies of Handel's works in his collection were copied expressly for him.[32] GB-Lcm MS 902

---

[29] A series of volumes given to the British Museum by Hawkins were apparently bound uniformly in marbled boards with calf spine and tips. The old covers of the first of this series are preserved as Add. MS 5319. It may well be that Hawkins himself had the various manuscripts rebound in this format.

[30] Dean, 'Handel's Early London Copyists', 81.

[31] W. Dean and J. M. Knapp, *Handel's Operas 1704–1726* (Oxford, 1987), 294.

[32] GB-Ob MS Tenbury 884 is one of several MSS formerly owned by Thomas Chilcot (c.1700–66). They are generally early copies, in upright II format, and they include the three volumes of Chandos Anthems GB-Ob MSS Tenbury 881–3 and the copy of *Muzio Scevola* from the Cummings Collection now in Japan, (Tn N-3, 18 MS 488). Most are bound in buff leather. They are unlikely to have been copied for Chilcot, who began his apprenticeship with the Bath organist Josias Priest only in July 1721 (see K. E. James, 'Concert Life in Eighteenth-century Bath', Ph.D. diss., (University of London, Royal Holloway College, 1987), 95). He must have acquired them—possibly as a group—from an early owner or owners. I suspect that

[*n. 32 continued on page 150*]

150   THE CHANDOS COLLECTION

(format IIa, paper B, copyist unknown), which contains twelve arias
with no recitatives, is bound in brown leather and labelled 'Amadis'
on the front cover and the spine. These remain possibilities, although
one wonders whether any cataloguer would designate a collection of
arias as an 'Opera in Score'. Other possibilities are GB-Lbl R.M.19.g.2
(format III, paper C1*, copyist RM2, complete without recitatives)
and BENcoke MS 15 (format II, copyists RM1, and one unknown).
So far as I can tell, there is no evidence to connect any of these
volumes to Cannons.

Item 130 in Pepusch's lost catalogue of the Cannons music-library
dated 23 October 1721—'The opera of Rhadamistus'—could refer
to a printed copy, since *Il Radamisto opera rapresentata nel Regio
Teatro d'Hay Market* was issued by Richard Meares and Christopher
Smith in December 1720, with a collection of *Arie aggiunte di
Radamisto* issued the following March. If the Duke of Chandos, as a
principal subscriber to the first season of the Royal Academy, acquired
a manuscript score, there are at least three possible candidates. One
is GB-Lcm MS 905, which contains the 1720 version in upright IIa
format in the hands of Smith and Gamma with December 1720 additions in the hand of H2. Since the previous item in the Cannons music-
library catalogue is item 129 'being the Opera of Astartus by Sr
Bononcini' which was in the middle of its initial Royal Academy run
in December 1720, one might expect the Cannons copy of *Radamisto*
to contain the December 1720 additions. It may be worth noting that
Smith and Gamma collaborated on the Malmesbury copy as well.
Unfortunately, the binding of Lcm MS 905 is marbled boards with a
calf spine, surely too plain for a Cannons binding. In addition, the
title-page reads 'Radamisto: / with additional Songs', so it is not clear
where the cataloguer would have found the spelling 'Rhadamistus'.

The only early copy of *Radamisto* I have found which calls the
work 'Radamistus' is GB-Lbl Add. MS 39180 (format upright II,
copyist BM1), and it does so only on the first page of music (fo.2)
which reads:

'Opera / Radamistus / Overture'. The title-page, however, reads:
'Opera da Radamisto'. This is a not especially neat copy (in a

they do not derive from Cannons, so the question arises as to which other early collection they
might have come from. The sale catalogue for the Henry Harrington collection dated 1816
indicates that it is not from that collection (i.e. Harrington is known to have possessed early
manuscript copies of the Chandos Anthems, *Esther* and *Acis and Galatea*, but they appear to
be accounted for by items 32 and 42 in the 1816 sale). Winton Dean has suggested that GB-Ob
MSS Tenbury 881–3 and GB-H MS R.X.XVI may be fugitives from Elizabeth Legh's
Collection. This is an attractive hypothesis, since they preserve between them a complete set of
the Chandos Anthems in their early forms, but there is nothing to connect the Tenbury and
Hereford volumes beyond format and shared scribal hands, and nothing at all to connect them
with Elizabeth Legh.

modern binding) which was subsequently owned by John Stanley, James Bartleman, and Edward Goddard. There is nothing to connect it with Cannons.

In some ways the most likely candidate for Cannons provenance would seem to be GB-Lbl Add. MS 31562, a neatly written copy in the hands of Smith, RM1, and an unidentified copyist, which preserves the April 1720 version of the text and which Dean dates from the same year on the basis of scribal hands.[33] It is bound in red morocco with gold tooling which is similar but not identical to that of the Stoneleigh Abbey volumes. The heading on the spine, however, is 'Radamiste / Opera', while that on the title-page (perhaps in a later hand) is 'Radamisto / Opera di G. F. Handel / 1720'. A further drawback to this manuscript is its oblong I format. The volume was subsequently owned by Edward Stephenson, Esq. of Farley Hill and Julian Marshall from whom it was purchased by the British Museum. Again there is nothing to tie it specifically to Cannons.

Item 131, 'Score of ye 3d Act of Mutius Scevola', has fewer candidates, if we assume the catalogue description to be correct in indicating that the manuscript contained only Handel's music. One might be D-B Am. Bibl. 439b, which is dated by the copyist Linike 'London Jun: ye 6 1721'. It is, however, in oblong I format and lacks the recitatives.[34] Another possible candidate would seem to be the former Cummings copy J-Tn N-3/18 MS 488, which also lacks the recitatives and includes some music by the other composers. The format is upright II, the copyists H1, H2, and RM1, and the manuscript is dated April 1721 by Dean on the basis of its predating the first performance.[35] It was subsequently owned by Thomas Chilcot and Thomas Field.[36]

After this inconclusive and generally discouraging look at early manuscript copies of Handel works not written specifically for Cannons, I would like to close by discussing how this search for fugitive Cannons library copies might be applied to two works composed specifically for the Duke of Chandos: *Esther* ('The Oratorium') and *Acis and Galatea*.

The easiest of the Noland catalogue items to identify should be item 123—'Oratorium for Voices and Instr:' Unfortunately, the only known early copies of the 1718 *Esther* which designate the work 'Oratorium' or 'The Oratorium' are the Malmesbury copy (containing

[33] Dean, 'Handel's Early London Copyists', 89.
[34] Dean and Knapp, *Handel's Operas*, 382, suggest this copy may have been made for the Prussian court.
[35] Dean, 'Handel's Early London Copyists', 89. See also Dean and Knapp, *Handel's Operas*, 379–80.
[36] See n. 32, above.

152 THE CHANDOS COLLECTION

Elizabeth Legh's signature and the date 1718 or 1719), and the copy in Manchester, MS 130 Hd4, vol. 93, (format I, paper Cb, copyist early Smith), from the Aylesford Collection. Of these copies, only the Malmesbury is in upright II format. There seems to be no obvious match here, although it is just possible that the GB-Mp manuscript could be early enough to be from Cannons if we allow for a different format and assume that it was subsequently acquired by Charles Jennens.

In the case of *Acis and Galatea* we have a tantalizing clue. The Noland catalogue entry for item 73 reads 'O the Pleasure of the Plain a Masque for 5 Voices and Instruments in Score'. It can be deduced from this wording that the manuscript in question lacked a title-page, and that the compiler of the catalogue leafed through the score until he found the opening chorus from which he took his title. A search through the early copies turns up two likely candidates— GB-BENcoke MS 1 and US-Wc M2.1/.H22/A3.[37] Both are early copies in the hand of Smith and datable as *c*.1719. Both lacked any sort of title-page in their original form, and both appear to have been copied from a posited lost conducting score.[38]

The BENcoke copy of *Acis and Galatea* is in upright II format on a combination of B and C paper in the hand of Smith, consistent with a date of *c*.1719. The binding is buff leather with tooling. Such a binding is common in the eighteenth century, but it is worth noting the similarity to the volumes later owned by Thomas Chilcot, many of which are very early copies.[39] The initials 'I:B' on the first page indicate the manuscript was once owned by the organist, composer, and copyist John Barker (1705/10–81), a Chapel Royal chorister under Croft until May 1724, organist of Holy Trinity, Coventry from 1731 and subsequently Vicar Choral of Lichfield Cathedral from the

[37] See Trowell, '*Acis, Galatea and Polyphemus*', 31–93, esp. table 1 on p. 34. See also Windszus, *Aci, Galatea e Polifemo*.

[38] The autograph (GB-Lbl R.M.20.a.2) also apparently lacked a title-page and a heading above the Sinfonia. The arguments for a lost conducting score (which presumably also lacks title page and heading) are given by Windszus, '*Aci, Galatea, e Polifemo*', 134, 138, 143–4, and summarized by Trowell, '*Acis, Galatea and Polyphemus*', 33. The GB-BENcoke and US-Wc copies were not known to Windszus in 1979 but are included in his unpublished revised Kritischer Bericht which I have not seen. According to Trowell, Windszus suggests that US-Wc M2.1/.H22/A3 might be the lost conducting score, but I can see nothing to support that hypothesis. Trowell suggests that the score listed in the Noland catalogue might be that conducting score, but this seems unlikely on the basis of the surviving Cannons MSS of Handel, Pepusch, and Haym anthems which all seem clearly to have been library copies. There must, of course, have been performing materials for works performed at Cannons, and probably conducting scores as well, but the scores and parts listed by Noland seem almost certainly to have been presentation copies. Whether the performance materials were kept at Cannons, remained in Handel's possession, or were stored somewhere else is unknown.

[39] See n. 32, above. I am grateful to Donald Burrows for providing information on this MS.

mid-1750s. He had no known connection with Cannons, but his hand is found in an early eighteenth-century musical miscellany from Stoneleigh Abbey which was sold in 1985.[40]

The US-Wc manuscript is in upright II format on Cb paper ruled I @ 8.5–9.0 mm and in the hand of Smith. It has been re-bound but the original binding has been retained and is just what one would have hoped for: dark red morocco leather with gold tooling in a style similar but not identical to the Stoneleigh Abbey anthem volumes. A later hand has added the following annotation to serve as a title page: 'Acis & Galatea / Set by Mr Hendel / Ex dono Nobilissimi Ducis Chandos 1719.' If we take 1719 to refer to the date of the gift, then this manuscript cannot be the one listed in Noland's catalogue of August 1720. If 1719 refers to something else—perhaps the presumed date of the first performance—then it could be.

The score was purchased by the Library of Congress in 1936 from Otto Haas acting as agent for Mrs Edward Speyer. Edward Speyer (1839–1934) inherited part of his collection of music from his father, the composer Wilhelm Speyer (1790–1878), but acquired most of the important pieces, including a large number of autographs, himself. There is no indication as to when this Handel manuscript became a part of the Speyer collection. The only indication of prior ownership is the inscription 'F-C- Grimston' on the inside cover in a hand which seems clearly to be different from that of the added title-page.[41] In any event, this manuscript is the only one I have found with any sort of contemporary annotation indicating a direct link to Cannons.

While there is no guarantee that either the GB-BENcoke or the US-Wc score of *Acis and Galatea* is the one mentioned in the Noland Catalogue, the possibility is tantalizing. Perhaps further research will prompt the discovery and/or identification of other missing volumes—including one or two more volumes of Chandos Anthems—from this small but important early English collection of Handel's works.

---

[40] Item 140 in Christie's sale of *Valuable Autograph Letters, Historical Documents and Music Manuscripts: The Property of The Stoneleigh Abbey Preservation Trust* . . . on Wednesday, 16 Oct. 1985: 'Manuscript Music Books, 3 vols., containing a Minuet by HANDEL, a song "With her alone I'll live" by Pepusch, a "Trumpet Aire" signed and dated by J. Barker, Jan. 10 1734, and other vocal and instrumental pieces by Bononcini, John Wether, Green, etc.' There is no knowing when these MS vols. became part of the library at Stoneleigh Abbey, nor when Barker acquired the BENcoke copy of *Acis and Galatea*. The connection is tangential at best.

[41] I am grateful to the staff of the US-Wc, and esp. to William Parsons, for their help in supplying this info. The order was placed in a letter to Otto Haas of 8 Aug. 1936, in which 9 items were ordered from the latter's Catalogue Speyer. This MS was apparently item 155 and the price was £41. The MS was given the accession no. 736920 and catalogued on 12 Feb. 1937 under the cataloguing no. 412733.

Appendix 1: Handel in the Cannons Music-Library

Cat. no. (US-SM ST 66)	Cannons item nos.	Title in Catalogue	Scoring in Catalogue	Present Location (if known)
1	1	Te Deum in Score for Voices and Instruments†	STTTB, 2 vn, ob, bc	GB-Lbl Add. MS 62099
2	2	O come let us Sing unto the Lord in score†	SSTTB, 2 vn, ob, bc	GB-Lbl Add. MS 62099
	3	O Praise the Lord with one Consent in score†	STTTB, 2 vn, ob, bc	GB-Lbl Add. MS 62099
	4	The Lord is my Light in score†	STTTB, 2 vn, ob, bc	GB-Lbl Add. MS 62099
	5	In the Lord put I my Trust in score†	STB, 2 vn, ob, bc	GB-Lbl Add. MS 62100
	6	I will magnifie thee o God my King in score†	STTTB, 2 vn, ob, bc	GB-Lbl Add. MS 62100
3	7	As Pants the Heart and	STTTB, 2 vn, ob, bn, bc	GB-Lbl Add. MS 62100
	8	O Sing unto the Lord both in score†	STB, 2 vn, ob, bn, bc	GB-Lbl Add. MS 62100
	9	My Song shall be always and	SATB, 2 vn, ob, bn, bc	GB-Lbl Add. MS 62099
4	10	Let God arise both in score†		GB-Lbl Add. MS 62100
	11	Have mercy on me o God and	STB, 2 vn, ob, bn, bc	GB-Lbl Add. MS 62100
5	12	Be Joyfull both in score†		
		The instruments of these twelve Anthems are written in 5 Books†	vn 1, vn 2, ob, bn, db	GB-BENcoke MS 109 (vn 1 and db only)
		The Voices of these 12 Anthems are written in three Books†	S, T1, B	
6	[19a]	A Score Book with a better cover than the rest of the Anthems†		GB-Lbl Add. MS 62101
		In thee O Lord put I my trust†		
9	36	I will magnifie thee†		
		Sento la che ristretto†	S, bc	GB-Lbl Add. MS 62102 fos. 60ᵛ–57 [sic: fo. nos. reversed]
11	63	The Songs in the opera of Rinaldo wth. ye Symphonys†		
13	73	O the Pleasure of the Plain a Masque Score the Voices and Instruments are coppy'd in Single Papers†	5 voices and instrs.	?US-Wc M 2.1/.H22/A3;
(16)	87	Amadis an Opera in Score†		?GB-BENcoke MS 1

Cat. no. ST 66	Cannons (US-SM item nos.)	Title in Catalogue	Scoring in Catalogue	Present Location (if known)
19	104	A Piece of Musick compos'd for Queen Ann's Birth Day†	SATB, instrs.	
	117	Sonata‡		
	121	Te Deum†	2 vn, ob, bc	
	122	Jubilate for Voices and Inst:†	SATB, 2 tpt, 2 ob,	
	123	Oratorium for Voices and Instr:†	2 vn, va, bc	
			SATB, 2 tpt, 2 vn, va, bc	
			SATTTBB, tpt, ob, 2 hn, 2 vn, va, vc, bc	
	130	Opera of Rhadamistus‡		
	131	Score of ye 3d Act of Mutius Scevola‡		
	132	Aetius (Walsh, 1732)§		Macnutt, Sale catalogue 1981
		Atalanta (Walsh, 1736)§		Macnutt, Sale catalogue 1981
		Partenope (Walsh & Hare, 1730)§		Macnutt, Sale catalogue 1981
		Sonatas or Chamber Aires for a German Flute, violin, or harpsicord (Walsh, c.1730–5)§		Fenyvres, Sale catalogue, 1981

† Item in Dr Noland's catalogue of 23 Aug. 1720.
‡ Item added in Dr Pepusch's catalogue of 23 Oct. 1721.
§ Item sold at Christie's 18 Nov. 1981, from the contents of Stoneleigh Abbey.

Appendix 2: Contents of the Cummings Manuscript (NL-DHgm MS A III 1)

Title (Taken from first page of each anthem or supplied editorially)†	Fo. nos.
ANTHEM / The First / COMPOSED BY / Mr HENDELL / O Sing unto the Lord	1–8ᵛ
ANTHEM / The Second / COMPOSED BY / Mr HENDELL / As pants the hart for cooling streams	9–20
ANTHEM / The III / COMPOSED BY / Mr HENDELL / My song shall be allways	21–33ᵛ
ANTHEM / The IV / Composed by / Mr Hendell / [Let God arise]	35–48
ANTHEM / The Vth / COMPOSED BY / Mr HENDELL / Have Mercy upon me	49–59
[ANTHEM / The Sixth / COMPOSED BY / Mr HENDELL / O be Joyfull]	61–76ᵛ
ANTHEM The Seventh / Composed by / Mr: Hendell / [In the Lord put I my trust]	77–87ᵛ
ANTHEM The VIII / Composed by / Mr Hendell / [I will magnifie thee O God my King]	89–103ᵛ
[ANTHEM / The Ninth / Composed by / Mr Hendell / O Come let us sing unto the Lord]	105–28ᵛ
[ANTHEM / The Tenth / Composed by / Mr Hendell / Wee praise thee o God]	130–63ᵛ

† The table of contents to this manuscript is a later addition. For those titles supplied editorially, I have attempted to use the style of the scribe who copied that particular anthem, or at least began its copying. In these cases, the style of the text *incipit* is taken from its first appearance in the body of the anthem.

Appendix 3: Contents of Cannons Music-Library, Items 23–5 (Identifiable Manuscripts)

Cat. no. (US-SM item no. ST 66)	Cannons Composer	Title	Scoring	Present GB Location
23[†]	T. Roseingrave	'Fragrant Flora, hast(e) appear'	S, 2 vn, bc	Lbl Add. MS 62103, fos. 1–8r
	T. Roseingrave	'When Love's soft passion'	S, fl, ob, 2 vn, bc	Lbl Add. MS 62103, fos. 8v–18v
	T. Roseingrave	'Cleora sat beneath a shade'	S, ob, vn, bc	Lbl Add. MS 62103, fos. 18v–27v
	T. Roseingrave	'Quem tu Melpemone'	S, 2 vn, bc	Lbl Add. MS 62103, fos. 28–37r
	T. Roseingrave	'Licori vezzosetta'	S, 2 vn, bc	Lbl Add. MS 62103, fos. 37v–45r
	T. Roseingrave	'Torna amore a consolarmi'	S, vn, ?va, bc	Lbl Add. MS 62103, fos. 45v–50v
	T. Roseingrave	'E si dolce il mio contente' (aria)	S, ob, 2 vn, bc	Lbl Add. MS 62103, fos. 51–55v
	T. Roseingrave	'S' innamora ancor per gioco' (aria)	S, 2 vn, va, bc	Lbl Add. MS 62103, fos. 55v–64r
	T. Roseingrave	'Amor, amante, addio'	S, ob, 2 vn, va, vc, kbd	Lbl Add. MS 62103, fos. 64v–73v
	T. Roseingrave	'Mentre il tutto è in furore'	S, tpt/ob, 2 vn, bc	Lbl Add. MS 62103, fos. 73v–85v
	T. Roseingrave	'Io m'ingannai a credervi'	S, 2 vn, va, bc	Lbl Add. MS 62103, fos. 86–95v
	T. Roseingrave	'Lunga stagion dolente'	S, 2 vn, va, bc	Lbl Add. MS 62103, fos. 95v–106
24[‡]	Pepusch	'No, no, vain world'	SS, 2 ob, 2 fl, 2 vn, va, bc	Lbl Add. MS 62103, fos. 1–16
	Pepusch	'Wake the harmonious voice and string'	SS, ob, fl, 2 vn, va	Lem 1097, fos. 17–28v
	Pepusch	'While pale Britannia pensive sate'	S, tpt, fl, 2 vn, bc	Lem 1097, fos. 29–36r
	Pepusch	'Vorrei scoprir'	S, vn, bc	Lem 1097, fos. 36v–41r
	Pepusch	'Menaleas, once the gayest swain'	S, fl, bc	Lem 1097, fos. 41v–44v
	Pepusch	'S' io peno e gemo'	S, ob, bc	Lem 1097, fos. 45–49v
	Pepusch	'Twas on the eve of a fair summer's day'	S, bc	Lem 1097, fos. 50–54v
	Pepusch	'To joy, to triumph dedicate the day'	SS, ob, fl, hp, 2 vn, va, kbd	Lem 1097, fos. 55–57v, 82–85
25[§]	Galliard	'Chi fra lacci avvinto ha il core'	S, fl, bc	Lem 1097, fos. 78–81v

[†] Catalogue description: 'Two Books full of Cantatas for one voice and Instruments by Mr. Rosengrave'. 1 vol. of cantatas by Roseingrave apparently does not survive.
[‡] Catalogue description: 'One Book full of Cantatas 3 of them for two Voices and Instruments one for a Voice and Instruments 4 for one Voice alone by J. C. Pepusch'. The Instrumental Parts of these 3 books in Score are copyy'd in 4 Books and all are bound up in ruff Leather.' The instr. pts. apparently do not survive. The binding of GB-Lbl Add. MS 62103 matches the description given here, which also describes the binding of the
[§] Catalogue description: 'One for one Voice and a Hautboi by Mr Galliard.' GB-Lam MS 1097 has evidently been re-bound.
GB-BENcoke copy of *Acis and Galatea* and a number of MSS owned by Thomas Chilcot.

8

The Shaw-Hellier Collection

PERCY YOUNG[1]

⟨⟩

AMONG those whose present reputation depends on their foresight in having collected works by Handel, Samuel Hellier (1736–84) stands out as an exceptional figure. His library of music, his collection of orchestral instruments, and the organs which he had Abraham Adcock to build, were all assembled and cared for as much in public as private interest. Hellier did not compose a formal essay explaining his philosophical views on the social value of the arts in society, but he did leave in documentary form evidence of a strong conviction that music was a necessary ingredient in the life of the community. The little world of which he was in this particular its cultural engine was the village of Wombourne, four miles from Wolverhampton, in Staffordshire, where his home was the house known since the Middle Ages as The Woodhouse. Here for two centuries was preserved his memorial, the Shaw-Hellier Collection of music and of instruments. The music is now preserved, on permanent loan, in the Music Library of the Barber Institute of Fine Arts in the University of Birmingham.

It will be evident that the use made of both sections of his Collection during his lifetime entitles Hellier to be ranked among the valuable pioneers of popular musical education in this country. Sir Samuel, as he unmeritoriously became in September 1762, when—as High Sheriff of Worcestershire—he made a speech congratulating George III on the birth of the Prince of Wales, would be, I suspect, somewhat surprised so to be regarded by posterity. He collected music for its own sake, for the pleasure it might ensure, and for its usefulness in the context of his fairly remote provinciality. His respect for Handel was profound, but Handel was accompanied into his affections by many other composers—some acquaintances of Handel, some of Hellier, and some of both—whose presence

---

[1] See also id., 'The Shaw-Hellier Collection' *Brio*, 23: 2 (autumn/winter 1986), 65; '"A sweet pretty instrument", Sir Samuel Hellier's Obsession' *Bios Journal*, 12 (1988) 51; 'Samuel Hellier: A Collector with a Purpose', *Book Collector*, 39: 3 (1990), 350.

makes for a genuine representation of general musical life in provincial England in the mid-Georgian era.

Hellier was not absolutely possessed by music, for his library, built up by his grandfather and father (Samuel I and Samuel II)—containing items of considerable historical value in respect of family Jacobite sympathies, early printed Bibles, and valuable seventeenth- and eighteenth-century texts, as well as general works—was well maintained, and augmented. In a countryside where horticulture was represented conspicuously by Hellier's near-neighbour, the poet William Shenstone, the grounds of the Woodhouse were cared for with imagination and also, to some extent, for the common good.

Hellier's musical zeal developed out of psychological necessity. It was (so far as we are permitted to suggest) genetically indicated, for his father was musical and, in this respect—and briefly—encouraging. Samuel's talents flourished and with them confidence; the violin became a tool in the hands of a modestly revolutionary student of the 1760s. His surviving manuscript book of violin exercises is dated 1752.

Although heir to a not inconsiderable estate—the main part in Wombourne, but with other properties in Worcestershire—Samuel was not born under a genial star. Before he was 15 both mother and father were dead. He was therefore made a ward in Chancery and then was assigned to the guardianship of Charles Lyttleton, Dean of Exeter. Of a distinguished Worcestershire family, Lyttleton was well known in the Hellier circle. From the time of the death of his parents Samuel was constantly subjected to the disapproval of a tyrannic grandmother, whose malignant influence persisted for the rest of his life. She died aged 103 in 1783, a year before Samuel himself.

Dean Lyttleton encountered Samuel in 1753 as a Gentleman Commoner in Exeter College, Oxford, of which he himself was a graduate. In January 1754 Samuel resumed studying the violin—which, inspired by his father's enthusiasm for the instrument, he had started with a Wolverhampton teacher—with a teacher in Oxford. His college tutor, Dr Benjamin Kennicott, found his industriousness in this particular highly commendable, but in any proper academic area invariably absent. Samuel (who was to become the master of his estate at his coming-of-age) was harassed on all sides. His rebelliousness—of which high spending was a significant part—and its consequences are well described in the family documents. Some part of this high spending, it may be said in mitigation, was accounted for by purchases of music and musical instruments.

The leading musician at Oxford during Hellier's time was William Hayes, who also had a power-base in the Three Choirs' Festival, in which Hellier too developed a lifelong interest. Under the general

oversight of Richard Church, a body of copyists—from whose pens came most of Hellier's Handel material—was kept exceedingly busy. One member of this team maintained connection with Hellier in later life. 'I've been last week to Oxford,' wrote Hellier to John Rogers on 1 April 1769, 'Saw Mr [John] Lamborn [*sic*] He is writing the other Coronation anthems which you have not yet got for your people and [I] shall send them for you very soon.' Hellier appears to have been acquainted also with William Walond, to whose setting of Pope's *Ode on St Cecilia's Day* he subscribed. On the same subscription list were John Lambourn, the Musical Society at Stourbridge in Worcestershire (a set of six of John Stanley's concertos in Hellier's library are stamped with the mark of this society), and John Alcock, organist of Lichfield, who as a boy had sung in the first performance of Handel's anthems for the coronation of George II.

Hellier continued as a student at a leisurely pace, passing one not difficult hurdle in 1758 by graduating as MA, and becoming a Doctor of Civil Law in 1760. By the time he was ready to return home to take control of the estate of which he had become master, he had acquired such a collection of music that the suggestion that he had been prodigal with his funds was probably justified. But there is no doubt that Hellier's experiences in early life taught him that music was a useful balm to a bruised spirit and even an afflicted body. For he experienced two fractured love affairs; the second of which, ending with a horse-whipping by the irate father of the girl, marked the end of Hellier's amorous career. He never married.

Among other works he had acquired while at Oxford Hellier took home with him printed copies of the Op. 2 and Op. 5 Sonatas, the *Water Music* and *Fireworks Music*; and manuscript scores and miscellaneous parts of *Messiah*, *Alexander's Feast*, *Judas Maccabaeus*, and *L'Allegro*. All these copies bear the date of acquisition. So too do a large number of other works catholicizing the Collection, and in one way or another seeming to indicate the areas of interest he intended in due course to serve. A volume of Hasse's 12 Concertos (with the inscription 'Exon. Coll. Oxon, 1750') had been acquired from its previous owner, who was also of Exeter College. From another college acquaintance, named Stevens, Hellier had five volumes of Arne songs. Boyce's Violin Sonatas of 1745 were added to his Collection in 1753. For the kind of choir which he might have expected in due course to develop in Wombourne the *Ten Anthems for Country Choirs* purchased in 1756 would have been serviceable. To John Alcock's *The Pious Soul's Heavenly Exercise* of 1756— another work for those with simple faith and modest ability—Hellier was a subscriber. In 1757 he bought Salvatore Lanzetti's Sonatas

for two violoncellos from 'Mr [Laurence] Sterne, Prebendary of York and author of Tristram Shandy and Yorick's sermons ec.'. In the same year an attractive and, on account of the associated poets and dedicatees, more than ordinarily interesting collection of songs, published in Birmingham, was acquired. The composer, John Pixell, friend of Jennens, of Addison, and of Shenstone, was the vicar of Edgbaston. Other minor masters of the Midlands supported by Hellier, as well as John Alcock, included Capel Bond of Coventry, William Bond and James Lyndon of Wolverhampton, and Barnabas Gunn of Birmingham.

The further development of the music collection and the continuing purchase of instruments, as well as the musical life of the country as experienced by Hellier, are interwoven with many matters of a practical nature concerning estate management and much local gossip. All are contained in a set of 165 letters (in the possession of Mr and Mrs Phillips), written by Hellier between 1763 and 1784 to his agent John Rogers at Wombourne. Throughout his life, for some part of each year, Hellier, a non-practising barrister, lived in London, from his rooms in the Inner Temple noticing the musical life of the capital as well as other of its attractions, and also detailing management requirements in respect of his house and estates. These letters to John Rogers denote an unusual relationship, for English squires of the eighteenth century were not conspicuous either for an absorbing interest in music or for their concern to further the capacity of their employees for cultural advancement. The first extant communication is a fragment of a letter written on Christmas Day 1766. As with all Hellier's letters the tone is somewhat breathless. On the home front, it is clear, various orchestral reinforcements were expected. 'They are' writes Hellier, 'so busy here [in London] making Trumpets for the Army I almost despair off [sic] getting French Horns in a reasonable time'. Rogers was promised, however, that some hautboys were on their way on the London–Wolverhampton coach, as well as a book and a barrel of oysters for a friend. In this first fragmentary despatch Hellier was also giving news of the organ which would soon be ready for Wombourne church, and from which Rogers, as Kapellmeister elect, would be expected to direct the music of the village and the surrounding countryside.

From this point, the surviving letters are mostly long and detailed, if inelegantly composed. On 3 January 1767 there was this peremptory injunction: 'Pray take care to be perfect in the singing of Te deum Messiah etc as we shall call upon you to perform Easter Monday or in the week at the opening of the organ.' But Hellier had not finished. 'You do not say one word concerning whether you are in the mind

162   THE SHAW-HELLIER COLLECTION

to learn Hautboys Horns and bassoons. However shall hasten them all in my Power and send them down.'

On 15 January supplementary information was sent to Rogers. Repeating his intention to send down the instruments named in the previous letter, Hellier begins a new disposal of his agricultural work-force. Bassoons, he said, were temporarily difficult to obtain, so 'Jonah [worker] must wait a little, for he is unquestionably the man for that instrument; your brother Sam for one hautboy and you must find me another and also for the Horns. But be sure they are People who have ears and will take Pains.' A second thought gives rise to the suggestion that Jonah Cartwright, seeming anxious to begin, could be referred to Mr Eller, a Birmingham music-teacher, who— having a bassoon loaned to him by Hellier—perhaps could spare it until a replacement came from London. For hautboy reeds and for tuition Mark Beaman at Wolverhampton should be consulted: 'to him I recommend you for Reeds to play with as the best can suit your lips and they must be made accordingly or no fine smooth Tone can be had from that Instrument.'

Hellier continued zestfully to keep his workers to their musical commitments. So on 15 February 1770:

I have also sent an ivory mute for your brother Samuels violin, a hautboy reed case for Ned Peter, a mute for your brother Daniel's horn or trumpet and a new top or mouthpiece to be given to young Bowater for the 1st clarinet, as that which Abel Cartwright made was of different wood—these trifles with a Concerto I beg the Wombourn band to accept off—I shall send your brother Daniel a silver mouthpiece and a few more musical things as fast as I can get them.

John Stanley, organist of the Temple Church where Hellier worshipped when in London, was one of his particular heroes. Having bought a set of his voluntaries he notified Rogers on 15 January 1767 of his intention to send them down by the next coach. 'If I do,' he wrote, 'you must practise them. I purpose a Voluntary on the organ after the Psalms, then sing an anthem or Psalm with organ before the communion Service and again as the Parson goes into the pulpit and after church play the people out. That's the way.' Three days later, however, second thoughts prevailed. 'I have look'd over Stanley's Voluntaries and find they are Difficult for you at Present. So have not sent them. But will have you apply to Mr Bond at Wolverhampton, as you are to commence organist soon, and beg him to write you down two or three easy ones to shew the Trumpet stop, the Cornet, and the French Horn which is done by playing the French Horn manner with the stopd and open Diapason and has a

pretty effect.' In due course the Stanley voluntaries arrived in Wombourne, while, among other music, on New Year's Day 1769 Rogers was given Walond's 'exceeding pretty' voluntaries and a year later six Handel overtures, 'being proper pieces for the improvement of the hand'.

One of the consequences of a mid-century concern for deprived and neglected children, advertised by Handel's interest in the Foundling Hospital, was the spread of a wider concern for 'charity children'. Broadly speaking, in the village of Wombourne, that suggested all children except those few of the neighbouring gentry and superior clergy. Hellier spent a considerable amount of money, much of his own, and some also of Rogers's time and energy, in organizing and funding a local charity school. The children were clothed and instructed according to Hellier's wishes, with their musical education a matter of priority, so that the boys, on Sundays in surplices and wearing bands, were able to be active as choristers: 'I have this School so greatly at heart I will establish it to my intire satisfaction to endure for ages to come when you and I are mouldering in Wombourn Churchyard.' In fact, the school did not last as long as that and, through lack of support from other of the gentry, dissolved after some three years.

Hellier's beneficence also extended to a London charity school in the neighbourhood of St Paul's, Covent Garden. Edward Clark, organist of that church, published a charity anthem 'All ye nations of the earth' in 1770, to which Hellier subscribed, and so too did Rogers, whose credentials 'Organist of Wombourn' were so inscribed. By this time an active musical society (noted among the subscribers to a volume of anthems by Lyndon of Wolverhampton) had taken official form, and was busy rehearsing the Dettingen Te Deum and the Coronation Anthems. The parish clerk meanwhile was writing out as many Psalm tunes as he could into the 'Red Book' said Hellier 'I gave him to give out.'

Music was rarely absent from Hellier's mind. At times the congestion of his ideas is bewildering. A characteristic passage from a letter of 16 January 1768 indicates the difficulties experienced by him as he obliged himself to write into his musical ambitions and intentions his social and domestic responsibilities.

I have sent you a Box by the Wolverhampton coach will be down on Wednesday: The Messiah. I have sent a very fine copy of it. I have bought it for myself so shall lend it your singers. Pray keep it quite clean and don't lend it from Wombourn. If they will not lend us the Church I will have an oratorio done in the wood. I have sent a book for the organ which you will like and some cane to make clarinet reeds when wanted but not for

hautboys. Its [*sic*] difficult to get and promised some soon and the gun barrel and bassoon shall send down next week. I expect the serpent in a day or two.—One of the little dogs which we brought to town—the small white one died of fatigue of so long a journey the other is well. How are those which I keep are they well. I think if Nanny [a servant] was to send and know if the old Lady [his grandmother] has he[a]r'd from me etc. Do it slyly. Perhaps one might hear why she does not write.

Hellier's friendship with Rogers extended to the point of insisting in the spring of 1768 that he should come up to London for a cultural holiday: 'You should be provided with an organist to play while you are gone to London. Lent is not far off. You'll have abundance to see. I can assure you.'

For his part, however, Rogers was doubtful whether he could leave his estate duties. But Hellier, determined on no refusal to his invitation, promptly advised, 'If you talk too much about it you will never get away. Slip up at once. I will have no denials. The King and Queen have commanded the oratorio of Samson for the first to begin Lent with.' Not only was there the oratorio to look forward to, but also the music at the Temple Church: 'The Temple Organ [*the organists Jones and Stanley*] is the very finest Instrument I ever heard in all my life'.

The London trip was clearly a success. No sooner had Rogers returned to the Woodhouse than he was instructed (19 March 1768) to let his master know if the gardener had attended to the walk to the temple: 'it should be grass very smooth and nice and not only laurels but as spring comes on flowers to be planted.' 'Have you', Hellier asks again, 'had a Practice of the Te deum since you came down. Remember how well it went at St Margaret's Westminster and your Messiah.' The temple was a monument, designed by James Gandon, being raised to Handel's memory and intended to stand near a bust of Shakespeare. In the same letter he writes how a harpsichord is due to arrive from London.

Hellier was both ingenious in and proud of his efforts to provide culture for his neighbours. Towards the end of April he began to plan for the better weather, when the grounds of the Woodhouse would be an attraction for visitors:

I shall be glad to hear when the wood is in full leaf and quite in perfection, and if any persons of note come to see it endeavour to get their names and send me word . . . Remember to put the serpent to rights where it is hurt in carriage . . . to clean the picture of the Hen and Chickens in the best room. Remember to polish the organ case and have the music room new painted—people will be coming every day to see it so pray set some of them to do it and remember the boat house.

As Handel's Temple is an intire new design and as Mr Gandon has drawn it and exhibited it to publick view I am very anxious to have it quite completed out of hand for which reason pray forward it with great expedition. Sand the outside and well paint of a light stone colour the inside and behind the figure paint it dark and remember to take particular care to prevent its raining in. Stop it effectually and make the bracketts for the Bustos larger that they may stand firm, and make the gardner widen the walk directly as we settled it when I was on the spot.

Hellier was involved in musical affairs throughout the Midlands, extending his interests to Stafford in the north and Coventry in the south; to Lichfield in the east and Worcester in the west. In September 1768 Geast, organist in Dudley, asked to borrow Hellier's kettledrums for a Festival performance. The instruction went to Rogers, 'You may lend Mr Geast the kettle drums. Let them be packed up in the baskets with straw as we intended them and very great care taken that they may not be wet or any way bruised or damaged.'

This was a busy season and there was some confusion of dates with the Birmingham Festival.

As to Mr Holden and the Birmingham people if they are angry let them be pleas'd again for all I care. Am I to be their slave and packhorse upon all occasions to be subject to their humours? No. I know this much that they are never ready to assist us and we can at all times hire for money a band of musick without being beholden to them.

At Wombourne the Dettingen or Purcell Te Deum and *Messiah* were in rehearsal. Geast was to supply help, so Rogers must speak to him. 'I depend intire on his help and assistance for our musick so you must keep him in good humour and please him—for otherwise we can not have a performance and I've always remarked that the Sons of harmony have usually the greatest share of discord belonging to them.'

Hellier all his life was fascinated with the sound of music, particularly of unusual instruments or unusual combinations of instruments: sheep-bells tuned to chords on the harpsichord, which he heard on southern country estates; the Sticcado Pastorelli—a 'whimsical thing' of which he requested Rogers to make one for him 'in his leisure time'; 'the Cuckow such as children play' which was—on a July night—to be hidden high up in the thickest part of the wood, and which 'would please the company'; his little volume, *The Bird Fancier's Delight, with tunes to teach to singing birds after the Flageolet or Flute.* He concerned himself with the pealing of bells in Wombourne church, with the preparation of those of his workers who played the trumpets for the procession of the High Sheriff to the Assizes in Stafford.

He supervised the building of his own organs and took a lively interest in organ construction generally. He was an early enthusiast for the clarinet, seeking teachers for his own musicians from Wolverhampton or Shrewsbury. As for music *en plein air* Hellier organized his workers for the purpose of playing on the lake in his own grounds. Once he proposed a musical excursion on the 'Navigation'—the new route opened by the Staffordshire–Worcestershire canal of 1762 connecting to the canalized Severn down to Bristol.

As one feels that the Romantic movement stirred early in the Midlands with the example of Shenstone, so one suspects that Hellier himself had all the correct sentiments. So on 16 November 1780 he enthused to Rogers:

I must not conclude my Letter without mentioning to you a wonderful improvement made to Harpsichords—it is the greatest discovery ever produced, and the effect is beyond conception, surprisingly great indeed! and is said to be what the late cellebrated Mr Handel was anxious to have brought to light before his death, but could not accomplish his wishes—but it is now done to a great degree of perfection, and by very simple plain means, and can with great ease be put to any harpsichord in Town or Country—and removed at pleasure. I do not exceed truth when I declare it is equal, if not superior to most common organs—the Treble excells the finest organ swell, which played on as it should be, and represents a fine trumpet, Brilliant and clear. The middle part a fine bass viol, or violoncello, and the lower part a strong full bass, like the double bass, but may be softened at pleasure. It is called the celestino, or heavenly stop, what is more surprizing is, it has not the least connexion with the instrument itself, longer than it is made use of,—and may be taken away or put to the harpsichord without the least injury, or detriment to the instrument . . ., and what renders it even yet more agreeable, is, it is not very expensive.

Hellier bequeathed his estate to Thomas Shaw, an old friend and his executor. A beneficed clergyman, vicar of three parishes *in absentia*, Shaw had for years acted as Hellier's business adviser. By the terms of the will he was required to take the name and style of Hellier, and 'to keep and preserve . . . my Pictures, Drawings Books of Musick and Instruments of Musick and other Books . . . and to ensure that the Music Room, organ, Wood and Hermitage be preserved and kept in good order and condition as in my life time.'

It was the great-grandson of Thomas Shaw-Hellier, Thomas Bradney Shaw-Hellier, who, having added modestly to the music collection drew general attention to the instruments that remained from the eighteenth century. Educated at Winchester and Oxford, Shaw-Hellier, soldier and musician, became commandant of the Royal Military School of Music at Kneller Hall, holding that office from 1883 to 1893. In 1890 he was responsible for a collection of wind

instruments displayed at the Military Exhibition, Chelsea; in 1900 was on the committee of the Loan Exhibition of Musical Instruments at the Crystal Palace; and in 1904 helped in the selection and exhibition of instruments at the International Loan Exhibition presented by the Worshipful Company of Musicians at Fishmongers' Hall. On each occasion instruments from the Woodhouse were on view. In 1900 they were 'on view in the Handelian Court, having been used in connection with some of the earlier performances of Handel's works known to have taken place in this country.' There is there, perhaps, a tinge of wishful thinking. None the less the remaining instruments of Samuel Hellier and the music of his Collection are a living memorial to a particular area of modest culture in the time of and under the influence of Handel.

Appendix: Handel Items in the Shaw-Hellier Collection

Within each section of the appendix, the order in which the items are listed is that of the numbers stamped on the original bindings, followed by those which were not bound and so have no number. The library numbers pencilled in each item use the same order.

The symbol 'SH' indicates that the item has the bookplate of Samuel Hellier, with 'Ex: Coll: Oxon'; those with 'SH sig' have his signature; a date under a manuscript entry shows that there is a handwritten date.

For the printed works the publisher is John Walsh unless otherwise indicated. Each edition is identified by its number in the relevant entry in W. C. Smith, *Handel: A Descriptive Catalogue of the Early Editions* (London, 1960; 2nd edn., Oxford, 1970), and the publication date given by Smith is shown; a date given thus: 1732+, means that the copy may be a later impression of an edition first issued in 1732 (see entry in Smith). The entry 'with MS inserts' almost always means that a printed edition containing arias only has been expanded with MS pages containing recitatives and choruses, to produce a copy of the complete work.

Items are full scores unless indicated as keyboard or parts; sets of parts are not always complete.

1. Manuscripts

Two Chandos Anthems, HWV 248, 253.
Judas Maccabaeus (overture printed), 3 vols. SH, 1762.
Dettingen Te Deum (with Houbraken engraved portrait of Handel), SH.
'Duetti [and Trios] del Sigr: G. F. Handel', HWV 194, 198, 184, 183, 180,
 199, 178, 191, 196, 185, 197, 188, 193, 201, 200.
L'Allegro, beginning with 'Overture in L'Allegro Penseroso' (= *Admeto*,
 Overture Act 2, HWV 22/14), pts., SH, 1759.
Coronation Anthems, v. and instr. pts.

168 THE SHAW-HELLIER COLLECTION

Dettingen Te Deum, with *L'Allegro*, 'Zadok the Priest', and 'Rule Britannia', v. pts.[†]

Dettingen Te Deum, with *L'Allegro* (with Overture as above), 'Rule Britannia' and Marches in *Saul* and *Judas Maccabaeus*, instr. pts.,[†] SH.

Dettingen Te Deum, with *L'Allegro*, extra v. and instr. pts.

Alexander's Feast, with *Judas Maccabaeus*, v. and instr. pts.; cemb. pt. (end): 'June ye 17th 1761'.

Messiah; handwritten: 'S. Hellier Exon: Coll: Oxon 1760'.

Overture in the *Occasional Oratorio*, with Dead March in *Saul.*

'Hallelujah' chorus in *Messiah,* instr. pts., SH.

Last chorus in Messiah, instr. pts.

'Hautboy Concerto ye 4th' (= Op. 3, No. 4), pts.

'March in Scipio' in D, pts.

'March in Scipio' in G, pts.

'March in Saul', pts.

'March in Rinaldo' pts. (2 cl, 2 hn, bc).

'Bass Song in Rhadamistus' (= 'Tutta rea la vita umana', *Scipione,* Act 3, Scene 1), instr. pts.

[†] Some have also a trio 'Fly hence, grim melancholy train', probably not Handel.

2. *Printed Editions*

Title	Smith No.	Date	Bookplate	MS Date
Church Music				
⎰ Coronation Anthems, vol i	2	1743	SH	1756
⎱ Funeral Anthem for Queen Caroline	2	1743		
Coronation Anthems vol i	2	1743	SH	
Utrecht Te Deum and Jubilate	2	1732+		1756[†]
Dettingen Te Deum	1	1763	SH	1764
Chandos Anthem, HWV 251b (Birchall and Beardmore) (incomplete)	1	1783		
'Celebrated Coronation Anthem' (= 'Zadok the Priest'), v. and hpd, (William Randall)	5	*c.*1775		
Oratorios, Odes, etc.				
Alexander's Feast	6	*c.*1750	SH	1760
Messiah (Randall & Abell)	2	1767		
The Choice of Hercules (with MS inserts)	2	1751+	SH	
Acis and Galatea	6	1743	SH	
Samson (with MS inserts), 3 vols.	4	*c.*1746	SH	
'Handel's Songs selected from his Oratorios':				
vol. i	17	*c.*1755	SH	
vol. iii	17	*c.*1755		
vol. iv	18	1758		
vol. v	19	1759		

[†] this date is written on the 2nd item in the vol., Purcell's Te Deum and Jubilate (Walsh, *c.*1737).

Title	Smith No.	Date	Bookplate	MS Date
L'Allegro (with MS inserts, including Overture as above)	9	*c.*1747	SH	1756
'Handel's Songs selected from his latest Oratorios for Concerts', pts.	20	*c.*1760		
'Six Grand Chorusses From Mr Handel's Oratorios Adapted for the Organ or Harpsichord by Mr Hook', (William Randall) (with Houbraken portrait)	1	1778		
Operas				
'Six celebrated songs . . . for French Horns perform'd in the several operas', pts. (no title-pages, bound with Concertos, Op. 6)	1/2	1731–2		
Instrumental				
Organ Concertos, Op. 4, pts. (bound with concertos by Corelli, Geminiani, Sammartini)	8	1753	SH	
{ Organ Concertos, Op. 4, kbd	7	*c.*1750	SH	
{ Organ Concertos, 2nd set, kbd	1	1740+		
{ *Water Music*, pts.	4	*c.*1750	SH	
{ *Fireworks Music*, pts. (1 pt. inscribed 'Exeter College Oxford 175[ ])	4	*c.*1750+		
{ Trio Sonatas, Op. 5	1	1739+	SH, SH sig.	1756
{ Trio Sonatas, Op. 2	3	1733–4+		
'Overtures . . . in four parts', pts.	43	1760	SH	
{ 'XXIV Overtures', kbd	10	*c.*1750	SH, SH sig.	
{ 'Six overtures'	12	*c.*1749+		
Overtures, kbd (vol. ii)	14,16,18, 20, 23	*c.*1749– *c.*1760		
Six Fugues (bound with voluntaries by John Bennett)	1	1735+		
'Sixty Overtures . . . in 8 parts', pts.	38	*c.*1758	SH	
Grand Concertos, Op. 6, pts.	4	1746	SH	
Concerti grossi, Op. 3, pts.	5	*c.*1752	SH	
Organ Concertos, Op. 4 (bound with concertos by Sammartini, Greene, and Felton), pts. (ob1, ob2).	8	1753	SH	
'Sixty Overtures . . . in 8 parts', pts. (a 2nd copy, with an annotation in the va pt. 'belonging to the Music Society at Stourbridge Worcestershire 1758', similar in bn pt.)	38	*c.*1758		
'Six overtures set for the Organ'	19	1747	'John Rogers his book 1770'	

Title	Smith No.	Date	Bookplate	MS Date
'Six concertos for the Harpsichord or Organ', kbd (H. Wright)	17	c.1785		
Librettos				
Esther		n.d. [post-1759]		
Esther		n.d.		
Esther, MS copy of 1732 print				
Occasional Oratorio		n.d. [post-1759]		
Joseph		1747		
Alexander's Feast		n.d.		
Joshua (Oxford)		1756		
Triumph of time and truth		1758		
Theodora		1759		
Messiah (Gloucester)		1760		
Athalia (Gloucester)		1763		

9

The Hall Collection

J. MERRILL KNAPP

IT is not often that a scholar has the opportunity to be in direct touch with the founder of a collection—particularly of one that deals, not with the twentieth century, but with Handel and the eighteenth. Many years ago, as a young American faculty member working in England, I had the privilege of meeting Dr James Hall through his old friend William C. Smith of the British Museum. Dr Hall (1899–1973), a busy physician of Deal and Walmer in Kent, was not a professional musician, scholar, or bibliographer, but an avid Handel enthusiast who had managed during an unbelievably active lifetime of medical practice to assemble bit by bit a large collection of printed editions of Handel's works—at a time when they could usually be picked up for a few shillings—and also contemporary manuscripts, some of which were made for Frederick, Prince of Wales in the 1740s. All this was accomplished by a man of modest means and no inherited wealth who, besides his musical activities (he was an organist and choir-master, and directed over a hundred performances for his local choral society), had a distinguished career during World War II as a sea surgeon, jumping on and off ships in the English Channel to perform emergency operations, notably during the evacuation from Dunkirk.

I was fortunate enough to spend a weekend in Deal with Dr Hall and his charming family, and to see his impressive Collection, which took up every nook and cranny of a modest-sized library-room in his house, and spilled over into his surgery, where one presumably had the privilege of seeing handsome eighteenth-century buckram and gilt lettering on the shelves during physical examination. He had also built up a vast lending library of Novello vocal scores, on which, I am told, many English choral societies and churches depended for their performances in past years.

It is not directly pertinent to relate how this Collection ended up in Princeton University in 1974 through the generosity of alumni and friends of music, except to say that after numerous transatlantic negotiations it did so, and we are the richer for it.

9.1. First page of the Sinfonia, Act 3, *Alexander Balus* (Hall Handel Collection).

The bulk of the Collection consists of printed editions of operas, oratorios, and other vocal works, and instrumental music (including sets of parts), altogether about 425 volumes published between 1714 and the middle of the nineteenth century. There is also a complete set of Samuel Arnold's edition; nine volumes of *Apollo's Feast*; Mainwaring, all of Burney, and much more. Outside the British Library, the Coke Collection, the Schoelcher Collection in Paris, and the Library of Congress, this Collection of printed editions is probably the largest of its kind anywhere; little work has yet been done on it, apart from the listing by William C. Smith.[1] A good example of what is found in the Collection is a copy of the 1748 Walsh edition of *Alexander Balus*.[2] Dr Hall and his son Martin note that the copy contains corrections to the music in an eighteenth-century hand very similar to that of the elder J. C. Smith, as well as manuscript insertions of the names of characters at the beginning of arias. The identification of J. C. Smith derives partly from a pencilled note inside the front cover which reads: 'Stated to be corrected in the hand writing of Christopher Smith Handel's amanuensis.' There are thirty-three corrections listed by page, stave, and bar. All but three agree with the original score: they are mostly corrections of printing errors, but some are actually altered notes. The source used for the alterations is not mentioned, and they are not to be found in the first printed full score (Wright, 1787).[3] The most interesting page is in the Sinfonia that opens Act 3 (Illus. 1). On Walsh's page 75, the missing viola part in bar 9 is inserted in a hand that resembles Handel's—stems to the right of the notes, and the kind of note-filling on the stave associated with his notation. The Halls declared that the insertion was indeed by Handel, and suggested that the copy might have been used for an abridged performance in a private home, as had been the case on other occasions. I am sceptical about the identification, particularly since two of the four notes are different in the autograph, which has c'–g–e'–e'; it is conceivable, of course, that the other reading was a later thought. Whatever the truth may be in this case, it demonstrates the need for a thorough examination of all the printed music in the collection.

Among the manuscripts are three volumes, *Belshazzar*, *Alexander Balus*, and *Joseph and his brethren*, which once belonged to Frederick, Prince of Wales, father of George III. They are labelled Vols. VIII, XIII, X, showing that other volumes of this nature must have been

[1] W. C. Smith, *Handel: A Catalogue of the Early Editions* (London, 1960; 2nd edn., Oxford, 1970).

[2] Ibid., 89, no. 2.

[3] Dr Hall adds in his notes: 'Purchased from a Brighton bookseller (Holleyman & Teacher) in November, 1954. Bound with Walsh copy of *Occasional Oratorio* (not evident today).'

174   THE HALL COLLECTION

commissioned and copied for Frederick. The volumes are large folios
in a handsome red morocco binding with tooling on the spine, gilt
edging, and inside covers of marbled paper. *Belshazzar* is entirely in
the hand of Smith senior, and was copied about 1746–7. It contains
a rather confused version of the music composed for the 1745 performances, derived partly from the autograph and partly from the
performing-score. The binding is labelled 'Handel's Belshazzar / An /
Oratorio. Vol. VIII.' Inside the front cover is the bookplate of
W. M. Moseley, whom we know to have been an eighteenth-century
collector of books and music. He wrote below:

This Oratorio with the others of the same Sett were written by Smith who
was assistant to Handel in the Directorship of the Opera. They were copied
from the author's MSS at the desire of the late Prince of Wales (Father of
George 3rd) and were deposited in his Collection, till he made a present of
them to Mr Denoyer. Sometime afterwards they were bought by Mr
Pocklington of Hatton Garden, & at his death, his Music being sold by
auction, they came into the possession of Mr Goodison, from whom I
purchased them in 1796. See Mr G's Lett. of Jan 21, 1796.'[4]

Illus. 2 shows the first page of the score.

Alexander Balus and *Joseph* are in the hand of the copyist S5, and
the watermarks give a date of c.1747.[5] On the flyleaf of Joseph the
copyist has left an account of his work—£6. 16s for 273 pages. There is
also a large folio copy of *Israel in Egypt* in various hands which may
date from around 1760. Perhaps its most interesting feature is a set

   [4] The Halls added: '252 pages with the final instruction: "Ends with the Anthem, I will
magnifie thee O God my King." Watermark (Larsen C), i.e. fleur-de-lis with shield and L.V.G.
below (countermark IV). Handel's supply of this paper seems to have run out in 1741/1742.
Suggests that this copy was made soon after the completion of Handel's autograph in Sept.
1744, for Vol. X (*Joseph*, 1744) and *Alexander Balus*, Vol. XIII (1748) are copied on later
paper.' They also pointed out that Denoyer may be the one recorded in O. E. Deutsch, *Handel: A
Documentary Biography* (London, 1955), 238, 252 (and *Händel-Handbuch* iv. *Dokumente zu Leben
und Schaffen* (Leipzig, 1985), 170, 178) as a ballet-master; Pocklington has not been traced.
Benjamin Goodison, a London lawyer (Smith and Humphries, *A Bibliography of the Musical
Works published by the firm of John Walsh, 1721–1766* (London, 1968), 156) published musical
works between 1787 and 1790. The address given is James St, Westminster. The Halls also say
that the manuscript corresponds to the second state of the performing score, when Beard sang
Gobrias as well as Belshazzar, but Daniel's part remains in the original keys written for Mrs
Cibber, even though they were transposed up a tone for Miss Robinson in the performance. *Ed.'s
Note*: The Halls' description of the WMs has, of course, been superseded by the more detailed
paper-studies of Hans Dieter Clausen and Donald Burrows. Dr Burrows has kindly supplied
information about the paper of the *Belshazzar* MS as follows: WMs Ci, Ck; rastra 16 @ 4 75.5,
20 @ 4 56.5, 22 @ 4 56.5 (× 5) + @ 2 24. See D. Burrows, 'A Handlist of the Paper Characteristics
of Handel's English Autographs', typescript (The Open University, 1982); and H. D. Clausen,
Händels Direktionspartituren ('*Handexemplare*') (Hamburg, 1972). The identification of the
sources used for the copying of the *Belshazzar* MS was also provided by Dr Burrows.
   [5] Paper details from Donald Burrows: Joseph: WMs Ck, Bl, Cl; rastra 18 @ 5 90 (× 3) +
@ 3 51–, 16 @ 4 72.5, 20 @ 4 56.5; *Alexander Balus*: watermarks C2, ?Ch; rastra 16 @ 4 75, 20
?@ 5 74–, 22 unidentified (total span 172–).

9.2. First page of the score of *Belshazzar* (Hall Handel Collection).

176   THE HALL COLLECTION

of separate trombone parts added at the end, which have pencil marks
on them, and clarifications of notes as if they had once been used in
performance; the pencil hand seems to be a nineteenth-century one.
Another contemporary manuscript contains the *Ode for St Cecilia's
Day* and *Ode for Queen Anne's Birthday*, and some smaller items,
written by several copyists, one of whom appears to be an amateur;
this volume also has pencilled corrections.

Three manuscripts bear the label of the Aylesford Collection.
They are a second violin part for *Joshua*, and a second violin and a
bass part for a collection of 'Thirty Songs from the Operas' (mostly
before 1724). Dr Hall is careful to say inside the front cover that the
attribution comes from Cecil Hopkinson of the First Edition
Bookshop. There is some doubt about the provenance here: according
to Arthur D. Walker's catalogue[6] there is already a second violin
part for *Joshua* in the Flower Collection in Manchester, and it seems
unlikely that two sets of orchestral parts were made for Charles
Jennens; nor is there an indication in either Walker's or Dr Hall's
manuscript catalogues that a manuscript of 'Thirty Songs from the
Operas' was part of the Aylesford Collection.

Another interesting manuscript volume contains operatic arias
by Pescetti, Veracini, Leo, Greene, and Handel, dating from *c*.1734
to 1743.[7] The Handel items are from *Rossane*, an adaptation of
Alessandro performed in 1743; the first has the heading 'Aria nel
Rossane (del Sigr Handel)', and most are copied with an indication
of the singer or the character:

Sigr. Monticelli—Ah no, non voler mio ben[†] [Act 2, Scene 4]
Sigr. Monticelli—Il cor mio [Act 2, Scene 7]
Sigra. Mancini—La gloria e la fortuna[†] [Act 1, Scene 2]
Sigra. Visconti—Lusinghe più care [Act 1, Scene 2]
Coro—Fra le guerre [Act 1, Scene 3]
[Alessandro]—Men fedele [Act 1, Scene 4]
Rossane/Lisaura—Placa l'alma [Act 1, Scene 5]
Alessandro/Lisaura—[Act 2, Scene 2] ending with
[Alessandro]—Son quelli vaghi rai[†]
Sigra. Frasi—Sempre fido e disprezzato [Act 2, Scene 3]
Sigra. Visconti—Alla sua gabbia d'oro [Act 2, Scene 4]
Alessandro/Lisaura—In generoso onor [Act 3, Scene 4] without Coro

All but the three arias marked [†] and some recitatives from Act 2,
Scene 2 are from *Alessandro*; the music of 'Ah no, non voler mio ben'

___
[6] *Handel, The Newman Flower Collection: A Catalogue* (Manchester, 1972).
[7] It is a folio vol., 11.5 × 9 inches, bound in full calf, with gold ornaments back and front;
a tag '127' in faded ink on the front board (= an auction number?); 12-stave paper, 276 pages.
The binding is loose, and there is no title on the cover.

is that of 'Return O God of Hosts' in *Samson*, 'Son quelli vaghi rai' is 'Là dove gli occhi' in *Admeto*, but 'La gloria e la fortuna' is not known elsewhere—it could well be by Lampugnani, who contributed music to *Rossane*.[8] The other contents include two arias from *Vello d'oro* by Pescetti (1738); four from *Partenio* by Veracini (1739); two from *Diana ed Endimione* by Pescetti (1739); an unidentified one by Leo; seven from Maurice Greene's pastoral *Florimel* (1734), not identified as such; and other pieces, some of which were copied with the volume reversed.

Another manuscript is a *Messiah* and Coronation Anthems part-book for a bass, whose name may have been William Thompson. It dates from the mid-century. These vocal partbooks are scarce, because individuals either lost them or they were scattered after use. This one contains the bass part and continuo of choruses in *Messiah* in an arbitrary order, and similar parts for the Coronation Anthems.

Of lesser importance, but of interest nevertheless, are a manuscript copy of the Utrecht Te Deum and Jubilate and the Dettingen Te Deum, which can be dated *c.*1807; *Lessons for the Harpsicord*, dated 1755 by a Miss Baring, and containing six Handel pieces in keyboard arrangements; and a manuscript book which belonged to M. Le Tellier, copyist to Louis XVI, containing the Minuet in *Samson,* and a flute part for 'Fixed in His everlasting seat'.

As well as the printed music and the manuscripts, the Collection includes some forty eighteenth-century librettos of operas and oratorios; about half of them are from Handel's lifetime, including one for the last performance of *Messiah* in which the composer himself was involved, on 6 April 1759; and there are five rare ones for provincial performances of the oratorio in Gloucester, Salisbury (2), Newcastle, and York, between 1757 and 1791.

An unusual item of a somewhat humorous kind is the back of a *Muzio Scevola* libretto in Princeton University Library, which is not strictly in the Hall Collection, but may have belonged to Handel. It contains what is presumably a laundry list by one of his domestics, and was identified many years ago by William H. Cummings, to whom the libretto once belonged. The items are difficult to read, but the first is '12 shifts', and the others include a hood and some small coats. At the bottom appears the name 'Handl', to show that the items belonged to him (Illus. 3).

---

[8] For *Rossane,* see Deutsch, *Handel,* 572, and *Händel-Handbuch* iv, 366, 8 Nov. 1743; B. Baselt, *Händel-Handbuch,* i, *Thematisch-systematisches Verzeichnis* (Leipzig, 1978), 273; and the libretto, printed in *The Librettos of Handel's Operas,* ed. E. T. Harris (New York, 1989), xiii. [*Ed.'s Note*: The identification of the Maurice Greene items and of the music of 'Ah, no, non voler', together with other information on this manuscript, has been kindly communicated to me by Anthony Hicks.]

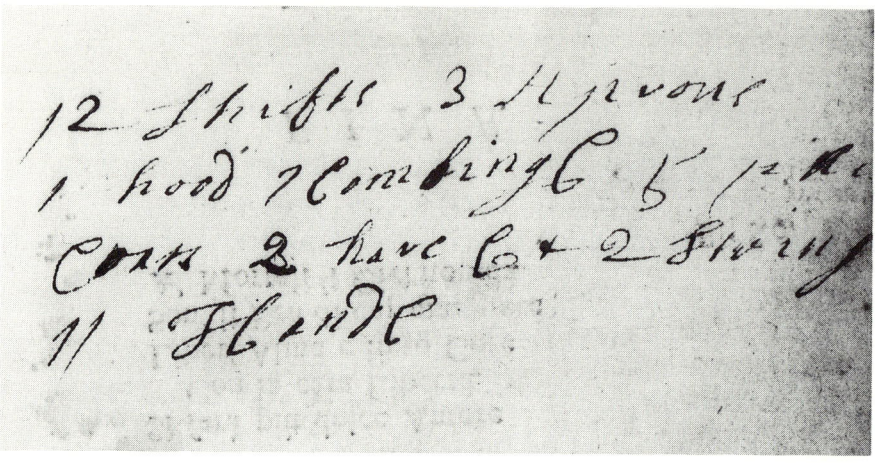

9.3. Back of a libretto of *Muzio Scevola*, showing Handel's laundry list (Hall Handel Collection).

In the course of his study, Dr Hall also compiled with painstaking care a number of typed catalogues to help him in his work. There are detailed ones of the Fonds Schoelcher Handel Collection, now in the Bibliothèque Nationale in Paris, and the Newman Flower Collection, now in the Henry Watson Music Library in the Central Public Library in Manchester, another of the Julian Marshall Handel Collection in the National Library of Scotland; also alphabetical indices of all Italian and French titles in Handel's work. A good deal of this has, of course, been superseded by more recent research, but quite original at the time was James and Martin Hall's work on the John Christopher Smiths, father and son: their origin and family background, where they lived in London, and their links with Handel.

There is a small collection of eighteenth-century newspapers containing references to Handel, a volume of eighteenth-century single-sheet songs (including two by him), a scrapbook of mainly nineteenth-century material, a watercolour of Covent Garden before its destruction in 1808, and various prints, mainly of Handel. Finally, there are twenty boxes of Hall's correspondence with Handelians all over the world; Dr Hall was indefatigable in asking and answering questions about his favourite composer.

Altogether, the Collection is fascinating because of its variety. Its founder could accumulate only what came up for auction and at odd private sales in the 1920s, 1930s, and 1940s. The true spirit of the collector is a passion for his subject and a willingness to go to any reasonable lengths—and often unreasonable ones—to acquire what he wanted. Much of this spirit is reflected in James Hall's activity

J. MERRILL KNAPP 179

and in what he was able to accomplish in his lifetime. One can only admire his zest and say; more power to him, and to those like him!

Appendix: Printed Handel Items in the Hall Collection

Items are identified by their numbers (and sometimes pages) in W. C. Smith's *A Catalogue of the Early Editions*; if they do not appear in Smith they are indicated separately, and the place of publication is London unless indicated otherwise; the same applies to librettos.

The Collection has one complete set of the Arnold edition; in addition there are second copies of many individual items, and these are listed. There are also thirteen of the fourteen volumes published by the Handel Society in London between 1843 and 1858 (*Jephtha* is missing); these are listed as 'HS'.

Items listed as 'arias' are eighteenth-century editions of separate numbers, usually consisting of a few pages of music, with no date of publication, and not listed by Smith.

There are a number of librettos in photocopy: these are not listed if they can be identified as copies of originals extant elsewhere.

Acis and Galatea: nos. 5, 6, 8, 10, 11, 12, 14, 17, 18, 20; 2 arias, i (J. Bland, n.d.); ii (n.p., n.d.); trio (J. Bland, n.d.); v.s. (London, n.d.); recit. and aria, v.s. (Berlin, 1828); HS; libretto (n.p., 1762; Edinburgh, 1753).
Admeto: nos. 1, 18.
Agrippina: no. 1.
Alceste: no. 1.
Alcina: nos. 4, 5, 9, 11; libretto (1735).
Alessandro: nos. 1, 5, 12.
Alexander Balus: nos. 2, 3; 1 aria (J. Bland, n.d.).
Alexander's Feast: nos. 1, 3, 4, 7, 8, 9, 11, 13; 2 arias (J. Bland, n.d.); 2 v.s. (*c*.1800–10); libretto (n.d.; 1753; Newcastle, 1778).
L'Allegro: nos 2, 5, 5 and 6, 11, 12, 13, 15; 6 arias (i, ii: J. Bland, n.d.; iii–v: n.d., n.p.; vi: Randolph, n.d., n.p.); v.s. (*c*.1810); HS; libretto (1754).
Arbace: no. 1.
Arianna: nos. 1, 2, 5; 'Minuet in Ariadne: with variations', arr. (C. and S. Thompson, *c*.1770).
Ariodante: no. 1.
Arminio: no. 1.
Atalanta: no. 1.
Athalia: nos. 1, 5; 1 aria (Wright, n.d.).
Belshazzar: nos. 1, 5, 7; HS.
Berenice: no. 1.
'Cecilia, volgi': no. 1.
Chandos Anthems: nos. 4, 5, 6, 8; v.s. selections (J. Page, 1808).
The Choice of Hercules: nos. 2, 7.

Concertos:

Concerto grosso, HWV 318: nos. 4, 5.

Concerti grossi, Op. 3: nos. 1, 5 ('Tenor' [= va]), 7.

Concerti grossi, Op. 6: nos. 1, 3 (vn1 concertino), 4, 5, 6; kbd. arr. (c. 1824).

Organ Concertos, Op. 4: nos. 2 (without vn2 rip. and bc), 3, 7 (4 copies), 12, 13 (vn1 concertino, vn1 rip.), 16, 17, 18 (vn2 only), 19, 20, 21, (Bland & Weller), 22; Concerto 4 (separate edn., J. Bland, c.1785); whole set, ed. S. J. Noble (mid-19th cent.).

Organ Concertos, 2nd set: nos. 4, 6, 7, 8.

Organ Concertos, Op. 7: nos. 1, 5, 6, 8.

Organ Concertos, pts., combined vols.: Op. 4 (Smith 8), with 2nd set (Sm.3) and Op. 7 (Sm.2): vn1 rip. (5 copies), vn2 rip. (4 copies).

Organ Concertos, pts., combined vols.: Op. 4 (Sm. 4) with 2nd set (Sm.4) and Op. 7 (Sm.4—vn2 Sm.2).

Coronation Anthems: nos. 1, 2 (2 copies), 3, 5, 8; kbd arr. (c.1810); HS.

Deborah: nos. 1, 5, 6?, 7, 8, 10.

Deidamia: no. 2.

Dettingen Te Deum: nos. 1, 3, 5, 6, 7; HS.

Esther: nos. 2, 6, 7, 9; HS; libretto (n.d., 1757).

Ezio: no. 1.

Faramondo: no. 1.

Flavio: no. 1.

Floridante: nos. 1, 4, 8.

Six Fugues: nos. 1, 3, 4, 5, 6.

Funeral Anthem for Queen Caroline: nos. 1, 2, 5, 6, 7.

Gideon (pasticcio by Smith jun.): libretto (1769).

Giulio Cesare: nos. 1, 11, 12; duet and chorus (Birchall, c.1802).

Giustino: no. 1.

Hercules: nos. 1 (2 copies), 5; 2 arias (J. Bland, n.d.).

Israel in Egypt: no. 1; selections, arr. Boyce (n.p., c.1783); HS.

Italian Cantatas, Duets, and Trios: nos. 2, 8; HS.

Jephtha: nos. 1, 3, 7; 3 arias, i–ii (n.d., n.p.); iii (n.d.).

Joseph: nos. 1, 5; 4 arias, i (H. Wright, n.d.), ii (J. Bland, n.d.); iii, iv (n.d., n.p.), 1 duet (J. Bland, n.d.).

Joshua: nos. 1, 4, 8; libretto (1748) (2 copies).

Judas Maccabaeus: nos. 2, 4, 6, 7, 9; 8 arias, i–vii (J. Bland, n.d.); viii (n.d., n.p.); HS; libretto (n.d.; 1755; 1757; Newcastle, 1778; Dublin, 1778); v.s., London (c.1800–10).

Lotario: nos. 1, 3.

Messiah: nos. 4, 5, 6, 9, 11, 12, 13; selections, see Smith 'Overture and Songs': nos. 6, 10, 12, 16, 19; choruses (2 vols. (c.1800, n.d.)); Hallelujah (n.d.); Mozart's arr., score (Leipzig, Breitkopf & Härtel, 1803); score (D'Almaine & Co., c.1831); score, pt. 1 (c.1823); score (Novello, 1850) (see Smith, no. 11); v.s. (1812, 1844); v.s. in German (Schwenke, n.p., n.d.); HS; libretto (1758; 1759 (2 copies); 1767; 1782; 1784 (Handel Commem.); Gloucester, 1757; Salisbury, 1762, 1765; Newcastle, 1778; York, 1791; 1932, 1951; Berkhamsted, 1939).

Music for the Royal Fireworks: nos. 8, 9.

Muzio Scevola: no. 1.
Nabal (pasticcio by Smith jun.): libretto (1764).
Occasional Oratorio: nos. 2, 3, 4, 6.
Ode for Queen Anne's Birthday: no. 1.
Ode for St Cecilia's Day: nos. 1, 3, 4, 6; HS.
Omnipotence (pasticcio by S. Arnold): libretto (1773; 1774).
Operas, selections:
    pp. 305, 313, 318: vols. i, ii, iii; p. 217, no. 2 (vn2, va, fl, hn2).
    Handel's Most Celebrated Airs: p. 267 (pts.).
    Apollo's Feast: nos. 2, 5, 6, 7, 9, 10, 14, 16.
    Twelve Duets: p. 173, no. 1.
    Bass Songs: no. 1.
    Handel's Songs: p. 190 (top).
Oratorios, selections:
    Twelve English Duets: pp. 174–5, nos. 2, 3.
    Grand Choruses: p. 267, ll. 1–3.
    The Beauties of Handel (3 vols., Preston, n.d.).
    Six Grand Choruses: p. 265, no. 2.
    The Celebrated Choruses: p. 267.
    Songs selected from the Oratorios: pp. 190–200, nos. 1 (pts.—fl, ob, hp);
        5, 10, 11–13 (pts.—vn1, vn2, bc); 17–19 (v.s.); 20 (v.s., vol i only,
        imperfect); 20 (pts.—vn1, 2); 22 (v.s.); 23 (v.s.—vol v only); 23 (pts.—
        vn2 only); no ? (n.n., n.d., pts.—vc, tr, bn, timp, hn).
    Bass Songs: 4.
    Grand Collection of Celebrated English Songs: p. 177.
    'Songs, duets & trios . . . from the oratorios . . .' (D'Almaine & Co.,
        ?1837).
Orlando: no. 1.
Ottone: nos. 1, 3, 13, 19.
Overtures: kbd (Smith 'For Harpsichord'): nos. 9, 10, 11 (2 copies), 12, 13,
    15, 17, 19, 20, 22, 23, 26, 27, 28, 29, 30, 31; pf, fl/vn (Goulding, Phipps &
    D'Almaine [1800–4]); pf, fl/vn (Goulding, c.1810); 48 overtures (L. Lee
    [1836–63?]).
    Score: p. 280.
    Pts: nos. 2 (2nd treble, bass), 3 (vn1, vn2, ob1, bass), 4 (vn2, ob1, bc), 10
    (vn1, 2), 11 (vn1, 2, va), 15 (vn1, 2, va, ob1, 2, bc, hn1), 18 (vn/ob 1, 2,
    vn3, va), 22 (vn1, 2, va, ob1, 2, bc), 25 (vn1, 2, va, vc, org), 28, 30
    (vn1, 2, va), 34 (vn2, 3, ob1, 2), 35 (vn1, 2, 'T' [= va], 39, 43 (vn1, 2,
    bc: vn1 and bc with works by Corelli, Humphries, Bowman), 45;
    Handel's Overtures . . . in 4 parts (n.d.).
Partenope: no. 1; libretto (1730).
Il pastor fido: nos. 1, 2, 6.
Pièces pour le clavecin . . . Vᵉ Ouvrage: p. 276.
Poro: nos. 2, 6, 8; libretto (1731).
Prelude et chaconne [HWV 442] (Bonn, N. Simrock, 19th cent.).
Radamisto: nos. 1, 2; libretto (n.d. [photocopy]).
Redemption (pasticcio by S. Arnold): no. 1.

La resurrezione: no. 1.

Riccardo Primo: libretto (n.p., ?1727).

Rinaldo: nos. 1, 10.

Samson: nos. 2 (2 copies, 1 incomplete), 6, 7, 10, 11, 12; 5 arias (J. Bland, n.d.); HS; libretto (1743; n.p., 1752).

Saul: nos. 2, 6, 9; 2 arias, i (J. Bland, n.d.); ii (W. Randolph, n.d., n.p.); HS.

Scipione: no. 1.

Select Harmony [HWV 318, 301, 302a]: no. 1 (vn1).

Selections from oratorios, anthems, instr. music (4 vols., Harrison, 1780–90).

Selections from oratorios, v.s. or kbd (19th cent.).

Semele: nos 1, 6; libretto (n.p., 1752).

Serse: no. 1.

Siroe: libretto (1728).

Solomon: nos. 1, 3, 5; v.s. (Button, Whitaker, and Beadnall, *c*.1814); libretto (1749).

Solos for a German Flute (Sonatas or Chamber Airs): pp.305–27, no. 20 (vol. i); nos. 2, 4, 7, 11 (vol. iv); nos. 1, 2, 5 (vol. v); no. 6 (vol. vi).

Solo Sonatas, Op. 1: nos. 1, 3, 4.

Solos for Flute and Bass; p. 241, no. 1.

Sosarme: nos. 2, 3, 7; libretto (1732).

Suites de pièces, hpd: nos. 3, 5, 6, 10, 11, 12, 13; 1st set [HWV 426–33] (Paris *c*.1828); 3rd set (Arnold edn.) (Smith p. 238).

Susanna: nos. 1, 2.

Tamerlano: no. 1.

Teseo: no. 2.

Theodora: nos. 1, 4, 6; 1 aria (J. B. Bland, n.d.); libretto (1759).

Tolomeo: no. 6; libretto (1730).

Trio Sonatas, Op. 2: no. 3.

Trio Sonatas, Op. 5: no. 1.

Il trionfo del tempo e della verità: libretto (1737).

The triumph of time and truth: nos. 1, 5; 2 arias, i (J. Bland, n.d.); ii (n.d., n.p.).

Utrecht Te Deum and Jubilate: nos. 4, 6, 8, 9.

Water Music: nos. 1, 3, 8, 11; kbd arr. with some spurious items, 6 vols.: i–ii (n.p., n.d.); iii (J. Bland, n.d.); iv (Dublin, Lee, *c*.1778); v (Dublin, Hime, *c*.1800); vi (Paine and Hopkins, *c*.1850).

Miscellaneous:

'Handel's posthumous trios', vn, va, vc (arr. from oratorios) (Birchall, n.d.).

'Eighteen songs [from oratorios]', vc obbl. hpd (Oxford, Hardy, *c*.1798).

The Beauties of Handel (T. Williams, 19th cent.), vols. iii, iv, vi.

'Seventy-five new psalm tunes . . . by Dr. Arnold and Mr. Calcott, to which is added forty-three tunes selected from Handel, etc. . . . ' (W. Hodsoll, *c*.1800).

Sprigs of Laurel, 'a comic opera . . . consisting of German, Scotch, Irish & English airs . . . & others by Handel, etc.' (Longman & Broderip, *c*.1793).

'A collection of the most admired songs, duets & trios in score' (n.d. [18th cent.]).

'Handel's Hallelujah in the Messiah and Grand Coronation Anthems, to which are prefix'd Two New Fugues'; kbd 4 hands, by J. Marsh (R. Bremner, 1780).

Ten Songs, arr. Somervell (London, Curwen / New York, Schirmer, 1928).

Typescript catalogue of the complete Arnold edition in the Hall Collection.

10

The Santini Collection

HANS JOACHIM MARX

SHORTLY after 1900 a young English musician travelled from Cambridge to Münster in Westphalia, in search of manuscripts containing works by Alessandro Scarlatti that were said to be in the local Diocesan Museum. His attention may have been drawn to Münster by a handwritten catalogue in the British Museum that had been compiled by Vincent Novello in 1843. This listed some of the manuscripts and printed music in the library of the Abbate Santini in Rome. The young musicologist—it was Edward Dent—found far more than he had imagined. In addition to the Scarlatti manuscripts he was looking for, the music collection of the Diocesan Museum contained innumerable manuscripts and a large amount of printed music from the sixteenth, seventeenth, and eighteenth centuries. These holdings had been ignored by scholars for decades, and had been quietly gathering dust. Dent was the first musicologist to draw attention to the importance of this Collection.

A few years later Joseph Killing's Berlin dissertation[1] provided the first survey of the treasures of sacred music held by the library, which comprised 4,500 manuscripts and 1,000 items of printed music. In the decades that followed, Karl Gustav Fellerer[2] and the head of the School of Church Music in Münster, Rudolf Ewerhart,[3] drew attention to the Handel manuscripts in the Santini Collection. Ewerhart was the first to recognize the importance of this source-material for the transmission of Handel's early works.

In turning once more to the Santini Collection and the works by Handel it contains, I am concerned with the question of how Handel's autograph manuscripts and the copies made by his Roman copyists came into Santini's possession. This question, which primarily concerns

---

[1] *Kirchenmusikalische Schätze der Bibliothek des Abbate Fortunato Santini: Ein Beitrag zur Geschichte der katholischen Kirchenmusik in Italien* (Düsseldorf, 1910), with many music exx.

[2] 'Fortunato Santini als Sammler und Bearbeiter Händelscher Werke', *HjB* 2 (1929), 25–40.

[3] 'Die Händel-Handschriften der Santini-Biobliothek in Münster', *HjB* 6 (1960), 111–50.

problems of transmission, permits us to draw a number of conclusions about the authenticity and dating of certain of the composer's works. I should like to begin by describing briefly the reasons which led Santini to assemble his music library, the criteria he applied in doing so, and the manner in which the collection was acquired by the Bishop of Münster.

Fortunato Santini was born in Rome in 1778,[4] and was sent to an orphanage at the age of 7. He was taught music by Giuseppe Jannaconi, who subsequently became maestro di cappella at the Sistine Chapel. Santini then studied theology and philosophy, and took organ lessons with Giovanni Guidi, maestro di cappella at Santa Maria in Trastevere. He was ordained priest in 1801, though he seems never to have held an incumbency. In his youth he was more interested in music than in theology; above all, he studied with untiring diligence the strict Palestrina-based style of counterpoint championed by Jannaconi. By making scores and copying works of the Roman school he acquired a knowledge of composition, and also assembled a small collection of model examples that were to form the backbone of a music library which was destined to become famous throughout Europe.

It seems that initially he made the scores only for his own use. In time, however, reformers in the field of church music requested him to supply copies of certain works, and these he made when they were commissioned and paid for. In order to fulfil these commissions he attempted to locate the original sources in the libraries and archives of Roman churches and monasteries, and subsequently in the private collections of Roman noblemen.[5] Gaining access to these holdings was evidently no easier then than it is today; petty claims to ownership and small-minded envy repeatedly conspired to hinder Santini's work. In such situations it may have been of help that he was supported in a number of ways by the rich, influential, and extremely musical Cardinal Carlo Odeschalchi (1786–1841); for more than two decades Santini lived in the Cardinal's palace facing the church of SS. XII Apostoli. The palace also housed his growing library.

Killing's biographical research failed to answer the question of how and with what means Santini acquired the thousands of manuscript and printed items that he assembled within a relatively short space of time. Vladimir Stasov, the Russian music critic, who was a friend of Santini, points out in his book *L'Abbé Santini et sa collection musicale*

---

[4] For the best short biography of Santini see R. Ewerhart's article in *MGG* 11 (1963), 1381–3.

[5] On Santini's methods of working see Vladimir Stasov, *L'Abbé Santini et sa collection musicale à Rome* (Florence, 1854), 12.

à Rome that the owners of old manuscripts and music attached little importance to them, and that many monastery libraries were dissolved at the time of the French occupation of Italy.[6] Santini evidently took advantage of this state of affairs, buying what was offered to him or what he was able to find in out-of-the-way places. One example among many is a manuscript in the British Library (Add. MS 34054), which contains sacred works from the early eighteenth century, including an autograph of Alessandro Scarlatti dated 1708; the manuscript came from the archives in Frascati. It is likely that Santini acquired the musical holdings of the old library of the Casa Ruspoli in a similar way, a matter to which we will return.

In his researches in Roman archives and libraries he probably received moral and financial support from Cardinal Odeschalchi, who was not only Vice-Chancellor of the Church, but also, on account of his musical proclivities, Protector of the Congregation of Santa Cecilia.[7] At his recommendation Santini was made an honorary member of the Congregation in 1835, and shortly afterwards he was appointed to a commission headed by Spontini which propagated the revival of Gregorian chant and of 'ancient classical' polyphony.[8] In 1838, when the Cardinal joined the Jesuits, Santini left the palace on the Piazza SS. Apostoli and moved with his library to Via dell'Anima 50, close to the German National Church. Here, particularly in Lent, when strangers came to Rome in large numbers, he gave musical soirées at which, with both friends and strangers, he performed pieces from his collection. Liszt, Cramer, Hiller, and Mendelssohn were among his visitors.[9]

Santini's financial situation does not seem to have been very good during the 1830s and 1840s. He still employed a number of copyists in order to fulfil his commissions, which were largely from abroad, but he missed the vigorous support of his patron Odeschalchi. This may have been one of the reasons why he toyed with the idea of selling his library. Since the middle of the 1830s major libraries in Berlin, Bologna, Paris, Brussels, and St Petersburg had attempted to buy this unique collection, though it seemed that Santini did not want to part with it. Only in 1854, when Stasov's book alerted the musical world to the unique nature of the library, did Santini feel unable to refuse the offers that were made to him. Hitherto inaccesible

---

[6] Ibid. 13. See also Gerald Abraham's introd., 'V.V. Stasov: Man and Critic', in *Vladimir Vasilevich Stasov: Selected Essays on Music*, trans. Florence Jonas (London, 1968), 6–7.

[7] Concerning Carlo Cardinal Odeschalchi's function in the Congregazione di Santa Cecilia in Rome, see Remo Giazotto, *Quattro secoli di storia dell'Accademia Nazionale di Santa Cecilia*, ii (Verona, 1970), 77–9.

[8] On Santini, see ibid. 91, 155 f.

[9] See Killing, *Kirchenmusikalische Schätze*, 18.

documents in the Collegio Campo Santo in Rome reveal that Bernhard Quante, a priest from Münster, who was chaplain of the German National Church in Rome, Santa Maria dell'Anima, in the mid-1850s, and who thus knew Santini who was his immediate neighbour, bought the library at the behest of the Bishop of Münster in exchange for a *vitalitium* (a kind of annuity) of 465 *scudi* per annum. The Confraternity of the Campo Santo Teutonico had initially advanced the payments, and accommodated the library in its house directly next to St Peter's.[10] It became possible to send the library to Münster only after the death of Santini on 14 September 1861, and after payment of the outstanding expenses incurred (which included $5\frac{1}{3}$ per cent interest). In January the Confraternity acceded to the request of the Bishop of Münster,[11] and thereupon 'one of the most complete libraries of ancient Italian music', as Mendelssohn termed it,[12] made its way by train to northern Germany in about 125 boxes. Until 1923 it was housed provisionally in the Diocesan Museum, where Edward Dent found it, uncatalogued and in a state of disorder. Until after World War II it was deposited in the University Library in Münster; since then it has been incorporated into the library of the Episcopal Seminary for Priests. The greater part has been restored and made freely available to scholarship through Kindler's multi-volume catalogue.

With regard to the provenance of the manuscripts containing compositions by Handel collected by Santini, it must first of all be noted that of the total of fifty-five volumes only twenty-two come from Handel's Italian period (see App. 3). Five volumes were copied at a later date, some as late as the nineteenth century (App. 2, items marked ‡). The other twenty-eight volumes were copied by Santini himself; they contain arrangements and translations of English anthems and oratorios, and can thus be disregarded in the present context.[13]

The contemporary sources are without doubt of the greatest importance for Handel research, and their significance did not escape Santini's notice. In the handwritten catalogue which he sent to Vincent Novello in London in 1843 (GB-Lbl, Add. MS 33240) he added in a footnote: 'oltre che io possiedo di Händel. Tutti gli Oratorij e molte altre cose che forse non si conosceranno in Londra, perchè composte fuori del Regno Brittanico.' This is followed more

[10] See App. 1, doc. 1.
[11] See App. 1, doc. 2.
[12] Killing, *Kirchenmusikalische Schätze*, 14.
[13] The nos. of the Santini copies are D-MÜs Hs. 1864–72, 1874–6, 1878–86, 1889–92, 1904, 1909, and 1929, and were assigned by the library in Münster.

188   THE SANTINI COLLECTION

or less by the same titles that Stasov listed eleven years later in his printed catalogue.[14]

The most important contemporary manuscripts in the collection are three Handel autographs, which probably remained in Rome in connection with the work carried out by his Roman copyist Angelini. They are the scores of the motet 'O qualis de coelo' (HWV 239, Hs. 1888) written for Ruspoli at his country residence Vignanello; of the cantata with instruments 'Ah! crudel, nel pianto mio' (HWV 78, Hs. 1897) which was probably composed for Cardinal Ottoboni; and of the solo cantata to a text by Cardinal Pamphilj, 'Hendel, non può mia Musa' (HWV 117, Hs. 1898, fos. 1–4), the autograph of which was probably given by Pamphilj to the Marchese Ruspoli for a copy to be made, since it is in the group of manuscripts in Hs. 1898 which includes other cantatas copied for Ruspoli.

In five volumes which contain only copies of Roman compositions, Handel made a number of minor emendations and corrections. They demonstrate that he went through the copies carefully because they were to be used in performance; this is especially true of the two volumes of *La Resurrezione* (HWV 47, Hs. 1873 I/II), and also of the cantatas 'Da quel giorno fatale' (HWV 99, Hs. 1905), written for Pamphilj, and 'Arresta il passo' (HWV 83, Hs. 1912), which were probably composed as early as the spring of 1707.

The Santini Collection in Münster also contains a number of unique items of which the autographs are no longer extant. These include the motet composed for Ruspoli, 'Coelestis dum spirat' (HWV 231, Hs. 1887); the sacred cantata 'Donna, che in ciel', which Handel probably wrote in response to a commission from the city of Rome to commemorate the earthquake of 1703 (HWV 233, Hs. 1895); the secular cantata 'Amarilli vezzosa' (HWV 82, Hs. 1906); and the cantata 'Notte placida e cheta' (HWV 142, Hs. 1910, fos. 85–118), which can be assigned to the year 1707.

With regard to the cantatas copied in Angelini's workshop, Hs. 1898, 1899, and 1910 are of particular interest. All three consist of single cantata fascicles, which can have been bound together only after the period of Handel's sojourn in Rome, that is after 1709. Although the majority of works were copied for the Marchese Ruspoli, some, for instance the cantata 'Torna il core' (HWV 169, Hs. 1898, fos. 47–8), seem to have been copied for other purposes. 'Torna il core', according to the latest research, was copied by someone who may well be Alessandro Scarlatti's copyist Carl' Antonio Ferri. No other copy of music by Handel is in his hand.[15] The situation is much the

---

[14] See Stasov, *Santini*, 50. The works specified as 'Trios pour 2 violons et basse' and '6 concertos pour orgue avec instr.' refer to the Arnold edn., Santini Dr. 394 and Dr. 391.

[*See opposite page for n. 15*]

same in the case of several copies of cantatas in Hs. 1910, the provenance of which has not been clarified.

The five manuscripts marked with a double dagger in Appendix 2 were definitely copied after Handel's sojourn in Italy. The most problematical case is that of Hs. 1877; this contains the Marian cantata 'Il pianto di Maria' (HWV 234), which, according to the title-page, was performed 'davanti al Santo Sepolcro'. Although Handel is indicated as the composer, several criteria speak against his authorship. First, the title mentions a 'Stamperia di Musica G. Lorenzi' in Florence, which obviously hired out the manuscript score on a commercial basis; this would explain the existence of further copies of the cantata in Palermo, Rome, and Siena. Giuseppe Lorenzi is known to have started a printing business in Florence in 1812, which was acquired by Giovanni Ricordi seven years later;[16] so the copy of the score of HWV 234 was probably not made before 1812. This late date of origin is confirmed by the kind of paper used, by the idiosyncrasies of the script, and above all, as Anthony Hicks has pointed out,[17] by the rather amateurish nature of the treatment of the Gregorian chant. It could of course be objected that the existence of the cantata in Siena in 1709 is certified by diary entries of Francesco Maria Mannucci, which were published in 1964 by Mario Fabbri. Prince Ferdinando de' Medici is said to have expressly mentioned the work in a conversation with Mannucci and Perti. Mannucci's evidence would indeed be irrefutable if it had ever existed; however, Carlo Vitali and Antonello Furnari have demonstrated[18] that the diary, which was said to be in the Archivio di San Lorenzo in Florence, was merely a figment of its supposed discoverer's imagination. So we can safely delete the Siena Marian cantata, HWV 234, from the list of Handel's works.

As with Hs. 1877, which contains the Marian cantata incorrectly ascribed to Handel, the two volumes Hs. 1907 and 1908, which contain the twelve duets and the trio HWV 201b, probably originated in the Florence area. Santini later entered them in the 'Acquisitations-Katalog' (Hs. 4449, p. 101) with four other manuscripts, including Hasse's cantata 'Orfeo ed Euridice' (Hs. 3581), which is incorrectly assigned to Handel. The three volumes in question have three-digit

[15] See K. Watanabe and H. J. Marx, 'Händels italienische Kopisten', *Göttinger Händel–Beiträge*, 3 (1989), 217.

[16] See A. Z. Laterza, 'Lorenzi, Giuseppe', in D. W. Krummel and S. Sadie (eds.) *Music Printing and Publishing* (New Grove Handbooks in Music, London, 1990), 324.

[17] See the worklist compiled by A. Hicks in W. Dean, *The New Grove Handel* (London, 1982), 134.

[18] 'Händels Italienreise—Neue Dokumente, Hypothesen und Interpretationen', *Göttinger Händel–Beiträge*, 4 (1991), 41–66.

THE SANTINI COLLECTION

numbers (683, 666, and 667) in addition to the old Santini numbers, which enable us to deduce that they have a common origin. Furthermore, Hs. 1908 contains the duet 'Langue, geme, sospira' (HWV 188), which Handel wrote in London about 1722.[19] As the two volumes with the duets are by the same copyist, they cannot have been assembled before 1722. Santini may have acquired from the Florence area the somewhat mysterious volume Hs. 1911 with the two keyboard suites in D minor and F sharp minor (HWV *deest*), for which there is no corroborative evidence.[20]

So far we have discussed only the Handel manuscripts of the Santini Collection in Münster. The brief summary of Abbate Santini's biography at the beginning has shown that the international reputation of this passionate connoisseur and collector of early music led to requests from foreign colleagues. We know that Santini was friendly or corresponded with the most important librarians and bibliophiles all over Europe; they included Edward Goddard in Chichester, Fétis in Brussels, Bouttée de Toulmon in Paris, Kiesewetter and Aloys Fuchs in Vienna, Gaspari in Bologna, Proske in Regensburg, and many others. Through these contacts a number of Handel manuscripts, autographs and contemporary performing material reached collections north of the Alps. Appendix 4 shows that in the 1830s the Viennese collectors Kiesewetter and Fuchs acquired a number of autographs with secular cantatas that were later sold or given away, whilst the English clergyman Goddard acquired the performing material for the sacred works that Santini had obtained from the Casa Colonna in Rome: these are the ones written for the church of Santa Maria in Monte Santo, HWV 235, 237 and 238, and 240 and 243, some of which were recently auctioned by Sotheby's and are now in the Pierpont Morgan Library in New York.[21]

At the end of my brief account of the Santini Collection I will attempt to answer the question raised at the beginning, about the provenance of the Handel manuscripts acquired by Santini. It is probably safe to assume that all the manuscripts with works by Handel, to which in his library he assigned the shelf-marks 'S[ezione]. 12. D[ivisione]. 2', numbers 5 to 24,[22] came from music collections in the city of Rome. Most of the volumes no doubt came from the

---

[19] Concerning the provenance of HWV 188 see D. Burrows, 'Handel in Hanover', in P. Williams (ed.), *Bach, Handel, Scarlatti: Tercentenary Essays* (Cambridge, 1985), 57.

[20] *Incipits* in Ewerhart, 'Die Händel-Handschriften', 147 f. [*Ed.'s Note:* The Suites in D minor and F# minor are certainly not by Handel. The MS also contains copies of movements from the Suites in E major, F minor, and D minor from the first set (HWV 430, 433, and 428), undoubtedly copied from the Cluer edn. of 1720, or one of its later issues.]

[21] See Watanabe and Marx, 'Händels italienische Kopisten', table 2, p. 203.

[22] The following nos. are missing: 6–8, 11, 15, 21, 22.

Casa Ruspoli, for which, as is revealed by domestic account books, Handel worked for a considerable time. Santini was able to acquire four manuscripts containing copies of the cantatas HWV 99 and 170, and of the oratorio 'La bellezza raveduta nel trionfo del tempo [*Il trionfo del tempo e del disinganno*] (HWV 46a) from the Casa Pamphilj, whereas the performing material with the liturgical music for Santa Maria in Monte Santo no doubt came from the Casa Colonna. We can only speculate about the provenance of the cantatas 'Ah! crudel, nel pianto mio' (HWV 78) and 'Qual ti riveggio' (HWV 150). However, it is significant that to date none of the Handel manuscripts that Santini collected in Rome have been traced back to Cardinal Ottoboni, who was probably the most important Italian patron of music.

The present survey of the acquisition and the location of the Handel manuscripts collected by Fortunato Santini no doubt confirms the observation of Terentianus Maurus, 'habent sua fata libelli'. Even if Handel's anthems and oratorios, which he owned in the Arnold edition and which he arranged for his soirées musicales, supplying Italian texts when needed, were musically more pleasing to him than the cantatas, with their often erotic texts, it is to his credit that he should have recognized the eminent historical value of these sources. Without Santini's passion for collecting, many an immortal composition from Handel's youth would have been lost for ever.

Appendix 1: Documents on the Sale of the Santini Collection

Document 1: Meeting of 19 March 1855 (Archivio di Campo Santo Teutonico, libro 177, pp. 104–5.)

Der Hochw. Bernhard Quante, Priester der Diözese Münster, gegenwärtig Kaplan in S. Maria dell'Anima, machte die Mitteilung, daß er die musikalische Bibliothek des Herrn Abbate Santini für ein Vitalitium von vierhundertfünfundsechzig Scudi angekauft habe, und stellte folgende Bitte an die Congregation: 1. Sie möge erlauben, daß er die besagte Bibliothek in das Hospiz zu Campo Santo bringen lassen könne; 2. sie möge gleich das Vitalitium für das erste Jahr, welches vertragsgemäß im laufenden Monat erlegt werden müsse, bezahlen; 3. sie möge Bürgschaft leisten für die Auszahlung des besagten Vitalitiums, welches für die folgenden Jahre zu Anfang jedes Trimesters an den Abbate Santini mit einhundertsechzehn scudi und 25 bajocchi vorausbezahlt werden müsse. Unter den Gründen, welche die Congregation zur Gewährung seiner Bitte bestimmen könnten, hob der Bittsteller besonders hervor den großen Werth und die hohe

THE SANTINI COLLECTION

Wichtigkeit dieser Bibliothek für das Studium der Kirchenmusik und den großen Nutzen, den folglich die besagte Bibliothek der Kirche Deutschlands, wofür sie hauptsächlich bestimmt sei, bringen könne, da dieselbe, seiner Absicht gemäß, Allen, welche von den Bischöfen Deutschlands mit dem Studium der Kirchenmusik beauftragt seien, offenstehen sollte. Für die gleich zu erlegende Summe von 465 Scudi hätte die fromme Stiftung in der Bibliothek selbst hinlängliche Bürgschaft, und die späteren vierteljährigen Zahlungen würde er selbst pünktlich entrichten. Er schloß mit der Erklärung, den Hochw. Bischof von Münster sogleich von diesem Ankauf in Kenntnis zu setzen, damit dieser, vielleicht in Verbindung mit den anderen Hochw. Bischöfen Deutschlands, auf irgend eine Art die Zurückzahlung der für das Vitalitium des ersten Jahres ausgelegten Summe an Campo Santo bewirke.— In Erwägung dieser Gründe und des Umstandes, daß auch seine Eminenz, der Cardinal Fürst von Schwarzenberg, Protektor unserer Erzbruderschaft, dem diese Angelegenheit vom H. Camerlengo mitgeteilt worden, seine volle Zustimmung dazu gegeben, glaubte die Congregation der Bitte des Herrn Quante entsprechen zu können, mit der Bedingung jedoch, daß die Bibliothek nicht von Campo Santo weggenommen werden dürfe, wenn nicht vorher die ganze von der frommen Stiftung ausgelegte Summe samt den Zinsen, die sie von derselben erhalten haben würde, wenn sie das Geld zum Ankaufe von Cartelle del Consolidato verwendet hätte, an dieselbe Stiftung zurückgezahlt worden sei, und daß, im Falle der Herr Quante aus irgendwelchen Gründen diese Bibliothek wieder verkaufen wollte, der Hochw. Herr Bischof von Münster an erster Stelle, an zweiter aber die fromme Stiftung von Campo Santo Anspruch darauf machen könne. —

Hierauf wurde ballottiert mit dem Bemerken, daß die schwarzen Bohnen für, die weißen aber gegen das Bittgesuch des H. B. Quante sein sollten; es ergab sich, daß alle Stimmen für dasselbe waren. Schließlich wurde der Herr Camerlengo Joseph Spithöver bevollmächtigt, alles das zu bewerkstelligen, was zur gültigen Ausführung dieser Angelegenheit erforderlich sei.

The Right Reverend Bernhard Quante, Priest of the Diocese of Münster, at present Chaplain of S. Maria dell'Anima, announced that he had purchased the music library of the Abbate Santini for a *vitalitium* of 465 *scudi*, and made the following request to the Congregation: (1) that they would permit him to have the aforesaid library brought to the Hospice at Campo Santo; (2) that they would pay immediately the first year's *vitalitium*, which according to the agreement was due in the current month; (3) that they would guarantee the future payment of the aforesaid *vitalitium*, which for the following years was to be made in advance to the Abbate Santini at the beginning of each quarter, in the sum of 116 *scudi* 25 *bajocchi*. Among the reasons which might persuade the Congregation to grant his request, the petitioner particularly stressed the great value and outstanding importance of this library for the study of church music, and how useful, therefore, the said library would be to the Church in Germany, for which it was principally intended; for, in conformity with its purpose, it should be accessible to all those to whom the study of church music is assigned by the German bishops. For the sum of 465 *scudi* to be paid immediately the Foundation would have adequate

security in the library itself, and he would for his part make the subsequent quarterly payments promptly. He concluded with an undertaking to inform the Right Reverend the Bishop of Münster immediately about the purchase, so that he, perhaps in conjunction with the other Right Reverend Bishops in Germany, could arrange for Campo Santo to be reimbursed in some way for the sum paid out for the first year's *vitalitium*.

In view of these arguments, and of the fact that his Eminence Cardinal Fürst von Schwarzenberg, Protector of our Community, who had been informed of this matter by the Treasurer, had also given his full assent to it, the Congregation considered that it could agree to Herr Quante's request, on condition, however, that the library should not be removed from Campo Santo without the whole sum disbursed by the Foundation, including the interest which it would have received from it had it used the money for the purchase of gilt-edged stock, being first repaid to the Foundation, and that should Herr Quante for any reason wish to resell the library, the Right Reverend the Bishop of Münster should have first claim to it, but the Foundation of Campo Santo should have the second.

The matter was thereupon put to a ballot, on the basis that the black beans should be for Herr B. Quante's request, the white against; the result was that all votes were for it. Finally, Treasurer Joseph Spithöver was authorized to take all the necessary steps for the proper implementation of the matter.

Document 2: Meeting of 19 January 1862 (Archivio di Campo Santo Teutonico, libro 177, p. 185)

Der Herr Camerlengo teilte dann der Congregation ein Schrieben des Hochwürdigsten Herrn Bischofs von Münster an die Congregation mit, worin derselbe der Congregation von Campo Santo die Anzeige macht: daß der Überbringer des Schreibens der Hochw. Herr Dr. und geistliche Rat Bangen beauftragt und bevollmächtigt sei, im Namen des Hochwürdigsten Bischofs die Santinische musikalische Bibliothek, welche in Campo Santo aufbewahrt zu übernehmen, und die betreffenden, noch rückständigen Zahlungen zu leisten. Der Hochwürdigste Herr Bischof spricht dann in den verbindlichsten Ausdrücken der ehrwürdigen Congregation vom Campo Santo und besonders ihrem Camerlengo den inngisten Dank aus für die (. . .) Gefälligkeit, durch welche diese hochwichtige Sammlung für kirchliche Zwecke unseres deutschen Vaterlandes erhalten worden ist.

Der Herr Camerlengo bemerkt dann, daß die Summe, welche Campo Santo für diese Bibliothek ausgelegt, sich auf 808 belaufe, welche mit den Zinsen zu $5\frac{1}{3}\%$ bis heute ungefähr die Summe von 1000 scudi ausmache. Die Zahlung selbst würde nach Aussage des Herrn Geistlichen Rates Dr. Bangen noch einige Wochen anstehen, inzwischen forderte der Herr Camerlengo die versammelten Mitglieder auf darüber nachzudenken, auf welche Weise diese Summe am nützlichsten könne verwandt werden. Der Camerlengo sei der Meinung, daß, da dieses Geld aus verkauften Consolidati herrühre, man auch dafür wieder Consolidati ankaufen solle. Da dies jedoch

THE SANTINI COLLECTION

in Anbetracht der politischen Zeitverhältnisse von nicht geringer Wichtigkeit
für unsere Erzbruderschaft ist, und man auf die möglichst sichere Erhaltung
des Vermögens zu sehen habe, so habe er rechtzeitig die Aufmerksamkeit der
Congregazion auf diesen Gegenstand hinlenken wollen, und erwarte daher für
die nächste Congregation die Ansicht der Congregation darüber zu hören.

The Treasurer then informed the Congregation of a letter from the Right
Reverend the Bishop of Münster to the Congregation, in which he announces
to the Congregation of Campo Santo that the bearer of the letter, the Right
Reverend and Spiritual Counsellor Dr Bangen, is authorized and empowered,
in the name of the Right Reverend the Bishop, to take possession of the
Santini music library, which is deposited in Camp Santo, and to settle the
outstanding payments involved. The Right Reverend the Bishop also
expresses in the warmest terms to the venerable Congregation of Campo
Santo, and especially to its Treasurer, his profoundest thanks for the efforts
through which this most important collection has been acquired for the
ecclesiastical purposes of our German fatherland.

The Treasurer then observed that the sum which Campo Santo has
disbursed for this library comes to 808 [*scudi*], which with interest of 5⅓
per cent amounts to a current figure of around 1,000 *scudi*. The actual
payment would be delayed for a few weeks more, according to the Spiritual
Counsellor Dr Bangen; meanwhile the Treasurer asked the assembled
members to consider how this sum might be used to the best advantage.
The Treasurer was of the opinion that since this money came from the sale
of gilt-edged stock they should for that reason buy new stock. Since,
however, in view of the political situation, this is of no small importance for
our Community, and they had to look for the safest possible way of
protecting their assets, it had seemed to him timely to draw the attention of
the Congregation to this matter, and accordingly he expected to hear the
opinion of the Congregation about it at the next meeting.

Appendix 2: Handel MSS in D-MÜs.

Numbering new	old	Title	HWV	Provenance
1873 I–II	—	Oratorio *La Resurrezione*	47	Ruspoli Lib., with corrections by Handel.
1877‡	S2D2-187	Motet 'Il pianto di Maria'	234	title-page quotes the Florentine printer G. Lorenzi, early 19th-cent. misattribution.
1887	S2D2-13	Motet 'Coelestis dum spirat'	231†	Ruspoli Lib., Rome/Vignanello.
1888	S2D2-14	Motet 'O qualis de coelo'	239†	Ruspoli Lib., Rome/Vignanello; partly autograph.
1893	S2D2-20	Cantata 'Un'alma innamorata'	173	Ruspoli Lib., Rome.
1894	S2D2-18	Cantata 'Dietro l'orme fugaci'	105	Ruspoli Lib., Rome.
1895	—	Cantata 'Donna, che in ciel'	233†	?
1896	—	Oratorio *Il trionfo del tempo* (pt. 1)	46a	Pamphilj Lib., Rome.
1897	S2D2-16	Cantata 'Ah! crudel nel pianto mio'	78	?; autograph.
1898	S2D2-10	Solo cantatas	117, 145, 90, 127a, 161a, 169, 139a, 158a†, 84, 167b, 126a†, 129, 95†, 153, 144, 155	Ruspoli Lib., Rome; partly autograph.
1899	S2D2-9	Solo cantatas	133, 107, 100, 130, 104, 131, 120a, 157†, 159, 172, 148, 137, 152, 102b†, 114, 160a, 156, 140	Ruspoli Lib., Rome; partly autograph.
1900 I/II	—	Cantata 'Cor fedele'	96	Ruspoli Lib., Rome.
1902	S2D2-17	Cantata 'Clori, mia bella Clori'	92	Ruspoli Lib., Rome (?).
1903	—	Cantata 'Tra le fiamme'	170	Pamphilj Lib., Rome.
1905	S2D2-19	Cantata 'Da quel giorno fatale'	99	Pamphilj Lib., Rome; with corrections by Handel.
1906	—	Cantata 'Amarilli vezzosa'	82†	Ruspoli Lib., Rome.
1907‡	S1D1-7	Italian duets	184, 199, 178, 191, 197, 183	Florence?; after c.1722.

Numbering new	old	Title	HWV	Provenance
1908‡	S1D1–6,	8 Italian duets, trio	194, 198, 196, 188, 185, 180, 201b	Florence?; after c.1722.
1910	S2D2–12	Cantatas	153, 171, 173, 142†, 168, 90, 161a, 127a, 144, 107, 130, 115, 152, 117, 125a	?
1911‡	——	Suites for harpsichord	430, deest, deest, 433, 428	Florence? [after 1720]§
1912	S2D2–5	Cantata 'Aresta il passo'	83	Ruspoli Lib., Rome; partly autograph.
1913	S2D2–23	Cantata 'Tu fedel, tu costante?'	171	Ruspoli Lib., Rome.
1914	S2D2–24	Cantata 'Oh come chiare e belle'	143	Ruspoli Lib., Rome.
1914a	——	Oratorio: *Il trionfo del tempo* (pt. 2)	46a	Pamphilj Lib., Rome.
1924‡	S2D2–82	'Dixit Dominus'	232	Later copy of a source in. Colonna Lib., Rome.

† unique
‡ later than 1709
§ *Ed.'s Note*: The Suites in D minor and F♯ minor are certainly not by Handel.

Note: All MSS except nos. 1887, 1888, 1903, 1911, and 1924 are cited in V. Stasov, *L'Abbé Santini et sa collection musicale à Rome* (Florence, 1854), 50.

Appendix 3: Handel MSS formerly in the Santini Collection, Rome

Location	Title	HWV	Tradition	Remarks
A-Wgm IV 6670	Cantata 'Alla caccia'	79	Santini, Kiesewetter	Handel's autograph from Ruspoli Lib., Rome.
CH-Bfi	Cantata 'Qual ti riveggio' (fos. 1–16)	150	Santini, A. Fuchs, S. Thalberg, S. Ochs, L. Koch	Handel's autograph, from Ottoboni, Lib., Rome.
D-Bds Mus. ms. autogr. Händel 3	Cantata 'Alla caccia'	79	Santini, A. Fuchs, et al.	Handel's autograph, cf. A-Wgm IV 6670.
GB-Lbl Egerton MS 2458	'Nisi Dominus'	238	Santini, E. Goddard, GB-Lbm	Roman copies, from Colonna Lib., Rome.
J-Tn Ms.o.52.3	'Saeviat tellus'	240		
	'Gloria patri'	238	Santini, E. Goddard, Cummings, Tokugawa	Roman copy, lost, from Colonna Lib., Rome.
US-NYpm MS 120	Cantata 'Qual ti riveggio' (fos. 17–22)	150	Santini, A. Fuchs, C. F. Peters, US-NYpm	Handel's autograph, cf. CH-Bfi.
US-NYpm MS Pl 103–40	[Church music]	235, 237, 240, 243	Santini, E. Goddard, Cummings, Plummer, Koch, US-NYpm	Roman copies, from Colonna Lib., Rome.

I I

The Music-Paper used by Handel and his Copyists in Italy 1706–1710

KEIICHIRO WATANABE

THIS survey of Handel's Italian music-paper derives from the study of the Italian copyists which I carried out jointly with Dr Hans Joachim Marx in Hamburg in 1987. The results of our investigation of the rastra were not included in our thesis;[1] they are now set out for the first time. The survey will shed new light both on Handel's Italian autographs and on the copies made by the scribes who worked for him.

The item-numbers in the left-hand column of Table 1 are in roughly chronological order, though not strictly so. The capital letters A, B, C, etc. denote rastrum-types; a small letter after the capital indicates a subgroup within the type. For example, rastrum-type D has four staves drawn twice across the page, making eight staves in all; rastrum-type A, on the other hand, has eight staves drawn at one sweep. The total span of each rastration—the distance from the top line of the top stave to the bottom line of the bottom stave—is accurate to the nearest half-millimetre, with the symbols + and – to indicate fractionally greater or smaller measurements.

It is not enough, however, to classify these rastra only by their total span, because two rastra with the same span may nevertheless have other features which are different, such as the width of the spaces between the lines of each stave; for example, in rastrum Ei, which occurs in the autograph of the cantata 'Alla caccia', no. 54, the second space from the bottom of the fifth stave is always a little wider than the others, and this feature distinguishes it from Ej.

Some rastra and watermarks can be dated by correlating the manuscripts which contain them with references in contemporary

---

[1] K. Watanabe and H. J. Marx, 'Händels italienische Kopisten', in *Göttinger Händel-Beiträge*, 3 (1987), 195–234.

documents such as copyists' bills.[2] Parentheses among the item numbers indicate that the work is listed in such a document; if the extant manuscripts can be identified as the ones mentioned in the documents, the item numbers are inserted between the parentheses. For example, *Il Delirio Amoroso*, no. (14), is listed in the Pamphilj accounts and dated 12 February 1707; this can be taken to be the extant copy of the cantata, 'Da quel giorno fatale', in the Santini Library, no. 14. In the case of 'Salve Regina' (between no. 78 and no. 79) there is no extant copy which matches the entry in the Ruspoli accounts, so a blank is left between the parentheses.

Several of the documents list the number of folios used in the copies. The *originale*, that is the score, of the 'Cantata dell'Arminda', no. (87), is described as having five and a half *fogli*, which makes twenty-two folios by modern counting, and this is the exact number of folios in the extant copy by Angelini in the Santini Library. On the other hand the cantata 'Menzognere speranze', no. (92), from the same document, is shown as having one and a half *fogli*, that is six folios in modern terms, while the copy by Ginelli in the Santini Library amounts to only four folios; but the identification may nevertheless be correct, because the paper has the same watermark, fleur-de-lis in double circle (2 / C),[3] as those of the other manuscripts listed in the same copyist's bill. The document gives its date as 22 September 1707.

Sometimes, however, there are two extant copies, either of which could be identified with an entry in a document: 'Una Cantata consiste in 2. fogli', no. (95 or 96), could refer to either 'Del bel idolo mio', no. 95, or 'Sarai contento un dì', no. 96. The copies in the Santini Library, both written by Angelini, are written on paper with the same watermark, 2 / C, and the same rastrum, Dk, so it is not clear which one is being referred to.

There are six watermark-types from the period, listed at the beginning of Table 1: (1) three crescents (*tre mezze lune*), (2) fleur-de-lis in a double circle, (3) animal in a single circle, (4) fleur-de-lis in a single circle, (5) bird, and (6) sheep in a single circle; subgroups are indicated by the addition of capital letters, e.g. 1 / A, 1 / B. We will now survey Handel's Italian period on the basis of the watermarks.

The earliest type, three crescents (1), is Venetian, not Florentine as has long been believed. The autographs between nos. 1 and 15 (1–3,

---

[2] U. Kirkendale, 'Ruspoli Documents on Handel', *Journal of the American Musicological Society*, 20 (1976); H. J. Marx, 'Die "Giustificazioni della Casa Pamhpilj" als musikgeschichtliche Quelle', *Studi musicali*, 12 (1983), 121–87; id., 'Händel in Rom', *HjB* 29 (1983), 107–27.

[3] Cf. K. Watanabe, 'The Paper used by Handel and his Copyists during the time of 1706–1710', in *Journal of the Japanese Musicological Society*, 27 (1981), 129–71.

5–8, 10–12, 15) use this paper. As can be seen in Table 1, almost all the three-crescents papers have rastra of types B or C (see nos. 1–15 and 158–171). The highly developed technique of drawing many staves at once is characteristic of Venetian music-paper, though the paper itself was used widely in Austria and in northern Italy. My attention was drawn to this point by Paul Everett's study,[4] and with Hans Joachim Marx I have suggested the strong possibility that Handel came to Rome not from Florence but from Venice. Unfortunately we do not have any Florentine paper with Handel's handwriting on it; the Overture to the opera *Vincer se stesso è la maggior vittoria* or *Rodrigo*, no. 10, is written on the Venetian paper, but the rest of the opera is written on the Roman paper (between nos. 94 and 95). Some parts of the autograph of this opera were written not by Handel but by Angelini, his most important copyist in Rome; so the opera, performed in Florence in the autumn of 1707, was not composed in Florence but in Rome.[5] The first part of the autograph of 'Dixit Dominus', no. 15, is written on this Venetian paper, but the latter part on Roman paper. The work was completed in Rome on 4 April 1707.[6]

The next paper to be used is that with the watermark bird (5). The autographs of the two cantatas 'Occhi miei che faceste?', no. 16, and 'Qual ti riveggio, oh Dio', no. 17, as well as a part of the cantata 'Tu fedel? tu costante?', no. 29, are written on the rare paper with this watermark. The first two of these autographs have the rastrum Aa; they form a group with the following items, from 'Venne voglia ad amore', no. 18, to 'Allor ch'io dissi', no. 28, written on the paper without watermark (rastra Dq, Dl, El, and Ep), since Handel's handwriting is in the same early style in all of them. They are probably Venetian in origin, because the paper has characteristics which are similar to those of the paper with rastra Ba, Bd, and Be. This does not mean, however, that these cantatas, or part of the famous 'Tu fedel? tu costante?', no. 29, were composed in Venice; 'Tu fedel', no. 29, uses the Roman paper as well, and it was first copied on 16 May 1707 by Angelini and Ginelli for the Ruspoli Library (no. 61).

The Roman papers with the watermarks fleur-de-lis in a double circle (2) evidently originate in the Roman region. They were used for a long time: types C and D of this paper appear so randomly that it is scarcely possible to think of them as a pair. Only types A

---

[4] 'Vivaldi Concerto Manuscripts in Manchester: II', in *Informazioni e Studi Vivaldiani: Bollettino dell'Istituto Italiano Antonio Vivaldi*, 6 (1985), 8ff.

[5] R. Strohm, 'Händel in Italia: nuovi contributi', *Rivista italiana di musicologia*, 9 (1974), 152–74.

[6] The music of the psalm is characteristic of Venetian style. Cf. Watanabe and Marx, 'Händels italienische Kopisten', 201.

and B (an undoubted pair) are of early date; a copy of 'Da quel giorno fatale', no. 56, uses these papers, and it has the same rastra, Dd, Dm, etc., as those of another copy, no. 14. The copy of 'Aure soavi', no. 34, transcribed by the anonymous copyist Lon XIII, is also an early Roman copy. Many of the manuscripts of works of Alessandro Scarlatti composed at the end of the seventeenth and at the beginning of the eighteenth century were written on this paper; but the C and D watermark-types cannot be further distinguished without the help of the study of rastra.

From the autograph of *Aci, Galatea e Polifemo*, no. 106, dated 16 June 1708 in Naples, to the autograph of 'Cuopre tal volta', no. 111, the papers are Neapolitan, with the watermarks animal in a single circle and fleur-de-lis in a single circle (3 and 4). Further items between nos. 112 and 126 are on the Neapolitan paper, but we cannot be sure whether they were actually written in Naples, because the Suite in G minor, no. 113, and the arias from *Rodrigo*, no. 114, are written by Angelini, the Roman copyist; and the trio 'Se tu non lasci amore', no. 127, which was completed on 12 July 1708 in Naples, was written not on the Neapolitan but on the Roman paper. The papers with the rastra Er, Em, and G- are of Neapolitan origin.

At the end of his Italian sojourn Handel was again in Venice; but it is difficult to know how many visits he made there. There was one in the winter of 1706–7, and another in the winter of 1709–10; but was he there in the winters of 1707–8 and 1708–9? There were certainly at least two visits; it is clear that the Venetian papers were used again at the end of his Italian period, but how can we distinguish the later Venetian papers from the earlier ones? The autograph of *Agrippina*, no. 158, was written on the same paper (three crescents N) as 'Dunque sarà pur vero', no. 164, a part of 'La terra è liberata', no. 165, and 'Quando in calma ride amor', no. 169, and they have rastra Ca and Cb in common; the paper with the Ca rastrum was used in the autographs of the cantatas 'Un sospir', no. 159, 'Non sospirar', no. 160, 'Clori degl'occhi miei', no. 161, 'Ah! che pur troppo è vero', no. 162, 'Alpestre monte', no. 163, and the duettos 'Giù nei tartarei regni', no. 166, 'Che vai pensando', no. 167, and 'Amor gioje mi porge', no. 168. At first sight Handel's handwriting in these works may seem to be very early, and there are a few double hyphens in the autographs of *Agrippina* and the duettos 'Giù nei tartarei regni', and 'Quando in calma ride amor', no. 169 (see below). Nevertheless a close comparison of Handel's handwriting in *Agrippina* with that of these works proves them to be in the same style.

I have surveyed the autographs and copies mainly from the point of view of their watermarks, but we must now return to the rastra.

We have to consider whether the paper was sold already ruled, or was ruled after purchase to suit the particular needs of the court where it was used. The latter seems to have been the case with the Roman papers: some of the copies have blank spaces for ornate initials at the beginning of the music; this happens in the cantatas 'Sei pur bella', no, 57, (rastrum Dm), 'Se per fatal', no. 58, (rastrum Dh[a]), 'Udite il mio consiglio', no. 59, (rastrum Dm and Ed), 'Nella stagion', no. 62, (rastrum Di), 'Oh numi eterni', no. 65, (rastrum Di) and 'Del bel idolo mio', no. 95, (rastrum Dk). In other cases ornate initials are indeed written out in the blank spaces (or on the staves): 'Aure soavi', no. 60, (rastrum Db and Di), 'Ninfe e pastori', no. 64, (rastrum Di), 'Menzognere speranze', no. 92, (rastrum E-). In one case even an autograph has its ornate initial at the beginning: 'Aure soavi', no. 33, (rastrum Ed). These music-papers must surely have been ruled for the particular occasion; moreover, the rastrum Ha of the autographs of 'Arresta il passo' and 'Alla caccia', nos. 38 and 54, is in fact 'Di + 1'. It is hard to believe that such music-papers were sold already ruled.

The rastra in nos. 55 and 56 (copyist's bill: 14 May 1707, for Pamphilj), 57 to 63 (16 May 1707), 76 to 78 (30 June 1707, Ruspoli Library), 87 to 93 (22 September 1707, Ruspoli Library), and 95 or 96 (26 February 1708, Ruspoli Library) suggest that at least Dm, Di, Da, and Dk were in particular use at this period. These rastra differ significantly from those of the 'post-Neapolitan' period embracing nos. 128 to 135 (9 August 1708, Ruspoli Library), and 147 to 150 (28 August 1708, Ruspoli Library), where the predominant rastra are Dg and Df. There are two exceptions to this: Df in nos. 57 and 131, etc.; and Dk in nos. 95–6, etc., and 128. These two rastra extend from the pre-Neapolitan to the post-Neapolitan period.

The last music-papers to be considered are those with the rastrum Ca. As the autograph of the opera *Agrippina*, no. 158, performed in the winter of 1709–10, was written on paper with this rastrum, the other autographs having this rastrum—nos. 159–63, 166–8—must also be attributed to the years 1709–10. Part of the autograph of the cantata 'La terra è liberata', no. 165, is written on paper with the same watermark as that of the *Agrippina* autograph, three crescents N; so the rastrum Bc (nos. 165, 169) must belong here also. Furthermore, the copy of the cantata 'Sento là che ristretto', no. 171, is written on paper with the same watermark and rastrum as the copy of *Agrippina*, no. 170, so they could be attributed to the same period. The three-crescents papers have seventeen subgroups, from A to Q: of these, F and G , K and L, and possibly I and J form pairs; I, J, K, L, M, N, O, P, and Q have the rastra Ca, Cb, C-, or Bc, while A,

B, C, D, E, F, G, and H belong to the early period when Handel first came to Venice.

It is not enough to use only the rastra-types for establishing the chronological distribution of the music-papers; we must also examine the style and character of Handel's handwriting in the autographs, and I will survey the material again from this standpoint. The most obvious characteristic of Handel's writing in his earliest period is the use of double hyphens under melismas in the voice parts, to indicate sustained vowels; this habit lasted until about the beginning of May 1707. Furthermore, Handel wrote his name as 'Händel', with the Umlaut, in 'Oh numi eterni', no. 1, 'Sarai contenta un dì', no. 2, and 'Tacete, ohimè, no. 12; while his musical handwriting in the autographs between nos. 1 and 15 (1–3, 5–8, 10–12, 15), with fat note-heads and short quaver-stems, is most characteristic of his earliest period in Italy.

Handel's handwriting does not develop continuously but changes by stages. The styles from 'Occhi miei che faceste?', no. 16, to 'Vedendo amor', no. 19, and from 'E partirai, mia vita?', no. 20, to Sonata, no. 26, form other groups. 'Tu fedel', no. 29, has similarities with 'Occhi miei', no. 16. 'Ah crudel', no. 31, has a beautiful florid style with vertical note-stems, as do the next four numbers, 32, 33, 35, 36. The writing from 'Del bel idolo mio', no. 37, to 'Se per fatal destino', no. 42, is of similar character, with vertical note-stems. 'Un'alma innamorata', no. 44, 'Filli adorata', no. 52, 'Alla caccia', no. 54, 'O qualis de coelo', no. 66, 'Salve Regina', no. 67, resemble each other, with tall crotchets and quavers. 'Ah che troppo ineguali', no. 70, 'Tra le fiamme', no. 71, 'Clori mia bella', no. 72, 'Cor fedele', no. 74, and 'Hendel, non può mia musa', no. 75, again have common characteristics, with tall crotchets and quavers. 'No se emenderá', no. 84, 'Menzognere speranze', no. 85, and 'Sans y penser', no. 86, have fat handwriting.

Handel's separate notes seem to grow ever taller, but the autographs of 'Lungi dal mio bel nume', no. 98, 'Manca pur quanto sai', no. 99, 'Care selve', no. 100, and 'Lungi, lungi n'andò Fileno', no. 101, have a short, fat quaver, which is also found in *La Resurrezione*, no. 104. Neapolitan manuscripts have their own characteristics in accordance with their papers; the autograph of 'Oh come chiare e belle' no. 155, is distinguished by its minute calligraphy.

In his last Venetian period Handel again wrote short-stemmed notes; we find quavers of this type, but with somewhat oval note-heads, in the autograph of *Agrippina*, and again in the seven numbers from 'Un sospir a chi si muore', no. 159, to 'La terra è liberata', no. 165. Handel used double hyphens again in at least three

autographs: *Agrippina*, no. 158, (fos. 24^r, 37^v, and 76^r); 'Giù nei tartarei regni', no. 166, (fo. 27^r and ^{v}); and 'Quando in calma ride amor', no. 169 (pp. 9 and 10). As has been said, the handwriting of the autograph of 'La terra è liberata' looks at first sight as if Handel began to compose it very early; but close comparison with the *Agrippina* autograph shows that the composition of the cantata was begun at about the same time as the opera.

Were any of Handel's Roman works composed for Cardinal Ottoboni? In the many manuscript copies in D-MÜs of the works of Giuseppe Ottavio Pitoni, who from 1692 to 1731 was maestro di cappella of San Lorenzo in Damaso, in the Palazzo della Cancelleria of Pietro Cardinal Ottoboni, there are eleven copyists, none of whom can be identified with Handel's copyists; and none of the rastra in the autographs and copies of Handel's works coincide with those of Pitoni. It is difficult, therefore, at the present time, to indicate which of Handel's works may have been composed for Ottoboni.

Table 1

Key

† after item numbers	=	Autographs, of which copies are extant from the period 1706–10
‡after item numbers	=	Copies of works whose autographs are lost
(–)	=	Works in a copyist's bill
Item numbers in (–)	=	Copies identified as those listed in the copyists' bills
Rastra:	A =	1 × 8 staves
	B =	1 × 10 staves
	C =	1 × 12 staves
	D =	2 × 4 staves
	E =	2 × 5 staves
	F =	3 × 3 staves
	G =	4 × 4 staves
	H =	2 × 4 + 1 staves
Watermarks:	1 =	Three crescents
	2 =	Fleur-de-lis in double circle
	3 =	Animal in circle
	4 =	Fleur-de-lis in single circle
	5 =	Bird
	6 =	Sheep in single circle

Folios	Rastra	Watermarks	Copyists	Remarks
1.† 'Oh numi eterni', HWV145 (GB-Lbl R.M. 20.d.12, 20–3)				
20–1	B-)1×10/192.0 (unique)	I/A		'Händel';
22–3	B-)1×10/189.0 (unique)	I/A		Double hyphen.
2.† 'Sarai contenta un dì', HWV156 (GB-Lbl R.M. 20.d.12, 7–8)				
7–8	Bb)1×10/184.0+	I/B	Autograph	'Händel'; Double hyphen; handwriting like no. 1.
3.† 'Chi rapi la pace', HWV90 (GB-Lbl R.M. 20.d.11, 56–7)				
56–7	Bd)1×10/187.0 (1)	I/B	Autograph	Double hyphen; handwriting like no. 1.
4. 'Chi rapi la pace', HWV90 (GB-Lcm 698, 39–41)				
39–41	E-)2×5/88.5 (3) (unique)	2/C	Lon VI	Autograph = no. 3.
5. 'Figlio d'alte speranze', HWV113 (GB-Lbl R.M. 20.e.1, 52–7)				
52–7	Be)1×10/188.0+	I/H	Autograph	Double hyphen; handwriting like no. 1.
6.† 'Udite il mio consiglio', HWV172 (GB-Lbl R.M. 20.d.12, 1–6)				
1–6	B-)1×10/190.5+ (unique)	I/G	Autograph	Double hyphen; short notes; fo.6^v: handwriting different.
7. 'Caro autor', HWV182a (GB-Lbl R.M. 20.g.9, 21a–6)				
21a–6	B-)1×10/193.0 (unique)	I/D	Autograph	Double hyphen.
8.† 'Fra tante pene', HWV 116 (GB-Lbl R.M. 20.d.12, 17–19)				
17–19	Ba)1×10/177.5	I/H	Autograph	Fo.9: double hyphen; handwriting like no. 1.
9. 'Fra tante pene', HWV 116 (D-MÜs 1898, 57–8)				
57–8	Ba)1×10/177.5	I/B	Mü X^a	Autograph = no. 8.
10.† *Rodrigo*, HWV5 (GB-Lbl R.M. 20.c.5, 1–106)				
1–14	Bd)1×10/187.0 (1)	I/F	Autograph; fos. 43–4, 45–7: Angelini	Handwriting like no. 1.
49–52, 57–93, 102–6	Et)2×5/89.0	2/C		(fos. 15ff. composed autumn 1707)
15–48, 53–6, 94–101,	Eb)2×5/81.0+ (2)	2/C, 2/D		
11. Sonata a 5, HWV 288 (GB-Lbl R.M. 20.g.14, 11–20)				
11–12, 19–20	Bd)1×10/187.0 (1)	I/H		
13–18	1×10/187.0 (2) (unique)	I/F	Autograph	Handwriting like no. 1.

Folios	Rastra	Watermarks	Copyists	Remarks
12. 'Tacete ohimè', HWV 196 (GB-Cfm MU.MS. 253, pp. 25–32)				
pp. 25–32	Bb)1×10/184.0+	1/B	Autograph	'Händel'; double hyphen; handwriting like no. 1.
13‡. 'Torna il core al suo diletto', HWV 169 (D-MÜs 1898, 47–8)				
47–8	E–)2×5/84.0+ (unique)	2/D		
(14) [Il Delirio amoroso] = 'Da quel giorno fatale'				
14‡. 'Da quel giorno fatale', HWV 99 (D-MÜs 1905, 1–76)				
1–10	Dd)2×4/72.5–	2/C	Mü XIII[b] (Carl' Antonio Ferri?)	Copyist's bill: 12.2.07, for Pamphilj.
11–76	Dm)2×4/78.0+	2/D		
15†. 'Dixit Dominus', HWV 232 (GB-Lbl R.M. 20.f.1, 30–82)				
30–45	B–)1×10/188.5+ (unique)	1/E	Angelini, Ginelli, Mü II	Composed 4.4.07, double hyphen; handwriting like no. 1.
46–9, 58–61	B–)1×10/192.0+ (unique)	1/E, 1/H		
50–7, 62–5	Be)1×10/188.0+	1/E, 1/H		
66–9	Ek)2×5/83.0	2/A		
70–82	Ee)2×5/81.5+ (1)	2/D		
16. 'Occhi miei che faceste', HWV 146 (GB-Lbl R.M. 20.d.11, 20–3)				
20–3	Aa)1×8/168.0	5/A	Autograph	
17. 'Qual ti riveggio, oh Dio', HWV 150 (CH-Bfl, 1–16)				
1–16	Aa)1×8/168.0	5/B	Autograph	Double hyphen; handwriting like no. 16.
'Qual ti riveggio, oh Dio', HWV 150 (US-NYpm, 1–3)				
1–3	Aa)1×8/168.0	5/B	Autograph	
18. 'Venne voglia ad amore', HWV 176 (GB-Lbl R.M. 20.d.11, 32–4)				
32–4	Dq)2×4/80.05+	without WM (C)	Autograph	Fos. 33v–34: double hyphen; handwriting like no. 16.
19. 'Vedendo amor', HWV 175 (GB-Lbl R.M. 20.d.11, 35–9)				
35–9	Dq)2×4/80.05+	without WM (C)	Autograph	Double hyphen; handwriting like no. 16.
20. 'E partirai mia vita?', HWV 111a (GB-Lbl R.M. 20.d.11, 14a–19)				
14a–19	Dl)2×4/76.0+	without WM (A)	Autograph	
21. 'Dimmi, o mio cor', HWV 106 (GB-Lbl R.M. 20.d.11, 48–51)				
48–51	Dl)2×4/76.0+	without WM (A)	Autograph	Fo. 49: double hyphen; handwriting like no. 20.

Folios	Rastra	Watermarks	Copyists	Remarks
22. 'Spande ancor', HWV 165 (GB-Lbl R.M. 20.e.2, 48–55)				
48–55	D])2×4/76.0+	without WM (A)	Autograph	Handwriting like no. 20.
23.‡ 'Dalla guerra amorosa', HWV 102a (GB-Lbl R.M. 19.e.7, 95–8)				
95–8	D])2×4/76.0+	without WM (B)	Lon III	Space for ornate initial on 4 staves.
24.‡ 'Figli del mesto cor', HWV 112 (GB-Lbl R.M. 19.e.7, 99–101)				
99–101	D])2×4/76.0+	without WM (B)	Lon III	Space for ornate initial on 4 staves.
25. 'Nice, che fa? che pensa?', HWV 138 (GB-Lbl R.M. 20.d.11, 79–82)				
79–82	E])2×5/83.0+	without WM (A)	Lon III; with Handel's tempo mark.	
26. Sonatas HWV 358, 357, 405 (GB-Cfm MU. MS. 261, pp. 61–76)				
pp. 61–76	E])2×5/83.0+	without WM (B)	Autograph	Handwriting like no. 20.
27. 'Zeffiretto, arresta il volo', HWV 177 (GB-Lbl R.M. 20.d.11, 13–14)				
13–14	Ep)2×5/82.5 (3)	without WM (D)	Autograph	Fine quaver.
28. 'Allor ch'io dissi', HWV 80 (GB-Lbl R.M. 20.d.11, 58–60)				
58–60	Ep)2×5/82.5 (3)	without WM (D)	Autograph	Oval short head.
29.† 'Tu fedel, tu costante,' HWV 171 (GB-Lbl R.M. 20.e.2, 56–68a)				
56–7	Fa)3×3/49.5	2/C	Autograph	Fos. 58–61: double hyphen; handwriting like no. 16
58–61	B-J)1×10/189.5 (unique)	5/A		
62–8a	Eh)2×5/81.5+ (1c)	2/C		
30.‡ 'O lucenti', HWV 144 (GB-Lbl R.M. 19.e.7, 91–4)				
91–4	Ef)2×5/81.5+ (1b)	2/D	Angelini	Fo. 1: 'Sonata Avanti la Cantata [qualti riveggio *deleted*] A Crudel;' vertical notes, florid style.
31. 'Ah crudel', HWV 78 (D-MÜs 1897, 1–21)				
1–6	Ef)2×5/81.5+ (1b)		Autograph	Handwriting like no. 31.
7–21	Ed)2×5/81.5+ (1f)	2/D	Autograph	
32.† 'Nella stagion', HWV 137 (GB-Lbl R.M. 20.d.11, 5–8)				
5–8	Fa)3×3/49.5	2/C	Autograph	Partly double hyphen; with ornate initial 'A' in the blank space; handwriting like no. 31.
33.† 'Aure soavi e lieti', HWV 84 (GB-Lbl R.M. 20.d.11, 24–7)				
24–7	Ed)2×5/81.5+ (1f)	2/D	Autograph	

Folios	Rastra	Watermarks	Copyists	Remarks
34. 'Aure soavi e lieti', HWV 84 (GB-BENcoke MS 62)				
	E-)2×5/81.0 (1) (unique)	2/A, 2/B		Autograph = no. 33.
35.† 'Poichè giuraro amore', HWV 148 (GB-Lbl R.M. 20.d.11, 40–3)				
40–3	Fa)3×3/49.5	2/C		Handwriting like no. 31.
36.† 'Dietro l'orme fugaci', HWV 105 (GB-Lbl R.M. 20.e.2, 1–10)				
1–10	Ek)2×5/81.5+ (1)	2/D		
37.† 'Del bel idolo mio', HWV 104 (GB-Lbl R.M. 20.d.12, 40–2)				
40–2	Ej)2×5/82.5(2)	2/C		Partly double hyphen; handwriting like no. 31. Double hyphen; vertical notes.
38.† 'Arresta il passo', HWV 83 (GB-Lbl R.M. 20.e.3, 1–30, 65–71)				
1–2	Ha)2×4/74.1 + 1(Di + 1)	2/D	Autograph	Fos. 8, 13: double hyphen; vertical notes; handwriting like no. 37.ᶜ
3–30	Ek)2×5/83.0	2/D	Autograph	
65–71	Ej)2×5/82.5 (2)	2/D	Autograph	
39. 'Arresta il passo', HWV 83 (D-Mü̈s 1912, 1–162)				
1–4, 89–162	Dj)2×4/74.0+ (1)	2/D		For Pamphilj; Autograph = no. 38.
5–88	Dm)2×4/78.0+	2/D	Angelini, Ginelli, Mü II	
40.† 'Ninfe e pastori', HWV 139a (GB-Lbl R.M. 20.d.11, 9–12)				
9–12	Et)2×5/89.0	2/C	Autograph	Handwriting like no. 37.
41.† 'Stelle, perfide stelle', HWV 168 (GB-Lbl R.M. 20.d.11, 72–5)				
72–5	Et)2×5/89.0	2/D	Autograph	Handwriting like no. 37.
42.† 'Se per fatal destino', HWV 159 (GB-Lbl R.M. 20.d.12, 9–12)				
9–12	Ej)2×5/82.0+ (1)	2/D	Autograph	Handwriting like no. 37.
43. 'Nel dolce dell'oblio', HWV 134 (GB-Lbl R.M. 20.e.2, 26–9),				
26–9	Ej)2×5/82.0+ (1)	2/D	Autograph	Handwriting like no. 20.
44.† 'Un'alma innamorata', HWV 173 (GB-Lbl R.M. 20.e.2, 11–18)				
11–18	Fa)3×3/49.5	2/C	Autograph	Sometimes with tall crotchet.
45. 'Dixit Dominus', HWV 232 (D-Mü̈s 1924, 1–79)				
1–79	Ej)2×5/82.0+ (1)		Mü XII	Autograph = no. 15.

Folios	Rastra	Watermarks	Copyists	Remarks
46.‡ 'Donna che in ciel', HWV 233 (D-MÜs 1895, 1–80)				
1–4, 17–33, 36, 41–56	Di)2×4/74.0+ (1)	2C, 2D	Angelini, Ginelli, Mü II, Mü VI	First performance: 1.2.07.
5–13, 16, 21–32	Dm)2×4/78.0+			
34–5, 37–40	D-)2×4/72.0+ (unique)	2/C, 2/D		
57–60	Ei)2×5/82.0+ (1)	2/C		
61–80	E-)2×5/82.0+ (2) (unique)	2/C		
14–15	De)2×5/72.5 (1)	2/D		
47. 'Oh numi eterni', HWV 145 (GB-Lcm 685, 96–9)				
96–9	E-)2×5/82.5 (3) (unique)	2/C		
48.‡ 'Da sete ardente', HWV 100 (D-MÜs 1899, 25–7)				
25–7	Ee)2×5/81.5+ (1)	3/A?		
49.‡ 'Saeviat tellus', HWV 240 (GB-Lbl Eg. MS 2458, 2–39)				
2–5	Eu)2×5/89.5+	2/C	Mü IV	
6–39	Ee)2×5/81.5+ (1)	2/C, 2/D		
50.‡ 'Saeviat tellus', HWV 240 (US-NYpm MS Pl, 103–4)				
103	F-)3×3/?	?	Angelini, Ginelli, D. Castrucci	
104	H-)2×4/? + 1			
51‡. 'Sei pur bella', HWV 160a (GB-Lbl R.M. 19.e.7, 102–5)				
102–5	Eu)2×5/89.5+	2/C	Mü IV	
52.‡ 'Filli adorata', HWV 114 (GB-Lbl R.M. 20.d.11, 76–8a)				
76–8a	Eu)2×5/89.5+	2/D	Autograph	Tall crotchet.
53.‡ *Il trionfo*, HWV 46a (GB-Lbl R.M. 19.d.9, 1–138)				
1–10, 15–55, 58–62, 64–5, 67–97, 100–16, 125–38	Ef)2×5/81.5+ (1b)	2/C, 2/D	Ginelli, Angelini, Lon I, Lon II, Mü IV; Autograph: fos. 69–78	Fo. 1: 'Per la Madonna Ss.^{ma} del Carmine' by Mü II Autograph = no. 1.
11–14, 56–7, 63, 66, 98–9, 117–24	Eu)2×5/89.5+	2/C, 2/D		

Folios	Rastra	Watermarks	Copyists	Remarks
54. 'Alla caccia', HWV 79 (A-Wgm VI 66740 [A 186], 1–4)				
1–4	Ei)2×5/82.0+ (1)	2/D	Autograph	Sometimes with tall quaver. Composed 5.07.
'Alla caccia', HWV 79 (D-Bds, Mus.ms.autogr., Händel 3, 1–4)				
1	Ha)2×4/74.1 +1 (= Di + 1)	2/-	Autograph	
2–4	Ei)2×5/82.0+ (1)	2/C		
(55) [La Belezza Raveduta nel trionfo del Tempo e del Disinganno]				
55.‡ *Il trionfo*, HWV 46a, i (D-MÜs 1896, 1–186)				
1–4, 21–80, 85–118, 135–50, 167–86	Di)2×4/74.0+ (1)	2/D	Angelini, Ginelli, Mü IV	Copyist's bill: 14.5.07, for Pamphilj.
5–16, 81–4, 151–66	Db)2×4/71.0+	2/C, 2/D		
17–20	Dm)2×4/78.0+	2/D		
119–34	Ef)2×5/81.5+ (1b)	2/C		
Il trionfo, ii (D-MÜs 1914, 1–172)				
1–52, 73–108, 133–40, 145, 148, 153–72	Di)2×4/74.0+ (1)	2/D	Angelini, Ginelli, Mü IV	
109–32, 141–4, 146–7, 149–52	Db)2×4/71.0+	2/C		
53–72	Ef)2×5/81.5+ (1b)	2/C		
(56) [Il Delirio amoroso] = 'Da quel giorno fatale'				
56.‡ 'Da quel giorno fatale', HWV 99 (D-Hs, M A/198, 1–76)				
1–10	Dm)2×4/78.0+	2/D	Angelini	Copyist's bill: 14.5.07, for Pamphilj.
11–26, 31–4, 39–42, 75–6	Dd)2×4/72.5–	2/A, 2/B		
27–30, 35–8, 43–74	Di)2×4/74.0+ (1)	2/C, D		Copyist's bill: 16.5.07, Ruspoli Lib.
( ) [Una Cantata della caccia]				
(57) [Sei pur bella]				

Folios	Rastra	Watermarks	Copyists	Remarks
57.‡ 'Sei pur bella', HWV 160a (D-MÜs 1899, 123–30)				
123, 128–30	Dm)2×4/78.0+	2/D		Blank space for ornate initial.
124–7	Df)2×4/74.0+ (1)	2/C		
(58) [Se per fatal destino]				
58. 'Se per fatal destino', HWV 159 (D-MÜs 1899, 68–73)				
68, 71	Dh[a]) 2×4/73.5	2/C		Copyist's bill: 16.5.07, Ruspoli Lib.
69–70, 72–3	Dm)2×4/78.0+	2/D	Angelini	Autograph = no. 42; blank space for ornate initial.
(59) [Udite il mio consiglio]				
59. 'Udite il mio consiglio', HWV 172 (D-MÜs 1899, 74–82)				
74–8, 80–2	Dm)2×4/78.0+	2/D	Angelini, with Handel's corrections	Copyist's bill: 16.5.07, Ruspoli Lib.
79	Ed)2×5/81.5+ (1f)			Autograph = no. 6; blank space for ornate initial.
(60) [Aure soavi e lieti]				
60. 'Aure soavi', HWV 84 (D-MÜs 1898, 67–72)				
67, 72	Db)2×4/71.0+	2/C	Angelini, Mü II, Mü V	Copyist's bill: 16.5.07, Ruspoli Lib.
68–71	Di)2×4/74.0+ (1)	2/D		Autograph = no. 33; with ornate initial 'A' in the blank space.
(61) [Tù fedel]				
61. 'Tu fedel tu costante', HWV 171 (D-MÜs 1913, 1–38)				
1–4	Fa)3×3/49.5	2/C	Angelini, Ginelli	Copyist's bill: 16.5.07, Ruspoli Lib.
5–38	Di)2×4/74.0+ (1)	2/D		Autograph = no. 29.
(62) [Nella stagione]				
62. 'Nella stagion', HWV 137 (D-MÜs 1899, 91–8)				
91–8	Di)2×4/74.0+ (1)	2/D	Angelini	Copyist's bill: 16.5.07, Ruspoli Lib. Autograph = no. 32; blank space for ornate initial.
(63) [Poi che giuraro Amore]				Copyist's bill: 16.5.07, Ruspoli Lib.

Folios	Rastra	Watermarks	Copyists	Remarks
63. 'Poichè giuraro amore', HWV 148 (D-MÜs 1899, 83–90) 83, 86 84–5, 87–90	Dm)2x4/78.0+ Di)2x4/74.0+	2/D (1)	Angelini	Autograph = no. 35; blank space for ornate initial.
64. 'Ninfe e pastori', HWV 139a (D-MÜs 1898, 49–56) 49–56	Di)2x4/74.0+	(1)	D. Castrucci	Autograph = no. 40; with ornate initial 'N' in the blank space.
65. 'Oh numi eterni', HWV 145 (D-MÜs 1898, 5–16) 5–16	Di)2x4/74.0+	(1)		Autograph = no. 1; blank space for ornate initial.
66.† 'O qualis de coelo', HWV 239 (D-MÜs 1888, 1–8) 1–8	Eg)2x5/81.5+	(1a)	Mü V	For Pentecost service: 12.6.07; with tall quaver.
67. 'Salve Regina', HWV 241 (D-Bds, Mus.ms.autogr, Händel 2, 1–8) 1–8	Eg)2x5/81.5+	(1a)	Autograph	First performance: 19.6.07; handwriting like no. 66.
68.‡ 'Nisi Dominus', HWV 238 (GB-Lbm Eg. MS 2458, 80–99) 80–99	Ee)2x5/81.5+	(1) 2/-, 2/C	Autograph	Composed 13.7.07; for Colonna?
69.‡ 'Nisi Dominus', HWV 238 (US-NYpm MS 845)		2/C, 2/D	Ginelli, Mü II, Lon I, Lon II	
70. 'Ah che troppo ineguali', HWV 230 (GB-Lbl R.M. 20.e.3, 72–5) 72–5	Eg)2x5/81.5+	(1a)	Autograph	With tall crotchet and quaver.ᵉ
71.† 'Tra le fiamme', HWV 170 (GB-Lbl R.M. 20.d.13, 1–14a) 1–14a	Eg)2x5/81.5+	(1a)	Autograph	For Pamphilj.
72.† 'Clori, mia bella Clori', HWV 92 (GB-Lbl R.M. 20.e.2, 19–25a) 19–25a	Eg)2x5/81.5+	(1a)	Autograph	Handwriting like no. 70.
73.‡ 'O lucenti', HWV 144 (D-MÜs 1898, 107–10) 107–10	Eg)2x5/81.5+	(1a)	Mü II	Performed 26.6.07.
(74) [Una Cantata]				

Folios	Rastra	Watermarks	Copyists	Remarks
74.† 'Cor fedele', HWV 96 (GB-Lbl R.M. 20.e.3, 31–71a)				
31–8, 65–71a	Ej)2×5/82.5(2)	2/D	Autograph	Handwriting like no. 70.
39–57, 59–64	Eg)2×5/81.5+ (1a)	2/D		
[50		3/B]		
58	D–)2×4/70.0(unique)	2/C		
75.† 'Hendel, non può mia musa', HWV 117, (D-MÜs 1898, 1–4)				
1–4	Ej)2×5/81.5 (2)	2/D	Autograph	Tall crotchet and quaver; handwriting like no. 70. Copyist's bill: 30.6.07. Autograph = no. 44.
(76) [Un alma innamorata]				
76. 'Un'alma innamorata', HWV 173 (D-MÜs 1893, 1–12)				
1–12	Eg)2×5/81.5+ (1a)	2/D	Angelini	
(77 and 78) [Due Mottetti]				
77.‡ 'Coelestis dum spirat aura', HWV 231 (D-MÜs 1887, 1–18)				
1–2	Eg)2×5/81.5+ (1a)	2/D	Angelini	Copyist's bill: 30.6.07.
3–18	Db)2×4/71.0+	2/D		
78. 'O qualis de coelo sonus', HWV 239 (D-MÜs 1888, 1–18)				
1–18	Db)2×4/71.0+	2/D	Angelini	Autograph = no. 66.
( ) [Salve Regina]				
(79) [Una Cantata]'				
79. 'Tra le fiamme', HWV 170 (D-MÜs 1903, 1–58)				
1–28	Dk)2×4/74.0+ (3)	2/C, 2/D	Angelini	Autograph = no. 67. Performed before 6.7.07. For Pamphilj; Autograph = no. 71.
29–58	E–)2×5/81.5+ (1e) (unique)	2/C		
80.† 'Laudate pueri', HWV 237 (GB-Lbl R.M. 20.f.1, 1–29a)				
1–8, 10–13, 15–29a	Eg)2×5/81.5+ (1a)	2/D	Autograph	Composed 8.7.07; for Colonna; with tall crotchet and quaver. Autograph = no. 80; for Colonna.
9, 14	Fa)3×3/49.5	2/C		
81. 'Laudate pueri', HWV 237 (US-NYpm MS Pl, 105–22)				
105–22	F–)3×3/?	?	D. Castrucci, Mü II. Angelini, D. Castrucci, NY I	
	H–)2×4/? + 1 (upright size)	?		

Folios	Rastra	Watermarks	Copyists	Remarks
82.‡ 'Te decus virgineum', HWV 243 (US-NYpm MS Pl, 132–40) 132–40	F-)3×3/? H-)2×4/?+ 1 (upright size)	? ?	Angelini, Mü II	Performed 16.7.07; for Colonna; on the cover: 'Antifona Pma = Te decus virgineum = Per la Madonna del Carmine.'
83.‡ 'Haec est Regina Virginum', HWV 235 (US-NYpm MS Pl, 123–31) 123–31	F-)3×3/? H-)2×4/?+ 1 (upright size)	? ?	Angelini, Mü II	Performed: 16.7.07; for Colonna; in MS Pl, 131: 'Per la B.V. del Carmine' by Mü II; on the cover: 'Antifona Sda = Haec est Regina = Per la Madonna del Carmine'.
84.‡ 'No se emenderá jamás', HWV 140 (GB-Lbl R.M. 20.e.2, 69–74) 69–72 73–4	Eb)2×5/81.0+ (2) Da)2×4/70.0+	2/C 2/C	Autograph	Fat handwriting.
85.‡ 'Menzognere speranze', HWV 131 (GB-Lbl R.M. 20.d.11, 67–9a) 67–9a	Eb)2×5/81.0+ (2)	2/C	Autograph	Handwriting like no. 84.
86.‡ 'Sans y penser', HWV 155 (GB-Lbl R.M. 20.d.11, 61–6) 61–6	Da)2×4/70.0+	2/D	Autograph	Handwriting like no. 84.
(87) [Cantata dell'Arminda] = *Armida abbandonata* = 'Dietro l'orme fugaci', HWV 105 (D-MÜs 1894, 1–22) 1–16 17–22	Da)2×4/71.0+ Fa)3×3/49.5	2/C, 2/D	Angelini	Copyist's bill: 22.9.07. Autograph = no. 36.
(88) [Una Cantata francese] = 'Sans y penser', HWV 155 (D-MÜs 1898, 111–16) 111–16	Da)2×4/70.0+	2/C		Copyist's bill: 22.9.07. Autograph = no. 86.
(89) [Qual or l'egre pupille] 89.‡ 'Qualor l'egre pupille', HWV 152 (D-MÜs 1899, 99–106) 99–106	Da)2×4/70.0+	2/C	Angelini; text written by Handel	Copyist's bill: 22.9.07. Space for ornate initial on the 4 staves.

Folios	Rastra	Watermarks	Copyists	Remarks
(90) [Una Cantata Spagniola] = 'No se emenderá jamás'				
90. 'No se emenderá jamás', HWV 140 (D-MÜs 1899, 139–48)				
139–46	F-)3×3/52.0+ (unique)	2/D	Angelini; text written by Handel	Copyist's bill: 22.9.07. Autograph = no. 84.
147–8	F-)3×3/55.5– (unique)	2/C		
(91) [Sarei troppo felice]				
91.‡ 'Sarei troppo felice', HWV 157 (D-MÜs 1899, 56–67)				
56–67	Da)2×4/70.0+	2/C		Copyist's bill: 22.9.07. Space for ornate initial on the 4 staves.
(92) [Mensogniere speranze]				
92. 'Menzognere speranze', HWV 131 (D-MÜs 1899, 44–7)				
44–7	E-)2×5/85.0+ (unique)	2/C	Mü IV	Copyist's bill: 22.9.07. Autograph = no. 85; with ornate initial 'M' on the 4 staves.
(93) [Ne tuoi lumi]				
93.‡ 'Ne' tuoi lumi', HWV 133 (D-MÜs 1899, 1–16)				
1–16	Da)2×4/70.0+	2/C	Ginelli	Copyist's bill: 22.9.07. Space for ornate initial on the 4 staves.
(94) [Cantata a tre]				
94. 'Cor fedele', HWV 96, i (D-MÜs 1900 I, 1–166)				
1–166	Da)2×4/70.0+	2/C, 2/D	Mü IV	Copyist's bill: 14.10.07, Ruspoli Lib. Autograph = no. 74.
'Cor fedele', ii, (D-MÜs 1900 II, 1–166)				
1–145	Da)2×4/70.0+	2/C, 2/D	Angelini	
146–66	Dk)2×4/74.0+ (3)	2/C	Angelini, Ginelli, Mü II	
10. *Rodrigo*, HWV 5 (GB-Lbl R.M. 20.c.5, 1–106)				
[1–14]	Bd)1×10/187.0 (1)	1/F]		Autograph; fos. 43–4, 45–7: Angelini
49–52, 57–93, 102–6	Et)2×5/89.0	2/C		(Overture composed 1706–7; fos. 15ff. composed Rome; performed autumn 1707, in Florence; handwriting like no. 105. Copyist's bill: 26.2.08.
15–48, 53–6, 94–101,	Eb)2×5/81.0+ (2)	2/C, 2/D		
(95 or 96) [Una Cantata consiste in 2. fogli]				

Folios	Rastra	Watermarks	Copyists	Remarks
95. 'Del bel idolo mio', HWV 104 (D-MÜs 1899, 36–43) 36–43	Dk)2×4/74.0+ (3)	2/C, 2/D		Autograph = no. 37; blank space for ornate initial.
96. 'Sarai contenta un dì', HWV 156 (D-MÜs 1899, 131–8) 131–8	Dk)2×4/74.0+ (3)	2/C		Autograph = no. 2.
97.‡ 'Lungi da me', HWV 125a (D-MÜs 1910, 193–204) 193–204	Dk)2×4/74.0+ (3)	2/C, 2/D	Angelini	
98.† 'Lungi dal mio bel nume', HWV 127a (GB-Lbl Add. MS 30310, 2–7) 2–7	Ea)2×5/81.0+ (1)	2/C	Angelini	Blank space for ornate initial.
99.† 'Manca pur quanto sai', HWV 129 (GB-Lbl R.M. 20.d.11, 52–5) 52–5	Ea)2×5/81.0+ (1) Without WM (C)		Angelini	Composed 3.3.08; Handwriting like no. 98.[g]
100. 'Care selve', HWV 88 (GB-Lbl R.M. 20.d.11, 70–1) 70–1	Ea)2×5/81.0+ (1)	2/C	Angelini, Mü IV	Short fat quaver; separate notes vertical.
101. 'Lungi, lungi n'andò Fileno', HWV 128 (GB-Lbl R.M. 20.d.11, 44–7) 44–7	Ea)2×5/81.0+	2/C	Autograph	Handwriting like no. 98.
102. 'Lungi dal mio bel nume', HWV 127a (D-MÜs 1910, 141–52) 141–52	Dc)2×4/71.5	2/D	Autograph	Autograph = no. 98.
103.‡ 'Fra pensieri', HWV 115 (D-MÜs 1910, 177–82) 177–82	Dc)2×4/71.5	2/C	Mü II	
104.† La Resurrezione, HWV 47 (GB-Cfm MU. MS. 251, pp. 1–8) pp. 1–8	Eh)2×5/81.5+ (1c)	2/C	Autograph	Composed 3.4.08; separate notes are vertical; short notes.
La Resurrezione, (GB-Lbl R.M. 20.f.5, 1–79) 1–79	Eh)2×5/81.5+ (1c)	2/C, 2/D	Autograph	
105. La Resurrezione, HWV 47, i (D-MÜs 1873, 1–156) 1–56, 85–156	E-)2×5/81.0(2) (unique)	2/C, 2/D	Angelini, T. Lanciani, Mü Va	
La Resurrezione, (D-MÜs 1873a, 1–105) 57–84	Dj)2×4/74.0+ (2)	2/C	D. Castrucci, Mü Va	Copyist's bill: 9.4.08. Autograph = no. 104. Performed 14.4.08.
La Resurrezione, ii (D-MÜs 1873a, 1–105) 1–105	E-)2×5/81.0 (2) (unique)	2/C, 2/D	Fr. Lanciani	

Folios	Rastra	Watermarks	Copyists	Remarks
106. *Aci, Galatea e Polifemo*, HWV 72 (GB-Lbl R.M. 20.a.1, 1–58)				Composed 16.6.08 in Naples; short quaver, tall crotchet, fat oval head.
1–25	Er)2×5/88.5(1)	3/A, 4/A	Autograph	
26–58	Em)2×5/86.0		Autograph	
107. *Aci, Galatea e Polifemo*, HWV 72 (GB-Lbl Eg. MS 2953, 98–101)				
98–101	Em)2×5/86.0	4/A	Autograph	
108.‡ 'A voi torno, o selve care', HWV 161b (GB-Lbl R.M. 20.d.11, 1–4)				Handwriting like no. 106.
1–4	E-)2×5/89.0+ (unique)	3/C	Autograph	
108.‡ 'Sento là che ristretto', HWV deest (GB-Lbl Add. MS 14215, 116–19)				
116–19	Em)2×5/86.0	3/D	Lon XVII	
109.† 'Quando sperasti o core', HWV 153 (GB-Lbl R.M. 20.d.11, 28–31a)				Handwriting like no. 106.
28–31a	Er)2×5/88.5 (1)	4/B	Autograph	
110. 'Nell'africane selve', HWV 136a (GB-Lbl R.M. 20.d.11, 83–6)				Handwriting like no. 106.
83–6	Er)2×5/88.5(1)	4/B	Autograph	
111. 'Cuopre tal volta', HWV 98 (GB-Lbl R.M. 20.e.5, 4–7)				
4–7	G-)4×4/46.5 (unique)	4/B	Autograph	
112. 'Lungi dal mio bel nume', HWV 127a (GB-Lcm 685, 104–11)				Autograph = no. 98.
104–11	D-)2×4/77.0 (unique)	4/B	Lon XV	
113.‡ Suite g minor, HWV 451, 521, 537a, 540a (A-Wm MS XIV 743, 34–7)				
34–7	Dp)2×4/79.5 (3)	4/A	Angelini	
114. *Rodrigo*, HWV 5: Arias nos. 36b and 31 (A-Wm MS XIV 743, 38–9)				Autograph = no. 10.
38–9	Dp)2×4/79.5 (3)	4/A	Angelini	
115.‡ 'Se pari è la tua fè', HWV 158b (GB-Lbl Add. MS 14212, 2–8a)				
2–8a	Do)2×4/79.5 (2)	6/-	Lon VII	
116.‡ 'Sarei troppo felice', HWV 157 (GB-Lbl Add. MS 14212, 27–34)				
27–34	Do)2×4/79.5 (2)	6/-	Lon VII	
117.‡ 'Nel dolce tempo', HWV 135b (GB-Lbl Add. MS 14212, 35–42)				
35–42	Do)2×4/79.5(2)	6/-	Lon VII	
118.‡ 'Usignuol che tra le frondi', HWV deest (GB-Lbl Add. MS 14207, 180–5)				
180–5	D-)2x4/85.0 (unique)	6/-	Lon XI	
119.‡ 'Da sete ardente afflitto', HWV 100 (GB-Lbl Add. MS 14215, 108–11)				
108–11	En)2×5/87.0	6/-	Lon IX	

Folios	Rastra	Watermarks	Copyists	Remarks
120.‡ 'Sento là che ristretto', HWV 161a (GB-Lbl Add. MS 14215, 112–15) 112–15	En)2×5/87.0	6/-	Lon IX	
121. 'Lungi dal mio bel nume', HWV 127a (GB-Lbl Add. MS 14212, 9–14) 9–14	Eq)2×5/87.5+	4/-	Lon VIII	Autograph = no. 98.
122. 'Oh numi eterni', HWV 145 (GB-Lbl Add. MS 14212, 15–22) 15–22	Eq)2×5/87.5+	4/-	Lon VIII	Autograph = no. 1.
123.‡ 'Da sete ardente afflitto', HWV 100 (GB-Lbl Add. MS 14212, 23–6) 23–6	Eq)2×5/87.5+	4/-	Lon VIII	
124.‡ 'Se pari è la tua fè', HWV 158b (GB-Lcm 685, 92–5) 92–5	E-)2×5/88.0+ (unique)	6/-	Lon VII	
125.‡ 'Sarei troppo felice', HWV 157 (GB-Lcm 685, 112–15) 112–15	Es)2×5/88.5 (2)	6?/-	Lon XVI	
126.‡ 'Lungi da voi che siete', HWV 126c (GB-Lcm 685, 116–19) 116–19	Es)2×5/88.5 (2)	6?/-	Lon XVI	
127. 'Se tu non lasci amore', HWV 201a (CH-Bfl, 1–16) 1–16	D-)2×4/?	2/C, 2/D	Autograph	Composed 12.7.08.
(128) [Tù fedel]				Copyist's bill: 9.8.08, Ruspoli Lib.
128. 'Tu fedel, tu costante', HWV 171 (D-MÜs 1910, 7–50) 7–50	Dk)2×4/74.0+ (3)	2/C, 2/D	Angelini	Autograph = no. 29.
( ) [Aure soavi e lieti]				Copyist's bill: 9.8.08, Ruspoli Lib.
(129) [Hendel]				Copyist's bill: 9.8.08, Ruspoli Lib.
129. 'Hendel, non può mia musa, HWV 117 (D-MÜs 1910, 189–92) 189–92	Dh[b)]2×4/73.5	2/D	Mü XI	Autograph = no. 75.
( ) [Sarei troppo felice]				Copyist's bill: 9.8.08, Ruspoli Lib.
(130) [Manca pur quanto sai]				Copyist's bill: 9.8.08, Ruspoli Lib.

Folios	Rastra	Watermarks	Copyists	Remarks
130. 'Manca pur quanto saì', HWV 129 (D-MÜs 1898, 89–96)				Autograph = no. 99; space for ornate initial on the 4 staves. Copyist's bill: 9.8.08, or 28.8.08, Ruspoli Lib.
89–92	Dg)2×4/73.0	2/D		
93–6	Dj)2×4/74.0+ (2)	2/C		
(131a) [Ditemi ò piante ò fiori]				
131.‡ 'Ditemi o piante', HWV 107 (D-MÜs 1899, 17–24)				Space for ornate initial on the 2 staves. Copyist's bill: 9.8.08, Ruspoli Lib.
17–24	Df)2×4/72.5 (2)	2/D		
(132) [Lungi da voi che]				
132.‡ 'Lungi da voi che siete', HWV 126a (D-MÜs 1898, 81–8)			Angelini, Ginelli	With ornate initial 'L' on the 2 staves.
81–4	Dg)2×4/73.0	2/C		
85–8	Dj)2×4/74.0+ (2)	2/C		
( ) [Lamarciata]				
(133) [Clori vezzosa Clori]				
133.‡ 'Clori vezzosa', HWV 95 (D-MÜs 1898, 97–100)			Ginelli	Copyist's bill: 9.8.08, Ruspoli Lib.
97–100	Df)2×4/72.5 (2)	2/D		
(134) [Quando sperasti ò core]				
134. 'Quando sperasti o core', HWV 153 (D-MÜs 1898, 101–6)			Ginelli	Copyist's bill: 9.8.08, Ruspoli Lib.
101–6	Df)2×4/72.5 (2)	2/D		
(135) [Stanco di più sospire]				
135.‡ 'Stanco di più soffrire', HWV 167b (D-MÜs 1898, 73–80)			Angelini, Ginelli	Autograph = no. 109; with ornate initial 'Q' on the 2 staves. Copyist's bill: 9.8.08, Ruspoli Lib.
73–80	Dn)2×4/79.5 (1)	3/A		
136.‡ 'Ditemi o piante', HWV 107 (D-MÜs 1910, 159–68)			D. Castrucci	
159–68	Dg)2×4/73.0	2/C, 2/D		

Folios	Rastra	Watermarks	Copyists	Remarks
137. 'Clori, mia bella Clori', HWV 92 (D-MÜs 1902, 1–28) 1–28	Dg)2×4/73.0	2/C	Angelini, Ginelli	Autograph = no. 72.
138. 'Un'alma innamorata', HWV 173 (D-MÜs 1910, 51–84) 51–84	Dj)2×74.0+ (2)	2/C	Angelini, Ginelli, Mü II	Autograph = no. 44.
139.‡ 'Irene idolo mio', HWV 120a (D-MÜs 1899, 48–55) 48–55	Dj)2×4/74.0+ (2)	2/C	Ginelli	With ornate initial 'I' on the 2 staves.
140. 'Filli adorata e cara', HWV 114 (D-MÜs 1899, 115–22) 115–22	Dj)2×4/74.0+ (2)	2/C	Angelini, Ginelli	Autograph = no. 52.
141. 'Chi rapi la pace', HWV 90 (D-MÜs 1910, 125–32) 125–32	Dj)2×4/74.0+ (2)	2/D	Angelini, Mü IV	Autograph = no. 3.
142.‡ 'Notte placida e cheta', HWV 142 (D-MÜs 1910, 85–118) 85–104	De)2×4/72.5 (1)	2/C	Angelini	Autograph = no. 3.
105–18	Dj)2×4/74.0+ (2)	2/C, 2/D	Angelini, Mü II	
143. 'Chi rapi la pace', HWV 90 (D-MÜs 1898, 17–22) 17–22	Df)2×4/72.5 (2)	2/C	Angelini	Autograph = no. 3.
144. 'Lungi dal mio bel nume', HWV 127a (D-MÜs 1898, 23–34) 23–34	Df)2×4/72.5 (2)	2/C	Angelini	Autograph = no. 98.
145.‡ 'Sento là che ristretto', HWV 161a (D-MÜs 1898, 35–46) 35–46	Df)2×4/72.5 (2)	2/C	Angelini	
146. 'Quando sperasti o core', HWV 153 (D-MÜs 1910, 1–6) 1–6	Df)2×4/72.5 (2)	2/C	Angelini	Autograph = no. 109.
(147) [Due copie della Cantata Se pari è la tua fe]				Copyist's bill: 28.8.08, Ruspoli Lib.
147.‡ 'Se pari è la tua fè', HWV 158a (D-MÜs 1898, 59–66) 59–66	Df)2×4/72.5 (2)	2/C	Angelini, Ginelli	Copyist's bill: 28.8.08, or 9.8.08, Ruspoli Lib.
(131b) [Dite ò Piante ò fiori]				
131.‡ 'Ditemi o piante', HWV 107 (D-MÜs 1899, 17–24) 17–24	Df)2×4/72.5 (2)	2/D	Angelini, Ginelli	

Folios	Rastra	Watermarks	Copyists	Remarks
( ) [Clori vezzosa Clori]				Copyist's bill: 28.8.08, Ruspoli Lib.
( ) [Lungi n'andò Fileno]				Copyist's bill: 28.8.08, Ruspoli Lib.
(148 or 149) [Mentre tutto in furore]				Copyist's bill: 28.8.08, Ruspoli Lib.
148.‡ 'Mentre il tutto', HWV 130 (D-MÜs 1899, 28–35)				Copyist's bill: 28.8.08, Ruspoli Lib.
28–31	Df)2×4/72.5 (2)	2/C		
32–5	Dn)2×4/79.5 (1)	3/A		Ornate initial 'M' on the 2 staves.
149.‡ 'Mentre il tutto', HWV 130 (D-MÜs 1910, 169–76)				
169–76	Df)2×4/72.5 (2)	2/C	Angelini	
(150) [Una Cantata à voce sola con VV]				Copyist's bill: 28.8.08, Ruspoli Lib.
( ) [Il Duello amoroso Cantata a 2 Con VV] = 'Amarilli vezzosa'.				Copyist's bill: 28.8.08, Ruspoli Lib.
150.‡ 'Amarilli vezzosa', HWV 82 (D-MÜs 1906, 1–44)				
1–8	Dj)2×4/74.0+ (2)	2/C	Angelini, Ginelli	
9–44	Dg)2×4/73.0			
151. 'Stelle, perfide stelle', HWV 168 (D-MÜs 1910, 119–24)				
119–24	Df)2×4/72.5 (2)	2/C	Mü VI	Autograph = no. 41; with ornate initial 'S' on the 2 staves.
152.‡ 'Sento là che ristretto', HWV 161a (D-MÜs 1910, 133–40)				
133–40	Df)2×4/72.5 (2)	2/C	Angelini	With ornate initial 'O' on the 2 staves.
153. 'O lucenti', HWV 144 (D-MÜs 1910, 153–8)				
153–8	Df)2×4/72.5 (2)	2/C	Mü VI	With ornate initial 'Q' on the 2 staves.
154.‡ 'Qualor l'egre pupille', HWV 152 (D-MÜs 1910, 183–8)				
183–8	Df)2×4/72.5 (2)	2/D	Mü VI	
155.† 'Oh come chiare e belle', HWV 143 (GB-Lbl R.M. 20.e.2, 30–47)				
30–47	E-)2×5/81.0+ (3)	2/C	Autograph	Performed 9.9.08; minute fine calligraphy.

Folios	Rastra	Watermarks	Copyists	Remarks
156. 'Oh come chiare e belle', HWV 143 (D-MÜs 1914, 1–56)				
1–42	Df) 2×4/72.5 (2)	2/C	Angelini,	Copyist's bill: 10.9.08, Ruspoli Lib; Autograph = no. 155.
43–56	D–) 2×4/74.0+ (4) (unique)		Ginelli, Mü II	
( ) [Da sete ardente]				Copyist's bill: 31.8.09, Ruspoli Lib.
( ) [Se pari è la tua fe]				Copyist's bill: 31.8.09, Ruspoli Lib.
( ) [Chi rapì la pace]				Copyist's bill: 31.8.09, Ruspoli Lib.
( ) [Ninfe e pastori]				Copyist's bill: 31.8.09, Ruspoli Lib.
( ) [Aure soavi e liete]				Copyist's bill: 31.8.09, Ruspoli Lib.
( ) [Nella stagione]				Copyist's bill: 31.8.09, Ruspoli Lib.
( ) [Del bell'idolo mio]				Copyist's bill: 31.8.09, Ruspoli Lib.
( ) [Ne' tuoi lumi, ò bella]				Copyist's bill: 31.8.09, Ruspoli Lib.
( ) [Se per fatal destino]				Copyist's bill: 31.8.09, Ruspoli Lib.
( ) [Hendel non può]				Copyist's bill: 31.8.09, Ruspoli Lib.
( ) [Sei pur bella pur vezzosa]				Copyist's bill: 31.8.09, Ruspoli Lib.
( ) [Fra tante pene e tante]				Copyist's bill: 31.8.09, Ruspoli Lib.
( ) [Poiche giuraro amore]				Copyist's bill: 31.8.09, Ruspoli Lib.

Folios	Rastra	Watermarks	Copyists	Remarks
( ) [Filli Dorata e Cara]				Copyist's bill: 31.8.09, Ruspoli Lib.
(157) [Dalla guerra amorosa]				Copyist's bill: 31.8.09, Ruspoli Lib.
157.‡ 'Dalla guerra amorosa', HWV 102b (D-Müs 1899, 107–14) 107–14	Df)2×4/72.5 (2)	2/C	Fr. Lanciani	Copyist's bill: 31.8.09, Ruspoli Lib. With ornate initial 'D' on the 4 staves
( ) [Sento la che ristretto]				Copyist's bill: 31.8.09, Ruspoli Lib.
( ) [Lungi da te mio Nume]				Copyist's bill: 31.8.09, Ruspoli Lib.
( ) [Oh Numi eterni]				Copyist's bill: 31.8.09, Ruspoli Lib.
( ) [Lungi da me pensier tiranno]				Copyist's bill: 31.8.09, Ruspoli Lib.
( ) [Aurette vezzose] (HWV 177, no. 2)				Copyist's bill: 31.8.09, Ruspoli Lib.
( ) [Sans penser francese]				Copyist's bill: 31.8.09, Ruspoli Lib.
158.† *Agrippina*, HWV 6 (GB-Lbl R.M. 20.a.3, 1–121) 1–87, 102–21 88–101	Ca)1×12/188.5+ B-)1×12/194.0+	1/N		Double hyphen on fos. 24, 37ᵛ, 76; performed 1709–10; oval head, short quaver.
159. 'Un sospir a chi si muore', HWV 174 (GB-Lbl R.M. 20.d.12, 43–5) 43–5	Ca)1×12/188.5+	1/J	Autograph	Oval head; with thin ink; handwriting like no. 158.
160. 'Non sospirar, non piangere', HWV 141 (GB-Lbl R.M. 20.d.12, 45–6) 45–6	Ca)1×12/188.5+	1/J	Autograph	Handwriting like no. 158.
161. 'Clori degl'occhi miei', HWV 91a (GB-Lbl R.M. 20.d.12, 47–50) 47–50	Ca) 1×12/188.5+	1/L	Autograph	Handwriting like no. 158.
162. 'Ah! che pur troppo è vero', HWV 77 (GB-Lbl R.M. 20.d.12, 13–16) 13–16	Ca)1×12/188.5+	1/K	Autograph	Handwriting like no. 158.

Folios	Rastra	Watermarks	Copyists	Remarks
163. 'Alpestre monte', HWV 81 (GB-Lbl R.M. 20.e.1, 38–9)				
38–9	Ca)1×12/188.5+	1/J		Handwriting like no. 158.
164. 'Dunque sarà pur vero', HWV 110 (GB-Lbl R.M. 20.e.1, 40–51)				
40–3	Cb)1×12/194.0+	1/N	Autograph	Handwriting like no. 158.
44–51	C–)1×10/182.5 (unique)	1/M	Autograph	
165. 'La terra è liberata', HWV 122 (GB-Lbl R.M. 20.e.1, 1–37)				
1–6, 13–16, 21–4,	Bc)1×10/184.5+	1/N	Autograph	Completed 1710 in Hanover; handwriting like no. 158.
11, 17–19	E–)2×5/82.5 (1) (unique)		Autograph	
7–10, 12, 20, 25–37		Hanover paper without WM (F)	Autograph	
166. 'Giù nei tartarei regni', HWV 187 (GB-Lbl R.M. 20.g.9, 27–30)				
27–30	Ca)1×12/188.5+	1/L	Autograph	Handwriting like no. 158; oval head; fo. 1: double hyphen.
167. 'Che vai pensando', HWV 184 (GB-Cfm MU. MS. 253, pp. 9–16)				
pp. 9–16	Ca)1×12/188.5+	1/J	Autograph	Handwriting like no. 166.
168. 'Amor gioje mi porge', HWV 180 (GB-Cfm MU. MS. 253, pp. 17–24)				
pp. 17–24	Ca)1×12/188.5+	1/L	Autograph	Handwriting like no. 166.
169. 'Quando in calma ride amor', HWV 191 (GB-Cfm MU. MS. 253, pp. 1–8)				
pp. 1–8	Bc)1×10/184.5+	1/N	Autograph	pp. 6, 7: double hyphen; handwriting like no. 166. Autograph = no. 158; dated 1710.
170. *Agrippina*, HWV 6 (GB-Lbl Add. MS 16023, i, 1–161)				
i, 1–88, 93–161	Bf)1×10/189.0+	1/O	Lon V	1710
89–92	B–)1×10/186.5+ (unique)			
171.‡ 'Sento là che ristretto', HWV 161a (GB-Lam 93, 31–4)				
31–4	Bf)1×10/189.0+	1/O	Lon IV	Copyist's bill: 15.5.11, Ruspoli Lib.
( ) [Hendel non puo mia musa]				Copyist's bill: 22.5.11, Ruspoli Lib.
( ) [Ho un non so che nel cor] (HWV 47, no. 14)				Copyist's bill: 10.10.11, Ruspoli Lib.
( ) [Ah crudel]				

Folios	Rastra	Watermarks	Copyists	Remarks
172. 'Cor fedele', HWV 96, no. 5 (GB-Och MS 96, pp. 1–5)	?	?	Lon V	Autograph = no. 74.
173. *Rodrigo*, HWV 5: Aria no. 14 (GB-Och MS 96) pp. 1–5	?	?	Lon V	Autograph = no. 10.
174.‡ Suites for Harpsichord, HWV 430, 433, 428 (D-MÜs 1911, 1–16)	?	?	Mü XIV	After 1720.
1–4	B-)1×10/181.0+	(unique)		
5–8	B-)1×10/185.0+	(unique)		
9–16	B-)1×10/191.0+	(unique)		
175. 'Oh numi eterni', HWV 145 (GB-Cfm MU. MS. 56, 1–8)				
1–8	E-)2×5/82.0 (2) (unique)	1/Q 2/E	Cam I	Autograph = no. 1; dated 1710.
176.‡ 'Lungi da voi, che siete poli', HWV 126b (GB-BENcoke MS. 110, 23–33)				MS dated 1711.
23–33	Eo)2×5/87.0–87.5	without WM	Lon XII	
177. 'Lungi dal mio bel nume', HWV 127b (GB-BENcoke MS 110, 76–85)				
76–85	Eo)2×5/87.0–87.5	without WM	Lon XII	
178. 'Nel dolce tempo', HWV 135b (GB-BENcoke MS 110, 33–44)				
33–44	Eo)2×5/87.0–87.5	without WM	Lon XII	
179.‡ Sarei troppo felice', HWV 157 (GB-BENcoke MS 110, 44–53)				
44–53	Eo)2×5/87.0–87.5	without WM	Lon XII	

a Mü X, the anonymous copyist of 'Fra tante pene', no. 9, is Handel's first Italian copyist; he was perhaps Venetian.
b Mü XIII, the anonymous copyist of 'Torna il core', no. 13, was one of Handel's earliest Roman copyists; he was an important scribe of Alessandro Scarlatti's works.
c This cantata was composed in 1707, not in 1708, perhaps at a time not far removed from 'Dietro l'orme fugaci', no. 36.
d This was first performed on the 'Anniversario della liberazione di Roma dal terremoto'. Cf. R. Ewerhart, 'Die Händel-Handschriften der Santini-Bibliotek in Münster', *HJB* ii (1960), 120–2.
e 'Ah che troppo ineguali', no. 70, and 'Clori, mia bella Clori', no. 72, were composed at about the same time as 'Tra le fiamme', no. 71. 'Hendel, non può mia musa', no. 75, belongs to the same period, because of similarities in the handwriting to 'Tra le fiamme'.
f This cantata was 'Tra le fiamme', as Hans Joachim Marx suggests in the Critical Report of his edition of the *Cantate con Stromenti*, HHA V 3 and 4.
g 'Manca pur quanto sai', no. 99; 'Care selve', no. 100; and 'Lungi, lungi n'andò Fileno', no. 101, were composed at about the same time as 'Lungi dal mio bel nume', no. 98, which was written on 3 March 1708.
h Nos. 136 to 146 were copied around August 1708.
i Nos. 151 to 154 were copied summer to autumn 1708.

Table 2. *Music-papers of other composers common with those of Handel, 1706–1710*

Rastra Type	Span	Composer	Title	Date	Shelf-mark	Copyist	Watermark
Dd	2×4/72.5	A. Scarlatti	'Al pensiero miei sguardi'	July 1706, (in Casa Colonna)	D-MÜs Hs.3904, Mü II		2/C, 2/D
Ek	2×5/83.0	A. Scarlatti	*Le muse Urania e Clio*	1706	D-MÜs Hs.3925	D. Castrucci	2/-
Dh [a or b]	2×4/73.5	Barone di Astorga	'Presso i momenti eterni'	Jan. 1708	D-MÜs Hs.207	Fr. Lanciani	2/-
De	2×4/72.5[1]	A. Scarlatti	'Lunga stagion dolente'	1 June 1706	GB-Lbm Add. MS 29249, fos. 133–40	anon.	2/-
Dg	2×4/73.0	A. Scarlatti	'Per te Florinda bella'	July 1708	GB-Lbm Add. MS 31511, fos. 26–33	D. Castrucci	2/-

12

Italian Source-Studies and Handel

PAUL EVERETT

THE extent to which the appraisal of Handel manuscripts has aspects in common with the present writer's field—the investigation of Italian manuscript repertories, particularly those of Vivaldi's music—has not yet been determined. In principle, at least, studies in these two areas are similar and should therefore prove to be complementary and of assistance to each other, especially since Handel was intensely active in Italy for a short period. Some mutually useful evidence may emerge; certain Vivaldi and Handel documents might employ, for instance, the same Venetian paper-types, characterized by the generic watermark of three crescents (*tre mezze lune*), of the kind Dr Watanabe discusses elsewhere in this volume,[1] or similarly exhibit the handwriting of a particular Roman copyist. The existence of any connections of this kind which indicate the contemporaneity of particular Handel and Vivaldi sources seems doubtful, however, simply because the time when most Italian Handel manuscripts are likely to have been created is distinctly earlier than the period from around 1713 to which virtually all Vivaldi manuscripts belong.[2]

If, as this writer suspects, the concurrences of precise data gleaned from Handelian and Italian sources will prove to be few, it is more profitable at this stage for us to consider the real relationship between Handel source-studies and the investigation of contemporary Italian manuscript repertories. This is a relationship between our respective scholarly approaches, our comparable but significantly different

---

[1] See Ch. 11, above.

[2] There is, in any case, a dearth of autographs from the early phase of Vivaldi's career (before the late 1710s), in contrast to the many later sources which survive in the Foà and Giordano collections in I-Tn. It seems that the composer was slow to acquire the habit of preserving his works for future reference. A definitive list showing precisely which MSS are early ones is not yet available.

expectations of evidence which is available to be discovered, our methodology, and our interpretation and presentation of results. There is much that Vivaldi scholarship can learn from a field such as Handel studies, and *vice versa*, but our sense of scholarly separateness needs first to be minimized in anticipation of a time when the exchange of data to our mutual benefit is easier than it appears to be now.

The factor which most obviously unites our efforts is the need to evaluate whole manuscript collections as comprehensively as possible. The principles remain the same, whether a collection contains Handel's music or Vivaldi's, and, indeed, whether the documents are of Italian, English, or any other provenance. In examining these principles, some of the similarities and distinctions between our respective research objectives and findings will become apparent. The investigative methodology to which this discussion will refer requires little explanation, for today its universal application is generally understood. Most readers will be familiar with the reasons why the analysis of a collection's original materials and other non-textual characteristics (the collation of leaves, the handwritings of scribes, and the bindings of volumes) is an essential part of our research. In short, it is axiomatic that all non-textual features are manifestations, in one form or another, of the manuscripts' compilation and use. When carefully and comprehensively recorded, they regularly reveal or suggest relationships between sources that would never come to light solely through the examination of the documents' musical texts.

We would all acknowledge that the obvious and primary reason for studying any collection is to make use of the music it contains for all the various purposes of performance and scholarship. But in doing this one is normally dealing with each source in isolation and examining the features which make it unique: its variants, revisions, and any further textual factors which distinguish it from concordances and all other sources. To achieve the remaining principal objectives in studying a collection, as suggested in the list below, an opposite approach is taken: one habitually looks for features common to two or more textually discrete sources as evidence of their relationship, and it is in this capacity that the use of non-textual data comes into its own. In the absence of external evidence in the form of correspondence or contemporary catalogues which might account for the nature and history of a collection, non-textual data remain the only kind of information capable of indicating the circumstances in which a collection became assembled, and herein lies their great value.

Principal objectives in the study of a collection of manuscripts other than the use of the music are:

1. To discover relationships of provenance and apparent contemporaneity between sources, and to group the documents accordingly;
2. To discern, as far as possible, the chronological order of origin of the manuscripts (whether grouped or not), ideally with some precise dates;
3. To learn the circumstances of the collection's assembly, including the contributions of scribes and the process by which 'composite sources' came into being;
4. To understand all subsequent states in which the collection has existed, including the present one;
5. To investigate relationships between the collection under review and collections and isolated manuscripts preserved elsewhere.

Because handwritings and matters of presentation and calligraphy are directly associated with the notation of the music itself, scribal hands and their incidence within a collection may be said to be the non-textual characteristics of greatest importance, especially if the hand of the composer is exhibited. The soundness of the notion is unquestionable; but an assessment of handwritings gives only some glimpses—albeit highly significant ones—of the circumstances in which a collection came into existence. Most seriously, the evidence of handwritings alone fails to provide an adequate impression of the contemporaneity or distinct dating of the documents.[3] It may also be observed that handwritings, while being indisputable evidence of the involvement of particular persons, often fail to give any clue to relationships between one scribe and another and between certain scribes and the composer.

These stumbling-blocks can be overcome to some extent when the use of music-paper is taken into account. Indeed, it may be argued that a full and painstaking analysis of the use of music-paper is the key to some success in all of the objectives listed above except, perhaps, the fourth. It creates a context with chronological implications, based on the musicians' use of their materials, within which all other matters—the incidence of hands, for instance, or the possibility that certain manuscripts are closely related companions—may properly be judged.

The term 'music-paper' is used here to denote the kind of materials musicians of the time normally acquired from stationers or music-shops: quires of paper which were already ruled with staves. By classifying both the paper-type according to its watermarks and

---

[3] Unless, of course, actual dates were noted at the time of copying, and in this respect Handel scholarship is blessed by the existence of the composer's own dates in many manuscripts. Vivaldi was less considerate; out of the hundreds of autographs which survive, only one carries his date. See P. Everett, 'Towards a Vivaldi Chronology', in *Nuovi studi vivaldiani: edizione e cronologia critica delle opere*, A. Fanna and G. Morelli (eds.), 2 vols. (Florence, 1988) 729–57; 731–2.

other features and the pattern of rastrum-ruled staves or rastrography by the analytical technique usually known as rastrology, each variety of music-paper may be recorded.[4] Methods of stave-ruling varied considerably, even within one region, and one has to be certain about these technical matters and their implications before citing rastrographical data as evidence of anything. It seems, for instance, that the circumstances in which music-paper was prepared in England are significantly different from those which prevailed in Italian centres, and we must adapt our use of data accordingly. Some rastrographies, such as those exhibited by Roman manuscripts of the early eighteenth century, are regularly found on more than one type of paper, having been ruled, it would seem, by paper-dealers.[5] Others, notably the sophisticated rulings typically exhibited by the Venetian manuscripts of Vivaldi's music, are each exclusive to a single paper-type, having been imposed by the paper-manufacturer.[6] In any case, it is the rastrography which distinguishes one variety of music-paper from another, and it is also the rastrography, rather than the paper-type, which is the most significant evidence for dating Italian manuscripts of the time. All such claims should, of course, be fully explained and carefully qualified with numerous caveats; it would be foolish to believe, for instance, that a composer—even one as busy as Handel or Vivaldi—never retained unused quires of paper from one year to the next or even over a longer period.[7] For our present purposes it is enough to observe that a conclusion based on any non-textual data cannot be proposed as an indisputable fact—but this is equally true of many worthwhile conclusions drawn in all branches of musicology. Non-textual evidence normally proves nothing; it does, however, have considerable value as sometimes quite weighty circumstantial evidence which strongly supports a hypothesis.

The first and second objectives, related to each other, make the assumption—a logical and obvious one in most cases—that the origins of a collection are unlikely to be as diverse as the variety of constituent documents might otherwise suggest, simply because there are bound to be reasons why the sources have belonged together from or shortly after the period of their creation. The extent to which it is possible for manuscripts to be grouped according to non-textual criteria will itself reflect the circumstances in which they were

---

[4] See Everett, 'The Application and Usefulness of "Rastrology", with particular reference to Early Eighteenth-Century Italian Manuscripts', in M. Di Pasquale (ed.), *Musica e filologia* (Verona, 1983), 135–58.

[5] Everett, 'A Roman Concerto Repertory: Ottoboni's "what not"?', *Proceedings of the Royal Musical Association*, 110 (1983–4), 62–78.

[6] Id., 'Towards a Vivaldi Chronology', 744.

[7] For limitations one must place on the interpretation of rastrographical data, see ibid. 745.

compiled and used originally; naturally, more connections will be found between sources which were the products of a single creative activity than those between sources of diverse origins which had come together for reasons other than their original use.

In the case of the many autograph and copied manuscripts once possessed by Vivaldi and now preserved in the Foà and Giordano collections in the Biblioteca Nazionale Universitaria in Turin, it was not surprising to discover a large number of correlations between their materials. Almost all are sources which, for all their diversity in musical content and scribal hands, possess a common pedigree, having been created by or, seemingly, for the composer; and the few whose music-papers and handwritings are not found elsewhere among manuscripts of Vivaldi's music have unique characteristics perhaps because they were copied in circumstances outside the composer's activity before coming into his possession. It became clear that the groupings of manuscripts which emerged represent something of far greater significance than simply the similar provenance of certain sources. Each group, typically comprising no more that four or five manuscripts or portions of manuscripts, seems to represent Vivaldi's use of a particular batch of music-paper: a limited quantity of one variety, probably purchased from a dealer on one particular occasion and sufficient for little more than tasks in hand. By utilizing the evidence of Vivaldi's and his scribes' apparently simultaneous use of two or more batches, it has been possible to build a fairly comprehensive picture, naturally with some gaps still to be filled, of the composer's consumption of music-paper throughout his career from about 1713 to the late 1730s.

All this evidence has major implications for dating the manuscripts and thus for assembling the much-needed chronology of Vivaldi's music. Specific dates may be assigned to the use of certain batches of paper, by reference to the known dates of operas and other occasional compositions.[8] But even where a precise date cannot be assigned or even surmised, the identification of the batch itself serves as a date-substitute because it is probable, in most cases, that the manuscripts or portions of manuscripts compiled from the quires of paper in a single batch are approximately contemporaneous—datable, let's say, to within a few months of each other. Another merit of this investigative approach, one which is likely to benefit the study of any collection, is that it draws attention to factors common to manuscripts of all kinds, irrespective of the kinds of texts they possess. It encourages a pure, objective view of the sources, unencumbered by

---

[8] For a detailed discussion of 2 exx. of such source-groupings and relationships of apparent contemporaneity for the putative periods 1718–20 and 1727–8, see ibid. 746–8, 752–6.

preconceived notions of the functions of the texts and the musical genres they represent. For the first time, we are gaining a view of Vivaldi's creativity that is not compartmentalized: a chronological perception which only the composer himself could previously have had.

Work on two other collections of Italian sources—some of the manuscripts preserved in Manchester which once formed part of Cardinal Pietro Ottoboni's collection before being acquired by Charles Jennens, and surviving portions of the repertory of Venice's Ospedale della Pietà—has caused the present writer to be even more convinced of the value and reliability of the evidence of music-paper. Each collection is considerably more diverse that the sources directly connected with Vivaldi's activities, having been assembled from manuscripts of widely differing origins. The complexion of each is also distinctly more residual in the sense that what has come down to us represents merely a portion of various fragments of what was once a much larger collection. It is natural, therefore, for their materials to lack uniformity; the manuscripts bound together in the 'Manchester Concerto Partbooks',[9] for instance, show several generic classes of paper and regional styles of rastrography, together with many handwritings, all indicative of the fact that the repertory of Ottoboni's establishment regularly included some music performed from manuscripts compiled in Venice, Bologna, and other centres as well as Rome.

Because the constituent documents of a collection assembled in these circumstances or from which much music has been lost will yield relatively few concurrences in non-textual data, one senses that the use of a particular variety of music-paper for two or more manuscripts probably occurred because the sources are of identical origin and similar dating. One reaches this degree of conviction because the alternative possibility, that the concurrence of materials is purely coincidental, is scarcely credible—especially when more than one case is evident.[10]

It is not easy to generalize about the ways of achieving our third objective, when the circumstances in which collections were formed vary enormously. Most investigations of this kind would need, however, to take account of the activity of scribes and of the assembly of the kind of composite source commonly found in collections: a volume of a number of originally separate manuscripts which, at some stage, were bound in order to preserve them in a state suitable

---

[9] GB-Mp MS 580 Ct51 (13 vols.), and GB-Lbl R.M.22.c.28 (one vol.): the subject of Everett, *The Manchester Concerto Partbooks*, 2 vols. (New York, 1989).

[10] Such an argument, specific to a particular group of sources, is made in id., 'Roman Concerto Repertory', 71–3.

for shelving in a library.[11] Provided that the date of binding is not long after the period when the manuscripts were created, there is a good chance that the order in which the manuscripts are preserved in such a volume may reflect relationships between documents and the circumstances of their initial use. The order will be expected to show, of course, that the manuscripts were sorted to some extent and perhaps accidentally rearranged before becoming bound. But with knowledge of the varieties of music-paper, one has the means of analyzing the order of binding in relation to certain sources' likely contemporaneity. In both the case of the 'Manchester Concerto Partbooks', bound shortly after Jennens had received the documents from Italy, and the case of Vivaldi's manuscripts, bound in large volumes soon after the composer's death, layers of contiguously bound sources are regularly to be found whose adjacent locations could not have occurred either by chance or by a process of sorting on textual criteria. Since a person responsible for rearranging the documents prior to their being sent to the binder is hardly likely to have consulted the watermarks and taken cross-sections of the stave-rulings, we must conclude that the manuscripts in question are now preserved together in layers because they naturally belong together, and that they were originally kept together by someone who *knew* that they belonged together by virtue of their similar date. Only Vivaldi himself could have had this perception of the Turin manuscripts, and I would conclude, therefore, that the seemingly significant sequence of, for instance, the cantata scores throughout two Turin volumes (I–Tn Foà 27 and 28) arose from the manner in which he stored his music towards the end of his life.[12] Similarly, the order of Manchester items seems to relate, in part, to the state in which the various repertories may have been kept in the music-library of Cardinal Ottoboni.[13]

The number of handwritings exhibited in a collection of manuscripts can be perplexingly large: some scribal hands may appear frequently, while others each occur only here or there—or perhaps only once. There is often very little chance of discovering the identity of the persons themselves; even if suitable documentation exists, one would be lucky to put a name to more than one or two. But the identity of individual copyists is not the most important issue. What

[11] The 'Manchester Concerto Partbooks' are of this kind, as are the twenty-seven Foà and Giordano vols. of Vivaldi's MSS.

[12] Further exx. of the significant order in which Vivaldi's MSS are preserved are described in Everett, 'Vivaldi's Marginal Markings: Clues to Sets of Instrumental Works and their Chronology', in G. Gillen and H. White (eds.), *Irish Musical Studies, i: Musicology in Ireland* (Dublin, 1990), 248–63; 251, 253, 254, 257, 258.

[13] Everett, *Manchester Concerto Partbooks*, 76–9, 444–50.

234 ITALIAN SOURCE-STUDIES AND HANDEL

matters more is to reach a view of the status of each scribe and the nature of his association, if any, with a composer, to evaluate his contribution to the collection, and to determine the extent to which he collaborated with other scribes; and it is possible to draw such conclusions even if the persons' identities never come to light. Beginning with the evidence of sources which show, beyond doubt, that one scribe worked with another in the copying process, it is usually a straightforward matter to determine which persons were directly associated with the composer and to assess other cases of collaboration between two or more copyists. Beyond that, doubts will persist about the possible relationships between scribes, and these are frequently one of two kinds.

First, there is the case of a source which exhibits, side by side, two or more hands in a context where one cannot be certain that the scribes actually worked together; it may be equally possible that they penned their respective portions of the text at distinctly separate times. A typical case is a pasticcio score, which may well have been assembled in a piecemeal fashion; certain passages—the recitatives, perhaps—were freshly copied, while others—certain arias—were added at various stages and may even have been extracted from existing opera manuscripts or special aria collections. In certain pasticcio scores assembled by Vivaldi, the correlation between the incidence of hands, the arrangement of leaves, and the use of various music-papers enables us to distinguish between the portions likely to have been freshly notated for the production itself and the portions— normally arias seemingly extracted from existing manuscripts—which are likely to have been appended.[14]

Such conclusions are more reliable, because they are based on the corroborative evidence of the use of music-paper, than the mere suspicions that result from textual analysis alone. With this method one can distinguish, moreover, between the copyists who almost certainly worked with the composer (because they shared with him particular batches of paper) and those who almost certainly had nothing to do with him: those whose hands appear simply because arias from older manuscripts were reused.

The second kind of uncertainty—a common one—arises when several hands each appear only singly, in separate sources, within a collection. Although there is no evidence whatsoever of collaboration between one individual and another, this does not necessarily mean that the scribes were never professionally associated with each other.

[14] An assessment of the scores of *Il Bajazet*, *Dorilla in Tempe*, *Rosmira fedele*, *Il Teuzzone*, and G. A. Ristori's *Orlando furioso* is given in Everett, 'Vivaldi's Italian Copyists', *Informazioni e studi vivaldiani: Bollettino dell'Istituto Italiano Antonio Vivaldi*, 11 (1990), 27–88; 39–48.

Indeed, since the manuscripts belong together in a single collection, it is only natural to suspect that such copyists were collectively involved, perhaps simultaneously, in the creative activity to which the collection relates. Again, the correlation between hands and varieties of music-paper can be extremely illuminating. If two manuscripts, with utterly distinct texts and handwritings, employ precisely the same variety of music-paper, is this common factor necessarily a deeply significant one? Does it necessarily mean that the two documents are closely related in their circumstances and date of origin? Does it necessarily mean that the two scribes worked together, knew each other or were at least active at the same time? Perhaps not, but the separate use of identical music-paper could not have occurred purely by chance in every instance, especially if the manuscripts have co-existed in the same collection and may have other factors in common. In the case of Vivaldi manuscripts and other repertories with a large number of varieties of music-paper, such concurrences of non-textual data, far from being merely coincidental, seem to indicate the related and sometimes contemporaneous activity of two or more scribes.[15]

Knowledge of the varieties of music-paper tends not to contribute greatly to an understanding of the subsequent history of a collection—our fourth objective—because it usually relates only to the compilation of the manuscripts in the first place. It is useful, however, for isolating early portions of a collection from later ones and, as discussed above, for explaining the nature of volumes which contain originally separate sources. One would need, of course, to be aware of all relevant non-textual and textual factors in order to recognize any portion of a collection as one added at a date distinctly later than the time when the rest of the collection had been assembled.

It is more usual, generally speaking, to seek evidence of the history of a collection from the characteristics of bindings, from signs of the rearrangement of the contents, and from external documents relating to the use and dispersal of the collection: catalogues, letters, details of sales, and so forth. This brings us to the fifth and final objective. It is common for a surviving collection to be merely a portion of what was once a larger collection, and the reconstruction of the parent corpus of music presents an important scholarly challenge. For manuscripts, how can this be done without knowledge of the varieties of music-paper? Since the appearance of the composer's or certain copyists' hands—or, indeed, the appearance of the same paper-types—does not necessarily mean that manuscripts now preserved in separate collections originally belonged together, only

---

[15] This argument is central to 'Roman Concerto Repertory', 70–3.

rastrographical data can provide the circumstantial evidence of common origin which one seeks. Such evidence is also useful for refining and supplementing the findings that arise from the study of a single collection: results which might otherwise remain limited or inconclusive. An attempt to achieve the fifth objective must, indeed, increase the chances of successfully achieving the other four.

Connections between collections are not easy to find, and to search for them without good hunches about where to look is not a practical prospect. Of the few the present writer has stumbled upon, one is of particular interest. It concerns the Roman autograph score, preserved in Turin, of Vivaldi's opera *Il Giustino*,[16] produced, during the 1724 Carnival season, at the Teatro Capranica of which Ottoboni was an important patron. The rastrography of just one leaf (fo. 6), inserted into the score at a late stage, matches that of some of the separate parts for two concertos by Giuseppe Valentini preserved in Manchester.[17] This tiny piece of evidence is amazingly useful. It helps to corroborate the Ottobonian provenance of the whole Roman concerto repertory of forty-three items which includes the Valentini works, and supports the notion that Vivaldi completed the opera score in circumstances connected with his contact with Ottoboni's establishment. It further indicates the mid-1720s as the focal date for the compilation of the Roman concerto repertory, and gives credence to the view that Vivaldi was personally associated with the musicians of Ottoboni's court whose hands are exhibited both in the Valentini manuscripts and in closely related Roman manuscripts of six concertos of Vivaldi himself. This, in turn, helps to explain how at least sixteen Venetian manuscripts of Vivaldi concertos, several of them autograph, came into the possession of Ottoboni's *cappella*.

We may conclude that the potential for discovering highly significant links between the manuscripts in widely dispersed collections is enormous, because our use of non-textual data can transcend all the bounds of text and authorship which are often allowed to confine musicological studies. It is not simply a matter of analyzing Handel sources to the fullest extent; after all, the characteristics of, say, contemporary English sources of the music of other composers should provide plenty of evidence of the origin and dating of Handel manuscripts—and *vice versa*. It argues for a new kind of reference tool which facilitates scholars' access to the classifications of hands, paper-types, and rastrographies of collections already analysed. And,

---

[16] Foà 34, fos. 2–184.

[17] The 'Manchester Concerto Partbooks', items 25 (two parts) and 51 (one part); see Everett, 'Vivaldi Concerto Manuscripts in Manchester: III', *Informazioni e studi vivaldiani: Bollettino dell'Istituto Italiano Antonio Vivaldi*, 7 (1986) 5–34; 12.

for such findings to be ideally useful when disseminated, it argues also for a suitable degree of standardization of the methods by which the data are initially recorded and then represented. But, above all, it argues for a new mode of collaborative research which traverses traditionally delimited fields of study, simply because such wide-ranging investigations cannot possibly be completed by individual scholars working in isolation. It's an exciting prospect.

13

Early German Handel Editions during the Classical Period

BERND BASELT

WHEN Handel was buried in Westminster Abbey on 20 April 1759 last respects were paid to him by almost everyone in cultivated English society. He was looked upon as the greatest English composer of the age, who had made London's opera the centre of European musical culture, and had created in his oratorios the national art form of the English middle class; later he would be seen to have prepared the way in his instrumental music for the classical symphony and sonata.

His compositional legacy to posterity has remained constantly before the public; his works, almost every category of which had been widely available in printed editions in his lifetime, have not only been continuously available for performance, but have been the subject of detailed evaluation in the Handel literature. Hand in hand with the cultivation of Handel's music has gone the analytical study of it, made possible by the existence of separate editions[1] of his best-known works going back to 1710; this can be seen in the first biography of him, by John Mainwaring,[2] published a year after the composer's death, about which Mattheson could write in the preface to his German translation:

There is no mere *musicus practicus ecclesiastico-dramaticus*, of high standing as a Kapellmeister, and of the highest as an organist, who being neither singer nor actor, nor even a composer of masses, has ever in the world, before Handel, had a book written exclusively about his life, without having a hand in it himself; a book printed in a considerable number of copies, and full of very instructive judgements, and furthermore translated from one language into another by a distinguished colleague in the art. Those

---

[1]   W. C. Smith, *Handel: A Descriptive Catalogue of the Early Editions* (London, 1960; 2nd edn., Oxford, 1970).

[2]   *Memoirs of the Life of the Late George Frederic Handel. To which is added, A Catalogue of his Works, and Observations upon them* (London, 1760).

BERND BASELT

who follow and would emulate him, do not let this spur press hurtfully upon you.[3]

So Handel's music went on being discussed after his death. Editions of those of his compositions which were most often performed in England[4]—the instrumental works and the oratorios—were put on the market before the end of the century in ever-increasing numbers by English music publishers;[5] the cultivation of Handel was spread to the whole English speaking world by emigrants, and although there were easily obtainable Handel editions of English origin, a need soon developed in America for selected editions adapted to particular local conditions,[6] and so a vigorous publishing activity began even on the other side of the Atlantic.

It was above all German visitors to England who brought to the Continent a knowledge of and enthusiasm for Handel's music,[7] which led not only to many performances, but also very soon to attempts to make his works available in their entirety for study and performance. It is significant that around the turn of the century plans were drawn up for complete editions of Handel's works at almost the same time in England and in Germany.

On the occasion of the great Handel Commemoration of 1784 in Westminster Abbey, Charles Burney[8] advertised a subscription for the first complete edition; this was begun in 1786 by Samuel Arnold. Arnold (1740–1802) was respected in the England of his time not

---

[3] *Georg Friderich Händels Lebensbeschreibung, nebst einem Verzeichnisse seiner Ausübungs- werke und deren Beurtheilung; übersetzet, auch mit einigen Anmerkungen, absonderlich über den hamburgischen Artikel, versehen vom Legations-Rath Mattheson* (Hamburg, 1761; facs. edn., Leipzig, 1976), p. x.

[*Ed.'s Note*: The original German text of the quoted passage is as follows: 'Kein blosser Musicus practicus ecclesiastico-dramaticus, als Kapellmeister im hohen, und Organist im höchsten Grad, der weder Sänger noch Acteur, am wenigsten aber ein Messkünstler gewesen, hat es jemals in der Welt, vor Händel, dahin gebracht, dass, ohne sein Zuthun, ein besondres eigenes Buch, ansehnlicher Auflage, von seinem Leben geschrieben, mit sehr lehrreicher Beurtheilung versehen, und noch dazu, durch einen eben nicht gemeinen Kunstverwandten, aus einer Sprache in die andre übersetzet worden wäre. Wettlauffende Nachfolger! lasset euch diese antreibende Sporne nicht wehe thun.' In the final sentence Mattheson seems to be saying that the Handel biography is a unique phenomenon, and cannot be repeated for others; so musicians who come after him should not let themselves be troubled by a desire to achieve a similar distinction.]

[4] W. C. Smith, 'Händels Stellung und Einfluß in England', *Musica*, 13 (1959), 23.

[5] See id., *Catalogue*.

[6] R. T. Daniel, 'Handel Publications in Eighteenth-century America', *Musical Quarterly*, 45 (1959), 168 ff.

[7] W. Rackwitz, 'Zum Händel-Bild deutscher England-Reisender in der zweiten Hälfte des 18. Jahrhunderts', *HjB*, 12 (1966), 109 ff.

[8] *An Account of the Musical Performances in Westminster-Abbey and the Pantheon, May 26th, 27th, 29th; and June the 3d, 5th, 1784. In Commemoration of Handel* (London, 1785); *Dr. Karl Burney's Nachricht von G. F. Händel's Lebensumständen und der ihm zu London im Mai und Jun. 1784 angestellten Gedächtnisfeyer, Aus dem Englischen übersetzt von J. J. Eschenburg* (Berlin, 1785; facs. edn., Leipzig, 1965), p. lii.

240   EARLY GERMAN HANDEL EDITIONS

only as a notable composer and conductor, but as an authority in almost all aspects of practical musical life. In a commemorative article in the journal *Harmonicon*[9] it was recorded that he 'enjoyed in early life the benefit of Handel's notice, and indeed of his advice'; this early acquaintance with Handel undoubtedly contributed to his being considered by the musical public as a particularly well-qualified expert on the composer's works. Arnold was first employed as 'composer to the House' at Covent Garden Theatre between 1763 and 1776, and at the Haymarket from 1776 to 1783. Later King George III appointed him organist and composer to the Chapel Royal; in 1789 he became conductor of the Academy of Ancient Music, and finally in 1793 organist of Westminster Abbey, where he was buried in 1802. Arnold was one of the conductors of the 1784 Commemoration, and so was a suitable person to carry out, with royal support, the plan suggested by Burney for publishing an edition of 'The Works of Handel in Score'.

The Arnold edition was issued not in volumes, but in 180 parts, between 1787 and 1797. The subscription proposal appeared in the London press in June 1786, and some of the parts include a list of the subscribers (about 380), of whom the most prominent was the King, who took twenty-five copies. From the outset the external appearance of the edition was designed for two different purposes: while there was for connoisseurs and amateurs of bibliophile excellence an edition on 'Imperial' paper (a format of about 38 by 28 cm), some copies having ornamental titles, another edition was issued at the same time on 'ordinary' paper (a smaller format of about 33.5 by 24 cm) for practical use; the two styles were, of course, printed from the same plates.[10]

It is not easy to determine what sources Arnold used for his edition, for although he possessed a large number of manuscripts of Handel's music, and was also undoubtedly permitted to consult the autographs which John Christopher Smith junior had handed over to the Royal Library about 1772, it is primarily the contemporary prints, from Walsh through to Wright, Randall, and Birchall, which appear to have served him as sources. This circumstance gave rise to a large number of incorrect texts, which were soon recognized as such by Arnold himself; as a result he planned in 1801–2 a revised edition, for which, however, he could publish only the subscription proposal before his death on 22 October 1802, so that this attempt to arrive at a better form of 'The Works of Handel' came to nothing.

---

[9] iii (1830), 137 ff.

[10] P. Hirsch, 'Dr. Arnold's Handel Edition 1787–1797', *Music Review*, 8 (1947), 106 ff; Jacob M. Coopersmith, 'The First Gesamtausgabe: Dr Arnold's Edition of Handel's Works', *Notes*, 4 (1947), 277 ff., 439 ff. See also Siegfried Flesch, 'Zur Hallischen Händel-Ausgabe: Ein Beitrag zur Entwicklung der Händel-Gesamtausgaben', *Traditionen und Aufgaben der Hallischen Musikwissenschaft* (Halle, 1963), 83 ff.

Arnold's achievement has been variously evaluated in the Handel literature. Much later, Chrysander severely critized his predecessor, but it must be acknowledged that Arnold not only laid the foundations of the modern complete edition, but also included among his individual issues a whole series of first editions of Handel works which until then were hardly known even to experts, and had remained unperformed since the composer's death. In the first phase of the attempt to create a complete Handel edition we see the beginning of a tradition aimed above all at the practical availability of Handel's works; this was the primary concern of English musicians, for which they hoped that the London Handel Festivals would provide the justification.

On the other hand, in Germany at this same period, inspired by musicians such as Johann Friedrich Reichardt[11] and Johann Adam Hiller,[12] people were beginning to assess Handel's music no longer just as a living performing tradition, but also as a cultural heritage, the popularization and protection of which was now a national task. The upsurge in Handel biography in the German classical period, initiated by Johann Gottfried Herder,[13] brought with it an increasing awareness of editorial problems. Significant in this regard are the activities of Baron Gottfried van Swieten who, while Austrian Ambassador in London and Berlin, came into contact with Handel's music, made a collection of it,[14] and had performing versions prepared by Mozart in Vienna in the 1780s;[15] with the assistance of Georg August Griesinger he sought to place his collection at the disposal of the Leipzig firm of Breitkopf & Härtel for their planned complete edition of Handel's works.[16] From similar motives J. O. H. Schaum,[17] at the same period (1805), proposed, at Reichardt's instigation, to publish a 'deutsche Ausgabe der Händelschen Werke'; this began to appear about 1820, but failed after a few volumes.

---

[11] G. Hartung, 'Händel und sein Werk im musikalischen Denken J. F. Reichardts', *HjB* 10/11 (1964–5), 139 ff.

[12] W. Serauky, 'J. A. Hiller als Erwecker der Händel-Tradition im 18. Jahrhundert', *Festschrift zum 175jährigen Bestehen der Gewandhauskonzerte 1781–1956* (Leipzig, 1956), 37 ff.

[13] W. Siegmund-Schultze, 'Die Musik G. F. Händels im Urteil der deutchen Klassik', *HjB* 4 (X) (1958), 32 ff.

[14] A. Holschneider, 'Die Musikalische Bibliothek Gottfried van Swietens', *Bericht über den Internationalen Musikwissenschaftlichen Kongreß Kassel 1962* (Kassel, 1963), 174 ff.

[15] Id., *Händels 'Messias' in Mozarts Bearbeitung*, diss. (Tübingen University, 1960). See also W. Siegmund-Schultze, 'W. A. Mozart unter dem Einfluß G. F. Händels', *HjB* 2 (VIII) (1956), 21 ff.

[16] R. Bernhardt, 'W. A. Mozarts Messias-Bearbeitung und ihre Drucklegung in Leipzig 1802–1803', *Zeitschrift für Musikwissenschaft*, 12 (1929/30), 21 ff.

[17] 'Zur Hallischen Händel-Ausgabe: Einige Bemerkungen der Redaktion', *HjB* 4 (X) (1958), 139 ff: W. Siegmund-Schultze, 'Prinzipien einer musikalischen Klassikerausgabe am Beispiel G. F. Händels', *HjB* 18/19 (1972–3), 111 f.

The many publications and arrangements of Handel's works by Ignaz Franz Mosel and others,[18] which raised in particular the question of how much arrangement of the originals was involved, were replaced by a new phase of Handel editions in which around the middle of the nineteenth century the notion of a *Denkmäler-Publikation*, or definitive edition, gained ground. Through men like Anton Friedrich Justus Thibaut and Georg Gottfried Gervinus there arose a view of Handel's music which emphasized the 'museum' aspect,[19] a suitable basis for the performance of this music by amateur choral groups such as those which they directed. These developed logically into musical societies which felt themselves to be almost exclusively dedicated to the cultivation of the 'sacred art of Music', in particular to the works of certain of the great masters.

In this matter England was again first in the field: a Handel society was founded in London in 1843, and immediately invited subscriptions for a complete Handel edition. Germany followed a few years later; the spur for this was twofold: the founding of the Bach-Gesellschaft in Leipzig in 1850, and the preparations for the centenary of Handel's death.

It would be useful to describe the history of the German Händel-Gesellschaft edition, but this would be outside the date-limits of the present survey; it has, however, a prehistory in the publishing of Handel's works which coincides with the decades of the Viennese classical period. Whilst Viennese and North German Handel performances before 1800 relied essentially on manuscript materials, some of which still survive today,[20] we find soon after the turn of the century a relatively abundant supply of printed full and vocal scores of Handel's works which bear witness to the popularity of his oratorios among amateur concert and choral societies, both religious and secular. To our knowledge there has not been until now a comprehensive bibliography of those works which were published in German-speaking countries in the five decades from 1780 to 1830; it reveals that under some ten separate titles the best-known oratorios could be had in performing editions from German publishing-houses, and thirteen works of church music.

After hesitant attempts in the 1780s—editions of arias in *Alexander's Feast* by Johann Nikolaus Fleischmann,[21] and in *Messiah* and *Judas*

[18] H. Leichtentritt, *Händel* (Stuttgart, 1924), 248.
[19] 'unter "musealem" Aspekt': this term was used by M. Geck in *Studien zur Musikgeschichte des 19. Jahrhunderts*, ix. *Die Wiederentdeckung der Matthäuspassion im 19. Jahrhundert* (Regensburg, 1967), 12.
[20] See A. Holschneider, 'Die Judas-Maccabäus-Bearbeitungen der österreichischen National-Bibliothek', *Mozart-Jahrbuch* (1960/1), 173 ff; Theophil Antonicek, *Zur Pflege Händelscher Musik in der 2. Hälfte des 18. Jahrhunderts* (Vienna, 1966).
[21] (Göttingen, 1785).

Maccabaeus by Hiller,[22] who had already produced an edition of the Utrecht Te Deum for Schwickert of Leipzig in 1780—there was after 1800, and especially during the 1820s, considerable activity by editors in various publishing-houses, and a brief account of this follows.

In 1802 appeared in the *Intelligenzblatt zur Allgemeinen Musikalischen Zeitung* of Leipzig[23] a pre-publication offer by the firm of Breitkopf & Härtel, which invited subscriptions for the first edition of 'Händels Messias für unsere Zeiten brauchbar eingerichtet von W. A. Mozart' ('Handel's *Messiah* arranged for use in our times by W. A. Mozart'). With this edition, issued at the beginning of 1803, edited by Friedrich Rochlitz and August Eberhard Müller (later to be Thomaskantor), the Leipzig publishing-house sought to prepare the ground for a series of complete editions of the great masters of music, in which Handel was to take his place alongside Haydn and Mozart. It seemed to the publishers (who were anxious at the same time to acquire the rights of Haydn's *Creation*) that in the absence of other sources Mozart's arrangements were the most suitable means of bringing about a revival of Handel's great oratorios, especially since the publishers were in close association with van Swieten, who possessed the manuscripts of these arrangements and strongly supported Härtel's plan. Unfortunately van Swieten died shortly before the publication of the *Messiah* edition (1803), so the further plans of the Leipzig firm came to nothing.

Another important attempt at a more comprehensive or even a complete edition was that of J. O. H. Schaum, who in Reichardt's *Berlinische Musikalische Zeitung*[24] wrote a follow-up article entitled 'Über eine deutsche Ausgabe der Händelschen Werke', in which he bewailed the lack of suitable source-texts for the printing of Handel's works, and put forward a threefold objective for the proposed edition: it should be so arranged that it could be used (1) by professional musicians, for study (2) to be heard by a wider, mixed public (3) by directors of church music in towns, and if need be in villages as well. It is clear from this that for Schaum it was Handel's church music which was of the greatest interest; only four volumes of his edition appeared, between 1822 and 1826, under the general title *G. F. Händels Werke in vollständiger Original Partitur mit untergelegtem deutschen Texte* ('G. F. Handel's works in complete original score with German text underlaid'): this contained nine Chandos Anthems, based on the Arnold edition. At the same time Schaum published separate vocal scores of *Semele* (1820–1) and *Acis and Galatea* (1829). It is very likely that the reason why he proceeded no further with his edition

[22] (Dresden and Leipzig, 1789). [23] 4 (Nov. 1802), 13–15.
[24] 1 (1805), 335 ff., 339 ff.

was a lack of interest on the part of the public, since very few copies of the published volumes survive today.[25] It is in this context that we must see Schaum's appeal to the public, printed as the preface[26] to the second volume of his edition, in which he declares about the project:

The fourth Handel Psalm now appears as the first part of the second volume of the complete edition of Handel's works, although the German musical public has not yet supported this undertaking in such a way that the publisher can adequately cover his costs. Nevertheless, relying on the desirability of the thing itself, and on the praise bestowed on him by a reviewer of the first Psalm in the *Leipziger Musikalische Zeitung* of 1822 [26: 241], the editor and publisher have the well-founded hope that, if only the project can become better known to the musical public, they will take more interest in it; both of us will endeavour to persuade the public how much the aim of our undertaking is to promote a desirable objective, and is in no way just the usual money-making speculation.

In addition Schaum goes into questions of editorial techniques, which had been raised by the quoted reviewer of the *Allgemeine Musikalische Zeitung*; for instance, that concerning the translation of the text from English into German, which had earlier been a problem for Hiller, and the possibility of adapting it to the Latin text of the Psalms so that Handel's works might be made interconfessional. He represents, therefore—and this is remarkable in that 'age of arrangement'—the view which demands a correct edition based strictly on the sources, without any kind of additions by the modern editor, and on these grounds he criticizes quite severely Hiller's edition of the Utrecht Te Deum, in which, as was well known, there were many alterations to the score because of differences in declamation between the original English and the Latin text. Disapproving of this practice, Schaum insists that the translation of the text should fit the music, and that as far as possible no note of Handel's should be altered.

After the failure of Schaum's project, many other separate editions were issued by German publishers, in which Handel's original texts were more or less heavily arranged. A chronological list of the works published in Germany up to 1830 is given in the Appendix.

No less a person than Mendelssohn was the inspiration behind a further plan for a German Handel edition. In 1833 he had undertaken to conduct the Rhineland Music Festivals in Düsseldorf, where he was engaged as the city's musical director. In the years 1833–5 he conducted six Handel oratorios in Düsseldorf, Elberfeld, and Cologne, in versions which he had partly arranged himself. He already felt the lack of a correct edition of Handel's major works, and when on

---

[25] There is only 1 complete set of the 4 vols. in D-HAu.   [26] Dated 'Berlin, Febr. 1823'.

his departure from Düsseldorf the committee of the Rhineland Music Festivals presented him with a complete set of the Arnold edition, as a particularly apt recognition of his efforts, detailed study of these volumes soon aroused in him the desire to obtain a reliable text of at least Handel's major oratorios, so on 10 July 1838 he wrote to his publisher Peter Joseph Simrock in Bonn:

Should it not now be worthwhile for a publisher to engrave in Germany the original scores of some of Handel's greatest oratorios? It would have to be done on subscription, but I think it would attract considerable support, since we have not one of these scores at the moment. I had thought that I would write organ parts for this purpose, but these should be printed in small notes or in notes of a different colour, so that the user of the volume would have (1) the complete original Handel, if he so wished, (2) my organ part in addition, if he wanted to use it and had an organ available, and (3) an arrangement of the organ part for clarinets, bassoons, and other wind instruments of the modern orchestra in an appendix, to be used in the absence of an organ. Such a score could therefore be used by all organisations which perform oratorios, and we would at last have in Germany the authentic Handel, not one that has been first dipped in Mosel water, and soaked in it over and over again [*this is a punning reference to the heavily-arranged editions prepared by Mosel in Vienna*]. People in England have assured me that a significant number of subscribers could be found there as well for such a score; what do you think about it? You have already published vocal scores of several of these oratorios [*since 1824 vocal scores and chorus parts for* Alexander's Feast, Israel in Egypt, Messiah *and* Solomon], perhaps we could choose some of these. You will understand that I am asking you for your very frank and honest opinion of my suggestion, about which I am only writing to you because it has often occurred to me, and has now done so yet again.[27]

The most interesting things about this are the editorial principles suggested by Mendelssohn, which, for the practical editions he had in mind, seem very modern compared with those adopted in the arrangements available at that time, by Mosel, Breidenstein, and others. These principles were in fact put into practice in an edition only once: in spite of the criticism which Chrysander later directed at Mendelssohn, the latter's edition of *Israel in Egypt* for the English Handel Society (1845) is even today of much more than mere historical interest.

Unfortunately neither the firm of Simrock nor Breitkopf & Härtel, to whom Mendelssohn later applied with a similar suggestion, responded to his initiative. Simrock reacted negatively to the suggestion of a subscription proposal, which caused the composer to reply resignedly:

[27] *Briefe an deutsche Verleger*, ed. by Rudolf Elvers (Berlin, 1968), 219 f.

What you write to me about Handel has astonished me, for I would not have thought that there is so little demand for his works. An edition of the scores would indeed not be feasible under such circumstances, and I could not advise you to proceed with it. But should we not try setting up a subscription, so that we then know how many other subscribers there might be, and can abandon the whole enterprise if it turns out that there are too few?[28]

As a result, any further involvement by the German publishing world in Handel's complete works was ruled out for some time, especially since the English Handel Society was set up in 1843 with the objective of creating a new complete critical edition on a subscription basis, and of course it sought also to attract Handel enthusiasts and admirers in Germany. In the German subscription proposal it says therefore:

The importance of this undertaking must not be underrated. The earlier great English edition of Handel's works [the Arnold edition] is now a rarity, and furthermore is unsatisfactory because of many inaccuracies. Now a better one is offered on very reasonable terms, since the number of subscribers is already considerable, almost 700, and as it increases, so in accordance with the plan the cost of the purchase reduces for each individual subscriber. Moreover, the work will be printed only for the subscribers, and an upper limit of these has been fixed at 1,000.[29]

Although the Handel Society was dissolved after a few years, its editions ran on until 1858,[30] before eventually it ceased publication and remained incomplete.

Meanwhile, the Bach-Gesellschaft was founded in Leipzig on the occasion of the centenary of J. S. Bach's death; in spite of initial difficulties in getting under way, it devoted itself with great success as a corporate undertaking to the publication of Bach's works. As Handel's centenary was now drawing near, it was natural that his many admirers should get together for a similar purpose; that happened through the inspiration of Gervinus, who had the young music historian Friedrich Chrysander as his technical adviser—the moment of birth of modern Handel scholarship had arrived.[31]

---

[28] Ibid. 220: dated Berlin, 11 Aug. 1838.
[29] *Wiener allgemeine Musik-Zeitung*, 5 (1845), 272.
[30] Vol. xvi. *Jephtha*, ed. G. A. Macfarren.
[31] See B. Baselt, 'Händel-Edition im Verständnis des 19. Jahrhunderts (Beiträge zur Geschichte der Ausgabe der deutschen Händelgesellschaft, hrsg. von Friedrich Chrysander)', in W. Siegmund-Schultze (ed.), *Georg Friedrich Händel im Verständnis des 19. Jahrhunderts* (Halle, 1984), 46 ff.

Appendix: *Chronological Bibliography of the German Editions 1780–1830*

Only those editions have been listed which can be dated with some certainty. The dates given are on the original title-pages, except those printed in square brackets, which are arrived at from other evidence.

G. F. Händel's Te Deum laudamus, zur Utrechter Friedensfeyer ehemals in Engländischer Sprache componirt und nun mit dem bekannten lateinischen Texte herausgegeben von J. A. Hiller (Leipzig, Schwickert, 1780; v. s. by J. H. Clasing: Hamburg, A. Cranz, [1819/20]).

Arien, nebst einigen Accompagnements, einem Trio und einem Chor, aus dem Alexanderfeste von Händel, fürs Clavier gesetzt . . . von Joh. Nik. Fleischmann (Göttingen, Fleischmann, 1785).

VI Fugen von Händel für Componisten, Organisten und Liebhaber der höhern Musik (Darmstadt, s.n., 1787).

Auszug der vorzüglichsten Arien, Duette und Chöre aus G. F. Händels Messias und Judas Maccabäus, in claviermäßiger Form, von J. A. Hiller (Dresden and Leipzig, J. G. I. Breitkopf, 1789).

G. F. Händel's Oratorium: Der Messias, nach W. A. Mozart's Bearbeitung, 3pts., separately paginated (Leipzig, Breitkopf & Härtel, 1803).

Der 100ste Psalm Jauchze dem Herrn alle Welt [Utrecht Jubilate] (Leipzig, Breitkopf & Härtel, 1803; v. s. by J. H. Clasing: Hamburg, A. Cranz, [1819/20]).

Des Staubes Söhne trauern. Empfindungen am Grabe Jesu: Ein Oratorium von G. F. Händel [Funeral Anthem], *hrsg. von E. Müller* (Leipzig, Breitkopf & Härtel, 1805).

Händel's Oratorium: Der Messias, im Clavierauszuge von C. F. G. Schwencke mit deutschem Texte von Klopstock und Ebeling (Hamburg, Joh. Aug. Böhme, 1809).

Alexanders Fest, oder Die Gewalt der Musik. Eine grosse Cantate, aus dem Englischen des Dryden übersetzt von C. W. Ramler, in Musik gesetzt von G. F. Händel, mit neuer Bearbeitung von W. A. Mozart (Leipzig, A. Kühnel (full score and v. s.), 1812 (firm taken over by C. F. Peters, 1814).

Timotheus, oder Die Gewalt der Musick. Eine grosse Cantate, in Musick gesetzt von Haendel, im vollständigen Clavier-Auszug übersetzt . . . von P. J. Riotte (Vienna, P. Mecchetti, 1812/13: 2 edns., one a selection of arias for 4 hands).

Händel's Oratorium Judas Maccabäus, nach Mozart's Bearbeitung [not by Mozart, but J. Starzer, commissioned by van Swieten], *im Clavier Auszuge von Ludwig Hellwig* (Hamburg, J. A. Böhme, 1820).

Judas Maccabäus. Oratorium von G. F. Händel. Im Clavier-Auszuge von J. H. Clasing (Hamburg, A. Cranz, 1820 [also Bonn and Cologne, N. Simrock; Vienna, P. Mecchetti]).

Alexanders Fest, oder Die Gewalt der Musik. Eine grosse Cantate von G. F. Händel, im vollständigen Clavierauszug von J. P. Riotte (Hamburg, J. A. Böhme [c.1820]).

Semele Ein dramatisches Gedicht von Congreve in Musik gesetzt von G. F. Händel. Nach dem englischen Original bearbeitet, und der Musik im Klavierauszuge untergelegt von J. O. H. Schaum (Berlin, E. H. G. Christiani, [1820–1])).

Saul. Oratorium von G. F. Händel mit untergelegtem deutschen Text von C. D. E. [Ebeling]. Im vollständigen Klavierauszug von J. F. Naue (Leipzig, F. Hofmeister, 1821).

G. F. Händel's Werke in vollständiger Original Partitur mit untergelegtem deutschen Texte herausgegeben . . . von J. O. H. Schaum i–iv (Berlin, E. H. G. Christiani [1821/2–26]). i: 'Lobsinget Gott, ihr Engel des Herrn' ['O praise the Lord, ye angels of His', Anthem 12, spurious]; 'Kommt her, laßt uns singen unserm Gott' ['O come, let us sing', Anthem 8]; 'So wie der Hirsch nach Labung lechzt' ['As pants the hart', Anthem 6]; ii: 'Der Herr ist mein Licht' ['The Lord is my Light', Anthem 10] 'Herr mache dich auf' ['Let God arise', Anthem 11]; iii: 'Erbarme meiner dich, o Gott' ['Have mercy upon me', Anthem 3]; 'Mein Lied singet laut' ['My song shall be alway', Anthem 7]; iv: 'O preiset den Herrn' ['O praise the Lord with one consent', Anthem 9]; 'O singet unserem Gott' ['O sing unto the Lord a new song', Anthem 4].

*Josua. Großes Oratorium mit deutschem Texte von ***. Musik von G. F. Händel. Im vollständigen Clavierauszug von J. H. Clasing* (Hamburg, A. Cranz, 1823).

Josua. Oratorium von Händel im Clavier-Auszuge von J. C. F. Rex, Musik-Director an der Dreifaltigkeits-Kirche zu Berlin (Berlin, T. Trautwein, 1823).

Athalia. Geistliches Drama aus dem Englischen übersetzt von M: C. J. Crain, Musik von G. F. Händel, im vollständigen Klavierauszuge von J. H. Clasing (Leipzig, Breitkopf & Härtel, [1825/6]).

Israel in Egypten. Oratorium von G. F. Haendel. Uebersetzung und Clavierauszug von K. Breidenstein. Mit englischem und deutschem Texte, (Bonn and Cologne, N. Simrock, 1826).

Azis und Galathe. Eine Serenate von Georg Friedr. Händel. Klavierauszug und deutscher Text von J. O. H. Schaum (Berlin, T. Trautwein, 1829).

Salomon. Grosses Oratorium in drei Abtheilungen von G. F. Händel. Mit frei übersetztem deutschen Texte, im Clavierauszuge von Xav. Gleichauf (Bonn, N. Simrock, 1830).

Tema con LXII variationi per il clavicembalo composto dal Sigr. Händel. Dedicato al Sigr. L. v. Beethoven per l'editore [HWV 442] (Bonn, N. Simrock [c.1825]).

Te Deum zur Feier des Sieges bei Dettingen im Jahre 1743 . . . im Klavierauszuge von C. F. Rex (Berlin, T. Trautwein [c.1830]).

Index of Handel's Works

This index gives references to Handel's works as they are mentioned in the text and footnotes; it does not cover the contents-lists of the collections which are printed as Tables and Appendixes to Chs. 2–11.

Aci, Galatea e Polifemo 201
Acis and Galatea 14, 16, 21, 22, 30, 31,
    145 n., 150 n., 151–3, 157 n., 243, 248
Admeto 7, 22, 32, 34, 36, 41 n., 42 n., 50, 51,
    121 n.
Agrippina xiv, 41 n., 91, 93, 95, 128, 201,
    202, 203, 204
'Ah, che troppo ineguali' 203
Alceste 123
The Alchemist 5
Alcina 41, 42 n., 46, 112 n., 121 n.
Alessandro 33, 34, 64, 176–7
Alessandro Severo 20, 22, 121 n., 123 n.
Alexander Balus xiv, 43 n., 173, 174
Alexander's Feast 19, 46, 88, 93, 123, 127 n.,
    160, 242, 245, 247
L'Allegro, il Penseroso ed il Moderato 2, 9,
    40, 42, 43 n., 47, 51 n., 52, 92, 112 n.,
    160
Amadigi xii, 12, 14, 32, 41 n., 50, 51, 97,
    148, 149–50
Anthems for Cannons, *see* Chandos Anthems
Arianna 19, 31, 41, 46, 47, 52
Ariodante 20, 41, 42 n., 46, 48, 121 n.
Arminio 46, 48, 88
Arsace 44
Atalanta 43 n., 46, 127 n.
Athalia 4, 43 n., 91, 248

Belshazzar xi, xiv, 4, 40, 43, 43 n., 51 n., 63,
    173, 174
Brockes Passion 30, 31, 34, 41 n.,

Caio Fabbricio 44
Cantatas 1, 30, 97, 98, 120 n., 142, 188–91,
    198–204
Chandos Anthems 30, 63, 112 n., 115,
    120 n., 124, 139, 142–7, 149 n.,
    150 n., 153, 243, 244, 248
Chapel Royal Anthems 30, 63, 115
The Choice of Hercules 42, 50 n., 123 n.
Clock Music 64
'Coelestis dum spirat' 188
Comus 9, 64, 88–9, 90, 92, 96
Concertos Op. 3 30, 35, 115 n., 121 n.
Concertos Op. 4 93, 95, 111, 115 n.
Concertos Op. 6 46, 88, 93, 121, 123 n.
Concertos Op. 7 45, 95, 123
Concerto HWV 303 45

Concertos HWV 304 & 305 127
Concerto a due cori HWV 332 127
Coronation Anthems 30, 160, 163, 177

Daphne 64
Deborah 4, 43 n., 63, 91, 115, 116
Deidamia 43 n., 64, 118, 123
Dettingen Te Deum 43 n., 92, 123, 163, 165,
    177, 248
Didone 20, 22, 44
'Dixit Dominus' 200
Duets 14, 50, 189, 201, 203, 204

Elpidia 22
Esther 7, 16, 17, 30, 31, 43 n., 48, 145,
    150 n., 151
Ezio 22, 43

Faramondo 22, 46, 88
Fireworks Music 5, 127, 128, 160
Flavio 34, 41 n., 120 n.
Floridante 17, 18, 31, 32, 36, 41 n., 43, 55,
    143 n.
Florindo 64
Foundling Hospital Anthem xi, 51, 52, 63
Fugues for keyboard 30, 35, 90, 247
Funeral Anthem for Queen Caroline 64,
    120 n., 247

Giulio Cesare 29, 34, 41 n., 64, 112 n., 143 n.
Giustino 46, 88

'Haec est regina virginum' 190
Hercules 43 n., 48
Hornpipe HWV 356 52
Imeneo xii, 41, 118, 121
Israel in Egypt 4, 40, 43 n., 63, 64, 91, 127 n.,
    174, 245, 248

Jephtha 21, 28, 42, 90, 246 n.
Joseph and his brethren 16, 43, 120 n., 173,
    174
Joshua 2, 9, 22, 43 n., 92, 97, 176, 248
Jubilate (Utrecht) 30, 148, 149, 177, 247
Judas Maccabaeus 8, 48, 92, 94, 96, 98,
    119 n., 160, 242, 247

Keyboard music 30, 35, 43, 64, 248; *see also*
    Suites

250   INDEXES

'Laudate pueri' HWV 237 190
Lotario 127 n., 143 n.
'Love's but the frailty of the mind' 52
Lucio Papirio 20

Messiah xi, 2, 5, 7, 16, 22, 40, 41, 42,
43 n., 48, 60, 61, 63, 90, 92, 112 n.,
115, 118 n., 120 n., 160, 161, 163,
164, 165, 177, 241 n., 242, 243, 245,
247
Muzio Scevola xiv, 16, 17, 35, 36, 41 n., 60,
148, 149 n., 151, 177

'Nisi Dominus' 51, 52, 190

'O qualis de coelo sonus' 188, 203
Occasional oratorio 43 n., 123, 173 n.
Ode for Queen Anne's Birthday 30, 42 n.,
48, 50 n., 51, 52, 121, 123, 125 n.,
148, 176
Ode for St Cecilia's Day 43 n., 123, 176
Oreste 121 n., 123 n.
Orlando 18, 22
Ormisda 22
Ottone 22, 32, 34, 36, 41 n., 120 n.
Overtures (keyboard) 34, 35, 48 n., 127, 163

Il Parnasso in festa 120, 121 n., 126
Partenope 121 n.
Il pastor fido 12, 14, 17, 22, 33, 41 n., 43,
52, 55, 121 n.
Il pianto di Maria (spurious) 189
Poro 19, 20

Radamisto xi, xiv, 15, 16, 32, 35, 41 n., 137,
143 n., 148, 150–1
La Resurrezione 11, 41 n., 51, 52, 54, 188,
203
Rinaldo 2, 12, 14, 20, 22, 31, 33, 34, 54, 55,
97, 137, 148
Rodelinda 33
Rodrigo 41 n., 64, 97, 120, 200, 201
Rossane 176–7

'Saeviat tellus' 190
'Salve regina' 199, 203
Samson 4, 63, 90, 120 n., 164, 177
Saul xiii, 40, 41 n., 42, 63, 119, 127 n., 248
Scipione 15, 21, 32, 33
Semele 42, 123, 243, 248
Serse 126
Silla 41 n., 51, 52, 120
Sinfonie diverse 121 n.
Siroe 34
Solomon 42, 115, 116, 245, 248
Sonatas Op. 1 115 n.
Sonatas Op. 2 4, 30, 93, 115 n., 127, 160
Sonatas Op. 5 93, 115 n., 121 n., 127, 160
Sonata HWV 395 64
Sonata HWV 404 35, 147
Sonata HWV 405 203
Sosarme 22, 34, 41, 119
Suites (keyboard) 43, 52, 90, 137, 148, 190,
190 n., 201
Susanna 42, 90, 115, 116 n.

Tamerlano xi, 30 n., 41
'Te decus virgineum' 190
Te Deum (Chandos) 30, 34
Te Deum (Utrecht) 30, 148, 149, 177, 243,
244, 247
Te Deum HWV 280 51, 52
Te Deum HWV 282 123 n.
Terpsicore 121 n., 123 n.
Teseo 5, 12, 13, 14, 22, 32, 33, 34, 41 n.,
50, 51
Theodora 42, 90, 115, 116, 117
Tolomeo 41 n.
Il trionfo del tempo e del disinganno 11, 12,
191
Trios (vocal) 189, 201

Venceslao 17, 22
Water Music 5, 30, 35, 50, 51 n., 96, 121,
160
'Water Piece' 127
Wedding Anthems 63

General Index

Anecdotes of G. F. Handel and J. C. Smith [Coxe] 2, 114 n.
Arnold, Samuel 20, 22, 114, 117 n., 127 n., 144 n., 173, 179, 188 n., 191, 239–41, 243, 245, 246
Aylesford:
    Earls of 39, 54, 55, 56, 57
    2nd Earl of 46, 47 n.
    3rd Earl of 39, 46–9, 55
    4th Earl of 49, 52, 60
    6th Earl of 52, 57

Bach, J. S. v, 242, 246
Barrett Lennard, *see* Lennard
Brydges, *see* Chandos
Burney, Charles 6, 39, 50, 51, 52, 61 n., 99, 114, 173, 239, 240

Cannons 137, 139–42, 144, 145, 147, 148, 150–3
Chandos:
    James Brydges, 1st Duke of xi, 14, 137, 139, 140, 142, 149, 153
    Henry Brydges, 2nd Duke of 139, 140, 142
    James Brydges, 3rd Duke of 140
Chrysander, Friedrich 3, 10, 18, 19, 22, 23, 32, 33, 95, 117 n., 139, 241, 245, 246
Cluer, J. 91, 93, 95
Coke, Gerald vii, 1, 87, 92, 96, 97
Collections (*references in chapters other than the principal one for each collection*):
    Aylesford 2, 31, 88, 95, 108, 145, 152, 176, 178
    Coke 12, 14, 20, 30, 44, 46, 47, 48, 55 n., 92, 96, 97, 102, 107, 127, 142, 144, 145, 146, 152, 173
    Granville 31, 50–2, 60, 108, 112 n., 119, 120
    Lennard 31
    Malmesbury 8, 43, 108, 147, 148, 151
    Shaftesbury 2, 8–9, 31, 108
Copyists:
    ENGLISH:
    BM 1 150
    H1 16, 30, 34, 37, 38, 151
    H2 30, 37, 38, 150, 151
    H3 31, 34, 37, 38

H5 34, 37, 38
H8 38
Hb.1 35, 38, 130, 131
Lenn 1: 131
Lenn 2: 133
Lenn X: 132
Linike, D. 12, 13, 33, 34, 37, 38, 149, 151
Newman, T. 33, 37
RM 1 31, 32, 34, 37, 38, 150, 151
RM 2 150
RM 4 34, 38
RM 5/6 51
S1 20, 31, 34, 37, 38, 41, 112, 121 n., 130, 131, 133, 136
S2 31, 34, 35, 37, 38, 43, 47, 131
S3 34, 35, 38, 130, 144 n.
S4 118 n., 131
S5 121 n., 131, 132, 133, 136, 174
S7 121 n., 133
S9 121 n., 132
S13 51
Alpha 38
Beta 34, 38
Gamma 34, 37, 38, 150
Zeta 37
Eta 38
ITALIAN:
Angelini, A. G. 11, 13, 188, 199, 200, 201, 205–22
Castrucci, D. 209, 212, 213, 216, 219, 226
Ferri, C. A. 188
Ginelli, A. 199, 200, 206, 208–11, 215, 219–22
Lanciani, Fr. 216, 223, 226
Lanciani, T. 216
Lon. I–XVII, Mü II–XIV, NY I 205–26 *passim*
see also Smith, J. C., senior and junior

Cummings, W. H. 139, 141, 144 n., 145–7, 151, 156, 177, 197

Delany, Mrs, *see* Granville, Mary
Deutsch, O. E. 3, 87, 88, 89, 96

Flower, Newman 1, 39, 53, 59, 60, 63, 108

George III, King 50–2, 56, 60–1, 158, 164, 173, 174, 240
Granville, Bernard 50, 61 n., 108, 119 n.
Granville, Mary (Mrs Delany) 50–2, 87–8
Guernsey, Lord, *see* Aylesford, 3rd Earl of

Hall, James 55, 171, 173, 174 n., 176, 177, 178–9
Handel Commemoration:
    (1784) 6, 39, 115, 239, 240
    (1834) 111 n.
Harris, Thomas 8, 30
Hellier, Sir Samuel 158–67 *passim*
Holdsworth, Edward 7, 40, 44, 57, 58

Jennens, Charles vi, 2, 7, 30, 39–65 *passim*, 108, 152, 176, 232, 233

Lacy, M. Rophino 121 n., 127
Legh, Elizabeth 8, 29–30, 32, 34–6, 37, 108, 137, 139, 148, 150 n., 152
Lennard, Henry Barrett 108–10, 112, 113, 114 n., 123 n., 125–7

Mainwaring, John 88, 173, 238
Mattheson, Johann 238–9
Malmesbury, Earls of 8, 29–30, 36
Marshall, Julian 2, 22, 23, 113 n., 127 n., 151, 178
Marshall, Mrs Julian 50, 60, 112 n., 123 n.
Mendelssohn, Felix 186, 187, 244–6
Mozart, W. A. 1, 241, 243
Münster, Bishop of 185, 187, 191–4

Novello, Vincent 184, 187

Ottoboni, Cardinal 44, 58, 62, 63, 64–5, 188, 191, 197, 204, 230 n., 232, 233, 236

Packington Hall 46, 47, 48, 49 n., 52, 56
Pamphilj, Cardinal 188, 191, 195, 196, 199, 202, 206, 208, 210, 212, 213

Pepusch, J. C. 137, 141 n., 142–7, 148 n., 152 n., 153 n., 155 n., 157

Rivers, Henry 22
Rivers, Lady 22, 114 n.
Ruspoli, Marchese 186, 188, 191, 195–7, 199 n., 200, 202, 211, 215, 218–24

Santini, Abbate Fortunato 184–7, 190, 191, 197, 199
Scarlatti, Alessandro 44, 62, 63, 184, 186, 188, 201, 225 n.
Schoelcher, Victor 1, 23, 36, 112 n., 113, 114, 125 n., 127, 128, 173, 178
Shaftesbury:
    4th Earl of xiv, 8, 87–9, 90, 92, 93, 94, 96, 97, 98, 99
    7th Earl of 90, 92, 93, 94, 98, 99
    9th Earl of 89, 94–6
    10th Earl of 87, 89, 90–1, 94 n., 96
Smith, J. C., sen. 7, 8, 10, 13, 15–17, 18, 20, 21, 30, 31, 33, 34, 35, 37, 38, 40, 41, 43, 90, 92, 93–4, 96, 98, 110, 113, 114, 118, 121 n., 130, 131, 132, 133, 139, 144, 149, 150, 151, 152, 153, 173, 174, 178
Smith, J. C., jun. 4, 18, 21, 22, 23, 33, 34, 35, 36, 37, 38, 45, 50, 113, 114 n., 139, 178, 240
Smith, W. C. 1, 2, 3, 4, 5 n., 6–7, 30, 46, 48, 55, 88, 95, 102, 171, 173, 238

Vivaldi, Antonio xii, 44, 57, 200 n., 227, 228, 229 n., 230, 231–2, 233, 234, 235, 236

Walsh, John, (sen. and jun.) 41, 42, 45, 46, 47, 91, 92, 93, 95, 115, 116, 117, 119, 126, 127, 128, 173, 174 n., 240
Westminster Abbey 5, 29, 39, 111, 113 n., 238, 239, 240
Wright, Harman 115–17, 144 n., 173, 240